The Lives of Stanley B

The Lives of Stanley B

Mat Guy

1889 books

www.1889books.co.uk

ISBN: 978-1-915045-00-3

To Deb. And Ellie.

And dreamers everywhere

The Left Back

One

People always ask the question, even though they know how hard it is to answer. It is a question with no right or wrong answer, that often yields animated debate, and no satisfactory conclusion: 'Who is the best footballer you have ever seen play?'

It is almost impossible. For as soon as you pick one player, a squad of others begin to manifest in the mind's eye. Their endeavour and skill through the years betrayed, shoulders drooped in bygone kits at being overlooked. Their blood sweat and tears for your team, your country, or some distant, exotic outfit all seemingly for nought.

It is a self-inflicted guilt-trip through every moment that made your heart soar at a match, or in your front room, watching World Cups in some far away land. Every feint and cross, last ditch tackle, spectacular goal or save, sweeping team move that elicited a primeval roar from deep within you.

And you want me to pick just one source of such emotion? One moment? It is a cruel yet captivating question.

In truth, there can be a different answer in any given heartbeat, depending on your mood. It is a question I have tried to avoid as much as possible throughout my career, even during the interminable pre- and post-match hours crammed into a press box with too many other journalists, trying to find elbow space to bash out copy before print deadlines.

Then, questions as ethereal as that can seem quite attractive. Especially when the words aren't coming. The hyperbole over an uninspiring and meaningless end of season, mid-table, goalless draw drying up as fast as the dustbowl goalmouths. Baked earth beneath a hot May sun, the scars of a long hard season.

It was during one such stifling and frantic post-match press box session, over the sounds of whirring laptops and scattergun typing. The limp breeze of an unseasonably hot day rustling notes. The distant drone of lawnmowers cutting fresh strips into the pitch below, that one colleague put a slight spin on that perennial question.

'Forget the best for a minute,' he said, leaning back in his chair chewing the stub of a pencil, ignoring the blinking cursor at the end of his half-written piece.

'Who is the player you have never forgotten, for whatever reason? It could be through infamy, loyalty, passion, anything. One player.'

Silence. The press box lost in thought for a moment, looking out absently at the banks of empty seats in the far stand, its shadow stretching out across the pitch before a cacophony of procrastination. Tales of drinking sessions and bar fights, exquisite pranks and excruciating ego, heartbreak, injury, skill, endeavour, sacrifice and glory. It was all there. Football, good and bad.

And from somewhere, among the to and fro of tall tales came a name. A name I had not consciously thought of for at least twenty years: Tom Maskell.

From the company he kept in other people's answers, he had no real right to be a part of the conversation. A young lad with just five first team appearances for a struggling Fourth Division side, mingling with European Cup winners, league champions. Players who had stepped out for Juventus, Barcelona, Liverpool. Players who had been a part of that impeccable 1982 World Cup in Spain. The tournament that truly cemented my passion for football as a nine-year-old boy.

Socrates, Zico, Tardelli – those names should have come easily to me, so formative was that tournament.

I would run home from school as fast as I could that long hot summer of 82, knowing that if I did, I would catch the second half of the first televised match of the day. Breathlessly I would plonk myself in front of the television and watch whatever was on, whilst sticking into my World Cup Panini album the stickers swapped in the playground at lunch break. Obscure players from the periphery of world football rubbing shoulders with giants of the game. Faces to statistics beneath each blank space in my album. Strange-sounding birth places and unfamiliar club sides represented back home, or elsewhere, how many international appearances they had made adding meat to the bones of a snapshot of their footballing life. A national team shirt, standing proudly on some unnamed pitch before an expectant crowd. Heat hazes, floodlight glare, a relentless sun on a yellowing surface. A whole other world, out there, somewhere.

I remember El Salvador versus Hungary, that resulted in the heaviest World Cup finals defeat – ten-one in favour of the Magyars. At the time I felt sorry for El Salvador and cheered as they scored their only World Cup goal: Luis Ramirez Zapata wheeling away with such emotion at making it five-one.

It would be many years later that I discovered why he celebrated so. The team had been the only thing holding together a country torn apart by civil war. Stories of players turning up late for training, having stopped to help the injured and dying on the side of the road were commonplace. A devastating earthquake had only made matters worse. A lack of resources made their qualification for the World Cup all the more remarkable. The knowledge that national team matches were one of the only things to bring a respite to the fighting added an extra layer of responsibility. After all that, Zapata deserved his emotional moment, even in the face of crushing defeat.

El Salvador versus Hungary, Peru versus Cameroon, Kuwait versus Czechoslovakia, it made no odds to me who was playing that World Cup summer of 1982.

It was a spectacular festival of colour and exotic football from countries I had never heard of before then, and I wanted to absorb it all. Each unfamiliar kit, every unfamiliar name. Not just the Brazilians and the Italians, the fortunes of England and Scotland.

From there the seeds were sown. My future life mapped out, one football match at a time. In perpetuity.

But despite all that – Despite Luis Ramirez Zapata's obscure heroics, the breath-taking skill of the Brazilians, and the effervescent Italians, Tom Maskell was the name that rose to the surface that cramped press box afternoon. And things have never been quite the same since.

To most who cared about them they were just called 'Town,' or 'The Town.' A day or so before a home game you would hear people asking others if they were 'going up the Town on Saturday,' or 'what are Town's chances tomorrow.'

Often, both questions were met with a grumble of an answer, born out of love for the club, and a lifetime of support repaid with mediocrity at best, struggle the default.

'Bloody rubbish,' you would hear, more often than not. 'They've no chance.' A pause.

'See you Saturday?'

'Yeah,' with a sigh. 'See you Saturday.'

A small coastal town far enough away from anywhere else to be considered isolated, but not so far as to be thought of as remote, my home town was never designed to be a hotbed of football. Though that didn't mean that people didn't care deeply for the Town.

Through thin and thin they could depend on crowds of two or three thousand. Whether celebrating an unlikely promotion up into the Second Division in 1955 or fighting off coming dead last; ninety second out of ninety-two Football League clubs. A thing that had happened three times during my short life by that summer of 1982.

Neither my Mum nor Dad had any interest in football, but they embraced mine. Having seen me captivated in front of the television that World Cup summer, watching me take a ball out into the back garden to recreate each match as it finished, they did what they could to nurture my new-found passion, having watched washing baskets replace desperate last-ditch tackles from a stretched Argentinian defence. A ball rebounded off the shed, a defence splitting Brazilian pass. That iconic Tardelli goal celebration, complete with outstretched arms and a silent roar, muted by the excited exultations of the commentator and a distant Spanish crowd – the family cat lazing in the sun taking the place of the Italian bench. One eye opened to register her disdain, watching me warily as I celebrated in front of her.

With the World Cup over, and my half-full Panini sticker album (complete with haphazardly inscribed results roughly there or thereabouts the pre-printed boxes and columns designed to hold them) safely stowed in my bedside drawer along with all those intoxicating memories, my parents offered up two surprises.

Firstly, they enrolled me in the local Cub Scout troop. Not because I had ever showed any interest in tying knots or jamborees, but because they had a football team.

'All you have to do is go to the Cub Scout meetings every Tuesday and you can play in the Cub Scout league on Saturday mornings. What do you think?' It was a price worth paying.

We were not a good team. I distinctly remember my central-defensive partner and I would have a routine: we would fight with a tigerish fervour to defend our goal. But as we were a new team up against sides who had a good year or two on us, when the inevitable first goal came, we would look across to one another, shrug our shoulders and smile, before focusing back on trying to prevent another goal.

It was a routine that could sometimes play out into double figures some weeks. But it didn't stop us trying. And it didn't stop us from loving every single minute of it.

Then, after a season of defeat, with just two games to go, some of that World Cup magic played itself out in real life on a small scrub of a pitch behind our local church.

I remember it was a hot and humid evening in late May. One of those typical end of season fixtures, crammed in whenever and wherever to catch up with all the frozen off Saturdays of the winter just gone. I remember having to bat away clouds of mosquitoes that hung like an infuriating, writhing vapour beneath the thick tree line that hugged the pitch. Sucking in a lungful with every dash and tackle.

I remember it clearly because that otherwise nondescript early summer evening was the first time that I ever felt the rush of victory.

Conceding early, the team, and our long-suffering coach settled in for what we thought would be business as usual. But the next wave of attack was shut down by my defensive partner and I, and a long ball forward landed at an unsuspecting striker, who rushed forward and kicked with all his might. One all!

Then it happened again, and again. And at the final whistle and a three one win, our manager, lost in the emotion of it all, took off on a dash across the pitch – jumping and dancing, raising his fists to the air before, a safe distance from the team and their parents, a sweep of a hand across his eyes.

He would claim he was wiping away a mosquito. But we all knew better. We let him have his moment.

The second football surprise my parents gave me post World Cup 82 was a brand-new set of the Town kit.

'Well, you'll need something to wear to training won't you,' Dad said as he handed a set of the 82/83 season Town shirt, shorts and socks. I have the shirt still. All these years later. So important it was then and remains now. Colours faded from countless washes and long days outside, it was like a second skin to me. My shirt of choice after school, on the weekends, during the holidays; it is a miracle it didn't fall apart long before now.

In a homage to the iconic, unmistakable kit of Dutch masters Ajax, it had two thick red stripes sandwiching a single yellow one, the club badge embossed in the middle of the central block. It would be a colour scheme that defined my burgeoning footballing passion, and to this day still makes my heart skip a beat when I see the team run out in those colours (or a redesigned configuration of them).

The colours seemed to pop as I held that first kit in my hand – an actual professional football team's kit. And it was mine.

Pulling it on, looking down at that badge of my hometown, those colours felt so vibrant, exciting. Especially given the team photograph that came with it, complete with a list of that seasons upcoming fixtures. Professional footballers, organised into two rows, wearing that same kit and a serious look that suggested they meant business.

Without even seeing them play I felt a connection. That tribalism kicking in before any ball could be.

'We could go,' Dad said, nodding at the column of fixtures 'If you wanted?'

Town's Inchmery Road ground has always seemed ramshackle, existing in a perpetual state of acceptable decay. Ground staff along with a small army of volunteers maintaining it just the right side of characterful with little to no money or any other tangible resource. It is a minor miracle performed the length and breadth of the country around the lower leagues of the football pyramid.

A dizzying display of structural plate-spinning on creaking stadiums well into their second century of service, they are a labour of love. Handed down from one generation to the next, walls are bolstered. Failing floorboards replaced, broken seats nailed, glued, taped back into use. Pitches mown, re-seeded, advertising hoardings erected.

Turnstiles are oiled until they purr with that unmistakable clack of Victorian engineering, a siren song, an adrenalin rush, calling more toward their field of dreams.

For those with a head for heights, floodlights are scaled, and bulbs replaced. Running repairs on leaks in the main stand roof are undertaken from flimsy walkways that scale the structures lip.

No matter how many volunteers, there is always one more task than able body.

I remember so much of that first visit.

It was a blisteringly hot August afternoon. First day of the new season.

Instead of getting the bus, Dad had suggested walking. An accidental, but inspired choice that only helped to accelerate my love for the Town, and football.

As we drew closer, through the knit of terraced streets that surrounded Inchmery Road, the pavements slowly began to fill with other football supporters also making pilgrimage.

Children skipping a step or two to keep up with parents weaving between bodies, desperate to make the pub in time for a quick one before kick-off. The rich smell of tobacco, roll-ups, trailing conversations on the Town's chances, our new striker, whether the manager should have gone during the off-season. The odd burst of blue language punctuating a point, making me blush, not knowing what to do when confronted with swearing in my father's presence. He just smiled, held his finger to his lips and said:

'Just don't tell your mother!'

Rounding the corner into Inchmery Road and the floodlights hove into view – four sporting pillars as spectacular to a young boy as the Coliseum of Rome or the Parthenon of Athens, topping and tailing the hulking body of the main stand, its shadow stretching across the club's gated car park. The distant sounds of music being played over a crackling tannoy.

From then on it was an assault on the senses as we wove between a tangle of bodies outside the ground.

Patrons of the Crown pub opposite (a pub I would go on to drown a great many footballing sorrows in) spilled out into the street, some sitting along the front walls of the terraced houses that stretched away either side of the Crown. The smell of onions from a hot dog stand mingled with tobacco smoke and the heady scent of alcohol on their breath.

Beyond, and a man selling programmes advertised his wares with a constant call of:

'Ogrammes. Get your match day programme here. Ogrammes.'

I tugged on my Dad's arm, asked if I could get one. It would be the first in a collection now stretching into the thousands. Though none so precious as that first one.

On the bright red cover was a picture of a man shaking hands with another man in a Town shirt. The centre spread was that shiny, colourful team photo again. And among the advert heavy pages were lists of fixtures for the first and reserve teams. Last season's tables. Player appearances. The team line-ups on the back cover. A wealth of precious football information that I didn't have time to absorb.

Sensing his son slowing to a standstill to pore over that programme, he hurried me along. Not wanting me to get lost in the crowd.

'Pop it in your pocket for now. Come on.'

The bell on the door of the club shop rang as people came and went. New home and away kits in the window along with a display of scarves and other knick-knacks tempted me. But having just got an 'Ogramme' I didn't want to push my luck.

Beyond, and the chatter of the turnstiles catapulting supporters inside grew louder, as did the piped music, and we joined the queue to get in to the Inchmery Road terrace.

A line of people, some sporting Town scarves, filed toward their sporting fate.

A few smiled and ruffled my hair, looking down at me head to toe in my new kit. A few even commented: 'Good lad. I wish more would support their local team like you.'

I didn't know them. Had never met them before in my life. But in that moment, I felt a part of them, of the Town. I felt a flush of pride. I hadn't even set foot inside.

When it was our turn Dad paid the man, then nodded for me to go ahead through the turnstile, only being able to enter one at a time.

Through the clunking ironwork looking glass, I stood there on my own for a few seconds, waiting for Dad to join me. The cool air deep in the bowels of the Inchmery Road terrace giving a young lad in shirt and shorts the chills. Though nothing like those that greeted a first view of the pitch.

Up a steep flight of wooden steps, I stood blinking at the top. A shimmering billiard green expanse overlooked either side by the East and West Stands; two tiered constructions sporting simple benches on the lower, and rows of flip down wooden seats on the upper. The snap of occupied spots flipping back up as old friends stood to greet one another echoed about the upper levels as if someone had smuggled in a fistful of firecrackers.

At the far end, the smaller Victoria Road terrace was split into two fenced-off enclosures. The least attractive of the two, crammed beneath the half-time scoreboard close to the corner flag housed a small band of skulking visiting supporters.

And down on the pitch, two sets of players warmed up; the Town eleven sporting tracksuit tops in the clubs' colours, stretching out limbs, pinging balls across to one another.

It was a lower league cacophony of sight and sound.

It was overwhelming, supporters weaving around me patiently at the top of the steps as I took it all in. It had, after all, happened to them once upon a time – that first glimpse of what would come to mean so much.

After what seemed like an age staring wide-eyed at the scene, Dad gently tugged at my hand, and we made our way across the terrace until we found a vacant crush barrier, to lean against in his case, peer over in mine. Those now anachronistic crush barriers that were once a legal requirement on all terracing to prevent injury in a crowd surge, they appeared wholly redundant at Inchmery Road, where that opening day crowd of the 82/83 season; some three thousand, two hundred and forty three souls, could have been accommodated three or four times over before capacity had been reached. Crowd surges were, in reality, no more than a Chairman's fantasy in the lower reaches of the Fourth Division.

Over the next two or three seasons, that same barrier would be the spot Dad and I would find ourselves gravitating towards to watch the Town. By no great design. We just did. And would in the decades that followed, whenever the stars aligned for us both to be free on the same Saturday.

Even now, many years after his passing, if I can co-ordinate a visit to see mum with a match, it is that barrier I stand at.

The game itself was a bit of a blur. The red and yellow of the Town up against the all blue of Rochdale, the players hurled themselves into the fray. Last ditch tackles, long raking passes, rasping shots had me fumbling for my programme to put shirt number to name on the team sheet. Heroes in a Town shirt were being discovered. Their endeavours replicated in the back garden that evening. Socrates and Co. from the World Cup discarded in favour of these lower league journeymen.

Nobodies outside of Town, but to a ten-year-old boy they became everything.

The roar of the crowd at a near miss. The chants from a group somewhere behind us. The wave of applause at a decent pass. Tobacco smoke, hot sun, howls of despair at fluffed clearances. Silence as a Rochdale goal in front of the Inchmery Road End elicited roars of delight in the players, then a second or two later in the smattering of Dale supporters at the far end of the pitch. It was a heady mix that, to his credit, Dad bought into.

The game never meant to him what it does to me. He went because I think he liked seeing me so enthralled, so passionate about something. He liked that we had a thing we did together.

He cheered at the goals, clapped at the right times, looked suitably happy or sad depending on the result. But that was it. He hadn't been interested in football before I came along, and if I hadn't, I don't think he ever would have.

Ninety minutes passed by in a flash. A two-nil opening day defeat doing nothing to dampen my spirits on the way home. Chattering animatedly about this shot, or that save. Pointing out to Dad future fixtures from the programme in as subtle tones as an excited ten-year-old could muster.

'They are playing Torquay United on the 24th Dad. That would be a good one to watch wouldn't it, Dad? That will be a good game?'

The week after that first match, I found myself riding my bike across town, back to Inchmery Road. The hush of a benign Tuesday morning so different to that first bustling Saturday that seemed to be over in a flash.

Unable to pause to absorb it all on match day, I had all the time in the world. The stadium seemingly all to myself that lazy, sun baked morning. From somewhere in the weave of streets that surrounded Inchmery Road, the distant shouts and screams of children playing, the odd rumble of a car engine, the drone of a lawnmower from an unseen backyard echoing across the rooftops.

But right there, at the stadium itself, it was just me and my bike.

You couldn't do an entire loop of the ground, as the East stand ran flush against the backyards of Lepe Street. A fact that had me casting envious glances at that run of houses, imagining what it must feel like to have a professional football ground as your back wall.

But take a left before the shuttered turnstiles of the Inchmery Road terrace and you were free to wander through the car park and past the West Stand. Past the club shop, the small ticket office windows beyond, the heavyset main entrance doors into the bowels of the club beyond them, and back out again, onto Victoria Road, where the turnstiles for the small away supporter's paddock and the home fans enclosure looked out onto an equally quiet residential street.

Press yourself up against the exit gates of Victoria Road, focusing on the small gap between them, and you could see a sliver of pitch, a slice of the East Stand in shadow, and the Inchmery terrace basking in the sun.

From time to time a groundsman pushing a mower up and back across the pitch came into view, concentrating on his task. I knew then, as I still do now, that despite that looking like the best job on earth, I would be terrible at it. My fresh cut lines into the pitch all askew from getting lost in the scene about me – my eyes drifting up toward the banks of benches and seats, the steep sweep of terracing, the towering floodlights casting an intricate shadow across the turf.

Having found this sliver of a view, it would be a regular haunt that first summer, and the summers that followed. Providing some comfort during the interminably long off season of May, June, and July.

Back on Inchmery Road and the ring of the club shop bell seemed deafening in the hush.

Free from the constraints of my Dad deciding what constituted staring at one thing for too long, I remember consuming each and every inch of our small shop.

Three mannequins in the window sported the home and away kits for the season. The middle body wearing the away shirt, shorts and socks that were the same design as the home kit, but instead of red and yellow, two strips of dark blue sandwiched a column of lighter blue. It was love at first sight. And the only thing on my birthday list that September.

I think it was a small relief to my Mum and Dad, who would no longer have to bargain with sense and hygiene with their son when it came to negotiating the washing of that lone home kit. From then on there would be no histrionics, just a smooth transition from red to blue.

In the years to come it would be the block of pigeonholes behind the counter that would be the centre of attention for me. As the season wore on, issues of every Town programme, home and away, would begin to populate there, so as people like me could fill in the gaps in their ever-growing collection.

Match reports, visiting player pics and photos, interviews with Town players, action shots, reserve team round-ups, league tables, fixtures and results, appearance statistics – every issue was a vital addition to an ever-growing Town encyclopaedia. Holding precious facts about my beloved team as they did, they were the primary drain on my pocket money, and have been so ever since.

That first trip, however, the pigeonholes were empty, save for Saturday's programme, my copy of which had had to be placed under a couple of heavy books on our dining table at home to flatten it out – so crushed had it been in my excited grip at the match. Even now when I look through it, its crumpled state reminds me of the thrill of that day. A tactile testament to such a seminal moment in my life.

Pocket money carefully counted, I bought a team poster that featured in the centre pages of Saturdays programme, not wanting to defile my copy by removing it. I watched the lady behind the counter carefully roll it and fasten with an elastic band before handing it over. I thanked her meekly, holding it gingerly as the shop bell peeled away to nothing behind me. Spending one last moment, just me and the Town, the hush of stands, terraces, floodlights, before cycling away; casting one last glance back before Inchmery Road slipped back into the warren of streets around it.

Two

The Torquay United game of the 24th would not be my next taste of Town magic. Instead, I would learn the ritual of the vidiprinter, of sitting transfixed in front of the television on a Saturday afternoon, watching scores chunter along the foot of the screen while boxing bouts, rugby league matches, and motor racing played out in the background.

Unable to look away for fear of missing your team's score rattle through, it was an exercise in abstinence: forgoing food, drink, the toilet over that first glimpse of your footballing fate.

It was through the Grandstand vidiprinter that I recorded the first ever Town goal, and point, in my lifetime as a supporter. A Tommy Patterson header in a one all draw away to Northampton the Saturday after that Rochdale defeat had The Town up and running for the season.

A late Bob Larson goal against Torquay on the 24th salvaged a draw and did much to lift the disappointment of not being there in person. Jumping up and down as, with little more than two minutes to go, Larson and Town appeared on the screen, I would be out in the back garden the second full time was recorded to play out how I thought the action of the match went.

It would be a ritual after every match witnessed via the vidiprinter. Rain or shine. I remember vividly playing out with a foot of snow on the ground. The winter dusk illuminated by the snowfall's eerie glow enabling me to stay out longer, until Mum came to the backdoor pleading with me to come in.

It was only later at dinner that night of the Torquay match that the matter of not being at Inchmery Road came up.

I was a quiet kid. I didn't make a fuss. So, when no mention of going to the game came up, I kept my disappointment to myself. I tuned in to Grandstand like how Dad had shown me the week before.

We always had fish and chips from the chip shop on a Saturday night, eating them on our laps in front of the television, rather than dinner at the table with the TV off every other night.

'I got you a surprise,' Mum said, handing me an envelope.

Inside were three tickets for Town's Milk Cup game against Third Division Hull City the coming Tuesday. Three tickets for the West Stand. Three of those firecracker seats in the top tier.

'I wasn't sure where you'd like to go, but the lady at the club said these were good seats. I thought you and your Dad could show me what all the fuss is about.'

It had been a steep learning curve for Mum, that summer of 82. A footballing baptism of fire. When she did the maths on my World Cup sticker album, multiplying the cost of a packet of six stickers by the number of blank spaces looking back at me every time I leafed through it, she knew that pocket money would never cover it.

Knowing that her and Dad couldn't make up the difference – we weren't poor, but there wasn't any money left at the end of each month, especially not for football stickers – she bought me a small Ladybird book on the World Cup. With a green hard-back cover sporting the World Cup trophy, it more than filled in the blanks.

Pictures of the host stadiums, the flags of participating teams, national team kits, qualifying results, and a map on the inside cover detailing where in the world each team came from, it became the invaluable companion to my sticker album. And between the two we more or less had it covered. Though missing stickers were still mourned, players' faces forever hidden from view. Tantalising glimpses of exotic, unfamiliar shirts, and far-flung stadiums behind them lost to economics.

At the back of the book was a section to fill out with all the scores and group tables, building up an archive of every match and every goal at the World Cup.

It was a system never seen before by Mum, who did her best to give her son a statistical head-start while he was at school.

Filling out the Group A table after the first round of matches that had been played while I was still in lessons, I couldn't hide the horror on my face when she showed me.

Explaining that the table could only be filled in when we had all the scores for that group, Mum was mortified that she had ruined the book for me. Though she was somewhat consoled by me saying that we could just neatly cross the teams out and write over them in felt-tip when all was said and done.

From then on Mum would write the lunchtime scores down on a scrap of paper and watch me transcribe them into my book and sticker album. Even now, decades later, leafing through that book, seeing mum's wonderfully neat handwriting, and an equally neat line through it, I always feel a wave of emotion. Remembering that look of acute disappointment on her face, on defacing that precious little book of her son's.

She had just wanted, so very desperately, to be a part of this wonderful new thing that had enthralled her little boy. And Group A World Cup 82 aside, she really was.

It was Mum who came to every Cub Scout match, and then the boys' team I played for after graduating cubs, in wind, rain, and snow. It was Mum who made football themed birthday cakes. Who signed me up for the Junior Town supporters club, which ultimately set me up on a crash course with the career of a young Tom Maskell.

It was Mum who waited patiently for me at a Town open day a year or two after World Cup 82, nudging me on to the front of the throng of boys clamouring for autographs of their Town heroes, beaming as I turned back to her to show her my little brown autograph book, and my latest capture.

It was mum who walked around with me on the stadium tour, feigning interest at changing rooms, long corridors lined with old team photographs, the players' lounge, an indoor sports hall, the steep stairs that led down to the players' tunnel and the pitch.

It was Mum who sat, at the same open day, on the lower benches of the West Stand, trying to gently encourage me to put my boots on and join the training sessions for kids being conducted out on the Inchmery Road pitch.

I couldn't, by the way. I couldn't do it – so hallowed had that pitch become to me, the thought of making a single mistake on it, of knocking over just one cone on a dribbling exercise, of misplacing a pass, of missing the ball altogether – it sent lightning bolts of anxiety through me. It left me frozen with fear, my legs unable, or unwilling to propel me up the steps and out into the sunshine.

Instead, we both just sat there quietly, watching other kids play. Their excited shouts echoing about the rafters, until the final whistle sounded, and my anxiety lifted.

Opportunity missed, I felt a genuine surge of relief that the decision had been taken out of my hands, and we walked home to the soundtrack of me leafing through my autograph book, animatedly showing each scribble to Mum. Detailing who they were, and what they did in the team.

Mum, cautiously satisfied enough that the experience hadn't been a scarring one, smiled and nodded back at her boy.

To this day I still can't reconcile myself to saying that it was a wasted chance. I stand by my younger self, and his stance on keeping that Inchmery Road turf sacred, no matter how much he would have loved to have been out there.

It was Mum who did all this, to help nurture the footballing passion in me. And it was Mum who got me those tickets to my first ever floodlit football match. And an experience even more magical than that first game against Rochdale.

It was already, in my mind, going to be an exotic, intoxicating experience, this Milk Cup First Round, First Leg tie. Not simply because it would be my first taste of knock-out cup football, but because it would be against a team from the rarefied air of the Third Division. A lower league David and Goliath battle.

The days leading up to the game were spent memorising the classified results page of my parents' Sunday paper. Carefully extracted and placed on the dinner table for multiple views, the meticulously constructed columns of results and league tables, that tapered away into smaller print below the fold with the details of the non-league and Scotland's lower leagues, were a feast of football.

Permutations on the Hull City match were considered again and again, based on the cold hard, black and white facts of these fledgling league tables.

Down in the Fourth Division, Town's two draws from their first three games had them sixth from bottom. While Hull's win that Saturday meant they had yet to be beaten with one win and two draws. Tenth in Division three had them looking up at promotion, not over their shoulders at the threat of the bottom four in the basement division, and re-election come the following May.

While Town attracted just shy of three thousand for the match against Torquay, Hull drew in eleven thousand for a home win over Rotherham.

Despite it all, with ramifications complete, heart kept winning out over head. It would be a decent two-one win for the Town.

The streets, the winding walk among them were the same, but everything felt different. Heightened. A parallel footballing universe played out among dusky hues and dark skies. Crisp chills lurking among deep shadows.

As we drew closer a brilliant halo of light began to illuminate the night sky above Inchmery Road. Like some scene from a lower league nativity, guiding us on to our sporting saviour, the four great floodlights towering over each corner of the Inchmery Road ground burnt up into the darkness.

Their presence felt long before they finally came into view, they added a magic that lingers to this day. The excitement of a game under the lights; though that first experience, shimmering beneath such vivid luminescence was beyond intoxicating.

Climbing up the steps to our seats in the West Stand, that first glimpse of the pitch, cast a brilliant emerald green beneath the lights, set my heart racing. Taking a few moments for my eyes to adjust to the scene, blinking as I felt my way down the steps to our seats, everything seemed that little bit more special. The reds and yellows of the Town kit popped that little bit more when floodlit. The murmured chatter of the shadowy crowd that little bit more expectant as they cascaded down the steep, unlit stands during the warm-ups. The smell of tobacco, a little richer on the air. The crack of footballs being pinged from one side of the pitch to the other, sharper in the cool night air, propelled beneath the lights with a wicked, magical velocity.

It was the perfect setting to witness my first ever Town victory.

In front of a crowd of fifteen hundred (only the Town faithful bothering with a League Cup fixture that left the rest of the footballing world completely non-plussed) two second half goals from Tommy Patterson and Barry Cranmer overturned an early City strike, and even had Mum on her feet as that winning bullet header from our centre back found the back of the net.

It was a wonderful feeling, that wash of emotion, as those goals went in, and again at the final whistle. Town had won, and against Third Division opposition. It was the best moment ever.

It was also all for nought, as Town lost the second leg away at Boothferry Park three nil. It didn't matter. The magic of witnessing a match beneath the lights for the first time, and a first ever Town win, would elevate this obscure first round fixture in my mind forever.

It had also been a thrill to watch a match from such a lofty position. Being able to follow the play from end to end, barring the odd obstruction from the pillars that propped up the West Stand roof.

Getting a good view of both goals, of all the near misses and set pieces was a different experience than that on the Inchmery terrace, where a constant readjustment of position to keep a good view of the pitch between the throng of bodies ahead of you meant missing out on some of it.

For our family, and many others like it in the town, it was a simple question of economics. Seats in the upper tiers were at a premium, followed by the benches in the lower sections, where high balls could get lost behind the lip of the upper tier if you were sat nearer the back.

Cheapest of all to watch the Town were the Inchmery and Victoria Road terraces, where an adult and a child, a programme, two cups of tea, and a chocolate bar for half time came in at a manageable total for a family on a budget.

It's not that the West and East stands were so expensive. But if there was a cheaper option, then many counting down the days to the next pay packet would take it. For me, so long as I was there, I didn't care where I was situated. Though Dad's favourite crush barrier seemed the natural spot.

The terraces were also the most raucous spots in Inchmery Road. While the more reserved took to the benches and seats, the terraces seemed electric to a young boy. Coarse jokes aimed at the referee, followed by guttural laughter among those who heard it. Screams of fury at a bad decision, or a fluffed shot on an open goal, an unwanted linesman's flag. Celebrations at a Town goal, random men hugging one another, surging between the crush barriers down to the front to salute our goalscoring hero, roaring up into the afternoon their approval. Shouts coming from somewhere that I would later understand to be racism, where visiting black players could sometimes be subjected to extra attention and calls that I didn't understand at the time, but I felt the malice and hate in their intonations.

The chants of a small group of young men standing behind us, who never ceased to make me jump, the way they seemed to start up from nothing into a series of familiar Town songs.

It was all so loud, so chaotic, so dizzying and confusing. And sometimes scary.

We didn't see much of the hooliganism of the day all the way down in the Fourth Division. When we did it was mostly when bigger teams tumbled down through the leagues found themselves down among the small fry.

My first taste of it came when Sheffield United came to town the season after that Hull City match.

The game had been fractious, and the chants from the sizeable away following that we were all going home in an ambulance did nothing to ease the atmosphere.

Shortly after the exit gates had been opened (which usually happened with some fifteen minutes to go, though I once heard of a man whose sum football going experience came in the last quarter hour of every Town match – standing in his slippers with a mug of tea waiting for the exit gate opposite his house to open, he would wander in, chat to the steward, watching the last moments of the game play out) a section of the United support stormed the Inchmery terrace.

I remember the rush of bodies away down the terrace, of peering around Dad who was sheltering me behind him. Police sirens finally bringing some order.

We left as soon as it was safe, before the final whistle, only feeling a little more at ease once we had left a good few streets between us and the ground.

Thankfully, my Uncle, Mum's brother, calmed her down after Dad had said what happened. He was a Torquay United fan, and a real character. A freelance artist, he had formed 'The People's Republic of Chagford' – a group claiming sovereignty over their small town in Devon and had once got the name of his 'girlfriend' wrong when having to unexpectedly introduce her to us.

'This is Maureen,' he said to us confidently, trying to style out that we had arrived for our visit earlier than he had expected.

'Marie,' she corrected him with dagger eyes that suggested there would be no second 'sleepover.'

My Uncle had, he said on the phone to Mum nearly been 'duffed up' a few times trying to extricate himself from Plainmoor, the home of Torquay. He gave her a list of clubs in the Fourth Division that were a potential risk, and we would avoid them when they came to town, preferring the safety of Grandstand, the vidiprinter, and a kick about in the back garden.

Those hooligan curtailed football weekends would also be mitigated by Mum the following Monday, who would meet me after school with our bikes. We would cycle across town to Inchmery Road, and she would come in with me to the club shop and buy a copy of that Saturday's programme, knowing how much I treasured them.

'Just don't tell your Dad,' she would say every time, even though we both knew that Dad was fully aware of our expeditions and would not have minded one bit even if he wasn't.

While I quickly scanned the precious contents to see which player had been interviewed, and who featured in the action shots from a previous match, Mum would sometimes chat to the lady in charge of those precious pigeon-holes.

It was how she came to learn of 'Junior Town' – a club for children who supported the team.

On my birthday she beamed as she presented me with my laminated supporters club membership card. I stood there looking at my name next to the club badge, my membership number: 223.

'They organise trips. They run competitions. And they also do special surprises on your birthday,' she said, as she took down an envelope from the kitchen cupboard and handed it to me. Inside was a card with a watercolour painting of a pair of ducks on the cover.

The inscription inside read: 'Happy Birthday from all at the Town' and was surrounded by the autographs of the entire first team squad. I thought my heart was going to stop!

It wasn't until much later in life that the true naivety of a duck themed birthday card from a football club to one of its young supporters shone through.

In a marketing savvy age where every single object in the world can be embossed with a football club badge and deemed 'The Official toothbrush of Liverpool FC,' a simple card sporting a pair of Mallards, bought from a local newsagent's, showed the old-world innocence of the football of my childhood.

Too precious to have displayed on the mantelpiece, where anything could have befallen it, my birthday card from The Town sat first on my bedside cabinet, then was stowed inside the programme closest to my birthday in my top drawer.

Standing there that eleventh birthday, membership card in one hand, birthday card in the other, wearing a brand-new set of Town away kit that had been my main present, a lot of what Mum had said about my membership card had got lost in the fog of excitement.

Competitions I heard, something about trips during school holidays (the most memorable of which had been an excursion to London to visit Highbury and White Hart Lane, the homes of Arsenal and Tottenham Hotspur.

I remember a hot summer's day. Sitting on the coach next to a boy called Peter Peter.

"I know", I remember him saying with a shrug "I don't know why either. I suppose Mum and Dad really liked the name Peter".

I remember the beautiful Art Deco façade at Highbury. Vast marble halls that looked like a palace. The vast north bank terrace. Main stands that could have accommodated all of Inchmery Road three or four times over, gawping slack jawed as we walked the perimeter of the pitch.

Along the sun bleached, quiet, residential street outside, the small party of Junior Town members queued along to gain access to a souvenir kiosk – three programmes from the season just finished and a pencil was my lot at both stadiums. White Hart Lane a towering, shimmering wall of blue seats rising up into the Gods. Sprinklers hissing and twitching across a vast pitch).

But the element that had interested her most as she spoke to the lady in the club shop completely passed me by on my birthday:

Free entry to all reserve team games.

Despite devouring all the information in the programme on the reserve team, reading match reports and studying their league table, they remained an abstract. Out of sight, they were a precious part of The Town, but one that seemed to exist in obscurity. A footnote to a club that were, at best, a footnote to the greater footballing public at large.

But as my passion for football outpaced Dad's tolerance for attending a sport he had a limited interest in, an interest born solely out of his son's love for it, it would be those obscure reserves who began to take the load off him.

'They only get a hundred or so to watch the reserves,' Mum said to Dad as I stood staring at my card's birthday and membership. 'The lady said it was perfectly safe for a lad on his own to go.'

And so, it would become the Town reserves that sustained my footballing hunger, topped up by a first team game with Dad as often as time and money allowed.

Three

Those first few seasons supporting Town were a blur of excitement. Creating heroes from sides that mostly generated groans of disappointment from the more weathered souls on the Inchmery Road terrace, it was the thrill of the game, not points that inspired me. Just as well, as the Town finished in the bottom four twice, needing to apply for re-election to stay in the Football League both times.

But any team sporting the red and yellow of the Town, playing out on that Inchmery Road pitch took on a God-like status in my eyes. Because of it, transition from first to reserves came easily. It was gift, suddenly having two Town teams to support, not just the one.

Those first few seasons after the Sheffield United horror show took on a familiar routine. Mum and Dad would drop me off at Inchmery Road, before heading out to the big supermarket at the edge of town. Mum making me perform the standard hat, gloves, membership card check before letting me out the car, then not letting Dad pull away until I was safely inside the gates of the car park.

I would wave on the step of the club shop, and head in to spend my pocket money on programmes for my collection, before heading round to the only open turnstile on reserve team match days at the foot of the West Stand.

They didn't do a programme for reserve team matches, but they did do a team sheet, and I would feel a sense of satisfaction at handing over my two pence with my Junior Town card at the turnstile and securing my copy. They had been known to run out before kick off, so few were printed.

A simple sheet of A4, it sported the bare minimum of information: date, that it was a Combination League fixture, and the teams. It was still precious Town information. And being printed on a grainy, fibrous paper it felt satisfying to the touch. It had a weight to it that, to a young boy, suggested importance. No matter the lowly status of the fixture. Worthy of being safely stowed away with my sticker album, my first team programmes.

After all, the names on those team sheets were Town players. Wearing the Town badge, the Town colours. Even a career in the reserve team of a Fourth Division club being one that a young boy could only dream of.

With crowds barely into three digits some games, the rest of Inchmery Road sat dormant. The one functioning turnstile funnelling spectators up into the top tier of the West Stand, where a sole steward would smile and shrug, wave at the sea of empty seats and say 'Sit where you like pal' to every reserve team punter.

I would always be in situ a good half hour before kick-off. Revelling in the time to absorb the scene. I would pick out mine and Dad's crush barrier first, before letting Inchmery Road wash over me. Rows of empty benches, a page of a newspaper lurching and tumbling across vacant terracing. The shouts of the players warming up, clear and crisp without the tannoy system blaring out music.

It was so familiar, and yet so different to a first team game.

The anticipation felt the same. But the fact that a Combination League fixtures' main purpose was to give a run out to squad players not featuring in the first team, to regulars coming back from injury, to the odd player on trial, meant that the result was far from the be all and end all.

They were games played at a tempo, with endeavour and no small amount of skill. Some players desperate to show their worth to the reserve team manager in the hope of elevation. Sometimes trying too hard on the ball and looking as if they had found their level.

But with the base desire to secure the win and the points, to climb the league table removed, reserve team games could also sometimes slip into the pedestrian.

Players could relax a little, maybe express themselves a bit more, despite it being a game that no one really wanted to be a part of. All much preferring the cut and thrust of first team football, the roar of a crowd far more motivating than shouts to a colleague echoing about an empty stadium. Echoes that no doubt amplified the disappointment that this is not how they saw their football career being played out.

It was the same, but so different to first team Saturdays. Even the kits betrayed the fixtures lowly status: the sponsors name absent across the front of reserve team jerseys. No need to be there if no one is watching; another reminder to the players of just where they were.

I thought their shirts looked great, however. Devoid of *'Drover Tools,'* a local hardware store, across the middle they looked more colourful. More Town colour unspoilt by wording could only ever be a good thing to a young boy. Even my replica kits thought so too. Slowly peeling the felt wording away with multiple washes – washes long after *'Drover Tools'* stopped being the club's sponsor (I wore those first Town kits until I was physically too big to do so any more) – I have been left with mementos of that first Town love affair with *'Dover Too'* emblazoned across the front.

With the score not being the sole end game, supporters could relax a little too at reserve team matches. Watching a game of football for the sake of it. For the simple pleasures that that brings. Enjoying the ebb and flow from one goalmouth to the other without the underlying tensions that a conceded goal could see your team slump to foot of the entire football league.

The temptation to have a sneaky look through the programmes bought in the club shop was strong during a lull in the play. Picking at the white paper bag the lady in the shop wrapped them up in, taking a peek at the strange covers from away games. The desire was significant. But out of respect to the players before me, I couldn't. No matter how uninspiring the game had become.

I would wait until I got home to pore through those away programmes. Always getting a thrill from seeing our team photo, the players' pen pics there for the rest of the world, or a few thousand people in Darlington to see.

Many, many years later, on a busman's holiday in America, I caught a few minor league baseball games, thanks in no small part to the movie *Bull Durham*. A film about the trials and tribulations of a small-town baseball team called the Durham Bulls, it portrayed a sport so ingrained into the fabric of its community, so central to that sense of identity and belonging, that attending the ball-game transcended victory or defeat.

Aided by the security that you couldn't be relegated, the film played out to the backdrop of life in the bleachers. Of humid summer evenings spent among friends, the crack of ball on bat, the rippling of applause, organ music serenading between innings with peppy little ditties. And so too did my holiday experiences at places such as the Asheville Tourists and the Evansville Otters.

It reminded me of those afternoons spent at all those Combination League matches as a boy.

It made me realise that it wasn't just about the games themselves. They gave me the time and the space to fall in love with the fabric of The Town. And the very fabric of football itself.

Those Combination days gave me the time to see what it meant to really love football. Your team.

I made friends, sort of. Mostly nameless friends, where nods and smiles would be the sum total of our interactions. Regulars of the reserve team just like me. Characters much like those in the bleachers of *Bull Durham*.

People who had to be at Inchmery Road come Saturday, three pm. So important was it to who they were – going to the football, to see Town.

In a crowd of thousands, it was hard to see this deep-rooted sense of self in any great detail among the sea of familiar faces stood on their own particular spot, game after game. Cheers and groans, expectation, despair, hope and sorrow that washed across the Inchmery terrace, did so in a blur of noise and electricity and bustle on a match day that was thoroughly overwhelming to a young boy.

Though seeing those same faces, year after year, in the same spots on the terrace, sitting on the same stretch of wall outside the Crown pub, the same 'Ogramme sellers on the same pitches, the lady in the club shop who never seemed to go home – I knew that this shared experience, it was everything and more for each and every one of them.

It was just that at the reserve team games I had the time and the space to really see the minutiae of what supporting a team meant. Or could mean.

Of the smattering of support attending the Combination League games, there were four who stood out.

Four regulars who would dot themselves across the West Stand. Four small stories of footballing love and devotion, exposed once the tide of first team support had drained away.

Some had names, those that didn't I named. One of which was Transistor Man.

Transistor Man was a plain-looking gent in his fifties, who sat just to the left of the half-way line, and arrived, watched the game, and then left again, plugged into a small transistor radio he had stowed away in a coat pocket.

Ear plugs in from the moment he turned up, he would talk with a raised voice to the turnstile operator, the steward, anyone. Unable to regulate the volume of his own among the chatter from his radio, you would be able to hear him coming long before he arrived.

'ALL RIGHT MATE. YEAH FINE. IS FISHER PLAYING TODAY? CHEERS.'

Tuned into a football station in order to glean The Town's first team score before anyone else, he would sit and watch one game, while listening to another completely.

We would all learn of Town's fate through him, who would carry this onerous task with an emotionless stoicism. With a simple nod of the head.

'ONE NIL' would signal Town going behind.

'ONE NIL. PATTERSON,' would mean Town had taken the lead.

At half and full time, when the Town first team score was announced over the tannoy, he would nod his blessing. Content that they had got it right.

He could have listened to his radio at home. Watched Grandstand. But he clearly preferred to be at Inchmery Road, even if he couldn't fully engage with what was going on out there on the pitch before him, so wired in was he to the emotion of a match far, far away, and the fate of the first team.

But come rain, snow, or shine, he would be there. At every Combination League game.

Inchmery Road. On a Saturday. If there was a game on. He had to be there.

The second of my quartet was Mary, a fearsome character, and a legend around Inchmery Road. Well into her seventies, she usually sat on the benches behind the dugouts, and was famous for her withering putdowns of visiting managers and substitutes, should they ever leave the confines of their Perspex shelter.

Banging the back of the visiting dugout at every Town goal from the moment the goal was scored, to the moment the ball was placed back on the half-way line for the restart, she was a footballing force of nature, and a law unto herself.

No matter how many times a steward asked her not to bang on the dugout, she would again at the next Town goal, shrugging her shoulders at the luckless steward shuffling along the benches to ask her once more to stop. A wicked glint in her eyes from beneath a headscarf protecting her latest tight perm, she would look a nondescript frail old woman when you walked past her at the shops. But in Inchmery Road she was 'Crazy Mary.'

With her usual spot behind the dugouts on the lower tier closed for reserve team games, she would sit instead on the front row of the upper tier of the West Stand and glare at the unsuspecting visiting bench from there, who remained blissfully unaware of their luck. She didn't hate the opposition. I really don't think she cared who they were. She just loved the Town so much that anyone trying to thwart them was her enemy for ninety minutes or so. And she would bang her pleasure at a Town goal until their ears rang. When exiled from her usual seat she would make do with pounding the advertising hoardings hanging from the upper tier. Our lone steward smiling, shaking his head. Mary too far away from anyone to cause annoyance.

Programme Man was chubby, in his fifties, with balding hair and ruddy cheeks, who hid behind a pair of ill-fitting glasses that would slide down his nose and be forever pushed back in place with his forefinger.

I would often see him in the club shop before games, leafing through the discount boxes of old season programmes, as well as at the counter with a neatly written list of needs from the current season – the lady behind the counter pulling out the issues needed from the pigeon-holes.

He would sometimes cut a strange figure, standing patiently on first team match days for his turn on the boxes among a small crowd of schoolboys doing the same thing. A grown man who many may have thought should have grown out of programme collecting, he waited for his turn and did his thing.

Now that I am not far off his age, and still prone to waiting my turn for a leaf down memory lane through those bargain boxes, I remember Programme Man as a benign, lonely figure. The Town being a social lifeline, where you can belong without any prejudice, where you can be a part of something, regardless of your conversational awkwardness, your lack of words, even if no one knows your name.

Saturdays were his day. His paper bag of treasured programmes on his lap. At the Town. He was part of it all, for a few short hours, before dissolving away into anonymity, and isolation once more.

Some Saturdays after a game I would catch a glimpse of him sat alone in the corner of the local chip shop, looking out at his own reflection in the ever-darkening glass frontage of a cold winter evening, as if frozen in an English version of a Hopper painting.

I never spoke to him. I wish that I had.

May he still be out there somewhere, tending to his collection.

I remember those new programmes bought on reserve team match days all those years ago being too great a temptation for Programme Man. With the result of a Combination League fixture not carrying the importance of a first team game, and with the comforting noises of a match in play echoing about Inchmery Road, he would be drawn down to that paper bag stuffed with new issues. Taking them out, he would lean into them, hunched over their contents.

Lost in football statistics, he would be jolted back into the moment by the cheers and applause at a reserve team goal, Crazy Mary banging on the hoardings in front of her seat.

He would sit up quickly and begin clapping, pushing his glasses back up the bridge of his nose. Watching the restart and a few minutes of play, before being drawn back down toward the contents of that white paper bag.

Just like Transistor Man, Programme Man had to be there, even if the games sometimes passed him by.

Bill White happened to sit a few seats away from my usual spot near the front, where you could see both goals well, but the pillars obscured the corner flags on the near side of the pitch.

It would be fun trying to guess the flight of the ball at a corner, trying to spot it before it potentially met a head and was either sent toward goal or cleared out into midfield.

Bill was a large, broad-shouldered man in his seventies. When he sat down in his seat, you could almost hear the groan of the coarse weave of his coat as it tried to stretch across his vast frame.

With a flattened nose from multiple breaks, he looked every part the retired muscle for some criminal gang. That was until he smiled, which was infectious. A grin as broad as those shoulders, he was a gentle bear of a man, who would always have a half-time boiled sweet in his pocket for me, him, and anyone else close enough to receive his offering.

Our conversations wouldn't be extensive, both respecting each-other's need for some quiet reserve team reverie. Reverie often inter-cut with shrugs at a goal conceded, smiles at a goal scored, raised eyebrows and an intake of breath at a near miss.

But what our conversations lacked in length, they more than made up for in meaning, with Bill becoming one of my all-time Town heroes. Right up there with those first squads of the early to mid-eighties. With Tom Maskell…

'What a day,' he would often say as he sat down and got comfortable before kick-off, nodding and smiling at me. 'With a game ahead of us, in this beautiful old ground, we are living like kings, no? If you could show me a place that I'd rather be on a Saturday afternoon, well, that would have to be some place indeed. Beautiful,' he would say, drifting off and out across the pitch, looking at the empty terracing, the far stand, floodlights.

'I think I would be perfectly happy if I were just sitting here watching the groundsman cut the grass, up and back. The ground all to myself. I would do it if they let me. Anything to be sat here.

'Though you can't beat the anticipation of a game, and all it might bring. We are living like kings, sat here. Like kings.'

I don't remember how many matches. How many weeks and months had passed with us sitting in close proximity to one another, lost in the ebb and flow of a game before Bills' revelation.

He was mostly a man of few words. Few, but well-chosen words.

He would never talk for the sake of it. And he was not a man of ego.

I think if I had led Bill's life, talking to a young football fanatic, I would have been far less restrained.

I don't remember how the conversation came about, something about me wishing one day to play for the Town, when he said it, before looking out into the middle distance, and a place lost to time. Faint memories overlapping the present.

'You know, I played for the Town. Many years ago.'

I can only picture the look on my face. Wide eyed and slack jawed. It was enough to make Bill laugh before he told the story. Or a condensed version of it.

'I played in goal for a few games. Down there,' he pointed down at the pitch. 'I was decent enough as a back-up for The Town. I moved here from Plymouth Argyle reserves in 1953. I wasn't here that long. Maybe a season and a bit. But I fell in love with the place. And when I finally got to retire, I moved back here. And I've been here ever since. The club always look after me, even after all this time. It's a special place.'

It was a life re-told by a modest man and missed out much of the incredible elements of his story. A story that would only begin to emerge with a few trips to the local library.

I had found the book by accident, passing the time while Mum returned her latest stack of borrowed books. She would read ferociously, devouring whole volumes in a couple of days. And Mum and I would find ourselves at the library at least once a fortnight after school for her to choose her latest batch.

The library wasn't big enough to get lost in, so I had free reign to wander while Mum read the cover notes of prospective stories. I preferred the reference section and rows of heavy looking encyclopaedias, atlases, and the microfilm machines – peering over the shoulders of people scanning the illuminated pages of old newspapers and other preserved documents.

The tables and chairs in the reference section always smelled of the rich furniture polish used to keep their dark wooden frames in pristine condition. It was a heady smell, and every time I come across it in later life, it is the quiet, gloomy corner of that little library that materialises in my minds' eye.

'Town: A Complete Record. 1904 – 1979,' by a publisher called Breedon Books constituted a quarter of all football books in our library, and once discovered, it was the first and only port of call.

Containing a complete season by season record of every Town first team match since their formation, it also featured a short biography of nearly every player to have pulled on the red and yellow of the Town up until the year of publication. Where there was no biography, the book simply listed the players' statistics while representing the team.

Thanks to 'Town: A Complete Record,' Bill: a complete life began to emerge.

My heart raced when I found his name and entry. Some of the biographies had a photo of the player. Bills didn't, but it did confirm that he *had* moved to the Town from Plymouth in the summer of 1953 and *had* stayed at The Town for a little over a season.

But the devil, as always, was in the detail. And over a few short paragraphs, Bill's story revealed itself.

He had played for his hometown team, Saltash United of the Cornwall Senior League, for four years after the Second World War, where he had been a paratrooper at D-Day and had pushed all the way to Berlin.

Plymouth Argyle signed him in the summer of 1950, where he played for three seasons in their reserve side, all the while holding down his job from school at Morwellham Quay Copper mine and dock.

After impressive displays for Argyle's combination team, he signed his first and only professional contract with The Town in 1953, and he went on to play 18 first team games in the Third Division South that season, after first team regular Joe Henderson injured his hand.

The following season he started off in the Town reserves, before being loaned out to Torquay United – also of the Third Division South – to cover a couple of injuries. After five first team games for United, he played out the remainder of his loan in their combination side.

Contract up, he moved home and re-joined both Saltash and Morwellham

Quay. However, his playing career was ended after he broke his back in a partial pit collapse in 1959.

Unable to take out a reference book, the Librarian kindly photocopied the pages featuring Bill – I still have them – so as I could study the 53/54 season statistics at my leisure.

I would trace my finger down the column below Bill's name, pausing at every small '1' to indicate a performance in goal, tracking left to discover the match, the attendance, and the score.

He had played in front of more than seven thousand on Boxing Day 1953, in a two-nil defeat away to Newport County. He had played in a four-nil win over Bournemouth & Boscombe at Inchmery Road in October, and a five-two defeat away at old club Plymouth.

Along with all those precious appearances for Town in the league, he had also tended goal the night of the grand opening of Inchmery Road's first ever set of floodlights, where Town entertained the mighty Arsenal of the First Division in a friendly match. More than eight thousand watched an impressive two all draw beneath the lights.

It was a career and life worthy of far more than 'I played for Town a few times.'

I remember one match after my discovery, bringing my photocopies to show him. He chuckled and leafed through the statistics, pointing out the odd match, the odd memory that came with it, and blushed when I asked him if I could have his autograph.

'Really!' he had said, shaking his head. Concentrating as he took the pen that I had ready for him, signing his name neatly beneath the small, photocopied biography.

Those few sheets now live in a protective folder, and wrap around seven programmes from that 1953/54 season, all sporting Bill's name in goal on the team sheet. They were not easy to find.

But a lifetime of looking also secured a single copy of one of Bill's appearances at Torquay, and a Plymouth reserve team game against Portsmouth's second eleven.

Precious memories of a career unseen, and a kindly old man called Bill who would chat football during reserve team games, and always have a boiled sweet spare for the half-time break.

After my discovery I would watch him staring out at the Inchmery Road pitch all glassy eyed, seemingly looking beyond events in the present. Possibly to moments facing down the Arsenal beneath those floodlights. Fingertip saves bringing a wave of applause from the terrace behind the goal. The time he lived every school child's dream of being a professional footballer.

I wouldn't interrupt those moments. In fact, I would try and imagine them myself.

Many, many years later, after I had moved to London for my first job on a national newspaper, Dad sent me a clipping from the local paper chronicling Bill's passing. He was described as 'Ex-Town and a much-loved member of the community.'

Even now, leafing through those old programmes, through the reserve team sheets of games we shared, I can see that smile, that wink as he slid a humbug toward me.

I enjoyed his company at reserve team games. Just as I did Transistor Man, Crazy Mary, and Programme Man. We were a rag-tag band of football supporters.

We also discovered Tom Maskell together.

Four

The Town, when it came to players, were almost always thin on the ground. Crowds of two and three thousand meant that keeping the club's head above the financial waters was always a fine balancing act.

Any manager taking on the Town job knew the deal before he signed: work miracles with next to nothing.

A 16-man, first team squad would be supplemented by two loan singings, a handful of apprentices, and a few non-contract players plucked from local non-league football. Those non-contract players would receive nothing more than travel expenses to and from Inchmery Road. The opportunity to wear the red and yellow of The Town, play combination football in Football League grounds, and the chance to impress the management of the first eleven was seemingly payment enough.

Even in Town's lowly position, and with such a threadbare squad, taking a non-contract slot was a long shot to the professional ranks. While not impossible – Calvin Cranmer, younger brother of Town centre back, Barry made the leap, playing maybe a dozen first team games a season for two years in the late eighties, before dropping back into non-league – it was rare. But the overwhelming odds wouldn't stop young men daring to dream.

Every season, the first Town programme would feature the newly assembled first team squad photo across the centre spread, while later in the addition there would be a picture of that years' non-contract and apprentice players wearing the season's away kit.

While visiting team profiles in the programme could sometimes feature a squad picture sporting three or four rows of players, Town's first team barely had enough for two – one standing behind a smattering of the more senior players sat on a gym bench.

For the non-contract and apprentice players, there would be no team photograph. Rather, a snap of a line of men and boys, arms folded, standing awkwardly before the camera would suffice.

In a world of dire economics and only one substitute being allowed, so long as Town had twenty-four fit players come Saturday, they were a fully functioning professional football club – the Combination League team sheet a serene swan of twelve names, no matter the frenzied phone calling on Thursday and Friday, trying to fill the gaps left by call-ups to cover first team injuries and suspensions.

Tom Maskell appeared unannounced a few weeks into the 85/86 season, signing apprentice forms for the Town. Too late for the team photos and profiles, his name simply appeared as a substitute at a reserve team fixture in mid-September.

With a slightly better success rate than the non-contract players, apprentices were mostly seventeen and eighteen-year-old lads signed from youth team football. On £10 or £15 a week, the club would put them up with a local family, feed them, and introduce them to the world of professional football.

Training with the first team Monday to Friday, they would turn out for the reserves on a Saturday and carry out a series of jobs around the ground the rest of the time.

Sweeping the terraces, cleaning the boots of the first team, mopping out the changing rooms, helping in the ticket office, stocking up the club shop, they would do it all with a quiet humility, knowing this was the same path trodden by most of the games' greats.

But if, after their two-year apprenticeship was up, and they hadn't been able to force their way through to the first team, they were released. No matter how good they had become at stock rotation or unblocking toilets.

Maskell finally got some game time, after a few weeks warming the substitutes bench, in a Combination match against Northampton Town.

The last fifteen minutes of a reserve team game already lost hardly seems a fitting entrance for our hero. An entrance before less than two hundred souls, all deflated by a reserve team reverse, and Transistor Man's crushing updates on the first team's misfortunes far from home.

'THREE NIL HARTLEPOOL. GAME OVER.'

But that was what Tom Maskell had to work with that benign September afternoon.

Three goals down in a game memorable only for a seagull refusing to yield its spot near the Victoria Road goal. Furious at being disturbed while scavenging for worms, it only skittered out the way, circling up and over the empty terracing, squawking its displeasure when the play had got right on top of it.

Right from the off there was a quiet intensity about Maskell's play. Not one to shout and marshal like some players do, it was actions that defined his debut from left back.

Receiving the ball from midfield, this lad with a scruffy mop of brown hair looked up at his options. Seeing little in the way of movement from his strikers, he took a touch, knocked the ball past the winger, closing him down, and chased after it. Controlling it he played a quick ball into our non-contract midfielder Sean Saunders' feet, who laid it back once Maskell had raced past another opponent.

Another touch, another look-up, he took the ball forward before whipping a ball into the penalty area, where reserve striker Ian Thompson dived at it. Connecting with it plumb on his forehead, the ball cannoned off the bar and away to safety.

It had lasted no more than ten, fifteen seconds, but it had dragged the smattering of support up from their slumped position in their seats.

Every Northampton goal, along with Transistor Man's updates on the first teams failing up at Hartlepool had made shoulders sag – the weight of the footballing world crushing posture as well as those dreams of climbing the table.

But that short burst by Maskell drew them back up toward the play, eyes widening at the simple poetry of football played well.

Despite the bullet header not nestling in the back of the net, it inspired Crazy Mary to go to town on her hoarding, accompanying the applause from the rest of us.

Bill looked across at me, eyebrows raised.

'I think we've got a player my lad.'

Ian Thompson applauded the cross, as did Sanders and the rest of the team. Maskell didn't see, trotting as he was, head down, back into position. Hands on hips to catch his breath, he watched on as play restarted.

It finished three nil.

By 85/86 I mostly rode my bike to reserve team matches, only taking the bus if the weather was foul. Tom Maskell's debut had been on a nondescript, mild early autumn afternoon, and I had locked my bike up to the railing outside the club shop like I always did.

Normally I would have been long gone before the players started to leave, but a puncture had me running late.

Seeing the players come out in dribs and drabs, getting in cars and pulling away had me pause from my repairs. Even now, as a seasoned journalist whose job it is to interview players, I still get that rush of excitement as they shuffle out from changing rooms to the media area. Players who had just enthralled out on the pitch, standing before you like a normal person. And you are meant to talk to them as such. It always takes me back to my childhood at Inchmery Road. To moments like Tom Maskell's debut.

Sean Sanders, Ian Thompson, Martin Coffin, our reserve goalkeeper who had once played a handful of Second Division games for Portsmouth, and the rest drifted out from the players' entrance and began to disperse into the evening.

I almost missed him as I followed the players' cars out and away.

He cut a slight figure, hands stuffed into the pockets of a cardigan, head down, Tom Maskell looked a shadow of the lad who had made such an impression out on the pitch. He looked like just another kid on his way home from watching the football.

I was not a boy of instinct, of rash moments of action. It was a shock to hear his name called out as he walked past me.

'Tom.'

He stopped, turned round, looked at me.

I smiled weakly, blushed, rummaged furiously in my rucksack. Pulled out that afternoon's team sheet and handed it to him with a pen.

'Could I get your autograph please?'

He looked as surprised as I felt in hearing the words come out of my mouth.

'Gosh, sure,' he said, taking the pen and sheet. There followed a moment of awkwardness, where we both looked about us for some surface for him to press against. We settled on the paper bag of programmes, again from the rucksack, and Tom Maskell carefully signed his name beneath his position as substitute.

'Good game today Tom,' I said as he handed the sheet back to me.

'Thank you,' he said. I didn't know what to say next, so I said 'Thank you' back at him, as he smiled, turned and made his way out the Inchmery Road gates.

I didn't know back then if that had been his first ever autograph as a professional footballer. I liked to think so. And it gave it an extra resonance to me, that maybe I had become a small part of his professional career – the first autograph hunter. No matter that it was, up to that point, a short and modest professional career. A fact rubber stamped as, with puncture repaired, I passed Maskell waiting at a bus stop to take him back to his lodgings.

With copy filed, that stifling end of season press-box afternoon, I drove home and found myself leafing through the boxes of old football programmes beneath the spare bed.

In one labelled 'Town 82-87' I found it, that autographed team sheet from Maskell's reserve team debut, sat on top of a sheaf of team sheets chronicling his season in the reserves. Placing everything else back safely, I propped that debut team sheet up against my lap-top, poured myself a drink, and sat down, looking at his signature, pondering how, of all the names in my own personal journey through football, it was his that rose to the top. The most memorable player.

Maskell was a raw talent. For every barnstorming run down the wing, for every wicked cross into the box, there was also a frailty to his play.

While terrific in chasing back, making last ditch sliding tackles, he was also prone to not reading the game quickly enough. Only seeing the danger in an opposition attack a heartbeat too late, having to use his speed to try to recover the situation. Sometimes it would work. Sometimes it wouldn't.

The step up from youth and non-league football, even to the reserve team of a Fourth Division club, was stark. Professional players, even reserve team professionals, were fitter, stronger, and had more footballing savvy than their part-time counterparts. It took time to adapt.

He had a good centre back pairing of Steve Haysham and Roger Emms alongside him, who helped school him in the best starting positions for a left back, and the professional deceit he would face coming up against tricky wingers.

Both Haysham and Emms were players who could, and did every season, step up into the first team at a moment's notice, fitting in to cover injuries and suspensions comfortably.

In the twilight of their careers, and on failing legs, they used experience to outmanoeuvre younger, faster strikers. Indeed, back in the day, Haysham had appeared in a Cup semi-final whilst playing for Second Division Southampton. Emms had made more than one hundred First Division appearances for Nottingham Forest at the start of his career.

They were the lifeblood of professional squads, playing out their last few years by helping others develop. Just as someone had once done for them.

With every odd mistake by Maskell, Bill would nod, reassure me.

'That's why clubs have a reserve team. To help the young ones learn. Make mistakes. He is some player. Haysham and Emms know it. See how they talk to him all game? They wouldn't do it if he wasn't A – listening, and B – a talent. We've got some player on our hands here.'

And despite the mistakes, whenever Maskell played, it seemed like his life depended on it. No matter that it was a reserve team game played in front of just one hundred and fifty or so, and the odd territorial seagull. There was a first team intensity about his desire to express himself, to create sweeping moves forward, goalscoring opportunities. To launch into thunderous tackles that could be felt way up in the rafters. Every moment mattered. And I loved it.

There was something about the way he conducted himself out on the pitch that reminded me of that epic Brazilian team of the 1982 World Cup. The poise and vision. The almost balletic interplay with his team-mates. The way the ball seemed to fall naturally at his feet, never straying as he surged forward, jinking past the opposition.

It was intoxicating. Thrilling to watch. It made your heart soar – the way Maskell played. It was everything that football had come to stand for, ever since that summer of 1982.

It was exciting. It captured your imagination. It was pure poetry, the way he made the game sing and flow. The way he connected with the ball, his team-mates, the game, seemed to belie his tender age, a seventeen-year-old with such vision and composure. And seeing it live, right there in front of you, made it more special again. He was the first player I saw, with my own eyes, that made me feel that way.

'He has no fear out there,' Bill would say, nodding down at the pitch. 'Ah the joys of youth. I hope he never changes.'

'Some players do. As the years roll on. Having to fight to pick up a new contract almost every season, they can sometimes play it safe, rein it in, in preference for a reputation as a solid, reliable pro.' He shrugged his shoulders, never fully passing judgement on which path was the right one. Looking back now I think it was because he didn't think there was a right answer. Everyone's journey being their own to discover.

At first team games, the reserve team page in the programme would be my first port of call after the line-ups, pointing out any mention of Maskell to Dad from the reserve match reports.

If it detailed a game at Inchmery Road, I would fill in the gaps for Dad, adding flesh to the often-limited bones of a paragraph or two that had to chronicle a full ninety minutes.

From 'Thompson converted from a Maskell cross' I would paint the scene: how Maskell had played his way up into a crossing position, feinting back onto his weaker foot to lose his marker, before curling a ball between defender and keeper for Thompson to flick home.

If the reserve team page featured an away game, I would absorb the report greedily. Lost for a moment on the bustling Inchmery Road terrace, I would transport myself into the empty stands of some faraway football club. Trying to picture the team in our blue away kit, shorn of sponsors' logo, I would imagine how the game had played out. How young Maskell had done. Sometimes based solely on the fact that his name appeared at the line-up at the foot of the report.

As the season progressed, and the statistics built up, Tom Maskell's professional career accumulated on that reserve team page. A small, tabulated box into which Combination League, Combination Cup, and local County Cup appearances gathered, detailed how Maskell had fast become a reserve team regular. Sometimes starting, sometimes coming off the bench. It was turning into a solid first season for this young apprentice.

A first season topped off with a debut goal in professional football away at Bristol Rovers in December. 'A low drive planting itself into the far corner of the Rovers net,' the Town programme proclaimed.

Every time I popped into the club shop I would look through the postcard sized player photographs displayed in an ageing carousel that would squeal whenever it was turned. I had collected them all long before, the player's autograph at the foot of each headshot making them too precious to not buy.

From time to time I would strike up the courage to ask the lady behind the counter if she had a Tom Maskell one. She would always shake her head and apologise, not liking to fail one of her faithful regulars.

'They only do them at the start of the season. He came in a little later didn't he?'

Her name was Tina, and she was far more than just the lady behind the counter. In her time at Inchmery Road she had worked in the ticket office, been the secretary to the chairman, placed apprentices with their lodgings, and taken in a few herself. She ran the Junior Town club, arranged coaches to away matches if there was suitable demand, and had done stadium tours for local schoolchildren. Help from apprentices aside, she *was* the club shop, and at the time of her passing in 2017, she had been a season ticket holder for more than sixty years.

Legend had it that she would have that shop locked up safely on match days and be in her seat before five past three. She would then duck out just before the final whistle, using the labyrinth of corridors within the bowels of Inchmery Road to be back in position behind her counter in time for any post-match customers.

Tina's husband had also been a part-time groundsman for The Town, a full-time handyman, and long-time kitman for both Town teams.

Knowing that I was an avid lover of football programmes, and an ever-present at reserve team games, whenever her husband was tasked with going away with the reserve team, she would ask if he could try and pick up a team sheet for me.

Whenever he remembered, she would present it to me the next time I was in, apologising at its battered state.

Colin, her husband, was no curator of precious footballing artefacts: team sheets, programmes would be folded, stuffed inside a pocket until re-discovered some time after. Grubby and worn, dog-eared, it made no odds to me. They had lived a footballing life.

They had been in changing rooms and on team coaches, on the bench where Colin would sit during the match. They had been among the players themselves.

Their imperfections told a tale. A precious, albeit downtrodden snapshot. And now they were mine.

Some were as simple as the Town's. Some had club comments, fixtures, maybe even a Combination League table on the back. Swindon's was printed in red ink. Peterborough's on blue. Though the greatest treasure that Colin offered up was from that Bristol Rovers game – a memento of Maskell's first goal.

Each and every offering, like those bought at a match, or from the pigeonholes behind Tina, added to the ever-growing piles of fanaticism neatly stacked about my bedroom. Precious Town pictures, line-ups, statistics, reports – it was my own personal history of the team I loved. And at the middle of it, that 85/86 season, was Tom Maskell, a young lad barely four years older than me.

That season was an idyllic time. I had the reserves, Bill, Crazy Mary and the rest every other Saturday, and the first team as often as Mum deemed it safe to go – as sanctioned by 'The People's Republic of Chagford.'

Some savvy signings by manager Geoff Butler had helped to propel the Town up into the glorious obscurity of mid-table. It had been a season of calm, free from the fear of re-election, winning at home more regularly than not. The air of expectation around Inchmery Road as a consequence felt electric. Anticipation justified in a team who could play.

Town wouldn't be lifting silverware this, or any season for a good three decades after it. But that feeling, of knowing that your team were decent, would put on a show for you on a Saturday afternoon, would die for you, for the town; to me that felt more precious than any medal. A season of fifty plus tiny Town cup-finals, no matter how inconsequential to the outside world, and a team doing you proud – to a young boy, to that lad now in his fifties – that was award enough.

Those first seasons in the eighties were the best of my life. Their routine being my sole focus, it was a time of bike rides to peer through shuttered turnstiles, bargain boxes of old Town programmes, boiled sweets with Bill White, standing next to my Dad on the terraces, then telling Mum all about it over fish and chips.

Like school holidays over summer, it felt like it would last forever. But it never does. Time moves ever on.

Graduating to college, with new friends, it was they who would start to come along to Town games with me. With Dad left behind to tend the garden. Fake drivers' licences gaining entry to the Crown, and a pint or two sat on those terrace walls before and after the match.

I felt bad, leaving Dad behind. Yet I let it happen anyway. The pull of friends, of adulthood closing one door, pushing open another. Complete with away games on the train, or on the supporters' coach. Every mile travelled to far flung grounds, a rubber stamp of your devotion to the cause.

Heavy away defeats, arriving home late at night, worn with a badge of honour at college on the following Monday.

I hope Dad didn't feel too upset at not being needed, wanted any more. Life, growing up can be cruel. Especially for those left behind.

But we still had the odd game, finding our spot on Inchmery Road at least a couple of times a season. At least. And it was good. Like it had always been.

Moving on to university, however, saw me missing out on huge swathes of Town's year altogether, being too far away, and too absorbed in my studies to make the long trip back.

My programme collection slowing to early season fixtures before term had started, the odd away game that was easy to get to, and games at Christmas and Easter. Games that felt extra special, timeless, spending Boxing Day, New Year's Day with Dad on the terraces, just like we had always done.

With studies complete, and a newly acquired degree in English Literature, but no clear idea of what came next, it would be The Town who would indirectly set me on my way to becoming a sports' writer.

A job advertisement in the local paper for a junior position on the paper's sports desk came at the perfect time for me. My lifetime of devotion to The Town standing me out from the competition, and landing me a gig in which, irony of ironies, I got to write a weekly report on Town's reserve team matches.

While living back with Mum and Dad, I would travel home and away to cover the Combination League side, writing up reports in my notebook from my seat on the team bus before finding a pay phone at a service station, phoning through my copy while everyone else went to pick up something to eat, or go to the toilet.

For three years, every other Saturday, I would induce travel sickness in the writing of my three-hundred-word piece, then suffer a full bladder and empty stomach all the way home by filing it in time.

Glamorous it was not. But it was so much fun, and over the years I got to know some of the players quite well. To the point that I would be included in the banter on the way home after a victory. Players ribbing me to make sure I featured their pass, tackle, cross, goal.

Nearer the end of my time with the reserve team, I would barter a sandwich or a chocolate bar, in exchange for a few extra yards added to my report of a goal, or a few superlatives added to a fingertip save. That way, at least, I managed to fend off my hunger, if not my need for the toilet.

They were a good bunch of lads who, like every player in every professional team, went their separate ways across the country and beyond to find their next contract or opportunity.

Like all the players from my childhood, what they got up to after they had left Town was just as important as their efforts for my team. Once a player for The Town, always a player.

For some, the reserves constituted the high-water mark of their playing days. Dropping down into part-time football, they could always say they played for The Town. Some moved sideways, eking out a living on short-term contracts, scrubbing around the Fourth Division. A few moved on an upward trajectory.

During my three years, a young lad called Ian Chalk broke into the reserves, moved up into the first team, then was snapped up by Second Division Barnsley, playing more than two hundred games for The Tykes before switching to York City in the Third. He played seven times for the Wales National Team, including at a sold-out Hampden Park for a World Cup qualifier against Scotland.

Denny Mundee played maybe fifty first team games for Town after a season in the reserves. He then forged out a decent career abroad, playing in the summer leagues in Finland and Norway before a spell in Malta and two years playing in Hong Kong for the wonderfully named Happy Valley. Denny would often slide me a sandwich on the team bus in payment for an over-inflated description of an already impressive free-kick effort.

He was still in the first team when I received a promotion, to cover Town's Fourth Division team. After which we spent a few away trips home debating whether either had given each other a lift-up: me by waxing lyrical about his ability, him by encouraging me to add some extra flair to my reports!

It was a wrench to leave the local paper, to leave The Town, Mum and Dad. But when the opportunity to cover First Division Ipswich Town with the *East Anglian Daily Times* came up, we all knew that I had to take it.

From there, a move up into the national papers had me based in London, Manchester, and for a time in Glasgow, first travelling the country on assignment, then into Europe for European and UEFA cup matches, before the holy grail – covering World Cups.

Stadiums holding in excess of one hundred thousand febrile supporters, watching the best players in the world playing for the most iconic clubs and nations, the most important trophies in world football. It was a far cry from Inchmery Road.

In fact, it was nothing like The Town at all.

And that was absolutely fine by me.

I had the best of both worlds, travelling the globe, and being paid to do so, to report on the sport I loved. But also having that grounding in the grassroots, the true soul of the game.

Inchmery Road, no matter where I had been, was the place that I wanted to come back to. It is where I felt I truly belonged. My identity mixed into the very fabric of the place, like spiritual grouting. No matter the teams I had seen for work, the world's very best, the feeling of being back at the Town was different. Better. It was *my* team.

Trips back home were a treat, taking a few days off mid-week, football calendar permitting, to spend a little time with Mum and Dad. The odd game under the lights with Dad, a simple joy. No matter the score. The event itself far more important than the sum of its ninety minutes of endeavour.

I felt like I was a child again. And Dad could walk without the aid of a stick, with Bill White sitting somewhere up among the shadows of the West Stand. Tina, the lady behind the counter, sneaking in a little late, having shut up shop.

Time could stand still or reverse at The Town. It could be any time you liked, set against the unchanging backdrop of this dilapidated old ground. Ghosts of supporters past could rub shoulders with the present. Saturday afternoon, or Tuesday evening. For more than a century. Countless games. Countless personal moments ready to flood back given half a chance.

For me, in truth, it never stopped being the early to mid-eighties at Inchmery Road. It was my default. My happy place in time. And when Dad passed away suddenly in 2014, in the three weeks I spent at home to help Mum sort everything out, Inchmery Road brought me some comfort when I thought there could be none.

I would find myself, unable to sleep, wandering up to the Town in the dead of night. Milling about the turnstiles, sitting on the wall outside the Crown, I had it all to myself, like those lazy days of summer holidays past. I would sit and watch me and Dad – a young man and a little boy – turn in to Inchmery Road, stop to buy an 'Ogramme, pop into the club shop. The echo of that bell chiming in the dark. I would follow them to the turnstiles, watch as they queued, passed through, slipping away beyond those clunking ironworks. Wishing more than anything that I could follow.

A simple routine performed God knows how many times over the years, I would stand in the darkness, broken, wishing more than anything for just one last turn with Dad. One last afternoon at our barrier. Unable to fully comprehend yet that memories, ghosts, would be all I could ever have from now on.

During daylight hours, in between trips to file papers, to register the one thing I didn't want rubber stamped and made official, I would find myself regressing back to happier times via my box of eighties programmes. That crumpled issue from my first ever game, the old Bill White programmes I had found, his signature on that page of career statistics. Stacks of team sheets from reserve matches, all filed by season in plastic wallets. Re-reading managers' notes, player interviews, both extolling ambitions for a season that would inevitably fall short of the mark. Studying match reports, line-ups, league tables long since concluded – it was a comfort, getting lost in the past for a while. And among those halcyon days relived, there were none more special than that 85/86 season.

Proving my devotion week on week, year after year, I felt that I truly belonged by the time Tom Maskell signed for The Town. With three full seasons behind me, three seasons of flirting with disaster at the foot of the Fourth Division under my belt. Three seasons of barrier leaning and seat flipping watching both Town's sides, I considered myself a war-scarred Town lifer. I was barely fourteen.

And even though my tours of duty paled into insignificance compared to those who stood or sat around me on match days, I knew a good season when I saw one.

Geoff Butler's first eleven had been pushing toward the top at one point during the 85/86 season, before injuries to a threadbare squad began to bite.

The reserves had found a rhythm, thanks in no small part to Tom Maskell's youthful zest.

And whenever a reserve team player stepped up to fill a gap left by injury or suspension, I took great pride in being able to prep Dad, and anyone else who had been listening on the terraces to their strengths and weaknesses.

I remembered one game, against Scunthorpe, when reserve team right-winger Ricky Walker had been promoted.

'Give him half a yard and he will whip in a wicked cross,' I had proclaimed pre-match, only for him to do just that within the first ten minutes, resulting in a Town goal. I remember Dad looking down at me with raised eyebrows, a tacit acknowledgement that I really knew what I was talking about. A couple of regulars nearby ruffled my hair — the football supporters' universal sign of approval towards their younger colleagues.

'You should be in the dugout young man. As Butler's assistant.'

I thought my heart was going to burst out of my chest with pride. Men who I didn't know proclaiming my knowledge of The Town.

It was a pride matched one more time that season, as the campaign began to wind down in late April.

Tom Maskell, guided by Emms and Haysham, had moved on leaps and bounds as the season had progressed. Ironing out the mistakes. Learning to anticipate the play in front of him, make the right decisions at the right time. He was, at the tender age of seventeen, becoming the player Bill saw in him all those months earlier against Northampton.

He had, in the space of thirty-three reserve team appearances, inspired Crazy Mary to nearly bash her hoarding clean off the side of the West Stand. He had, from time to time, compelled Transistor Man to stop focusing on the commentary of the first team's match — proclaiming:

'GOOD BALL. THAT LEFT BACK CAN REALLY PLAY, EH?'

He had even stopped Programme Man from delving into his paper bag barely minutes after kick-off. Pushing his glasses up the bridge of his nose, he would lean into the play, in readiness for the next Maskell burst forward.

It was clear that injuries were beginning to bite by late March. Town's first team had been losing regulars like flies. A small squad and a long season beginning to catch up with weary joints, niggling knocks and knotting muscles meant that the team sheet for reserve games started to lose familiar names. Soon there weren't enough bodies to name a substitute for the Combination team, injuries during matches leaving the Town to battle on with just the ten.

In late April, even reserve team boss, Andy Groves, chalked up five appearances as the reserve team season wound down, despite having retired from playing a good four years earlier.

But despite all that, it was still a shock when it happened, when Maskell went up to the first team.

The first any of us reserve team regulars knew about it was on handing over our two pence for our team sheet at the last Combination match of the season at Inchmery Road.

I would always greedily scan the list of names, even before I had passed through the turnstile. This last game against Gillingham I stopped, looked up at the man taking the gate money.

'Maskell's not playing?'

He shook his head.

'He's gone with the first team. Elliot pulled up in training yesterday. They've taken just the bare eleven, so he will be starting.'

It was the talk of the stand before kick-off, with Transistor man confirming the team: Maskell started, along with two of the more senior non-contract players and another of the few reserve team regulars who hadn't already been promoted.

'BARE BONES. AND AGAINST TOP OF THE TABLE,' he said, shook his head.

A five-nil defeat that secured Doncaster's promotion came as no real surprise. The match report in the local paper confirming that the Town eleven fought valiantly, and put up a good footballing display, but were simply outgunned by a team that would go on to win the title.

'Young Maskell on his first team debut,' the report went on to say 'put on a good show. Not looking out of place in a Fourth Division setting.'

I couldn't wait for the following Saturday, so I rode my bike up to Inchmery Road during the week to pick up a copy of that Doncaster programme. And while I was disappointed not to see Maskell's name among the line-ups, his call-up coming so late in the day that the programme had long been sent off to print, I tucked the match report that I had cut out from the local paper inside it.

A precious memento of a first team debut for a player who had come to mean so much to Bill and me, to the other reserve team regulars. A player of humility, who took every opportunity to represent a professional team with a desire and passion that those of us not blessed with the talent to live out our dreams would have done.

A player of real flair, who could light up the dreariest of November afternoons with a moment of sublime ability, before trotting back into position in his quiet, unassuming way. A player who seemed to get the Town, who bought into the attitude needed to thrive in such humble surroundings.

He was ours – Programme Man, Crazy Mary, Transistor Man, Bill and me, and the smattering of others who had watched him play all season. And now our little reserve team secret had made the first team. And with some style. And we felt the pride in his achievement as if it had been our own. As if it had been us out there.

From the echoes of an empty Combination League match to the first team, no one deserved it more than Tom Maskell.

Due to postponements earlier in the season, Town would have to squeeze four games into the final eight days of the league campaign, playing Saturday, Tuesday, Thursday, Saturday to finish by the third of May. This would include three away trips in a row after a final home match to Carlisle.

And with injuries still biting, it would be those left standing who would finish off Town's season, Maskell included.

Seeing his name on the back of the programme, among the line-ups for the Carlisle game felt like a vindication of all my animated retellings of Maskell magic in the reserves. I had said he was good enough. So had Bill. And here he was, in the big time as I saw it.

I was excited for him. I was excited for me. I was excited for Dad, who would finally get to see what all the fuss was about. He didn't let anybody down.

In an otherwise meaningless end of season mid-table match, Town's injury crisis almost played in their favour, with just over two thousand home supporters giving the benefit of the doubt to the odd slack pass or shanked cross.

In fact, the patchwork nature of the team seemed to help some of the players too, Maskell included. With Emms alongside him in defence, and reserve team regular Sean Sanders a willing foil in midfield for Maskell's now trademark barnstorming runs, there was a familiarity that allowed them to play their usual game. He even had the tricksy movement of Ian Thompson to aim for up front. And find him he did.

It didn't matter that Town were already two nil down, and the shadow of the main stand had started to stretch across the worn pitch on a warm Spring afternoon – battle scarred and rutted from a long, bitter winter, bare in patches, a dust bowl in others – as the second half wound down, the supporters were still behind them. Enjoying a free-flowing game of football purely for the sake of it, Inchmery Road applauded endeavour, and when it came, they roared their pleasure.

It was a trademark reserve team move: Maskell to Sanders, to Maskell. A lung bursting run intercut with jinks and feints, before a withering cross into the path of Thompson – who took the ball on the half-volley, burying it into the top left-hand corner of the goal in front of the Inchmery End terrace. The place erupted.

I remember grabbing Dad's arm, screaming 'Maskell, Maskell' before calming down enough to form whole sentences.

'Did you see that Dad! Did you see that!'

It didn't register immediately, being so drunk on the moment: the merciless drumming of Crazy Mary's fists on the Carlisle dugout. It may have been the adrenalin coursing through me, but Mary sounded even more crazy than usual as she bashed out her pleasure mere inches above the Carlisle managements heads, as if needing to signify, above all other goals scored, the graduation of our reserve team secret.

I looked up into the rows of shadowy seats in the West Stand, trying to do the impossible and spot Bill, and both men: Transistor and Programme. In reality, and just like me, they may very well not have sat where they did for first team games. Looking back, I saw Bill as more of a bench man, somewhere among the lower tiers, while Programme man struck me as someone for the quieter, less animated reserve of the East Stand.

But it was to the West Stand I looked, imagining the pride and pleasure at seeing our hidden gem do so well. This quiet lad who would be waiting at the bus stop long after most had left Inchmery Road for his ride home.

Momentum changed, and Carlisle rocked back on their heels, Town pushed forward, desperate not to finish their home season with a defeat.

It was a curious thing, that psychological desire to finish on a high. As if a season of disappointment could be somehow softened by one last hurrah. A glimmer of optimism to sustain a supporter during the long summer months.

When it came, the equaliser felt like a winner, arriving in the very last minute. Bob Larson driving into the Carlisle box before slotting under the onrushing keeper.

With barely time to restart the game, the Town players sank to their knees on the final whistle with the effort of it all. The warm applause from all four corners of the ground lifting them back to their feet, propelling them on into the changing rooms.

In the bigger scheme of things, it was a meaningless end of season, mid-table draw way down in the Fourth Division. Its existence barely registering below the fold on the football classifieds page of Mum and Dad's Sunday paper.

To me it was everything. And even though it yielded nothing more than the score, scorers, and attendance, that little column of Fourth Division results was deemed worthy enough to be cut out and placed within the pages of my programme. The story of Tom Maskell setting up his first ever Fourth Division goal drifting between the lines of print.

With nothing but pride riding on those last three fixtures – Town's retained and released list having been published before the Carlisle game, meaning that contracts had already been won and lost – those players still standing did their best.

But the paucity of fit bodies, combined with the lack of recovery time between games, and the Herculean efforts to finish off the home season on a high resulted in three defeats. Three long bus journeys home, the two midweek trips stretching into the early hours of the following morning, yielding a three-nil loss at Darlington, a four-two reverse at Hereford, then a five-nil drubbing at Swindon on the final Saturday.

Maskell played in all three, coming off the bench at Swindon, and more than held his own every time, according to the match reports.

Season over, with Maskell's second year apprenticeship confirmed on the retained list, the squad drifted off their separate ways, and Inchmery Road wound down almost to a standstill. Leaving it free for young boys to press against exit gates, wander alleyways, listen to the sounds of quiet terrace streets. And dream.

Five

The slow, interminable grind of the off season tested my patience. It still does. Most childhood close seasons played out in the same way.

Days were filled with football in the back garden and imaginary seasons played out on my *Match Magazine* league ladder. A flimsy cardboard contraption, the ladder covered all four Football League divisions, with ninety-two slots into which a tab for each club could be placed.

Over the course of the year, I would religiously change every club's position, to the point that some slots and tabs would disintegrate, needing reinforcement with clumsily applied swathes of Sellotape.

Close season, all ninety-two tabs would be mixed up and twenty-four teams randomly selected for each division. Games would then be played out in the back garden, and league ladders updated. It was a world in which Town could win the Third Division title and get to the semi-finals of the FA Cup.

At least the close season of 1986 had the World Cup, and a brand-new Panini sticker album to embrace – complete with facts about obscure Paraguayan, South Korean, Iraqi and Moroccan players, and as many games on the television as I could get away with.

It was all exciting, and kept me going, but even World Cup finals didn't bring with it the same levels of electricity that fixtures day did every year. And the summer would drag by interminably until that magical day.

The local paper would, in a desperate attempt to fill up column inches on the sports pages during the off season, create football stories where there were none.

Transfer speculation, though Town rarely had any money to spend on the like. Lists of out of contract players that would, by and large, have no interest in a deal playing for us, but had numerous articles written about them, detailing how much they would improve the Town team.

'Where are they now' articles were a favourite of mine, where former Town players now playing in the summer leagues of Scandinavia, or in some other far-flung place, were interviewed on life over there, life at Inchmery Road, life elsewhere.

Pictures of them sporting exotic Swedish football kits littered with sponsorship logos, action shots frozen in front of the unfamiliar dimensions of foreign football grounds, reports on matches between teams with wonderfully bizarre names, and life among idyllic landscapes nestled on the sports pages among the equally unfamiliar look of the football pools fixtures.

For many, the football pools were as established a part of the football experience as programmes were to me.

Every week, for a nominal fee collected by a local Littlewoods' representative who would knock on your door and collect your pools slip, your twenty pence, you could pick ten fixtures that you thought would end in a score draw. If you won, you could win a life-changing sum of money. I have never met anyone who got anywhere close to winning the pools.

It wouldn't stop people poring over these columns of fixtures, forensically placing their ten x's on their coupon after multiple cups of tea, ruminating over potential outcomes.

We did it too, me and Mum. I would explain my rationale over every x – how Bolton had drawn away from home a couple of times before. How Grimsby were good for a goal, but were also leaky in defence, and Mum would nod seriously, humouring my attempts to decipher the future.

She would watch as I handed over our money, our coupon, to Terry, a cheery chap with a limp, who would do his rounds on a Thursday collecting up everyone's dreams of a better, richer life.

During the close season, not wanting to deprive the pools fanatics of their sport, Littlewoods would switch to the Australian semi-professional leagues for people to gamble on.

Matches from five divisions of the Victoria State League, and as many again from the New South Wales and Queensland leagues populated the foot of the sports page. Unfathomable rows of crosses, dashes and zeroes flanked each team name on the fixtures list. To those in the know they denoted past form for Geelong, Heidelburg United, Dandenong City and the like. It would be all anyone had to go on when forming a decision as to who was most likely to play out a one-all draw on the other side of the planet.

It seemed entirely likely that more people were betting on the scores of a Queensland League division five fixture every week than actually attending each game, that was barely more than an amateur match up, against the likes of Toowong and Kangaroo Point Rovers.

Interviews with former players, pools from far-away lands – during summertime it looked like the football page of the paper – but it was also strangely very alien. Familiar enough to read from top to bottom, it was also a jarring reminder that you were navigating the barren months of the close season, and a world shorn of the Town.

So, when it came – the day the new season's fixtures were released – it felt like the end was in sight. Your passing interest in the fortunes of Parramatta and Wollongong Wolves, or some winger from before your time playing for IFK Norrköping dissolved away.

Printed the length of the papers back page, forty-six Division Four fixtures mapped out more than nine months of your life. The opportunity to avenge heavy defeats from the season before, to face the four relegated teams from Division Three, to dare to dream that this year, just maybe, might be the year of a Town promotion push – fixtures day was a Godsend. And the back page would be cut out and preserved. A talisman to the future that couldn't come soon enough.

Pinned to my wall, that page would yellow and grow brittle over the course of the year, finally being thrown away once it had become immune to the properties of the blue tac holding it in place. Multiple re-fixings failed, and now obsolete thanks to the updated statistics page in the programme, I would always feel a sense of guilt in letting it go. Remembering back to those summer months when it was so precious. When it had been everything.

When it had been the first thing you looked at in the morning, and the last thing at night. The one thing keeping you going until that first game of the season…

After the World Cup, an extensive match league ladder tournament in the back garden, and hours idly perusing any snippet of football in the local paper, the opening day of the 86/87 season finally arrived. And as was now tradition, Dad and I walked across town to Inchmery Road for a game against Scunthorpe United.

Hopes were high as Scunthorpe had struggled last season, and Town had also secured the signing of two players who had been released by Third Division Reading. Brian Chambers and Grant Orchard had both played in more than thirty games each the year just gone, Chambers scoring seven goals from midfield. It was considered a real coup for Town to sign them, and I was looking forward to watching our new look team.

Programme secured from my now regular and 'lucky' seller by the main gates, Dad and I made our way through the turnstiles to our spot and absorbed that glorious first view of Inchmery Road as it began to come alive with the hope of a new season.

A shimmering green pitch ready for the spoils of war, supporters sporting short sleeves shielded their eyes from the summer sun with a cupped hand. Bodies inching along the rows of seats and benches in the stands greeted friends and settled down for another season's endeavour, while players stretched and passed balls to one another, zipping daisy cutters from one touchline to the other. It was a time to dream of cup runs and giant killings, of league titles. It was a time when all teams were equal, and anything seemed possible. Even if it wasn't.

I'm not sure what I was expecting as I scanned the line ups. Maskell had, after all, only achieved his five first team appearances due to a decimated squad. He was still only a second-year apprentice.

But his displays up in the rarefied air of the Fourth Division suggested to me that he might feature in the first team a lot more, and I felt a sense of disappointment when his name didn't even make the substitutes spot.

Worse still, as I flicked through the programme, Maskell was absent from both the first team and the apprentice/non-contract photographs. There was no mention of him anywhere, even among an article detailing the comings and goings at the Town over the summer.

He had disappeared.

As if he had never been there.

In the weeks that followed, as the wheels of the season began to spin and games came thick and fast, it was the Town team of the here and now that captured all the attention. Well, nearly all.

At the first reserve team game at Inchmery Road, those of us who had seen him grow into a player who caused Carlisle so many problems just a few months ago, we at least needed to mourn his absence.

Tina in the club shop had shrugged her shoulders, passed on what kitman husband Colin had told her – that Maskell had not reported back for the first day of training. Had not arrived at his apprentice's lodgings. Had not responded to the two letters sent by the club enquiring on his whereabouts. Phone calls went unanswered.

And slowly, the club gave up and moved on.

No matter how promising he had been, he was only an apprentice. There were plenty of young lads desperate to take his place.

Bill White seemed as saddened as anyone at Maskell's absence, knowing just how hard it was to make it into the professional leagues. And how hard it was to stay there.

'It just doesn't make any sense,' he said. 'The club will still have his registration, so it's not like he has gone elsewhere for a better contract. Without Town's consent he won't be able to play for any other team. It's such a shame.' The wasted opportunity, as he saw it, weighing heavily across his broad shoulders, sagging into his seat as he spoke.

'He really could have been someone,' he would say dolefully whenever Maskell's name cropped up in conversation that season, during afternoons with the reserves that seemed a little bit flat without Maskell's energy down the flanks.

No player or manager is ever bigger than the club. That is the mantra. They come and go while the supporters remain, generation after generation.

For a young boy, new heroes in red and yellow emerge. Their autographs sought, and performances recreated in back gardens and parks. But just like your first love, you never forget your first football infatuation. That first player to ignite your imagination, to send your emotions soaring, to turn sport into art.

For me, rather strangely, that player was a seventeen-year-old lad with just a handful of first team games behind him. A player who simply disappeared.

For the remainder of 86/87 (a season that flattered to deceive, with new signings Chambers and Orchard doing little to improve the team: the former due to a broken leg in October, the latter unable to get a decent run in the side) and the seasons that followed, we lived our Town lives as we had always done. Crazy Mary diverted her attention back to the opposition dugouts, and at reserve team games Messrs Transistor and Programme did what they always did.

But every now and then, conversation would turn back to young Tom Maskell.

Bill and I would ask Programme Man from time to time if he had ever come across Maskell's name among the many teams' programmes that populated his white paper bags. We would ask if Transistor Man ever heard the name as goals were relayed into his ear from across the length and breadth of the country. Neither had.

Afternoons in front of the vidiprinter would be spent following Town's scores, but also casting half an eye on the various names of goal-scorers chuntering across the foot of the screen – from the First Division in England to the basement league in Scotland, via Northern Ireland and Wales' domestic competitions – just in case.

The results page in the Sunday papers would also be scoured from top to bottom, with no joy.

It was an imperfect science, but to the best of our knowledge, young Tom Maskell was never heard of again in football circles.

An autograph, a handful of first team programmes and newspaper cuttings, bundled together with a stack of team sheets from the Combination League – the sum-total of one footballing life – began to gather dust.

Though the name was never truly forgotten. Popping into my head from somewhere the moment the question was asked that hot, press box afternoon decades later.

The fallow off-seasons where there are no European Championships or World Cups to report on are as tedious as a football correspondent as they are for a young boy.

While others transfer across to cover the cricket (a sport that leaves me cold) or some other summer endeavour, I put all my eggs in one basket when it came to sporting knowledge.

And while I can sit and watch the Tour de France or the Olympics from dawn to dusk, it is with an untrained eye. Enjoying the spectacle without any great desire to understand the mechanics of it all. I would feel a fraud if I tried to pretend that I was anything other than a fair-weather fan.

I could dive into the mire that is transfer speculation, but it is more like fiction writing than genuine sports journalism – imagining how good one team might become if player X joined them, then phoning for a comment from said team; turning 'We have had no contact with player X' to read 'Everton keeping close-lipped about player X' is a complete waste of time for everyone concerned.

Though on occasion, like an infinite number of monkeys trying to type Shakespeare, it sometimes throws up the right club and the right player, at the right time, giving you a scoop and an unfair tag of having 'your finger on the pulse.'

Spending my summers chasing an invisible tail left me feeling like that monkey plonked in front of a typewriter when I tried it. It wasn't for me. It was a part of football that didn't interest me in the slightest.

Probably the result of supporting a team who rarely had any money to buy a player.

No, it would be my local paper's approach, with their tried and tested summer-time formula that would help me fill my allotted column inches every week. It kept me occupied as boy, and I hope it does our readers.

The 'where are they now' features that I read as a boy must have been excruciating to research. In a time before the Internet, good old-fashioned leg work was the only way forward. Snippets of knowledge, Chinese whispers translating into laborious phone calls, letters, faxes sent out into the unknown, hoping for a bite.

These days you can pull up the squad list of pretty much any football team in the world in seconds. Wikipedia pages detail journeymen football careers. Social media accounts link you direct to football players of all abilities, Skype enabling you to have a face-to-face conversation with anywhere in the world.

In a productive week I could knock up three or four articles in this way. Articles on players who had left England and Scotland to take up contracts elsewhere, forging careers in Russia, Japan, Kuwait, Mexico and all other points on the globe.

Some trying to resurrect potential that had been squandered. Others simply having a wanderlust, wanting to use their abilities to travel and explore. Others still, having not quite made the grade in the UK venturing out to forge a rich and colourful life for themselves elsewhere.

Amazing stories of players who struggled to make it in professional football here ending up playing in Champions League and Europa League qualifiers, facing down some iconic teams whilst representing clubs from Iceland, the Faroe Islands, and Andorra.

One lad from Barrow, having been released by his National League North hometown team as an 18-year-old – the sixth tier of English football – took a contract playing for EB/Streymur in the Faroes.

Working part-time in a fish processing plant, he represented the villages of Eidi and Streymur – combined population six hundred – in the Faroese top-flight, plying his trade among the mountains and wild Atlantic storms of this remote archipelago. Two years running they qualified for Europe.

Which is how this young man came to face down the might of Fenerbahçe in Istanbul at the fifty thousand seater Sükrü Saracoğlu Stadium – a ground that can hold the entire population of the Faroe Islands and still have a few thousand seats left over.

The following season they played at the equally iconic, yet more sedate setting of Craven Cottage on the bank of the River Thames, home of then Premier League Fulham. Beaten by Athletico Madrid in the Europa league final a few short months earlier, Fulham won four-nil on the night. He was back in the fish processing plant the following day.

With a stockpile of these articles on my desk, and the name Tom Maskell nagging, I requested some time to do some real old-fashioned journalism.

To work on the ultimate, to me at least, 'where are they now.' One that has remained unanswered my entire life.

Six

Inchmery Road. A quiet summer's day. It could have been 1982 again, so little had changed. Laughter from an open window of the Crown, an afternoon pint going down well in the shadow of the old West Stand, the floodlights acting as a sundial across the hushed tangle of streets beyond.

Before heading to the main entrance, I couldn't help but linger outside the club shop for a moment, looking in at all the Town souvenirs inside. I couldn't help but press my face against the exit gates on Victoria Road. A sliver of pitch, of terracing. Always a thrill.

The timeless calm around the ground belied the trauma that Town had been through for more than a decade. When relegation replaced re-election at the foot of the Fourth Division, Town flirted with it on many an occasion, finally falling through the trapdoor into non-league in 2012.

Worse was to come a year later, with a second relegation into the sixth tier. At least from this all-time low came a unique experience – the one and only time Mum, Dad, and I got to celebrate Town winning some silverware together.

For the occasion of lifting the National League South title in 2014 Mum had bought us three tickets for the West Stand, and we watched the celebrations unfold from on high. The trophy being lifted, champagne bottles popped. For once celebrating something tangible. Something other than the simple, yet profound, joy of Town's very existence.

Mum bought us two tickets when Town secured the title in the National League in 2015, and promotion back into the Football League. It was bitter-sweet without Dad. He would have loved it, knowing The Town were back where they belonged – the obscurity of the Fourth Division.

I caught Mum wiping away a tear. She had said that she was just happy. But I knew that she wasn't. She was lonely. Bereft. Being at Inchmery Road making her feel that little bit closer to Dad, but at the same time highlighting the void left behind with his passing.

On the anniversary of his death every year Mum and I would place a small bouquet of flowers by his barrier on the Inchmery terrace, and that seemed to cheer her. Having never stood there with me and Dad, it was a place where she could imagine him without the painful tang of memory.

I didn't find out until a good while later, but Mum had been going to stand for a few moments at that barrier on a regular basis. Sometimes every week. It was one of the wonderful things about being a part of a small, community club: such empathy and accommodation.

One of the young assistants from the club shop would come round to meet her at reception and lead her through the warren of corridors, round the perimeter of the pitch, and up onto the terracing.

They would stand for a few moments, and Mum would tell them all about Dad, me and my love for Town. How Dad didn't really like football but loved being a part of my passion. She pointed at the benches where we sat that open day, me frozen with fear.

These young assistants would stand and smile, patiently listening to mum's stories, over and over, waiting for Mum as she stood quietly for a time with her thoughts, her memories of a happy life, before getting her a cup of tea from the canteen and sitting with her quietly as they watched people coming and going about them, before waving her off, watching as she wandered away to the same bus stop young Tom Maskell had used all those years ago.

It was that same sense of community that opened-up the club's antiquated filing system to me when I asked if I could research Tom Maskell's time at the club.

Filing system, it turned out, translated to a dusty old room choked with cabinets full of assorted papers, in no particular order. A room that still existed because the job to throw it all out had been forever usurped by more pressing and time-sensitive tasks.

Old receipts and invoices mingled with player contracts, various letters to and from the club, photographs with names scribbled on the back, team sheets, newspaper clippings, user instructions for manual typewriters, fax machines, photocopiers, itineraries for away trips, sheets detailing gate receipts, old Junior Town newsletters and decades of other paperwork clogged each cabinet drawer.

Trying to find details on a player who only mustered five first team appearances over a period of two weeks more than thirty years ago among that lot felt a daunting task. Daunting, but exhilarating, poring through the club's history. The day-to-day life of The Town revealing itself one page at a time. A fascinating haystack in which to search for one specific needle.

'Take your time,' Tina, the general manager had said. 'We're happy to have you.'

And take my time I did, enjoying not only the hours spent hunched over stacks of club papers, but also the time just being about Inchmery Road again. The time at home with Mum, sleeping in my childhood bedroom, absently kicking a ball about the garden like I used to, eating fish and chips together in front of the television. It was so precious.

When I finished sifting through it all, I had three volumes of the most interesting stuff bound and covered, presenting them to Tina as a thank you. Three volumes of papers, some dating back to before the war, all with the club crest embossed at the top. Papers offering contracts, informing others that they were being released. Offers of trials, a few letters banning supporters involved in trouble in and around the ground, financial breakdowns detailing the meagre resources The Town had to work with, and the income generated on random match-days.

Bob Larson's 1983 contract was an eye-opening read. A senior player in his third season with the club commanded an £80 weekly wage. Every goal scored earned him a £10 bonus, with the same again for a Town win. There would be a £50 bonus for reaching fifty points in the league.

Getting through to the third round of the FA Cup would earn Bob and the rest of the team a £100 bonus each, which would double for every round reached thereafter. In the unlikely event that Town got to the final, Bob and co. would pocket a £3,200 bonus!

Having never seen Town progress beyond round three in my entire life, Bob's contract bordered on the cruel, offering up such impossible riches.

Amazingly, improbably, among it all, I found Tom Maskell, and a letter sent to his home address on the Isle of Netton. The letter congratulated Tom on his apprenticeship, detailed his meagre £10 weekly wage, and confirmed that the club would provide accommodation and all meals.

It requested that Maskell arrive at his lodgings by the 28th of August, where he would be welcomed by housekeeper Ms Sarah Whittingham. The following day he was invited to Inchmery Road to meet Town manager Geoff Butler, and watch the Division Four match against Mansfield Town, before reporting for training on the 31st.

When I showed it to Tina, she shook her head, amazed that anything useful could be gleaned from that room of filing horrors. Mrs Whittingham, she confirmed, still lived at that address, and even though she was now well into her eighties, she still helped the Town out by putting up trialists for a few days while they tried to prove their worth.

'She had put up apprentices for decades before that. Long before your Maskell. She treated them like they were her own. I don't know if they ever knew it, but she would be in the stands at Inchmery Road for every game her boys played. Even if it was just the reserves. And legend has it, if they had had a shocker, she would be back at home by the time they returned, and she would give them an extra chocolate biscuit with their mug of tea. A subconscious arm around the shoulders,' she shook her head.

'God only knows how many fledgling careers she saw either take off or wither over the years. I'm sure she would be happy to talk with you, if you thought it might be useful?'

Sarah Whittingham sat dwarfed in her armchair, a slight curvature of the spine making her frail frame, her shoulders slump forward, as if gravity were trying to pull her to the floor. She took Tom's letter in her hands and read it carefully, muttering '1985' to herself before taking a sip of her tea.

'I remember all the boys who passed through here,' she said, her piercing blue eyes scanning the page.

'There are those who don't believe that, but it's true. I sometimes forget the names, but I always remember the faces. Though the years can get all jumbled up'

'I remember Tom. He was one of the few who made it to the first team while still an apprentice, while he was still here with me. They didn't usually make it that far, if at all, until after they'd moved out of lodgings and into their own place. After signing professionally.

'I remember Tom. A quiet lad. So very quiet. You would hardly get a peep out of him all day. He would sit with me and watch television in the evenings if the weather was foul. If it was fine, he would go out for long walks, sometimes sit out on the bench in the back yard,' she waved her hand vaguely behind her. 'He liked it out there.

'A nice lad,' she paused, then nodded as something came back to her.

'He didn't come back, did he? I remember now. He played those games for the Town, and never came back. It was a real shame. For him. For the Town. I wonder why?'

Over a cup of tea and a biscuit we talked all things Town. Sarah spoke of some of the players who had boarded with her.

Colin Worthington, a young lad from Cornwall, who was terribly homesick, went on to play in the First Division with Crystal Palace. Years after he had graduated from The Town, he sent her a signed Crystal Palace shirt and a lovely letter, thanking her for all the time she spent with him, keeping him busy, helping him overcome his homesickness, so as he could get into the Town first team, and then on to the big time.

She insisted on getting up, though it looked an arduous process, and ushered me through to her kitchen, where she had framed both shirt and letter, mounted it above the table that had seated all those young lads for breakfast, lunch and dinner.

She had never married, had no children of her own – 'These boys,' she said, pointing up at the white Palace shirt with its red and blue sash, Worthington's signature just beneath the club badge 'they were my family. Good boys they were.'

The more she spoke, the more memories seemed to flood back in a tangle of years and players.

'Imantis Bleidilis was a young lad from Latvia. I think in the late nineties. Spoke hardly a word of English. And my Russian was a bit rusty,' she cackled with an infectious laugh.

'We'd still natter away to one another though, pointing at things and miming things to fill in the gaps where we had no words. We'd have good conversations,' she smiled and shrugged 'Well I think we did. About growing up in the Soviet Union. Holidays along the Baltic coast. All sorts.

'He'd come from Southampton where he had been cut from their youth team. A speedy little winger, but easily knocked off the ball. He found English football tough to adapt to, though he gave every game a good go with our reserves. And God loves a trier don't you know. He only lasted a season before he went home.

'He struggled with English food as well. He ate whatever I put in front of him. But it was clear it was through politeness. One day he came home with a carrier bag of ingredients and said to me with his pigeon-English to "sit you, please" at the kitchen table.

'That night he cooked me and this young lad from Hull his favourite Latvian dish – the name of which I forget.

'It was lovely! And every week after that he would cook something from home, and I would learn how to do it, making some of it for him as a treat every now and then. I still cook it for myself from time to time.

'He went on to play for the Latvian National Team did Imantis. He played in World Cup and European Championship qualifiers. In big stadiums against some of the best national teams, the best players in the world. He won the Latvian league as well, a number of times.

'I would follow all their careers after they left us here, as best as I could, my boys. I learned how to use the Internet, and I would find them. See where they ended up. I doubt they remember me now, but I remember them. I remember them all, my boys.'

A second cup of tea was accompanied by Sarah sitting up in her chair as if she had been shocked.

'Gordie!' she announced, smacking the arm of her chair. 'That was his name!'

'Gordie?' I replied.

'Tom would talk about him, all the time, when I asked about home,' she leant down by her side and picked up Tom's letter from 1985, pointing at the address at the top. 'Netton. I remember now.'

'His Dad worked away on the oil rigs in the North Sea. He was never there. His Mum had died when he was little. He never really mentioned either. It was always Gordie.

'He worked on a boat, a ferry of sorts, transporting people and goods across Blackwater Lake. It is a lake, right in the middle of the island. Have you ever been? I did once, a long time ago. A beautiful place as I remember.'

I had been to The Isle of Netton, we had had a family holiday there one summer, back when it had been a popular tourist spot. Just off the southern coast of Devon and Cornwall, Netton had been a major draw for families working to a budget.

The ferry journey there made it feel exotic, like you were really going far away, as did Westlyn, the only town of any real size on the island. Palm trees lined the esplanade, while warm sand and gentle waves below demanded a young boys' attention.

Every day a man would walk the beach selling apple doughnuts, the like of which I have never tasted since. They would simply melt in your mouth.

Large, whitewashed Edwardian town houses looking out to sea had been converted into holiday apartments and guesthouses. Huge sash windows poured light into every room. Open them a sliver and the tantalising sounds of bells and horns could be heard from the arcade on the pier, signalling another win on the penny slots and the one-armed bandits.

I couldn't recall ever seeing a ferry on Blackwater Lake, but I remembered seeing the lake itself from the bus as we headed to Blackwater Chine – a self-titled 'Spectacular Adventure Park' on the southernmost tip of the island.

It was pure heaven for a little boy. They had a life-sized Wild West town, complete with cowboys who would, on the hour, every hour, perform a Wild West shoot out outside the saloon. Cap-guns cracking and smoking, the vanquished writhing on the floor. There were Native American Indian tee-pees, huge totem poles, piped chanting rising-up from hidden speakers every few minutes.

Blackwater Chine also boasted one of the largest mazes in Britain, its vast shrub walls twisting and turning towards the centre and a giant climbing frame from where you could see the heads of those still lost bobbing towards dead ends.

But the best bit for me was 'The Land of the Dinosaurs.' Huge model Diplodocuses, Tyrannosaurus Rex, Triceratops and others would loom into view from every turn. I knew they weren't real, but it didn't stop me from holding Mum's hand tightly, hiding behind her skirt every time one of these monsters materialised. It was pure, spine-tingling electricity, and at the end of the trail through 'The Land of the Dinosaurs,' there were a few smaller models that you could climb on.

The photograph of me sat on a scaled down brontosaurus, while Dad pretended to be being eaten by it remains my favourite picture of all time. He had positioned himself down by its mouth and had stuffed his arm inside, a pretend scream frozen as he looked up at the camera.

A few years ago, I saw a news clipping about Blackwater Chine, how it was under threat from soil erosion; landslides making parts of the park unsafe. An image of those giant model dinosaurs, having tumbled top over tail down a cliffside, resting on crumbling ledges, caught up in root bowls and tree branches, dangling precariously over the ocean and certain, inevitable oblivion onto the rocks below bringing on a genuine sadness. My own personal dinosaur extinction frozen for posterity; another piece of a happy childhood lost to time.

Sarah interrupted my momentary lapse of reverie as she put her teacup down on a small table beside her chair.

'They were neighbours, Gordie and Tom. He brought up Tom as much as anyone did, taking him out on his boat, letting him tie up on the jetties and the like. He would feed him, make sure he went off to school. He would take him to watch football. I am pretty sure he was the one who got Tom into playing as well.

'I never met the man. As far as I know he never made the long trip all the way out here. But the way Tom would talk about him, and write home to him every week, you could tell that he meant a lot to him. If you want to find out more about young Tom, then I think this Gordie is your man. If he is still going.

'If he does have anything to tell, would you be kind enough to share it with me? I should love to know that young Tom is well.'

Seven

It is amazing how certain sounds and smells can catapult you back in time. Triggering vivid memories. Two points in your life merging for the briefest of moments with equal clarity, making you wonder for a heartbeat which is real, and which is recollection.

The rumble of the powerful engines of the Netton ferry sent ripples across the surface of my coffee, reverberating my bones. The rich yet choking diesel fume stinging the nostrils out on deck when wind direction and funnel aligned. Timeless experiences from another life, where a little boy clung to the thrumming rails and watched the churn of the ocean created by vast, hidden propellers.

I left him to it, that little boy, and returned to my pile of Football League annuals borrowed from the newspaper's library. Ten years' worth of meticulous detail and statistic, accounting for every goal scored, every appearance made, from the top of the First Division to the bottom of the Fourth.

I paused at The Town's small entry in the 1986 edition; Maskell's five appearances sandwiched among the rest of that season's squad's statistics.

From there a small ruler helped me scan down every line of appearances made by every player across the Football Leagues' ninety-two teams, for ten years.

On occasion a familiar name would crop up. An ex-town player's humble career surfacing among the pages of other clubs, before disappearing altogether. Sometimes resurfacing among the pages of non-league annuals from the same time period. One last hurrah in the Gola League, or the GM Vauxhall Conference, the Isthmian League, the Multi-Part Northern League.

Denny Mundee, so it turned out, had ended up after his stint in Hong Kong playing for Southern League Salisbury before an unsuccessful attempt at player management with Worcester City.

Fascinating though it was, this journey through ten years of football yielded not a single appearance by a Tom Maskell, anywhere.

Tina, The Town's General Manager's hypothesis that Maskell's player registration had never left Inchmery Road – that it had either once been in that dusty old room of filing cabinets, or a similar room, getting lost over the decades seemed to hold water.

In the eyes of football officialdom, Maskell had simply vanished. Had never played again after that last substitute appearance at Swindon.

From out of the haze, the faint silhouette of a land mass began to emerge. Westlyn pier, the esplanade, rows of tall Edwardian town houses slowly materialised behind a lip of yellow sand. Tiny dot holiday-makers paddling at the shoreline, basking next to colourful windbreakers, precariously lodged umbrellas.

Sandcastles, ice creams, somewhere maybe a man selling apple doughnuts.

Westlyn seemed peculiarly familiar and strange at the same time. The benches and palm trees, the smell of candy floss and sun cream, shops selling inflatables, postcards, buckets and spades.

The same, and yet jaded, dulled by time. The vast Edwardian frontages weather-beaten and peeling, greying and jaundiced where vivid whitewash used to exist. As if, like a newspaper, my memories had been left on the car dashboard, the pages curling and yellowing, becoming brittle with age.

It still had its charm, but it had seen better days, like most seaside towns in Britain. The cheap package holiday abroad taking the profitability out of many, Westlyn no longer thrived. It survived at best and did little else. Its beaches far from packed as they once had been.

The closure of Blackwater Chine had hit Netton hard. Without it the southern half of the island held little else of interest to tourists, save a few small fishing villages and Blackwater Lake.

Ever shrinking seasonal tourist work remains the major employer on the island. With winter months becoming cold, dark, and lean among the bitter storms that roll in off the Atlantic.

Beyond the esplanade, beyond the rise of narrow terraced streets, is Seaview Park.

Looking down at Westlyn, the shimmering sea, a ferry pulling out and away back toward the mainland, it is the home of a large old bandstand. During the summer, rows of deck chairs seat those who enjoy the brass band that plays every day at 2pm. On still days you can hear wisps of it all the way down on the esplanade.

Surrounded by tall fir trees on the far side of the park is the home of Westlyn Town FC.

An old wooden stand painted in the club colours of blue and white has stood on this spot for more than 80 years, when the club was formed.

Though fenced off to prevent spectators from shirking the humble gate fee, the ground, also known as Seaview Park, is easy to access. A gate by the clubhouse squealed as it opened. Beyond it a gravel pathway led pitch side and lined the dimensions of Westlyn's hallowed turf along with a barrier, from which faded advertising hoardings hung.

The beams of the stand groaned beneath my feet. The handrails smooth from a recent off-season treatment. The heady smell of fresh paint indicating that a lot of love and attention has been put into this grand old relic.

Behind the goal to the right of the main stand a narrow stretch of exposed terracing curves away and round behind the corner flag, and up the far touchline. Its edges eroded by decades of shuffling supporters, little patches of rubbled scree built up on the steps below, crunching beneath your feet as you wandered.

The only break in the wooden fencing and fir trees that line Seaview Park occurs just to the right of the main stand, where iron gates open out onto a terraced street.

Facing opposite, standing on the curve of terracing, you can recreate one of the few photographs of Tom Maskell that I could find.

I found it twice actually: once in a Westlyn Town match programme from 1984, and then again accompanying an article in the Netton Gazette, detailing Maskell's apprenticeship with the Town in the August of 1985.

The online digital archiving of the Gazette proved to be a Godsend and gave up a few snippets of Maskell's playing career on the Island. An over-exposed and washed-out team photograph for a Freshwater FC saw a fifteen-year-old Maskell line up before the 1984 Netton Gold Cup Final. So much smaller than the rest of his team-mates, a broad smile beamed beneath that familiar wild crop of brown hair.

'Plucky Freshwater push Town all the way,' was the headline to an article that detailed how Island League Division Two side, Freshwater took the semi-professional Western League Westlyn to extra-time in the Gold Cup Final. A last-minute winner denied the amateurs but, the article continued, a number of the Freshwater players impressed the Westlyn manager enough to invite them to pre-season training that July, Maskell being one of them.

From the league tables supplied on the sports page in the Netton Gazette, and a map of the island, Freshwater was a village on the southern tip of Netton. Its football team had been no more than a solid middle table outfit in the ten team second division. A far cry from the semi-pros of Westlyn, who competed on the mainland in the Western League, populated by the reserve teams of Football League sides Plymouth, Torquay, and Exeter, the National League second strings of Yeovil and Weymouth, as well as the best non-league teams from Cornwall, Devon, and Somerset.

It was that Gazette image of Maskell as a Westlyn player in the autumn of 1984 that needed no caption detailing the players involved, so familiar was Maskell's gait. Holding the photograph up it was almost possible to line up the present-day Seaview Park perfectly with that of Maskell's, the best part of four decades earlier.

In it, Maskell is frozen in black and white as he shadows the advances of a Barnstaple winger, poised to slide in and pick the pocket of a player a good foot and a half taller than him. Beyond, a row of expectant faces shrouded in hats, scarves and coats look on from their spot in front of those large iron gates. A freezing fog dims the line of terraced houses beyond, and the bodies populating the sliver of main stand in shot.

It is a moment in time vivid enough to make you shiver, tricking you into forgetting the warm summer sun on your back.

It is an image that makes you want to know what happened next, sucking you in to this duel captured for posterity. A duel that dissolves with an aching arm, a cold, foggy November afternoon lost once more as the photograph dropped to my side.

Another 'what happened next' to add to my list, though at least with this one we know that Maskell's efforts were rewarded with a three-one win to move Westlyn up into fifth spot in the Western league.

Blackwater Lake is a large body of water, stretching from the Colbridge campsite on the edge of Westlyn all the way across to Durnford Downs and the southern part of the island.

Including the tributaries that snake down into Freshwater and out into Freshwater Bay, the lake is a mile long and a good two hundred metres across at its widest point. And with a depth of more than twenty fathoms in places, the lake takes its name from its dark, brooding waters.

In its hey-day, the wooden cabins that dot Blackwater Lake's shoreline were the preserve of the rich and wealthy. The rank-and-file holiday-maker contenting themselves with envious glances taken from small rowing boats that could be hired by the hour from the few campsites lining the lake.

Perfect looking families playing tennis on their private court, lounging on their very own pontoon, taking lunch on verandas looking out across the water. Watching them taking walks among the thick, secluded pine forests could potentially put a dampener on your own little slice of heaven; complete with sun burn, toddlers covered in ice cream, and a hangover from one too many at the guesthouse bar the night before.

In the intervening years, these cabins' fortunes, just like the rest of Netton, have been in decline. Becoming dark and gloomy as the forests about them grew, some have fallen into disrepair, the lines of tennis courts lost beneath decades of shed pine needles. Nets sagging from neglect.

Those cabins that continue to receive guests are not in such high demand that a last-minute booking in June couldn't be accommodated.

Choosing one a relatively sedate walk away from Blackwater Chine, a ramble through the forest presented a depressing sight.

Gates locked and overgrown, the sign above it that promised a 'Spectacular Adventure Park' stood faded, scarred with ivy, and broken, one panel swinging gently from a single un-breached fixture. Wild West towns, mazes, climbing frames beyond lost beneath unchecked creeper, shrub and tree. Reclaimed by nature, they awaited the same fate as their prehistoric brethren. The slow, inevitable failure of chalk cliffs on rough seas edging them closer to one final tumble into the ocean.

This was no way for someone's childhood to end up.

Later that evening a couple of whiskies, sat on my own private pontoon seemed a fitting wake for Blackwater Chine. And in the failing light I caught a first glimpse of Gordie and his boat.

I could hear her long before she hove into view around a small headland. The rhythmic chugging of her engine carrying across the still waters, echoing off the thick forest at the shoreline, belying her true position. Then a dark silhouette hugging the far shore. One dim green starboard light. A fan of ripples behind her the only chop on otherwise glassy waters. By the time they rolled in beneath my pontoon, breaking gently on the shingle, she was long gone. Heading on toward Freshwater.

By bicycle along a gravel forest track it takes ten minutes to reach Freshwater, a fishing village that straddles the river Ebb, connecting Blackwater Lake out to Freshwater Bay and the open ocean.

Freshwater was a forgotten place. Protected from the ocean by a sweeping arm of large grassy cliffs, a natural harbour wall to the village and its fishing boats, it remained hidden from view until you were on top of it.

With the closure of Blackwater Chine, there was little else to attract visitors to the southern tip of Netton and Freshwater. The trickle of tourists hiking up to the lighthouse on Saint Catherine's Point on the top of the bay kept the tea-room on the seafront, the boat taking tours out to the cliffs and its scores of nesting birds, just about in business.

A declining fishing fleet that could now be counted on one hand, and the closure of the island's spectacular adventure park meant that job opportunities were scarce.

Freshwater had an old-world charm of narrow alleyways, whitewashed fishermen's cottages, heaps of stacked lobster pots. But it was a world that had been left behind, and was being lost as families moved away, their homes turned into holiday lets. The permanent population shrinking.

From the tea-room, directions to Gordie were loosely discovered.

'Though you can never be sure where you'll find him,' the tired looking young waitress said.

'He works on Gordie time, which is not like your watch there. Unless you have a collection or delivery booked in with him you mostly stumble across him, or he stumbles across you.'

Gordie's ferry had him criss-crossing the lake, dropping off deliveries, picking up passengers and taking them up to Colbridge and Westlyn, or wherever they wanted to go, collecting anything ordered from the mainland from the Westlyn ferry, taking it where it needed to end up.

'He's been doing it for more than forty years,' the waitress added, shook her head. 'The silly old sod. God knows how he survives. Legend has it he has never changed his prices. It would cost you a pound to go from here to Westlyn on his boat back in the seventies. Guess how much it costs you today?

'You can't miss his cottage: it's the last one on the far side of the river, with an old anchor outside. There is a bench opposite with a bell, next to his mooring. Sit there and when you see his boat – you can't miss it, it's the boat that looks like it should have been scrapped years ago – ring the bell. He will come to you.

'Give it a good battering though, that bell. The sound travels well across the lake, but his hearing isn't what it once was. Cross the bridge just behind us and follow the river path. You'll find him.'

Gordie's cottage, his mooring, was the last of a row of small, single storey cottages that had once housed the jobbing fishermen that came in to help the fleet in season. Small windows in thickset walls suggested they were a gloomy place to call home. You could imagine the old wooden doors warped by time and weather rattling in their frames in winter storms, doing little to halt the bitter cold sweeping in off the lake.

A far cry from a warm June day, the bench a sun trap, lulling those with nowhere else to be into a heat induced daze of rustling reeds and bird song. So much so that the distant sounds of an engine didn't register for quite some time.

It didn't look like it had done the trick. The deep peal of the bell heavy enough to make your arm ache after a few rings, seemingly doing nothing to alter the course of the boat as it slipped across Blackwater Lake. Lactic acid building in my bicep I placed the bell back down on the bench, then watched as the bow swung round to port and began in toward me.

It was a forty-foot pleasure cruiser, built at the Thorneycroft boatyard, Southampton in 1930. A low-slung day cruiser, a wheelhouse sheltered by a primitive wooden frame covered in an old canvas, stood on top a cabin housed in her bow. Steps down from the wheelhouse led to a similarly covered deck, lined with benches, strewn with coils of rope and boxes. Stretched across the aged wooden frame, sun bleached a silvery grey, the fraying canvas displaying the patchwork scars of countless repair jobs protected the deck from the elements.

On his skipper's chair bolted to the wheelhouse floor Gordie Macrae skilfully manoeuvred the boat to come alongside, then beckoned me aboard.

'That'll be a pound,' he said, a Glaswegian accent undiluted from decades of Netton living. As he gunned the engines and carefully pulled back out into open water, I offered him my pound. He nodded at an old tin hanging from a nail by the cabin door.

'Pop it in there and that's you. Where to?'

Unsure just how to start, I said nothing, I opened up my backpack and carefully took out that autographed team sheet from Maskell's reserve team debut against Northampton, I handed it to Gordie.

He didn't say anything for a moment, he stared down at it, before handing it back and nodding out at the lake.

'I have to away to Colbridge, to collect some parts for the garage. Take a seat.'

For a vessel well into a ninth decade of service, Gordie's boat seemed to glide across the water, the smooth turnover of the engine an indicator of the love, sweat, and tears that had clearly been poured into it, giving it a smooth ride.

But for the jaded paintwork of the hull, where a lifetime of mooring against dock and pontoon had created a pattern of scuffs and blemishes, and the outdated, primitive wooden frame protecting wheelhouse and deck, you might think she was a fraction of her age, having been so well looked after.

For the most part she had the lake to herself. A few small sailing boats limped along on the insipid breeze closer to shore. One or two hire boats ventured further out into the deeper waters, the chop from which slapped her sides, the spray drifting across deck pleasant in the sun.

Moored up at Colbridge we walked to the campsite office, where he waved at a lad sat inside, who pointed at two boxes of car parts just inside the door. Gordie nodded to me, then the boxes.

'Will you help me with one of these? It will save a trip.' I nodded and we took a box each, and as we walked back through the campsite to the boat he nodded at my backpack.

'Where did you get that: Tom's signature?' he said, then listened as I told him my story.

He walked with a heavy limp, the box of parts lurched to one side as he carried it between the pitched tents, rows of camper vans, its contents clunking together as his bad knee buckled beneath him every other step. Not saying a word until we had stowed everything onboard, he nodded for me to take a seat.

'Are you hungry?'

Moored alongside his cottage, a neighbour's cat sunbathed on Gordie's bench, leaning against the heavy hand bell that must have felt nice and warm. Unfazed by the clatter of bowls and pans drifting up from below deck, the tabby was a picture of contentment, eyes scrunched shut, face turned up toward the sun.

Gordie cut a slight figure, a weather-beaten face betraying a life lived. His oversized overalls turned up in the leg and arm; one cuff kept unravelling as he poured out two bowls of soup that had been warming on the small stove in the ship's cabin.

'That's where I first saw him, that bench,' Gordie said as he ripped off two chunks of bread from a farmhouse loaf and handed me one. 'He wasnae more than seven, eight years old. Him and his dad had moved in two doors down. Simon Maskell worked out on the oil rigs. Six weeks on, six weeks off. Though you couldnae tell which was which. He rarely left the house when he was home. He would just sit inside.

'Tom fended for himself, whether his dad was here or not. God knows what Social Services or his school would have said if they had known that he was left all alone for such a length of time. But they never did, so good was he at keeping himself neat and tidy, fed.

'He had lost his mum when he was a toddler, and I think he didnae want to lose his dad as well, no matter how absent he was from his life. So, he made sure no one at school would ever suspect that he spent so much time on his own.

'I don't think his dad ever recovered from losing his wife. Life, bringing up a child on his own, too overwhelming a task to do well. It was like he wasnae at work, he was on pause, waiting to go back.'

'Tom seemed fascinated by the boat right from the off,' he said looking about him.

'After they had moved in, I would see him watching me, the Stanley B, all the time. When I set off, or moored up, he would be peering out his window, watching me come and go. Then one day, after quite a time of watching me off across the lake, he got up the courage to sit on that bench. To say hello.

'He was a boy of few words. A product of a solitary life I imagine, but we got to talking. About nothing in particular. Just this and that.

'After that he would almost always be waiting for me of an evening as I came home, and I would throw him a line as I came alongside, which would thrill him, and he would tie the boat up just as I showed him.'

'I would invite him onboard, where he would love to explore, peering down into the cabin, the engine room. He would sit on my seat and pretend to steer, and he would swish his hand in the water sitting down on the deck. He was a nice lad, quiet, very polite and friendly, and we struck up a friendship.

'We would sit around in the evenings, and he would play quietly in the cabin, drawing in a little pad he had, or he would sit on the deck, pretending that we were out at sea, looking out at imagined, faraway lands, strange sea creatures. Or wherever he imagined. He would draw maps of these places in his book, sketches of his sea monsters.

'Then he started helping me out with my work on the boat after school and on weekends. He would come on trips with me and tie the boat up at each dock we stopped at.

'When his Dad was away, we would sit and have dinner in this very cabin. He would do his homework at that table. And he would help me out around the boat. He could soon tie up at dock and set off again faster than I ever could.

'During the summer holidays he would take that tin round the deck to make sure that all the tourists paid their fare, back when there were plenty who wanted a spin around the lake. He would sit and watch me fix the engine, passing me the tools from my toolbox, and he learnt how to darn holes that had appeared in the canvas roof.

'And before I knew it, Tom had kind of adopted me.

'He would take my washing with his to the launderette. I would fix anything that needed it in his house, and we would keep each other company on the boat in between.

'He would laugh when I tried to help him with his homework. He was smarter than me, even back then. My help was no help at all, but it entertained him to see me try and fathom equations and the like. I learnt quite a lot watching Tom learn. But maths, forget it,' he smiled, to no one in particular, staring down into his soup. 'They were happy times.'

'He had this battered old football, with fraying seams. He would play keepy uppies on the towpath outside his house, chipping it against the wall of the cottage before juggling it again from one foot to the other. During the summer he would kick up this plume of dust from the path. A cloud of flailing arms and legs. Rarely would he drop it. And on the odd occasion he did, and it bounced into the river, we cobbled together a net, gaffer taped to a broom handle so as he could fish it out before the current took it out through town and into the bay. It is still out there, propped up against my cottage,' he said pointing at the cabin's small portholes. A net long since passed its ball catching heyday, hung limply from a splintering handle. Its weave frayed and perished over time, it looked as if it would dissolve if plunged back into the River Ebb.

'I couldnae throw it out, so there it stays,' he said, sat quietly for a moment.

'Tom loved to play with that ball. When its seams finally gave out and the bladder inside began to poke through, he still tried to use it, though its shape had started to resemble a peanut. When I couldnae bear to watch any longer, I ordered a ball for him from the mainland – that beautiful looking ball that was used at the 1978 World Cup, with those black and white panels.

'Being a Scot, it brought back bitter-sweet memories, having seen my team humiliated three-one by Peru with it, then even worse, only managing a draw against Iran. But at the same time, I watched those games with Tom on a small set I had bought just for the World Cup. He had helped me with the aerial, and he loved watching all the games he could with me. He cheered our three two victory over Holland just as loudly as I did, even though it was too little, too late that competition. And that ball really was a thing of beauty.

'He was absolutely made-up with it. He wouldnae use it on the towpath. He didnae want to scuff it up, or it go in the river. So, we would go to the park after I'd finished for the day, and I would watch him chase around with it on the grass. He would always towel it down when we got back, cleaning off any mud or grass stains as best he could, before putting it to bed in a small chest in his bedroom.

'He had a real talent. That ball would stick to his feet. But more importantly to me, he loved it. He loved to play. He would smile, laugh, be a little boy having a great time. He was happy. It was a big deal to me,' he took up our empty bowls and dropped them in a wee sink next to the stove.

'If you want to learn about Tom, then I need to show you something, if you have the time?'

Car parts safely stowed on a makeshift trolley made of old wheelbarrow wheels attached to the underside of a wooden pallet, I followed behind him as he dragged his contraption along the towpath by a length of rope draped over his shoulder, tugging at it as a wheel snagged in undergrowth, or faltered on a stone.

Parts delivered, he leant it up against the side of the garage and nodded away across the village.

'This way,' he said.

Shooters Meadow, the former home of Freshwater FC stood as both a memorial to what had been lost, and a celebration of ingenuity.

Founded in 1885, Freshwater had been the oldest club on Netton. And while being far from the most decorated team on the island, it represented the few villages along the south coast with distinction in the Island League. In its heyday it ran three sides, despite a limited pool of players to choose from, with first team matches attracting healthy crowds.

The closure of Blackwater Chine, then the local cottage industries that used to supply it, drove unemployment up and forced families elsewhere, in search of a living.

Freshwater FC struggled for numbers, first losing the reserve team, then substitutes for the first team. Finally, a succession of Saturdays being forfeit, unable to raise a side, saw this proud old club fold in 2013 – one hundred and twenty-eight years after its formation.

Despite that, Freshwater could not, would not, just let Shooters Meadow fall into ruin. Just in case.

Sagging goalposts remained in situ, as did the hoardings lining the pitch – faded reminders of failed local businesses. The small main stand still looked out on a field of dreams now dotted with a few caravans, tents, and camper vans.

'It does OK as a campsite. You would be surprised how many people prefer the quiet and isolation of here over the bustle of Colbridge. Enough at least to keep it going. They put that screen up at the front of the stand, and during the summer, in the evenings, they play movies for the campers on it. They sell popcorn, everything.'

The changing rooms on the ground floor of the old pavilion next to the stand had been converted into shower blocks, toilets and a small laundry, while beyond the far goal, benches and barbecues stood for summertime outdoor eating.

A small, narrow stair led up to the top floor of the pavilion and a makeshift café where Freshwater's clubhouse once stood.

Old photographs, team pictures and pennants still hung from the walls – no one having had the stomach to remove more than a century of history – looking down at tables ready to host Shooters Meadow's new patrons.

Gordie wove between the tables to a spot by the large windows looking out at the pitch, pointed at a familiar picture of that Freshwater team of the 1984 Netton Gold Cup Final on the wall.

'There he is,' he said proudly 'That's Tom.'

A young girl called Sandy stepped out from a small kitchen and greeted Gordie warmly, taking our order for two teas.

'I come here in the evenings during the summer; you can have a beer or whatever. Sandy even got a bottle of whisky for me, though I'm not much of a drinker these days. It's nice to see the place being used still. You can sit here with the windows open and listen to the movie, watch the kids playing in the goals. Over where Tom used to play.

'He would dribble the length of the pitch before banging his ball into the net, turning to me and raising his arms above his head. He would drive down the left channel, cut in, and leather it for all his might. He absolutely loved it, chasing after his ball if it flew past the goal.

'After he had played, we would have to walk around the ground so as he could wander up into the stand, spend a few moments looking down at the pitch. Then he would always linger by the entrance, where they used to put a large poster with all the upcoming fixtures on it. He never said a word, but you could tell he was itching to go to a game.'

Gordie sipped at his tea when Sandy dropped it off and looked down at the pitch.

'It was hard at the start of the season. August was a busy month. But when the tourists drained away, I would moor up for a couple of hours and we would go to see Freshwater play. He loved it. They were a solid first division side back then, and most of the village would turn out. It was a great atmosphere, and Tom always wanted to sit up at the back of the stand, so he could see it all. Then he would sneak under the barrier at half time and play with his ball, making sure not to interfere with the substitutes' warm-ups. And after the match we would have to hang around until they presented the man of the match award, which was a fresh caught lobster from out in the bay. He loved seeing the non-fishermen trying to hold it without being nipped while their photograph was taken for the paper,' he smiled. 'It would make him laugh so. Though when a player offered it to him to hold, he would squeal and hide behind me. They were fun days,' he said, trailing away into a moment of quiet contemplation, that photograph of Tom's team from 1984 over his shoulder. That beaming grin.

'I'd noticed in the programme that Freshwater had a couple of junior sides.

They didnae have enough players to fill every year group, but they ran an under thirteen and an under fifteen team. So, when Tom turned ten, I asked if he could join in. Just for the training.

'We went up to Westlyn to buy him a pair of boots, and he held that shoe box so tightly all the way home. Sometimes he would carefully peel back the tissue paper to take a look, before tucking them back in. He cleaned them after every training session, putting them back in that box, covering them back up with the paper. He cherished them so much. It was something to see.

'He would find me on the boat after training and tell me all about it. Football had been so important to me in another life, had captivated me entirely, and it was hard not to get caught up in his enthusiasm.'

'Maybe a month or so after he had started, the under-thirteens' manager stopped me one Saturday and said that he wanted to put Tom in the team. Despite him being a good two or three years younger than some of the other boys, he had impressed so much in the training games he wanted to put him in at left back.

'He showed no fear. He loved it. And when I could get away from the boat, I would watch him play. Watch him bounce off the bigger boys when tackling, dust himself down, and go again. But when he got the ball at his feet, his speed would see him past them before finding a team-mate to pass to.

'Age twelve, he had been sent up to the under fifteen team. Age fourteen he was on the bench for the first team, playing against men.

'I used to take the team out to some of the away games on the boat, when they were playing a team from Westlyn, or one of the villages along the eastern shore. And as luck would have it, the game he made his first team debut, I had no other jobs on the boat, so could go along and watch.

'Away at Woodford it was. Away up there on Shanklin Point. He came on for the last fifteen minutes, dwarfed among all the men. But he got his tackles in, passed the ball well. He just loved to play. I still have the programme from that game, back on the boat. I have them all, for every game he played.

'If I couldnae get to the game myself, I would ask the Assistant Manager Ernie if he would get one for me. And if Tom got on, I would keep it. It was such a feeling to see his name among the line-ups: that wee boy lost in a cloud of dust, playing keepy uppies with that old, battered ball.

'The following season he started nearly every game in the first team. Helped them to the Gold Cup Final,' he said and turned to glance at the picture behind him.

'The boat was packed for that match, and despite it being the biggest game of his young career – against the semi-pros of Westlyn – he still went about making sure everybody put their fifty pence in the tin; locals paying half-price,' he looked at me and chuckled. 'Sorry about that.'

'And against a team featuring a number of ex pro's he did so well. He set up one goal, saw a rasping shot edge just wide of the mark, and he stood his ground against the Westlyn winger, virtually playing him out of the game.

'He did enough for the Westlyn manager to invite him to pre-season training during the summer,' he stopped and watched a young girl wading through the long grass around the old dugouts on the far side of the pitch. Lost in a game known only to her. He stirred a spoon around in his empty tea mug, looked at me.

'More tea?'

'He didnae want to go. He wanted to stay with Freshwater. But even at the tender age of fifteen he had outgrown the second division of the Island League. Westlyn's reserves regularly won the first division, and their first team battled for honours in the Western League every season back then.

'All he ever talked about doing was becoming a professional footballer, playing football all day, every day, and that wouldnae happen playing for Freshwater.

'Westlyn trained Tuesday and Thursday evenings, and he got so nervous beforehand. He would go all pale, very quiet on the way. I would take him up there, go for a walk around Seaview Park, sometimes down onto the esplanade while he trained, then listen to Tom talking animatedly about it on the way back, his nerves evaporated after the fact.

'They were good people at Westlyn. They looked after him. The senior players took him in as one of their own. And he did well. He was offered a semi-pro contract. Twenty pounds a week. He started the next season a Westlyn Town player.

'A month in the reserves and he went up to the first team. I missed his debut as a substitute against Taunton Town but saw his first start a month or so later against Bideford.

'Crowds of 300 were the norm, which created a real atmosphere. The trees around the ground seemed to amplify the cheers and howls of derision, trapping it inside.

'Whenever Town scored, two old timers who were allowed to park their cars just inside the gates and watch from the comfort of behind their steering wheel, would lean on their car horns, not stopping until the game kicked off again. It made for quite an atmosphere.

'They took to Tom right from the start. Such a young lad thundering into tackles, springing up after one had been landed on him, getting stuck back in right away. He was possessed by playing. No matter if it was on his own on the towpath as a young boy, or in a blood and thunder Western League game. The way he played it was as if everything happening around him had disappeared. No crowds, no car horns. Just him, the ball, and a stretch of grass to run into.

'We would get up at the crack of dawn when Westlyn were playing away, take the boat up to Colbridge to get him to the ferry on time. It would be a long day for the team, travelling the length and breadth of the West Country once they had made the mainland. Some days it wouldnae be until gone ten at night that a weary Tom would materialise back at Colbridge dock, falling asleep in the cabin before the campsite's lights had faded into the darkness.

'I hated missing Tom's games, but it's hard making a living on this lake, especially once the tourists have left, so any job, no matter how big or small, is an important job. But if I knew I couldnae spare the time to watch his match, I would always take a break a little before kick-off, wander up to Seaview Park to listen to the atmosphere inside, to the team being announced over the tannoy, to Tom's name.

'I knew the feller on the gate. He would sometimes arrange with me transport for the reserve team down to Canford Cliffs and Weathertop. I would buy a programme from him, even though I wasnae going in, and he would save me a copy of any away games that Tom played in.

'I had never been bothered with that sort of stuff during my playing days, but with Tom it was different. I was so proud of what he was doing that I needed a record of sorts. I'd cut out any clippings from the Gazette as well.'

'He found it all one day,' he said, nodding across Shooters Meadow, 'Stowed away in the boat. A programme from nearly every single first team game he had played in. He didnae say anything as such, just smiled as he leafed through it, and when he got the move to the mainland, he made sure to write to me every week, tucking in a team sheet from all his reserve team games in the Football Combination, then his first Football League appearance up at Doncaster. All at just age seventeen, this quiet wee lad from the towpath,' he paused, the animation in his face drained away for a moment. A sadness passed across him like a scudding cloud. The story nearly told.

'No one understood how the local pro teams didn't pick him up. They played against him in the Western League home and away after all. But nothing came of it. When other lads his age were getting apprenticeships up and down the country, Tom just carried on at Westlyn, with me on the boat. I thought maybe his chance had gone. And then it came, the letter, a good few weeks after the 1985 season had started.

'Westlyn had played your team while they were on a pre-season tour of the West Country and had sent a scout to the first three Western League games of the new season. Then, out of the blue, the letter came. An apprenticeship in the Football League.

'Things moved fast. He had a week to decide what to do before he needed to be on that ferry. No time at all really. No time to overthink things. And on the day, I took him across with an hour to spare, watched him away through Colbridge until he was gone. Off on his football adventure,' he smiled. 'I don't mind telling you that I cried on the way back. I was so proud of him, but the boat felt empty knowing he wasnae coming back. Not for a long while at least. The football calendar meant no time off until the season's end.

'He coped better than I did, I think,' he shook his head. 'He had been looking after himself for such a long time by that point that I think he adapted all right. His letters home told of missing it all, but he had been so busy with training and his apprentice chores around the football ground that he didnae have a lot of time to feel homesick. At Christmas the apprentices would travel with the first team to keep them busy, take their minds off being away from home, as well as for the experience. I think it really helped Tom cope.

'He wrote that at his lodgings there was an old garden bench in the back yard. And he would sit on it and close his eyes and imagine that he was back on my old bench on the towpath. He wrote about all the things he saw in his mind's eye. Things we used to do – fishing in the river, sailing away across the lake on our chores, sitting and watching the light from the lighthouse up on Saint Catherine's Point swish across the night sky. Dinner in the cabin, telling tall tales about monsters lurking in the deepest parts of Blackwater Lake.

'He had read a book about the Loch Ness Monster. He loved it when mist crept out from the forest and sat across the water, the shadows thickening among the trees. It spooked him so as he would only peek his head out of the cabin, peering at the water as dusk fell, as he told me stories from his book of monsters of the deeps.'

'He would write and ask about the boat, checking to make sure I was taking everyone's fare, joking that I must have been struggling tying the boat up dockside, so used was I to him doing it.

'He would always ask after Freshwater, and how the team was doing. That if I was at a game to make sure to say hello from him to anyone that he knew.

'But most of all his letters were bursting with excitement. At playing alongside Emms and Haysham, players who had played in the First Division, in cup finals. At playing in grand old football stadiums, even if they were empty. At scoring his goal against Bristol Rovers. At the thought of coming home, being able to tell me all about it in person.

'It was a dream come true for him. Maybe a humble dream to some – an apprentice at a Fourth Division team – but it was his dream. And he was living it.

'And as excited as he was about it all, at his first team debut, and another four appearances in quick succession – he was just as thrilled as you were at his cross for that goal against Carlisle, by the way – he was equally excited to come home, back to Freshwater, back to the boat and the lake.'

He stopped, watched a camper stepping out from the converted changing rooms, following the same path out onto the pitch as Tom Maskell had done all those years before. The memory of one taking up their position at left back, the other in the present stepping up into a small caravan in the centre circle, disappearing from view.

He smiled weakly as Sandy took up our empty mugs. A shadow, a sadness had descended across him as he took one last look out across Shooters Meadow, then he turned to me.

'That's enough for today. If you dinae mind. I should head back to the boat, just in case,' I nodded and thanked him for his time, stood up, followed him down the narrow staircase.

'If you like,' he said 'you can join me tomorrow. Have a go at what Tom did on the boat. Live a day as he did. You never know, I may even wave the pound fare for you, if you do a good job. Which cabin are you staying at? I can be waiting at your pontoon for ten.'

Eight

The mist from Tom's scary stories, that had lingered on the lake all night, parted as Gordie's boat rounded the headland in the morning, her hull finally catching up with the chug of her engine that had long since been echoing about the hushed forests along the shoreline.

Gordie throttled back the engines perfectly, bringing her port side flush with my cabin's pontoon. Years of experience leaving an inch or two between.

'Jump on,' he said, 'before she starts to drift.' Safely aboard he edged her out and away and back into the deep waters in the middle of Blackwater Lake.

The icy chill from the water crested the bow as the boat picked up speed, the morning sun not yet up above the tree line to take the edge off.

'Job number one,' he said, 'pour out a couple of mugs of coffee from the flask down there,' he nodded down into the cabin. 'You canae work on cold bones.'

'I'll carry anything, take anyone anywhere. I'm not precious. Anything to keep fuel in the tank and food on the table,' he said as he edged the boat toward Woodford on the eastern shore and a consignment of oysters bound for the sea food restaurants along Westlyn Esplanade.

'Believe it or not, but we used to take a flock of sheep from Widdett's farm across to pasture on the Durnford Downs. Tom loved that one.

'They had, for centuries, driven them around the lake, down past Freshwater and up. It would take them three days. But on the boat, it would only take half a day to get the whole flock across.

'They were bred for their wool and would live to a ripe old age. And despite being skittish creatures by nature, they trusted old Andy Widdett implicitly, and the guidance of his dogs, through years of kindness and nurturing. It was a thing to see.

'Old Andy would bring one of his dogs on first, then he would carry the sheep on board, one at a time, nine or ten a trip. And they were no little things mind. But when he scooped them up, they wouldnae struggle. They just hung limp in his arms until he let them down again, where if anyone else had tried it, they would have bucked and bleated and kicked up a storm. He did it well into his eighties, lugging them across onto deck.

'Then he, his dog, his sheep would sit still as we took them over. Sometimes seven or eight trips to get them all across. Then a few months later, seven or eight to get them back for shearing.

'Tom thought it was brilliant. Watching them huddle around old Andy for safety. He didnae even mind washing down the deck after, clearing everything of mud, hay, and sheep shit.

'One year, Andy dropped off a couple of thick jumpers and two bobble hats that his wife had made for me and Tom. From their sheep. By God they were warm. We both pretty much lived in them in winter. Mine only fell apart a few years ago. That thing got me through more than thirty winters. I still have the hat,' he said and leant down, rummaging by his side, pulling it out.

'When Andy died, they stopped farming sheep. Turned to crops. I still get to take their sacks of produce up to town every now and then. The roads around the island have always been narrow and winding. They can be a real headache. Sending stuff with me can sometimes save a lot of time and money for people. That's if I can dock safely, keep people and their produce above the water, not in it,' he said nodding at the fast-approaching Woodford dock.

'Let's see what you are made of eh?' he said and pointed at the bow line 'You remember what I told you?'

It was far from smooth, but I managed to jump across onto the dock, tie the boat up, pull it into the mooring without Gordie needing to gun the engines too much. As we loaded the crates of oysters caught that morning off Shanklin Point onto the deck, Gordie talked about how Tom made everything on the boat look easy.

'He would walk across from boat to dock, tie her up in one seamless motion,' he said 'timing it perfectly. I had to throttle away a little just then, to keep her from drifting. Tom would have the bow line secured and would be on the stern line, would be bringing her in to rest before I could even think.

'He would also dive under the boat, cut away anything that had got tangled in the propeller. He could tie the prop up when it needed replacing, unbolting it so as we could pull her up onto deck. Then he would dive back under and secure the new one.

'It's funny,' he said, and smiled. 'When it came to the boat, he would be in the water in a flash. But if we were just fishing, or taking a dip when it was hot, he would squeal if he touched the reeds in the shallows. Claiming that it was those monsters of his.' He shook his head. 'But for the boat, he would do anything.'

'The boat,' I asked him, 'or you?'

He shook his head, again.

'I don't know,' he said quietly, paused for a moment. 'We were good friends. We kept each other company. It was a blessing, being with Tom. They were happy days. And whether it was me, the boat, or whatever doesnae really matter. What matters is that it all came together, and we had our time.'

He paused.

'We were happy. And it was a blessing.'

Gordie turned, took the last of the crates on board, shells clinking as his limp shifted them from side to side.

'Come on,' he said. 'You'd best throw those lines. We should be away.'

As Woodford shrank away behind us, picture postcard cottages, a tea shop with bright awnings, a thatched pub looking out on the dock fading away, I found myself slipping into a habit formed all the way back in my childhood – that if I knew there was a football ground close by – I would crane to see if I could spot a floodlight pylon, a stand, a goalpost, anything to pinpoint its location – in this instance, the home of Woodford FC, the ground in which Tom Maskell made his debut in men's football.

But there was nothing. No sign. And Woodford drifted away.

Anywhere else and it would have cut a strange sight – an old man towing crates of oysters up the pavement on a pallet construction on wheels, weaving between retirees on lazy walks, locals on their chores, young children transfixed on their ice cream cone. Not on Netton however, as Gordie dropped off his load at the fish restaurants along the esplanade, an island institution forty years in the making.

And as we threaded our way back through Colbridge campsite, he became like the pied piper, passengers for his boat filing in behind him. Six twitchers off to watch the migrating birds on Canford Cliffs, a young family of four off to Woodford for a cream tea and a walk along the beach there, a couple of hikers off up to the Saint Catherine's Point lighthouse at Freshwater.

All safely aboard I threw the lines and we pulled away, Gordie looking at me, then nodding at the tin.

'Off you go. Adults a pound, kids fifty pence.'

Fares safely collected I sat on the steps as he steered the boat across the lake.

'It's a thought,' he said after a time spent in silence, the thrumming engines easily lulling you into daydreams, idly watching the woods as they passed, the shimmering sun on the water, 'But had you taken a ride across the lake when you came as a little boy, you would have handed your fifty pence to Tom. It's strange, no? How you nearly crossed paths, and then years later, far from here, he became your special left back.'

The day done, with the sun falling behind Durnford Downs, Gordie Macrae eased his boat dockside outside his cottage, stretched in his skipper's seat, then stepped down into the cabin below and poured us both a whisky.

He pulled out an old hand-made wooden box and placed it on the cabin table. A little larger than a handyman's toolbox, in another life it had been painted black and varnished, though time had dulled both. Scuffs and scratches exposed the pine beneath. Flakes and splinters of wood, like worn threads in a shirt, threatened to undermine the boxes structural integrity over time. But for now, in this lifetime, it held firm, its hinges groaning as Gordie opened it up, and took out a small parcel wrapped in paper, bound together by string.

'I call it the ship's log,' he said, nodding at the box. 'It's where things of significance have been put, since long before my time on this boat. It is her memory. Her heart. Her soul. The people who loved and lived her,' he said, peering down into its contents 'they can be found in here.'

He closed the lid and pointed at initials carved haphazardly into the wood.

'Each one has a connection to her somehow. They played their part. See,' he said 'there I am – GM. And down here is Tom,' he traced his finger across the scratch marks made by a young boy and a pen-knife.

'It took him ages to etch his initials. He wanted it to be just right. Neat and tidy. It meant a great deal to him, to be on this box.

'And it seemed the right place for all his things.

'I put all his programmes in here. And that is how he came across them. All those years ago.

'He would love to pore through this box, delve through all the "treasures" as he called them. Photographs, bundles of letters, postcards, old pamphlets, notebooks, documents, papers, envelopes, little parcels of this and that, bits that make up a patchwork history of this boat, going back a very long way.

'And he would love to rummage and wonder through it all, right the way down to the bottom.

'Some things have no obvious explanations. Would make no sense to anyone who didnae know about them. Photographs of nameless people. A scrap of rope. A small conch-shell. There is a matchbook from a bar in Havana, Cuba, with an address scribbled inside for a "Martha" of Whitby. There is a bolt that has been sheered in two, and an old baseball cap with the letter 'B' on the front,' he nodded 'All important to someone, at some time or other. Worthy of being put in here, even if the meaning of some of them have got lost along the way. But there they stay, all the same.'

He took out a handful of Tom's things and placed them on the table, sorting through them. The programme to Maskell's first ever senior game against Woodford, a newspaper clipping from a Westlyn Town match, a photograph of Shooter's Meadow blanketed in snow, a young Tom no more than ten or eleven kicking his ball toward goal, wading through virgin snow that came up over his shins.

A black and white moment made all the more striking by the dark and shadowy main stand silhouetted against the vivid white of the wintry scene.

'His last letter home before the end of his season at the Town said that he had something for me, for the box,' he placed his hand gently on the paper parcel.

'I don't know who was more excited for him coming home, me or him. I couldnae wait at Colbridge, so I went all the way to the Westlyn ferry to meet him, trying to spot him on deck as it docked. I remember giving him this huge hug. It just happened. I hadnae planned it. I was just so happy to see him.

'He hadnae changed one bit. He was still the humble, quiet little boy I first met all those years earlier, despite him coming home a professional footballer.

'I canae remember the number of times he was stopped on the way back to Colbridge – former team-mates, Westlyn Town supporters, and other friends via the boat and football – all wanting to shake his hand, slap him on the back, congratulate him. One of our own had made it.

'I joked with him, asked if he was too much of a big time Charlie to cast off the lines any more. And he put a pound in the tin when he came aboard, saying that he couldnae be sure I hadn't replaced him on the crew, that he wasn't just another passenger.

'He was so happy to be home, to be back on the Stanley B. He didnae want to be dropped off. He wanted to help with the rest of the day's work, skipping off and on to tie up dockside like he had never been away. And that night, when we had finished for the day, he gave me this.'

He carefully undid the string, peeled back the paper, took out the bundle of Tom's letters home and put them to one side, before unfolding and holding up a Town shirt. Its reds and yellows dulled with age and a life lived. Its collar stiff from decades of inactivity, the embroidered Town badge warped on the front, creating undulations across the material. The shirt of my childhood.

'It's his reserve team top,' he said. 'The club were changing strips the following year and had no need for it any more. Tom asked if he could have it, for me, for the boat.'

He turned it round to show off the number three on the back, then carefully draped it across the table.

'He scored his goal in that, against Bristol Rovers. He played in it all around the Combination League, at all those football grounds. He played in it in front of you, your friends. It's something, isn't it.'

I found myself involuntarily reaching out for it, rubbing the material slowly between my fingers.

A relic from those obscure reserve team games at Inchmery Road, it had, with Tom's help, captivated me, Bill White, Crazy Mary, and the smattering of others who had watched Maskell develop into that fearless little first team player come the April and May of 1986.

Those colours, that design, woven among its threads were the sounds of turnstiles chattering, the rich smell of tobacco, the smack of ball on boot echoing about empty stands. The chill of a shadowy main stand in winter, players shouting to one another beneath strengthening floodlights, the rasping of ball on net beyond an outstretched keeper.

Pieces of footballing poetry, those sweeping passages of pass and move from Maskell to Sanders, to Maskell, to Thompson. Those wicked crosses and perfectly timed sliding tackles, thunderous strikes on goal, all performed with a buccaneering vibrancy. All performed in that shirt.

Dad, Mum, Bill White, Tina from the club shop.

Strangers ruffling my hair, sitting on the wall outside the Crown.

Programme Man bent over his latest paper bag of treasures.

Hull City in the Milk Cup, promotion back into the Football League, Mum's quiet moments at Dad's spot on the terrace. Me looking up at him beneath snow flurries that made those wintry games so memorable, Dad leant up against his barrier, looking out at the play, enjoying his afternoon with his boy at the football. Such wonderful times.

It all flooded back with a touch of that shirt.

As I wiped a tear away, Gordie shifted in his seat.

'A whisky?' he said gently.

Tom's letters were all printed in a sweeping upper case – big, broad pen-strokes a physical manifestation of the excitement contained within.

Stories of long away trips, descriptions of grand old football stadiums and players played against, mingled with reminders to Gordie to check the oil pressure on the Stanley B, and requests for tales of life aboard. He wanted to know about Freshwater, Westlyn Town, how they were doing in the league. He checked up on Gordie every letter, whether he was managing without him.

He wrote about Mrs Whittingham, how she looked after him, her bench in the back yard where he would imagine being back on Gordie's bench on the towpath. Two pages every week, neatly folded around a team sheet or two from his games.

Gordie shot up in his chair, his eyes wide.

'Jesus,' he exclaimed and began rummaging through the envelopes on the table, looking at the date stamps added by a sorting office between here and there.

'Here,' he said, handing me what he had been looking for. 'Read.'

It was a letter about his reserve team debut, wrapped around the team sheet for that three-nil defeat to Northampton. He was so excited about getting on. How it happened in a flash, that he didn't have time to get nervous. One minute he was sat in the dugout, the next he was stripped off and jogging out toward the East Stand.

He wrote about it all being a blur, that he just tried to imagine that he was having a kickabout with Gordie down at Shooter's Meadow. That he thought he did all right. He listed all the players on the team sheet who had been serious professionals in their hey-day, writing that he couldn't believe that he had shared the same pitch as them.

Then I sat upright, looked at Gordie.

'Go on,' he said, nodding at the pages in my hands.

I carried on reading.

"You won't believe what happened after the game. As I was leaving for the bus, a young lad stopped me outside the ground. He asked for my autograph! Can you imagine! I was in such a fluster I don't think I got my words out properly! But I just about managed to sign my name! What a day. My first appearance for Town, and then my first autograph. Anyone would think I was a proper professional footballer, not just an apprentice!"

'You made his day,' Gordie said, watching me take out that signed team sheet from my bag. 'And there it is,' he said and shook his head, 'all this time later, here on our boat.'

'He worked on the boat all summer, just like how we used to. Taking fares, helping with deliveries. He was so happy. Happy to be home, but also excited for what the following season might bring. His manager had been impressed with him when he stepped up into the first team, and he had loved playing in front of big crowds – well big crowds for a lad from Freshwater. There had been more than ten thousand up at Doncaster when they clinched promotion.

'I didnae want the summer to end, but I knew that call back to pre-season training would come, sooner or later. And when it did, he would have to away again.

'Tom said that it had been so hard to walk away from the boat at Colbridge the year before. That he had looked over his shoulder more than once. Thought about turning back.

'And when notice came, we made plans to get him up to the ferry on time. It needed an early start, and the boat was the fastest way.

'When the day came, I got up, warmed the engines, expecting Tom to arrive shortly after. After half an hour of idling I knocked on his door. But he wasnae in. It took me a while to spot the note tucked under the hand bell.

'He couldnae bear to say goodbye again, it said, to take care. He thanked me. For everything, the note said. And with that, he was gone.'

Gordie Macrae looked down at Maskell's sporting life strewn across the table, gently tried to flatten out a dog-eared corner of an old Freshwater programme.

'It wasnae until a couple of weeks later that things began to not sit right,' he said.

'Pre-season was always busy. Double training sessions. Long cross country runs. So, I wasnae that surprised that he hadnae written. He had mentioned a boot camp where the team were going to be put through their paces by the army. I remember pre-season's when I was a lad, legs feeling like lead, barely being able to keep my eyes open in the evening, let alone do anything else.

'It was around three weeks or so after he left that I answered the bell being rung out there on the towpath. It was the postman. He had a letter for Tom that needed signing for.

'By that time his dad hardly ever turned up at the cottage, whether he was away on the oil rigs or no. He just gave up on it, on Tom. I heard that he died a good few years back now. Drank himself to death they said. Somewhere on the mainland.

'The letter was from the club. It had the Town badge embossed on the front. I didnae know what to do, so I opened it.

'It said how disappointed the club was in him not reporting for training on time, that if Tom didnae arrive at the club by the end of the week, his contract would be terminated.

'I rang the club from the phone box in the village. Spoke to someone. Told them that he had left weeks ago. They said they would pass it on and have someone get back to me, though they never did.

'It was a shock, that letter. Tom hadnae turned up?'

'Well, where was he then? Was he all right? Nobody had any answers.'

'I asked around at the Westlyn ferry. If anyone had seen him, the day he was due to leave. Some of the crew were ex-team-mates of his at Westlyn Town, others were supporters of either Westlyn or one of the Football League teams on the mainland. They all knew Tom through football. None of the shifts saw him. Not that day, or any after. And you would have thought that they would have.

'The ferry is the only way off or on Netton. And they hadnae seen him. But he wasnae here either. He had just vanished.'

'I gave the letter to the police. I didnae know what else to do.'

'They looked into it. But people came and went from the island all the time back then. Seasonal workers at Blackwater Chine, on the fishing boats, the camp sites. All the tourists. For so many, Netton was a place from which you moved on.

'Tom was nearly eighteen. A master of his own fate. There was nothing to go on other than a missed appointment. And just a vacuum in between. There was nothing suspicious. Nothing out of place, other than Tom.

'No ripples on the water.

'He was happy, healthy, well-liked.

'Tom simply disappeared. Became a needle in a haystack. Lost. A statistic in a file somewhere.

'He was as excited about what the future held for him as he was sad to be leaving Freshwater, the boat,' he paused, shook his head, looked across the table at me.

'I dinae know what to say. I never stopped looking for him. On the touchline up at Shooters Meadow. Dockside at Colbridge, Woodford, Canford Cliffs. Along the towpath here. Among the trees along the shore. Always looking.

'But Tom was gone. Lost somewhere between these two perfect worlds of his – football and Netton. Neither here nor there,' he leant across the table for my glass, poured another whisky for us both.

'All this stuff here,' he nodded down at the table 'makes then feel like now.

'I open up this box and the sights, sounds, smells – I am there again. Young Tom skipping on and off our boat, kicking up a dust storm with that old ball, crunching into tackles up at Seaview Park. It is so vivid, so rich, sometimes it is hard to distinguish memory from the here and now. Like they are so bound together they canae be told apart. One happening over the other.'

'He's gone, but he's not,' he took a sip. 'At least in this box. The memories are so real. Everything is so sharp.

'It's as if he couldnae decide on his future path, so he retreated here,' he tapped on the lid of the box, 'where he could be both places at once.'

'It sounds stupid. The mutterings of a silly old fool. But I still talk to him, out on the boat. About all sorts, just like we used to. When I look through all his stuff, head up to Shooter's Meadow or Westlyn Town, it feels like then, not now. Like he is here,' he paused. Shrugged his shoulders and took a drink.

'I went up to the police station in Westlyn every week. For years. One of the desk sergeants was on the committee at Westlyn Town. He would have a cup of tea with me. Talk about the club, Tom's season up there.

'He told me in confidence that a couple of detectives had gone all the way out to Inchmery Road. To try and piece things together. Working their way from the mainland ferry terminal up.

'He told me that there wasnae any unidentified bodies lying in mortuaries from here to there. That there was nothing to suggest any kind of foul play, he had said, was a good thing.

'That most likely Tom was out there, somewhere. Just not here. And not there.'

'He had been reduced to a statistic. A file. A photograph in a sea of files and photographs. Just one of thousands of missing people. Cold cases. Getting colder. Neither open nor closed. In limbo.'

Gordie pulled the shirt toward him and looked down at the club badge on the front, letting his fingers trace across the embroidery.

'I went there once,' he said, nodding at the badge. 'A few seasons after he had disappeared.

'We had been talking about me coming up, to see him play. We just never got round to it that season of his.

'I really wanted to, but it was hard to leave the boat for a few days.

'I thought we had all the time in the world.

'I went up on a reserve team game. That had seemed right. I found his old digs, but I didn't summon up the courage to knock on the door.

'So many of the places felt familiar, even though I had never been there before, Tom had described them so well in his letters.

'He loved Inchmery Road. I could see why. It seemed a timeless, ramshackle old ground. Full of character. It felt important to be there. To sit up in the stand and look down at the pitch that Tom had played on.

'I may not have seen him play in person, but I could imagine him tearing down the wing, that little boy with his World Cup 78 football, just like he did on Shooter's Meadow.

'By being there I felt like I had fulfilled my promise to him, or as best I could. It will always be a regret that I didn't get up there for him that season.

'After that little trip, I came home, back to the boat. And that is where I have been ever since. Working, waiting, hoping.'

He stopped, shrugged, looked at me.

'And that,' he said 'As far as I know, is the story of young Tom Maskell.

'I am sorry I dinae have a happier ending for you. For your article.

'He was a wonderful young lad, and I miss him every day. They were nine great years together, on this boat.

'No one will ever be able to fathom just how precious they were to me' he paused.

'I guess most stories, in truth, never end with a full-stop. I still hope that, maybe, one day, I will find him back on the towpath, sat on that old bench,' he looked out at the darkening skies, shadows thickening around his cottage, Tom's net dissolving into darkness.

'Until then,' he said, raising his glass 'I have all this.'

We clinked whisky glasses together above a table strewn with Maskell's footballing life and toasted the young man who had brought us together. Who had unknowingly captivated Bill White, Transistor Man, Crazy Mary, Programme Man and who knows who else in his year at Inchmery Road.

A young boy who had lit up Seaview Park, Shooter's Meadow, Gordie's boat with his infectious enthusiasm and passion. Who had overcome a lost mother and absent father, who had built for himself a life truly worth living – and then lived it to the full.

Five first team games in professional football, registering nothing more than a footnote in one out of one hundred and twenty-five seasons of an anonymous lower league club, Maskell's career appears, at best, underwhelming.

But beyond the black and white columns of statistics lies a tangle of people, friendships and stories, moments that have lived in the memories of those that experienced them. Moments of footballing poetry that compelled them to rise-up out of their seats.

Small interactions, hands shaken, autographs collected, smiles exchanged, kinships, moments over a cup of tea and a biscuit. Early mornings on Blackwater Lake, evening kickabouts at Shooter's Meadow, and so much more. All bound together by a young man called Tom Maskell.

Some measure success by trophies won, money earned, houses lived in. Young Tom Maskell had none of that.

But what he had, who can put a price on?

Maybe, one day, Maskell will return, and do just that.

Nine

We sat quietly drinking whisky well into the evening, leafing through all of Tom's memories. His name in the line-ups of long since forgotten Island and Western league fixtures, hammered out in old typewriter fonts. Match reports detailed his past. League tables and fixture lists pointed toward his future. Hopes and achievements chronicled in piles of letters and Combination League team sheets, that small stack of first team programmes.

From time to time, one of us would peer into that old wooden box, pull out something else to look at, to add to the life of young Tom Maskell.

Slipped down the side of the box was an old brown manila envelope, its edges thinning, gone completely in parts, it just about kept its contents stowed safely together.

Inside, newspaper clippings, photographs, and a couple of football programmes spilled out; three from Cowdenbeath, and one from Glasgow Rangers, all from the sixties.

Three black and white Cowdenbeath team photographs, from 1964, 65, and 66 contained rows of young men in their kits posed in front of a modest main stand, chests puffed out, arms folded, a serious look on their faces that meant business.

'What's all this?' I found myself saying, looking up at Gordie who had been lost within the pages of a Westlyn Town programme. He leant across the table to see what I had found, then sat back.

'So,' he said, 'You've found me have you.'

I shook my head.

'I don't understand?'

He took up the Rangers programme, from a cup replay against Cowdenbeath at Ibrox Stadium in 1965, and opened it up to the centre pages, at the line ups.

'Number eight for Cowdenbeath,' he said, tapping the page with his finger.

'Macrae,' I said, none the wiser. I looked across at him and he took a sip of whisky, raised his eyebrows, shrugged his shoulders.'

'Go on,' he said. I looked back down at the programme, then it clicked.

'Macrae? Gordie Macrae? Is that you?'

He flicked through the programme until he found a folded page from a newspaper. Yellowed and brittle he carefully opened it to reveal a match report from the game which ended three two to Rangers.

The image to accompany the piece was of a player letting loose a shot. His leg fully extended, having followed through after the ball that was a blur in the far corner of the picture, the player was a vision of focus, watching the ball on its way. Beneath the picture a caption read:

'Cowdenbeath's Gordie Macrae scores a last-minute screamer to put the fear into Rangers.'

The face was etched in concentration, contorted with the exertion of holding off a Rangers defender. Putting all his might into his shot, he was cast into shadow a little by the floodlights from the towering main stand behind him that housed a part of the forty-six thousand spectators in attendance.

A Rangers arm from a desperate last second attempt at blocking his shot obscured a little of his profile.

But there he was. A young Gordie Macrae.

'Jesus, Gordie! You scored at Ibrox! You were a footballer too? You kept that quiet!'

'Well,' he said 'you were asking after Tom, not me. It never came up. And I didnae mention it. Anyway, it was more than a lifetime ago.'

'All the same,' I said, trailing away as I scanned the team pictures. 'Where are you in these?' He pointed to his younger self in all three.

'Happy days,' he said.

I peered back into the box.

'Is there any more in here?'

'No, that's your lot. I didnae really keep anything like that, just these few pictures, those programmes from the two cup games against Rangers, and a few from the end of season that had all the year's appearances and goals tallied up. I wasn't really one for collecting stuff like that back then.'

The end of season programmes detailed a young Gordie Macrae playing in most of Cowdenbeath's Division Two matches in 64/65 and 65/66, with the odd goal thrown in from out on the right wing.

In the home tie with Rangers, that ended a one all draw on a mud bath of a pitch at Central Park, the programme mentioned that Gordie Macrae, a former Rangers junior, would be coming up against his old team for the first time since his release.

'I never played for the first team, or the reserves at Rangers. Just the colts.

'When they let me go, I was devastated. All I had ever wanted to do was play for Rangers.

'They were my dad's team. They were my team.

'I used to sneak under the turnstiles to go see them play on my own, as my dad would always go with his mates from the shipyard.

'If you were small enough you could dive through when a paying punter was let in. Me and my school mates, or those who had made it in would meet right down the front behind the Copland Road goal. We would give the visiting keeper hell when Rangers scored.

'All I ever wanted to do was be out on that pitch, play for Rangers. And I did a few times, when the youth team were lucky enough to play on it. But I really wanted to be out there for those big games against Celtic, or in Europe, where the noise of the crowd reverberated in your chest, it was deafening.

'When I was let go, I didnae know what to do. I thought I was going to be at Rangers forever.

'My dad never said anything, but I could tell how disappointed he was. He used to tell his mates how I played for Rangers. And when I didnae any more, when I turned up to work at the shipyard like everyone else, he seemed to take it as a personal insult.

'I was a rivet catcher. I left school and went straight to Rangers. I had no trade out in the real world, so I became a rivet catcher.

'They would forge these great rivets for the ships in the fires, then toss them out at people like me, who would catch them in tin buckets, run them through the shipyard, up onto the great scaffolds that grew with the ship.

'You would have to get them to the shipbuilders in double time, so as when they drove them into the hull, they would still be steaming hot. That way they would expand at the end with the all the hammering and seal the two plates.

'It was tiring work, but it kept me in shape. God knows how far I ran every day. And when the call came from Cowdenbeath I was fit and sharp and ready to take my chance.

'They were only part-time, training Tuesdays and Thursdays. And it damn near killed me, working a full day, getting the train across, training two hours, coming home again.

'The day after midweek games and training were a real slog on little sleep.

'But the extra money from playing was welcome. I had a wife and a wee bairn.

'We were nothing special, Cowdenbeath. We never threatened to get up into the top league, but we could play.

'I remember when the draw for the cup came out there was a bit of a buzz around the shipyard. I remember getting slaughtered as I ran through the yard with my rivets. You would hear from the scaffolding things like "you're going to get pumped, you Rangers reject", and "F-off back to Cowdenbeath Macrae".

'To them, like my dad, as soon as I had left Rangers, I was nothing to them.'

'The first game was a real battle in the mud. We scored first. They equalised. We held on for dear life, and somehow, thanks to the woodwork and some inspired saves from our goalie, we held out for a one all draw and a trip to play at Ibrox.

'Out there, among the hurly burly of the game that was all mud and thunder, I had heard them. I had recognised their voices – some of Dad's shipyard and Ibrox pals – piping up whenever I got close to the touchline – "F-off you Rangers reject", "You're useless, Macrae". It really hurt. Dad was there with them. He did nothing. And he could have if he wanted. He was well respected both on the scaffolds and the terrace. You didn't mess with him on either.

'It carried on the following Monday at work, raining down from the scaffolds, from Dad's pals, then again the day of the replay on the Tuesday.

'By the time I stepped out on the pitch I was possessed. I played like my life depended on it. We all did. And at three-one down with fifteen minutes to go I got my chance. All the taunting, all the frustrations of being let go went into that shot. I absolutely leathered it, and it flew in. It silenced Ibrox. All forty-six thousand of them.

'I stood there, staring into the Copland Road end. I knew they were there, my abusers, with dad, staring back.

'For a few seconds, before I was swamped by my team-mates, I had my moment,' he looked down at the newspaper cutting. At that picture.

'And this time it was Rangers who were holding on by the final whistle. We had the game of our lives. We nearly pegged them back. A few minutes longer and we may very well have. It all came together that night. I lived my dream, although it was against Rangers and not for them. It didnae matter.

'And the next day, I was back catching rivets. And the scaffolding was silent, save for the sounds of shipbuilding,' he flicked through the Rangers programme, leaving it open on a photograph of the Cowdenbeath team, a young Gordie Macrae stood in the back row.

'As far as I know, those two games were the only time my dad saw me play for Cowdenbeath. It was Ibrox or nothing for him. He never said a word to me about the games. The goal. Nothing,' he shrugged his shoulders.

'The following season, barely into October I dislocated my knee-cap in a game. It tore all the ligaments and tendons as it went. It even broke a bone. It was a real mess. I nearly lost my leg because of it.

'It finished my playing days. I had just turned twenty-one. And it left me with this wicked limp,' he looked down at his hand that had instinctively started to rub his damaged knee, a force of habit whenever recounting his traumatic tale.

'I couldnae play. Or work. I lost my job at the shipyard,' he looked down at the cabin table 'All that was left was this. A few bits and pieces that can fit inside a single envelope,' he looked up at me, then smiled faintly, his eyes drifting off to a moment in time, captured beneath the floodlights.

'All the same,' he said, 'It was one hell of a goal.'
Outside, the Saint Catherine's Point lighthouse swept across the night sky. A door rattled, and closed, a light flicked on in a cottage further up the towpath.

A small fishing boat chugged past, on down the estuary toward the bay. Swell slapped at the hull of the boat, sending her rocking a little as Gordie carefully brought together the contents of the box on the cabin table. Stowing memories of that goal against Rangers away, before tying Tom's shirt, his letters home back up into a little paper parcel. Programmes, photographs, and clippings shuffled together into a neat pile and placed carefully back into the box.

I washed up our whisky glasses in the sink, shook his hand warmly when offered it, followed him out and up onto the towpath, the warm night air just as intoxicating as the half bottle drunk below deck.

'But how,' I said 'how did a rivet catcher and Cowdenbeath winger, the scorer of a wonder goal at Ibrox find himself here, all the way down here on Netton? Skippering a boat?'

Gordie waved his hand, batting away one too many questions for one night in the same manner he did the mosquitos that had gathered at the riverside at dusk.

'A story for another time. Maybe,' he said as he opened the door to his cottage.

'Good night. Are you all right to cycle back?'

'Not a problem. I'll take it easy. Good night Gordie. And thank you.'

'Nae bother,' he said, turned. And with that he slipped away.

The Rangers Reject

Ten

I bought a ticket for the next train. It didnae matter where it was going. So long as it was leaving Glasgow.

I just knew that if I stayed, that would be the end of me.

The injury had knocked me for six. I lost my job in the shipyard, and I lost the ability to play the game that had been my entire life. It had been everything to me. I was football, and little else.

Cowdenbeath had been fantastic. They got me some money from their insurance, and they paid my contract up for that season, even though we had barely played ten games by the time that late tackle clattered into me down at Berwick Rangers.

I remember big Tommy Tynan blocking my view of my leg, which was a mess. I could tell how bad it was by the looks on my team-mates, the Berwick players' faces. Most couldnae look after an initial glance, the colour draining from their faces. Alex Brae, our centre forward, stood in the centre circle, on his own, and cried.

It is funny what you remember in moments like that. Tommy holding my hand, talking to me constantly, Alex in the centre circle, the Berwick left back who had caught me just a fraction too late, on his knees, head in his hands, frozen in the horror of it. I remember lying back on the grass while people rushed about me, looking up at the large silos behind the main stand at Shielfield Park. I remember wondering what was stored inside them, why they were there, of all places.

It was like an out of body experience. My career was over. My leg was hanging in the balance. The pain was so intense waves of nausea washed over me, my head fogging so as I thought I was going to pass out. And among it all there was that distraction, like my brain was going into self-preservation mode, keeping me out of the moment I was in.

Were they grain silos? Maybe they were part of some aggregate plant? Could they be part of a dairy farm, something like that?

I remember a plane high up in the sky and wondering where it was going. Two young ball boys behind the far goal having a kickabout. Too far away to know what was going on with me.

Among it all, among the pain and shock that had made my breathing so shallow I couldnae scream the way I wanted to, there was this moment of calm that sometimes comes with such a profound moment of chaos.

It was a calm I didnae feel again until I stepped onto the 10.14 train for Birmingham some eighteen months later.

Between these two moments my life fell apart.

Recovery was excruciating, and to me wasnae a recovery. Being just about able to walk with the aid of a stick didnae feel like getting back to who I was. I had been a young man making his way in football, scoring at Ibrox. I felt I had another chance at the very top in me if I just kept working hard with Cowdenbeath.

Then, in a heartbeat, it was gone. It was like losing your very identity, your personality, who you were.

I had a wife, a young girl. That should have been enough. It could have been, and Lord knows how much I wanted it to be, but somewhere along the way I had fallen into this thick fog.

Long days of recovery with nothing to do, nowhere to go just blurred into one. Some days I couldnae even get up out of bed, so pointless it seemed.

Others I felt as if I was still asleep while being awake, lost to the world at the kitchen table. Remote, out of reach, like some far away island. I didnae hear what people were saying to me. Some days I felt nothing, saw nothing that was happening around me. I was there, but far away.

And the days I did feel something, it was dread. All meaning lost, I felt rudderless, helpless, in a storm that never seemed to calm. I felt a heaviness in my chest. A dead weight. The world around me blurred, out of focus. Sometimes much too loud, other times stifled, distant.

I didnae know where I was, or how to get back.

Today you would call it depression. Back then it was simply a sign of weakness, being unable to pull yourself together.

The days that I made it out the flat to do my exercise it was even worse.

Painful hobbles past the shipyard, standing and listening to the bustle of industry, great showers of sparks cascading from the scaffolding as welders welded, the hammering of rivets being driven into place, it only made me feel more isolated from life. I wasnae even fit for work on the simplest of tasks.

Wandering aimlessly, if I turned a corner and found myself in the shadow of Ibrox, I would turn back right away. Unable even to look on it. Once a Cathedral of hope and passion it stood now as a symbol of everything that I was not. And never would be. Not any more.

I knew my life as I knew it had gone completely one afternoon. I knew then it was over.

It had been a day when the thought of drawing the curtains, of sitting up, was simply too much to bear. I had no idea of time. It was either light or dark. My knee either hurt a lot, or a little. That was it.

I heard the door push open a sliver, little Eilish's face peering in at me. She was just shy of her fourth birthday. I sat up, went to get out of bed, to go to her. She stepped back, then screamed, ran away down the hall crying.

I was no longer Daddy to her. I was some shadowy monster, lurking away in the gloom of the back room. I had lost her.

Finally, Eilish, my wife Shannon, they couldnae live with me any more. The pain of being unable to reach me, help me, live around me became too much. It must have been very scary. Shannon took Eilish to stay with her mother, and when the divorce papers came, I signed them, then sat in an empty flat until the rent ran out.

Despite pushing her away, shutting her out, leaving her to fend for a wee bairn on her own, Shannon still took the time to make up a bag of my things, put the last of the Cowdenbeath money in a little envelope in the front. A final goodbye. A final act of love for a man who had left her, broken her heart. Even if he, above everything else, never ever wanted to.

I was just lost. In a maze. That I couldnae get out of.

As the train pulled out of Glasgow, I didnae look back. I sat and looked down at the small bag on my lap. What was left of my life. Inside, clothes neatly folded. A wash bag. A brown manila envelope. She had put my team pictures, programmes, the newspaper cutting of my goal at Ibrox, all those things that had made her proud of me inside.

Unable, I think, even then, to give up entirely on the man, even though our lives were now forever set on separate paths.

As the train began to pick up speed, as Glasgow blurred, I began to cry.

I saw it in the pages of a discarded newspaper, left on an adjacent seat by someone on the earlier commuter service.

'Come to the Lake District,' the advert read, the words hovering above an intricate black and white line drawing of a vast lake overlooked by a great mountain. Passengers on a sightseeing boat beamed in the foreground. A little sailing boat in the distance. People walking along a narrow road near the shoreline, looking in the windows of pretty little shops. An old-fashioned bus trundling down past them.

It was such a peaceful scene, so benign and calming that I stared at it for a good long while, losing myself completely, until at one of the stops, as the train squealed and slowed to a halt, the tannoy on the platform said to change here for Windermere and the great lakes.

I found myself standing up, stepping out onto the platform, newspaper still in hand, waiting for the train to Windermere.

I got myself a room in a guesthouse and paid for a week, spending my days wandering about the pretty high street, staring into shop windows, taking ferries up to Ambleside, walking around there; sitting on benches breathing in the sharp, fresh air, watching the world go by, sailing boats drifting away to the forested far shore. Trying to dissolve into that picture of tranquillity from the advertisement.

One day I found myself getting off the ferry at a small cove. A neat strip of grass, a line of benches looked out on the water. The other side of a narrow road, a small, neat, white-washed hotel was doing a grand business in cream teas.

I didnae see the little sign, the cut among the trees. I dinae think many people would, save for those who had been seeking it out. And every now and then, a small group would leave the tea-rooms, take a right, then slip past the little sign and disappear into the woods.

Having sat over my pot of tea for as long as I possibly could, the last dregs too cold to drink, and with nothing better to do, I found myself getting up, following as another couple turned and slipped away into the trees.

The sign simply read 'Gardens,' the narrow gravel track overgrown by thick scrub, to the point that you would have to hold your arms above your head in places, to squeeze through without being scratched by large thorns and bramble.

A five-minute walk beneath a thick canopy of trees, spent largely trying to keep my distance from the couple ahead and nettle stings to my arms down to a minimum, finally opened out into a small gravel car park dotted with a few cars, and three large peacocks patrolling the scene.

Beyond, a cottage largely consumed by ivy stood flanked by a couple of dilapidated barns. A picket fence led round to a wooden stake with an arrow nailed to the top, pointing toward a gate with that word again, 'Gardens' painted on it.

The couple made for it, opened the gate, slipped inside. I followed them in.

Beyond, and a series of grass paths fanned out into a sprawl of chaotic, beautiful gardens.

Huge swathes of tree-ferns sheltering beneath enormous ginkgo trees, like a prehistoric frieze.

Enclosures of fennel so thick and tall you quickly lost yourself along the maze of paths that wove between them. Pastures of huge sunflowers with stalks as thick as your arm, swaying gently on the breeze. Expanses of wildflowers, a riot of colour. A sea of butterflies and bumblebees flitting above.

Boardwalks rose up into an expanse of mature oak trees; a series of wooden walkways lined with rope handrails to keep your balance, bridged one to the next. Platforms around each gnarled trunk dotted with tree log stools, all a good twenty feet above the mossy floor. A little warren of pathways up among the boughs.

Five acres or so of sculpted land, sheltered by the woods around them created a habitat in which plant life could flourish. Lanes flanked by poppies that went up to your waist. Expanses of grass speckled with clouds of daisies. Impenetrable thickets of raspberries. Old vegetable patches and greenhouses overgrown with shrub and creeper, reclaimed by the land.

Great trees and towering rhododendron shrubs created a dizzying maze of seemingly never-ending pathways, cul-de-sacs, and openings to secret gardens, secluded benches, beds of rosemary and thyme. All bordered along one edge by a slow running river. Reed beds rippling on a slow-moving current. Grand gunnera leaves forming a canopy beneath which dragonflies and mosquitos skittered.

It was a beautiful assault on the mind, only occasionally disturbed by stumbling across others lost in their own bewildering journey through archways of roses and warrens of grass walkways lined thick with shoulder high dahlia plants, topped off with large, colourful blooms the size of your fist.

Somewhere among it all, a large glass house stood in front of a patch of grass littered with more peacocks. A piercing screech, suspicious looks, and fans of beautiful feathers splaying out behind them, greeted anyone who strayed too close. Seeing them on their way before settling back down.

Beyond the rickety door, the glasshouse revealed what had once been an opulent looking swimming pool and summer house. A large pool, complete with diving boards and a slide, had long since been transformed into a wilderness of grand lily pads and reeds, clumps of bulrushes, great slicks of spawning algae.

Creeping vines had clawed their way along the diving boards and dangled down toward the water.

Large moss-scarred terracotta pots lined the poolside – home to delicate fruit trees, ferns and bamboo. On top of the slide, an old stone cherub statue had been placed. Forever pondering whether to risk the murky waters beneath.

Looking out on it all, a series of old garden furniture had been converted into seating for a makeshift café. A group of three sat quietly drinking tea out of miss-matched china, taking in the view from the damp cool of the glasshouse – aided by the mildew and moss that had dulled many of the panes of glass in the roof – making the air feel earthy, heavy, like we were deep underground in a cave.

Above, ivy crept across and over the roof, scarring the glass like cracks. Though in truth, it had no doubt been keeping failing panes in place for years. A natural preservative of this grand old structure. Clearing it away would quite possibly have condemned the glasshouse to almost certain ruin.

In the far corner, busying herself in a small kitchen, Maisie Buchanan cut, then carried three slices of cake over to her guests.

Well into her seventies, with long grey hair styled loosely into a plait that curled over one shoulder and down the front of an old, oversized men's shirt, she dropped off the cake, stood chatting for a time, before she noticed me.

'Oh, my goodness,' she proclaimed and wiped at her brow with the crook of her wrist, waved over to me 'we're so busy today. I'm sorry, love,' she said as she wove between the mish-mash of seating while I glanced about the otherwise empty glasshouse.

'Are you enjoying the gardens?' she asked. I said that I was, but I didnae know where to pay. She smiled.

'It's free to walk around. Everyone is welcome. But we do have a donations box,' she said, nodding at an old tea trolley by the door, at a large, glazed moneybox in the shape of a windmill. Postcards and pamphlets lay strewn about it, a handwritten sign saying 'help yourself, donations welcome' tacked to the front of the trolley.

'Are you thirsty? Hungry? We don't have a menu as such. We just do tea and a slice of home-made cake. How does that sound? And if you enjoy it,' she said, nodding back at the trolley 'you know what to do.' She smiled and turned back toward her little kitchen.

The calm, the cool of the glasshouse, shaded by the creeping ivy and a thicket of grand old oak trees behind it seemed to slow time. Drops of condensation from the glasshouse roof seemed to tumble forever before landing in the reclaimed pool. Ripples fanning out between lily pads taking an age to reach and silently break against the edge. The quiet only interrupted by the dragging of chairs, Maisie Buchanan's only other guests getting up to leave, the clinking of coins into the windmill. The creaking of the glasshouse door as they stepped out into the day, a precautionary shriek of a peacock monitoring their progress.

For the first time, maybe since that final game away at Berwick, my head felt quiet, still, unburdened. It was breathless, blissful. Overwhelming.

Standing up to leave and Maisie was nowhere to be seen. The glasshouse, the pool, still, decrepit, abandoned.

The cake and the tea, Maisie Buchanan and her guests, all of a sudden it felt like I had imagined it all. That it had simply been a mirage, a daydream, a memory of some forgotten place.

An absent moment.

Among the old postcards of Lake District beauty spots on the trolley, a pamphlet yellowed and wrinkled by sunlight and condensation poked through. The basic cover sported a delicate pencil drawing of some flowers. Above it the pamphlet's title: 'The Gardens of Five Acre Cottage.'

On the back was a sepia photograph of a man in a Fedora hat and Maisie, twenty, twenty-five years younger, wearing dungarees, a warm smile, a trowel in hand; the photographer disturbing a session of planting in a raised border lined with wooden logs.

Inside, black and white photographs detailed the gardens in a less chaotic state than they had been on my walk round.

Orchards and pastures, borders and beds, secret gardens bursting with life, mysterious shaded pathways covered by trellis and hanging baskets. One photograph was of Maisie sat in the boardwalk labyrinth high up among the trees, her legs dangling over the side. A grand smile raining down.

I fished out some money. Paid for the gardens, the tea, the pamphlet, and left. But I found myself back there the following day. And the day after that.

I had no idea what I was going to do after my week was up at the guesthouse. I had no plan of what to do, where to go. I just knew that right there, right at that moment, I just wanted the calm, the tumbledown beauty of the gardens at Five Acre Cottage. Losing myself among its myriad pathways.

'Back again!' Maisie would greet me, then scoff as I apologised. I didnae know how to put it into words, I told her. I just liked being there – better than being anywhere else. I had never seen anything like it.

I had been lost in my thoughts when Maisie had come to clear up my empty mug and plate, watching a couple of blackbirds scratching about on the glasshouse roof, scrubbing for mites among the patches of moss clinging to the framework.

'I am glad you like it. And in that case, well, I mean, I don't know how you are fixed,' she had said. 'It might not be for you. But take a look, just in case,' she pointed toward the door, to a wrinkled sheet of paper tacked to the glass beyond the trolley.

From the outside it was fogged up and virtually unreadable, to the point that I, nor anyone else, had even noticed it, so sun bleached and faded was it, contorted and stained from what looked like years of damage from condensation and hot summer sun.

The ink had run and smudged, like a spider had lurched scattergun across it whilst still wet. Once neat rows of handwriting drifted and blurred, but free from the fog of the glass, the message was just about readable, though I stopped at the first line: 'Help wanted.'

I had wandered a few paces outside, stopped, turned around. I closed the glasshouse door behind me and stood by the trolley until Maisie appeared from out the back. I didnae say anything. I just held the notice up. She nodded.

'Are you free this evening? Could you come back then? I will cook some dinner and we can talk.'

It wasnae a paying job as such, she said. There would be some pocket money every week, and all meals and board would be included. There was a little cabin in the gardens with a bed, a desk and sink, with an outhouse behind, complete with a toilet and a shower that was fed by the river at the bottom of the gardens.

'There is a wood burner that keeps it cosy, and it heats the water for the shower in the winters. The sun keeps the water tank hot during the summer months. It's a beautiful little spot, away by the far boundary, next to the birch copse.'

In return, I would tend to the gardens. Mow the grass. Cut back what needed cutting back. Fixing, as best it could be, anything that had broken.

I had limited skills, I told her. And a bad leg that slowed me down.

'Skills can be learnt,' she replied. 'And I'm in no hurry.'

Her husband had passed away five years earlier, and they had been struggling with the upkeep for years before that. Large gardens being, she had said, a young person's game.

'You could help me keep it together. Not let it fade away. I would hate to see that happen. It was such a special place to Charlie. He lived and breathed it.'

'Well, you think on it tonight,' she had said. 'And if in the morning it is still of interest, well, you know where to find me.'

Having missed the last boat back to Windermere, the five-mile walk went by in a blur. I packed my things before I went to bed, and left the guesthouse right after breakfast, a full day before my week was due to be up.

The cabin had a small shelf on which I propped up that newspaper advertisement for the Lake District. Next to it I stored my bag and my pile of clothes.

From the small hand-made wooden desk beneath the window you could see a dense copse of silver birch, the brilliant white bark of their trunks shimmered at night like an apparition.

From the desk I read the pamphlet, over and over. Paragraphs detailing many of the different sections of the garden became my guide to help try and restore areas that had become overgrown. Trying to place myself where the photographer had stood, to find the right spot, the right dimensions.

Long days of grass cutting, hedge trimming, turning over soil, were interspersed with sandwiches and a slice of cake in the glasshouse at lunch, a tall glass of lemonade at three.

I would change my gardening plans, or at least take a wide berth when the peacocks took too close an attention to what I had been doing. They appeared very territorial, very protective of their garden, their spot in front of the glasshouse, and I was not yet trusted.

Long days of log cutting, scrub clearing, seed sowing, though: no weeding, were the instructions.

'Charlie always said that weeds are just plants that are in the wrong place. He loved how things self-seeded where they wanted. It wasn't for him to say where nature should go, that's what he always said. Even if it did encroach across his vision sometimes. We try to leave them be, as much as possible.'

It was all-consuming. There would be scrambled eggs and cereal at the kitchen table in the cottage at eight in the morning, dinner at seven thirty at night, where Maisie and I would talk about what needed doing, and how I would go about doing it.

After breakfast I would watch her head off to the glasshouse around nine, where she would always disappear for an hour or so, where to I could never tell, before returning to start baking for any potential guests.

As she walked away, I would fill up a wheelbarrow of tools that I might possibly need from a shed next to the cottage, heading off into the warren of walkways, pastures, beds and thickets that needed tending to.

It brought a calm that I hadnae felt since my playing days; where my mind could clear for a moment or two, lost in the task at hand, bees and flitting butterflies my only companions.

It was a life of sorts, if not a living. The satisfaction at a chore completed, a flowerbed liberated, a pathway freed, brought with it a feeling I hadnae experienced for a long time: a kind of contentment, a pride in achieving something. No matter how small. And that calmness. For a while.

Sunday evenings I would write a letter to Eilish, addressing it to Shannon's parents, telling her all about the secret gardens, the maze of Fennel, the walkways among the trees, how I missed her so much. How sorry I was, that things had gone so wrong. And that I hadnae been able to do anything about it.

First thing Monday morning I would walk with Maisie to the road and catch a bus to Ambleside, where she would pick up supplies.

I would go to the post office and post Eilish's letter, pick up the previous week's that had been returned to sender, unopened. The pile of unread letters on my cabin shelf slowly growing as weeks turned into months.

It hurt, seeing them come back unopened. These slightest of lifelines to Eilish. But deep down I didn't think I deserved much better. I had abandoned them, no matter how desperately I hadnae wanted to, long before Shannon abandoned me.

Leaving them unopened, I saw it as an act of self-preservation, of protection. Keeping little Eilish safe from further harm. From whatever might be inside. The darkness I had inhabited.

I hated it. But I understood it.

I wish that just one letter… Shannon might have taken a chance. Opened it up. But she never did.

And again, I didnae blame her.

Maisie found me one Monday, sat outside the post office, staring at the big red lines scored through the address. She was a very perceptive person. She saw more than you ever realised.

Later that evening, at our weekly bonfire where we burnt everything that couldnae be composted or cut up for firewood, she mentioned it.

I would pile up everything on a patch of scrub near the cabin, next to the birch copse, and we would light it at dusk. She always brought two large glasses of whisky for us.

'Why bring a small glass when you can bring a large one?' she would always say with a smile, and we would sip at them while the flames grew.

'Do you still have it?' she said, breaking the silence that had grown while listening to the crackle and pop of a heap of fir branches catching light.

'The letter,' she said when she saw the look of confusion on my face.

I nodded.

'Good,' she said 'that's good. Because there is more than one way to send a message, you know. To those who can't, or don't want to receive them.

'When my Grandmother lost my Grandfather, she would always be writing notes to him. Long or short, inane or heartfelt. Every day. She would fold them up, toss them on the fire. She told me how the embers would take them up to him, wherever he was. "They always manage to find a way", she would say. "I can tell. Don't ask me how. That he has received them".

"The Tibetans, high up in the Himalayan Mountains have prayer flags. People write messages on them, hang them out, and the wind catches them, spirits them up into the mountains, to God. They have the wind, and God. Me, I have my fire. It's just a pity that no one can answer", she used to say.

'I've been known to send the odd letter, in my time,' Maisie said, looked at me.

'It sounds silly maybe. But I had great faith in my Grandmother's faith. I still do.

'I didn't need to believe. I saw the conviction in her eyes. She was talking to Grandad. And I believed in her. Enough to send my own letters, just in case.

'If you can't get through, maybe you can still get through?'

After that, I still sent my letters. Knowing that they had actually been there, had dropped onto the doormat, had maybe been picked up by Eilish, that meant an awful lot.

I would rub them between my hands, imagine her holding them, looking down at my handwriting. I would stretch my fingers out across the envelope, eyes closed, hoping beyond hope to feel her hand. The slightest of brushes.

I would hold them tightly on the bus, then let them go in the fire, watching them catch and curl in the flame, breaking apart, the embers rising up on the heat, dancing up into the night sky. Hopefully finding their way.

As the fires burned, Maisie would talk about the cottage, the gardens, Charlie. She had met him while she had been sailing solo around the British Isles in 1947 – another story entirely, she said. A stop-off in Whitehaven and a week's walking had resulted in a chance encounter in a hotel bar in Keswick.

Charlie had been a carpenter, a very good carpenter, specialising in bespoke staircases and balustrades. From small rustic cottages to the grand spaces of opulent lake-side hotel foyers, where he had been measuring up for a new job when they met.

'We hit it off immediately, and to cut a long courtship short, I never set sail again from Whitehaven. I never finished my journey. Instead, I started another. Though I always had it in my head that I would finish what I had set out to do,' she shrugged, looked into the fire 'But the years, they fly by. And I never have.

'I got a job maintaining the walking trails about the lakes. Mending stiles and gates, fences, bridges, whatever needed doing.

'I didn't need to. Charlie's wage could have kept us comfortable. But I have never been a kept woman. I have always paid my own way. And nothing will ever change that. So, I found my job.

'It was hard work. You would sometimes have to camp out for a few days, so remote were some of the spots. For those jobs you would have to carry up your tools, any materials you needed. You were on your own. Out in all weather. A lot of people tried the job. A lot of people gave up. They couldn't see past the downpours, the sodden clothes, the bitter winds, so they missed out on breath-taking sunrises and sunsets, watching weather fronts sweeping across the mountains trailing veils of rain, fogs that shrouded everything in a stunning otherworldly shadow. Shafts of sunlight bursting between breaks in cloud, plummeting from the heavens and anchoring to mountainsides.

'It wasn't for some, that was clear. But for me it was perfect. I kept at it a fair few years after Charlie sold up his business.

'While he loved carpentry, he had always dreamed of spending his days creating something special here, in the gardens. He had all these plans that he had sketched out. He would often sit and leaf through them. He could lose himself for hours.

'He had grown up in the house, but his parents had seen the garden as an object to be looked at, a symbol of status, not a child's plaything full of exploration and adventures.

He had been an only child. Tree houses and dens were nothing but a pipedream – out of the question. But he would imagine adventures out in the gardens, draw them out. And it was those drawings that inspired him. All the work you are doing now is keeping that little boy's imagination alive.

'You could often find him up amongst the walkways he built in the trees. Making up for lost time he would always say. And it is where I go when I want to feel close to him. That little boy who never really ever grew up.'

Life settled into a busy routine of long days in the gardens, lost among the task at hand. A long hot summer brought a steady stream of visitors to Maisie's glasshouse for cups of tea and slices of cake. They would startle me when they came across my patch of work, as I would get so absorbed in the calm of my work that I never saw them coming. I would blink and smile as they asked questions about plants to which I had no answer.

In the evenings, after dinner, I would sit outside my cabin, wander among the birch copse, walk down by the riverbank where you could sometimes see an otter, a water vole. From time-to-time Maisie would invite me to the hotel by the lake for a glass of ale, the walk through the woods much easier after I had spent a day cutting the bramble back from the path – a day of dappled sunlight, distant sounds of boat engines thrumming away to nothing, the clinking of glasses, laughter from the beer garden.

We would sit outside watching the last ferry pull away and head down to Windermere. The last of the days sailing boats gliding across the darkening waters, returning to the shore.

Sun dappled days lost in undergrowth, pushing a mower along winding walkways, staking up bowing sunflowers – summertime passed by slowly, breathlessly beneath a hot sun. Thunderstorms gathered among black, menacing clouds as booming thunderclaps rumbled, lightning forked across the gloom and charged the air. Large raindrops becoming a downpour, sending visitors skittering toward the glasshouse and Maisie's tea and cake.

In the evenings as dusk fell, I would watch bats flit and sweep across the sky, picking off gnats and flies as they dive-bombed down toward the ground, and I would walk about the gardens – parched, yellowing grass crackling and scrunching beneath my feet. The shadowy figures of peacocks watching me pass in an uneasy standoff.

I would lose myself in the gardens, hushed, still in the dead calm of a hot summer's night. I would walk. On and on. Round the next corner, through archways and secret enclosures, slight breezes tugging gently at my opened shirt.

Then on to the next one.

Eleven

With autumn, long days of grass cutting were replaced with leaf collecting, with running repairs to things damaged by ever strengthening storms. Maisie would seek me out in heavy downpours and wild squalls, scold me for being outside, and after a cup of tea in the glasshouse, if the weather had set in for the day, I would sit in my cabin listening to the rain drumming on the roof, the wind whistling through the trees. The gardens distorting and blurring beyond my rain-streaked window.

As the year turned colder and visitors dwindled to the point that some days you wouldnae see a single soul, Maisie would call me up to the cottage on a Sunday morning, where she had the Sunday papers and a large pot of coffee set out across the table.

And while she slowly prepared a roast dinner, par-boiling the potatoes that I would peel for her, we would drink coffee, chat, spend long hours in silence reading the paper. Though, in truth, I rarely strayed far beyond the sports section, lingering over the page of football results and tables, my finger tracing along each result from each division, then looking to see what that had done to the league table.

It was the only part of the paper that I had ever engaged with, those complex-looking league tables. Rows of numbers detailing a team's fortunes, each row denoting, to those who knew the order, a specific element of the play to date. Blocks of statistics, of ever-increasing numbers – as incomprehensible to some as the pages of stocks and shares in the financial section were to me.

From time to time, among the Scottish League results, I would recognise a name on the scoresheet, a player I had played against, played with, their humble careers, their new clubs revealed down among the small print below the fold of a Sunday newspaper.

It didnae hurt any more, that lost career. Two and a half years playing for Cowdenbeath, scoring a goal at Ibrox in front of all those people was a lot more than many ever got to achieve. And besides, being unable to play football any more was nothing compared to what else had been lost.

Reading those results, imagining the grounds they had been played in, that I had played in, recalling the sights, the sounds, helped me feel a little closer to Eilish. She had, mostly unbeknownst to her, being so young, been at Central Park for many a Cowdenbeath match, swaddled up in the stands.

It became a comfort of sorts, reading the results each Sunday, as among the stretches of terracing, the stands that materialised in my mind the length and breadth of Scotland's lower leagues, so too did Eilish, sat way up at the back. Her face so vivid, just for a moment.

'You must know it all by heart by now,' Maisie said one rainy Sunday, looking down at me leant over the page, staring into the rows and columns of tables and results. 'Are you a big fan?'

I told her that I used to play before I hurt my knee. That I used to be out on the streets around the shipyard in Govan, playing football from dawn till dusk when I was a little boy. She smiled.

'That sounds familiar,' she said. 'My boy was much the same. He would sleep with a ball in his bed. Though I kept telling him that it would still be there in the morning if he left it by his bedside table. He was inseparable. He would dribble it wherever we went.

'I had never liked football. Or never been introduced to it before my son. But I came to love it, through him.

'He was born in Southampton. I was born in Southampton. Southampton was our local team. He would be down at The Dell whenever we could afford it. All the children would gather right down the front of the Milton Road end so as they could see. Even when he allowed me to tag along.

'When they scored, he would push back up through the bodies between us and give me a hug, before jinking between the forest of legs and coats, back down behind the goal.

'I would get some funny looks. Women going to the football, standing shoulder to shoulder on the terraces, unaccompanied by a man was a rarity. But I didn't waste any time worrying about the opinions of others, or societies norms. If I wanted to go with my boy to the football, then no man, or terraces of men, could stop me.

'Did you ever have a favourite part of the season?' she asked me.

I said that the first few games were the best, while it was still warm and light. They felt so good after a long, horrendous pre-season of hill climbing, sit-ups and running drills. A reward for getting through all the lung-bursting. For those first few games anything was possible with a fresh fixture list ahead. We were going to win the league, the cup. We were going to do it all. Until we didnae.

Maisie smiled.

'It was always Christmas for me. Boxing Day games. New Year's Day games. And any that fell in between.

'It would just be Stanley and me at Christmas. There was no one else. And with him being such a lover of football I would save up a little extra money, and we would go to as many matches as we could. If Southampton were playing at home, we would go there on Boxing Day, after watching our local Hampshire League team play in the morning. Once we took the train into the New Forest to watch Brockenhurst play Lymington in the local derby. We also went up to Salisbury to see the Corinthians play one New Year's Day. He loved train journeys.

'Games at Christmas always felt different to me. They felt special. The atmosphere charged somehow. They always felt like occasions that were bigger than simply winning points, scoring goals. More a celebration. Of the game. Of being alive. Friends and family. It was a real gift to have these special moments with Stanley. It was a joy to see how excited he used to get,' she paused.

'Wonderful times,' she said, staring down, staring beyond the kitchen table for a few moments, before snapping back into the present.

'Right,' she said, 'enough of that. Are you all right to peel the carrots?'

Winter brought heavy snow flurries and drifts built up by bitter arctic squalls. Days were spent clearing paths, digging out the entrance to the small barn that the peacocks sheltered in, teetering on ladders trying to clear the thick blanket of snow putting a strain on the glasshouse.

Inside was otherworldly before I cleared it all away, the world outside lost beneath a white pall. There was absolute silence, save for the odd creak and groan of the glasshouse frame labouring beneath the extra weight. It was like stepping inside a snow globe – the glasshouse illuminated a pallid, dusky white beneath the drifts. Wisps of mist rising from the frozen pool. Lily pads trapped in a sheet of ice. The cherub on the slide looking doubtfully at the wintry scene below.

Inside, beneath the blanket of snow, time stood still, which did nothing to help the integrity of such an ageing structure, desperately in need of some relief beneath the extra weight.

Maisie would hold the ladder while I leant as far as I could, casting a soft bristle broom in front of me like a fishing line, dragging blocks of snow toward me and down to the ground, crumpling with a heavy thud that had Maisie skittering away so as not to get hit.

It was an arduous task, especially among the wild overgrowth behind the glasshouse where there was no space for Maisie to hold the ladder. Though the heavy scrub and thick snow would have cushioned any fall.

With the worst of it done we would sit inside and drink tea, watching our mugs, our breath trailing up into the dusting of snow left behind, knowing that the next flurry wouldnae be far away, and with it the need to repeat the chore.

Days were spent in the cabin, watching snow flurries so dense that the birch copse, the gardens dissolved away to the faintest of apparitions, while listening to the crackle and spit of the logs in the wood burner. The chill of the far corners of the cabin bit when you turned away from the fire. Though not as much as the dash out the door and round the back to the shower, the toilet.

I wrote letters to Eilish while the light held, sitting in the dark, watching the shadows of the flame dancing across the walls when I could no longer see my pencil on the paper.

I would walk around the gardens at night, after dinner. The covering of snow made everything glimmer in the darkness with an eerie half-light glow. It felt otherworldly. Magical. Pathways to secret gardens, to shadowy thickets shimmering like something from a spooky bedtime story. The scene somehow diminished in the light of day, retracing my steps in the snow.

Mondays would still involve a trip to Ambleside. If the buses couldnae run due to the drifts on the roads, we would walk the five miles, skirting round the worst of the snow. We would nod and head our separate ways, kicking off the slush from our boots as we disappeared into the post office, wherever we needed to go.

Maisie would open up the windmill money box in the glasshouse every Sunday night and count out that week's donations, from which she would fill a little brown envelope with twenty, sometimes twenty-five pounds, and hand it to me on the bus into town.

'Thank you,' she would say as she did so, 'for all your help. It's really appreciated.'

She would talk about how the money from the windmill was special, how it was the product of simple moments of wonder, as people explored the nooks and crannies of the gardens.

'Remember how you felt when you first walked round, how it made you come back, day after day? Well, that is a little envelope of feelings just like yours. Your work, it made them happy. It let them lose themselves in exploration, in their imaginations. To me, its special money.'

No matter how quiet the gardens became, and in the harsh weeks of winter you could sometimes count the number of visitors on one hand, there would always be twenty pounds or so in the envelope every Monday.

Gone our separate ways in town, the envelope would go on stamps, envelopes, and paper in the post office, warm winter jumpers and woollen gloves from the market.

Near the top of town there was a small gift shop that specialised in snow globes, the small display window crammed with rows upon rows of domes containing scenes from around the Lake District and beyond. The name of each particular place beautifully handwritten in miniature at the front of each scene. Sailing boats, churches, lakes lined with trees and mountains, Dove Cottage, the former home of William Wordsworth, whole high streets. Every facet of the region shrunk down to size, encased in globes of varying sizes.

The old man inside made them in a little back room and agreed to make two for me from sketches I had made. And two weeks before Christmas, just as he had promised, they were ready. The first was a scene of the walkways up among the trees. A beautifully delicate reproduction of the warren of paths and rope handrails, all beneath a canopy of boughs that became dusted in snow when the globe was shaken. The contents lost for a time in a swirling flurry.

For Eilish he made a reproduction of the contents of the glasshouse. Miniature lily pads painstakingly painted a vibrant green. The cherub on the slide. Creeper and vine wrapped around the diving board. Peacocks standing poolside among the pots of plants for dramatic effect. There was even a tiny me and a tiny Maisie frozen in work poses. Intricate tables and chairs, and when it was shaken it looked just like how I had tried to describe in my letters when the snowstorms hit; feeling like being trapped inside a giant snow globe as the flurries grew so thick that everything else outside the glasshouse dissolved away to nothing.

When it came back in the post the following week it sat on my shelf in the cabin, where I would shake it every now and then, and imagine what Eilish might have thought, if she had ever been able to look down into it.

On Christmas morning Maisie had decked out the kitchen with a tree, covered in baubles, tinsel, and fir cones. Paper chains had been hung around the roaring fireplace, and beneath the tree was a large, warm, patchwork quilt that she had made for me herself, and a small parcel of colourful Tibetan prayer flags on a length of rough string. I hung them up through the birch copse, so as I could see them from the cabin fluttering on the winds. In time the colours faded, the flags fraying in the winter storms. Prayers safely sent on their way.

She had sat quietly in a chair by the fire for a few moments, shaking the snow globe when I had presented it to her, watching the contents slowly settling, revealing the miniature labyrinth of boardwalks suspended in the trees.

'It's beautiful,' she said, 'Thank you.'

After lunch, as I was about to leave, she called me back from the door.

'Tomorrow,' she said 'Come to breakfast early. And wrap up warm. I have a surprise.'

We set off for Windermere along the lakeside path, the rest of the world hushed so early on Boxing Day morning. From there we had a cup of tea while waiting for the train to Barrow, then a couple of ales and a roast dinner for lunch in a pub overlooking Barrow Park. Slowly it began to fill with people, the excited chatter of families, friends meeting up soon grew to a din. And when, as if by some secret signal, they all began to drain back out into the street, Maisie nodded.

'Drink up. We're off.'

All roads led to Holker Street. The stream of bodies on the pavements thickened the closer we got, a set of floodlights slowly rising above the terraced houses. Holker Street stadium, the home of Barrow AFC was beginning to fill ahead of a Third Division Boxing Day clash against Southport.

Maisie looked at me, nodded.

'It's been too long,' she said 'I suspect for both of us. Stanley would love that I was here.'

She paid for us through the turnstiles, jostled through the crowds on the terraces until she found a spot she liked, applauded as the teams ran out, then turned to me.

'Happy Christmas,' she said, smiled, then became lost in the game, lost elsewhere. Memories of Boxing Day games past with her son mingling with that cold, overcast day in Barrow.

It was a right old ding-dong match. End to end stuff that you couldnae help but find yourself getting sucked into. A smart half-volley into the bottom corner of the Southport goal saw the crowd leave happy with a one nil win for Barrow. Groups of friends and families drained away home, back into the pubs as we made for the train station and the last service of the day, the roar of the crowd still ringing in my ears. Months of quiet working in the gardens making the ebb and flow of the terraces feel electric, deafening, overwhelming. Exhilarating.

The following day we retraced our steps back down to Windermere, this time taking a train north to Carlisle and the paddock in front of the main stand at Brunton Park. From there we watched Carlisle United beat Norwich in the Second Division, the thunderous roar from the vaulted Warwick Road terrace hitting you like a shockwave with every Carlisle goal.

The bustle of the crowd, the electricity in the air, the crunching tackles and lung bursting runs lifted Maisie up onto her tip toes to keep an uninterrupted view of the play.

A sparkle from a bygone age re-ignited in her eyes, for ninety minutes at least, complete with wild gestures at bad tackles, howls of derision at the referee. Cheers and the twirling of her scarf above her head with every goal.

It affected me too. I had always been a terrible spectator once I had become a player; sitting in the stands when I hadnae been in the team felt like torture. But now, with all that removed, the simple joys of the game returned. The joys that had first captivated me behind the Copland Road goal as a young boy. The play sweeping from end-to-end absorbing all, troubles dissolving away, for a time at least.

In the years that followed, trips to the football became a Christmas ritual, taking us back to Barrow and Carlisle, as well as across to the other local team, Workington. It could be the second division and Carlisle one day, then the Fourth Division and Workington the next. Packed paddocks at Brunton Park, then the chill winds blowing in off the River Derwent at Borough Park, Workington. Newcastle and Preston being replaced by Hartlepool, Bournemouth, and Crewe as the opposition. It didnae matter. The games were always absorbing, their drama captivating all.

But more importantly, it was everything else around them that made those trips so special. Resurrecting feelings, memories from another time, people and places lost along the way, returned so vividly for a short ninety minutes among the familiar setting of terrace and floodlight.

And as I drifted off up north, Maisie would be right there with me, but also far, far away herself. Down in Southampton. With her boy. Lost in memory. A goal shaking us both from our reverie and back into the present.

For my second Christmas at Five Acre Gardens, I got her a scarf from each of our three teams as a present, taking the train on quiet days in the gardens to each ground to collect them.

I would linger in those club shops, breathing in the rich smell of brand-new football leather from the balls on display. Replica shirts feeling rough to the touch, like my old Cowdenbeath jersey used to, getting heavier on my shoulders as it absorbed the mud and rain.

Displays of team pictures, individual photographs of players proudly sporting their clubs' colours lay beneath glass counters next to the tills.

No matter the division, the size of the ground and the crowds that populated them, these images of their heroes deserved their place beneath the glass, like precious artefacts in a museum. Only being released from captivity once they had been bought. Pictures of those lucky enough to live out the dream of so many more in playing Fourth Division football for their beloved Workington Reds.

Browsing it all, absorbing the reverence and adulation bestowed by supporter on their club, I felt a sense of rare pride that I had once been a part of that. Had once been behind the glass.

I also took great satisfaction in Maisie's happiness at those scarves, smiling as she twirled them in the air at Christmas matches, always mindful to take the right coloured scarf for the occasion.

They would appear, our Christmas games, as tiny, inconsequential entries among a sea of others on the football classifieds page of Maisie's paper. But being there, feeling the energy of the crowd, the animation of the game, the unbridled joy at a goal for, the sharp intake of breath at a goal against. The anguished cries of an entire terrace at a shot just wide of the mark, their attempts at willing the ball the right side of the post falling just short beneath darkening Cumbrian skies – this was all far from inconsequential to those who cared, who lived and breathed their team no matter how lowly or unfashionable.

For Maisie, for me, they were anything but inconsequential as well. They were lifelines to another time, and the people that had become lost along the way. Standing shoulder to shoulder with others in the present, while looking out for familiar, cherished faces in the crowd – apparitions, faint, fading. Always fading. Ever more so.

Twelve

As the snows began to thaw after a long, chilling winter that first year, days were spent once more, from morning to night, lost among the many jobs that needed doing about the gardens. Though there was one, a big one, that kept nagging at me every lunchtime as I sat eating my sandwiches in the glasshouse.

Out the front, either side of the glasshouse door, Maisie had, many years earlier, dug a border, and planted rows of sunflowers that grew to monstrous heights, sheltered as they were from the elements in the lee of the glasshouse. It looked as if it had, at one time, extended right the way round the structure. Though the border had become lost among the wild thickets and scrub that had grown up unchecked as soon as it strayed away from the little gravel path, and on round the side and back.

Some of the thicket had grown so dense and big over the years that large branches as thick as my arm pressed up against the glass and threatened to punch through with the next storm. It needed clearing and would create a nice-shaded spot beneath the oaks, as well as freeing Maisie's sunflowers to once more circle the glasshouse.

It was back-breaking work, cutting away the foliage, sawing off the larger limbs, then digging out deep and stubborn root systems. But slowly, day by day, more of the glasshouse began to appear, revealing new views through fogged, mildew-stained panes, of the pool, the tumble of tables and chairs. Maisie busying herself in readiness for any hardy souls that might need feeding.

The shadow began to loom out of the scrub the further I cut away. An indistinct shape slowly growing in form as more light reached it with every downed limb. The bow of a boat, trapped in a sea of ferns, tree saplings, and creeper, that clawed at the hull like the tentacles of some sea creature trying to pull it down into the earthy depths.

It had seen better days, sections of the hull rusted and corroded, clawing up through the flaking paintwork beneath a row of gloomy portholes.

The more I cleared the more of the boat appeared, propped up on a cradle of iron supports with splintering wooden buffers holding her firm.

Trailing away into the undergrowth, she was a decent sized pleasure cruiser. Or had been in another life, the glass panes of her wheelhouse still intact in their wooden framework, windscreen wipers long since perished, frozen into position, looking out at warped wooden decking on the bow.

The wheelhouse roof hadnae been as lucky, having been caved in by a fallen tree branch from some long-forgotten storm, buckling the flimsy wooden framework that covered the aft deck, sending it lurching to starboard.

Clearing more foliage away, a makeshift set of steps appeared made up of overturned milk crates lodged up against the hull, and from them a narrow pathway stamped down out of the dense overgrowth snaked away into the gloom behind the glasshouse.

She was structurally sound, or she felt it, as I stepped carefully up into the wheelhouse, crouching down to avoid the roof. A few steps led down to the deck, where you could stand up fully, stretch out your back, walk across its sturdy wooden decking to the stern that was hemmed in by a large, thick-set fir tree. A dense canopy of scrub shrouding the outside world.

A large oak log had been lodged beneath the sagging roof of the wheelhouse, propping it up just enough to be able to clamber down the few steps into the cabin that appeared to have been untouched by time and decay.

In the half-light afforded by the runs of four portholes to port and starboard, padded benches lined a table right up into the bow. Work surfaces and a stove were polished and clear, a couple of mugs, a kettle, and a jar of coffee stood on top, free from dust and cobweb. A sink and cupboards portside stood neat and tidy, doors and hinges tight and flush. Rugs on the floor free from the years of decay littering the deck.

On the table was a wooden box, painted a fading, scuffed and peeling, black, with a series of initials scored roughly into the top. Inside, a collection of letters, photographs, booklets, all manner of bits and bobs barely discernible in the gloom. Sitting there, looking into the box, out at the lovingly tended cabin, it became clear that this had been, and was still a special place. Maybe a private place. A place I suddenly no longer felt comfortable in.

Maybe the boat was meant to be hidden, had been lost to the outside world by design? I stepped out carefully, picked up all my tools, made my way to another job elsewhere in the gardens.

That evening, after dinner, I apologised to Maisie, explained what I had done, the job I had been doing, what I had found. She listened quietly, then nodded.

'No, Gordie,' she said 'No need to apologise. I'm glad you found her. It is a good thing,' she nodded again. 'It's something I've been meaning to get round to for such a long time. But the task, well, it just began to feel so big, overwhelming, I didn't know where to start,' she said, pouring out two large glasses of whisky, handing me one and a torch from the kitchen pantry. She took up another and checked that it worked, before putting on her coat, slipping out the door.

After a few moments she popped her head back round at me.

'Well,' she said, 'are you coming to see?'

The glasshouse at night was an eerie place. A three-quarter moon illuminating shadow that lingered in deeper recesses.

We wove between the chairs and out the back into Maisie's storeroom, then out a door into the scrub, our torch beams flitting across a narrow pathway scratching at our arms until they hit upon the boat looming out of the darkness.

'There she is,' she said. 'Our boat – the Stanley B.'

She gingerly climbed up onto the deck, beckoned me aboard. 'Careful though. Mind how you go,' she said before disappearing down into the cabin.

The paraffin lantern grew stronger, filled the cabin with a warm glow as Maisie hooked it into the fitting in the ceiling, letting it gently swing to a stop of its own accord while she eased herself down onto a bench at the table. She took a sip of whisky, drew the wooden box toward her, gently caressed the lid, letting her fingers trace across the indentations of the initials carved into it.

'Come,' she said 'sit,' as she opened the box, and began rummaging among its contents.

'This is my boat. The one I travelled round the coastline of Britain with. Well, most of it anyway,' she said as she leant over the lip of the box.

'I say it is my boat. It is our boat. Mine and my son's. And what a life it has lived. Here,' she pulled out a photograph and slid it across the table 'That's us.'

It was a picture of a very young Maisie, maybe still in her twenties, long brown hair tied in a familiar-looking plait, standing next to a young boy with a beaming smile. He was holding Maisie's hand, and they were stood on a dock, squinting at the photographer beneath a fierce sun that bleached out the picture in bright whites and greys.

Behind them the unmistakeable shape of the boat that I had been cutting out of the forest of scrub.

Wheelhouse roof intact, paintwork gleaming, the sunlight off the water dappling the hull, it was a handsome looking boat.

A second picture had them both standing at the wheel in the wheelhouse. Both holding it steady, smiling, looking forward, the boy on tiptoe trying to see up and over it, out the windows and beyond the bow. On the back of both, in flourishing handwriting was the date – 'July 1932.'

'He would have been not quite nine in that picture, my Stanley. He loved this boat. Adored it. Would be on it, morning, noon, and night, at least when he wasn't out playing football.

She has seen some things I can tell you. Her, me, and Stanley. Those pictures are from the day we took her out onto the Solent for the very first time.'

She rooted around in the box, taking out a small, dog-eared hardback notebook. The pages warped from water damage, and full of writing, drawings, glued in pictures torn from magazines, they burst out of the binding, refusing to let the covers settle neatly together on the table.

'I couldn't leave her in Whitehaven, when I met Charlie. She stayed there for a time, until I was satisfied that Charlie was genuine. That what we had was serious.

'And when I couldn't afford the mooring fees any more, and I had to make a decision to either pull up anchor and move on, or stay, I let Charlie pay for her to be hoisted up on a low bed truck and moved to here. To this very spot.

'I hated not being able to pay my own way. I had never relied on a man for anything. Still haven't. But I wouldn't leave her behind. Never. So, I saw it as Charlie's grand gesture.

'Instead of a diamond ring, an expensive wedding, he brought the Stanley B to me. Safe and sound behind the glasshouse. That was back in 1947. And now here we are, with you discovering her, nearly twenty-five years later.'

She leafed through the dog-eared notebook, pausing at a particular drawing or entry, taking up a photograph of her with a young woman stood in front of an imposing ruin on top of a cliff. On the back the words, in the same flourishing writing – 'With Martha, Whitby Abbey, September 1946.'

'I hate to see her in this state,' she said nodding toward the portholes, the decaying hull beyond. 'I never meant for her to fall into such disrepair. She doesn't deserve it.

'I've kept the cabin up together. I come in here most mornings for a quiet cup of coffee, and a few moments with Stanley, the Stanley B.

'But my job, then the gardens, and then Charlie starting to get ill, there always seemed to be something else just that little bit more pressing. Plus, I'm not as strong as I used to be. I worry that some of the jobs might be beyond me now.

'It would be such a sad thing if the forest took her. She has lived such a life. Done things and been places worthy of a better fate than this. She gave so much to me, to Stanley. She deserves better.'

She trailed away for a moment, and we sat quietly, listening to branches scraping across the wheelhouse roof on the breeze.

'I named her the Stanley B after Stanley, Stanley Buchanan, because they became inseparable, the boat and him. He knew her inside out. He wanted to learn about every single piece of her. Every moving part. Every Fixture.

'He loved everything about her. She was his passion. Or one of them. Children seem to have a never-ending supply of the stuff.

'He had always dreamed of being a professional footballer. Of turning out for Southampton at the Dell in the Second Division. But he had also been a realist, probably as a result of us always living a hand to mouth existence, just me and him. It was tough at times, providing for us both.

'He loved to dream, but not into the realms of complete fantasy. He knew he wasn't good enough to play at such a high standard, so when the Stanley B came along, he found a vocation he both loved and had a natural aptitude for. We would run sightseeing trips out on Southampton Water and down to the Solent, sometimes across to the Isle of Wight.

'He was such a good kid.'

She placed her hand on the notebook, flicked at the pages with her thumb.

'Our little Stanley B gave him so much. It also helped him when the war came. It gave him hope, something to cling on to when all hope seemed lost,' she slid the notebook toward me.

'We stopped our sightseeing trips and became part of the war effort, ferrying parts to the Spitfire factory and the shipyards making navy frigates and support vessels. Whatever was needed of us. And while we did that, he made this for us. Something to do when the war was over.

'He lost himself in it for hours, down in the bomb shelters, while all hell was breaking loose outside. Southampton got it bad during the Blitz. It felt like the end of the world every night as the bombs fell. He would flinch with every impact, dusting away the plaster that would fall from the ceiling with every blast, carry on writing in the book. He was just a little boy back then. And when the book was finished, he gave it to me. Something to look forward to, he said, for the future. Even though at times, as the bombs fell, it sometimes felt that there could be no future, for us, for anyone.'

Inside the front cover was a neat and painstakingly accurate hand drawn map of the British Isles. Littered around the coastline and about the outlying islands were dots accompanied by a number. Each dot and number had a corresponding page, with the name of a place of interest that they represented at the top, a sketch of a church, monument, bridge, ruin, whatever it was primarily known for beneath.

Handwritten notes, little map drawings, pictures cut out from magazines and glued in place were crammed onto each page. Where there was a little space left over, and only when relevant, the badge of a local football team had been carefully traced and coloured in – Stanley's other passion getting the better of him.

On many of the pages, held in place with a paper clip, a small photograph not too much bigger than a passport picture. A photograph of the sketch that Stanley had drawn.

The binding groaned with every turn of a page, the crinkling of warped paper, the cracking of brittle glue just about holding everything in place. The odd entrance ticket to a castle or monument skittered across a page as it turned, and I was careful to leave them in their rightful place before turning to another entry.

Towards the end of the book the pages grew neater, less water damaged, and free from paperclips and photographs. The last few pages held an intricately designed set of tables. Hand drawn columns with their own headings: Place, date visited, notes.

Beneath 'place,' every dot, every preceding page was named, written out in black ink. Beneath 'date visited,' in various hues of blue, black, and red, days and dates had been filled in. From a visit to the Needles on the Isle of Wight on April 16th, 1946 to Whitehaven, Lake District on September 23rd, 1947. The next entry, Morecambe, and those beneath it all the way down to the last dot, the last row – 'Saint Catherine's Lighthouse, Freshwater, Netton' remained blank.

In the notes section, entries had been inscribed in varying colours. Some longer than others, some with sentences crammed in so small it was hard to read.

Dot thirty-seven, Lindisfarne Castle on Holy Isle simply read: 'You would have loved it Stanley, it drifted in and out of a thick fog,' while dot thirty-two, Whitby Abbey was a blur of words:

'I met Martha, Stanley. She agreed to meet me, even though I just turned up out of the blue. What a beautiful, wonderful girl. You two would have been so happy together. My heart breaks that it was all snatched away from you.'

I leant across the table to the photograph, looked at Maisie.

'Martha from Whitby,' I said 'She knew Stanley?' Maisie nodded.

'It was a strange quirk of fate, that all those years before, Stanley included Whitby in his book. When he finished it, he gave it to me, said that when the war was over, we would take the Stanley B, travel round to all the places, to celebrate peacetime, enjoy a life without bombs and horror.

'He would talk about all the places that he had read about when we were down in the bomb shelters. He had this nervous chatter that wouldn't stop when he got started. He would talk and talk about the places in his notebook, his voice cracking, becoming lost when the bombs drew too close, became deafening. But he would carry on, flicking through it, trying to picture us somewhere else, somewhere safe.'

She leant into the box, rummaged around until she brought out a matchbook and handed it to me. On the cover the words 'Copacabana, Havana' he been embossed in a faux gold. Inside had been written 'Martha, Whitby,' and an address in the town.

'When he turned eighteen, Stanley enlisted in the merchant navy for a year and was on a ship carrying supplies from the Americas back to Britain. Dangerous work.

And that is how he met Martha, whilst on shore leave. They only had four days together initially, but when he wrote home, he wrote about being in love. Of long walks with Martha along the Malecon, watching the Caribbean lap against the sea wall, while intoxicating, rhythmic son and salsa music drifted from open windows. He wrote of dancing all night at the Copacabana, watching the sun come up as they left. He sent this matchbook with a letter, asked me to keep it safe, that they had promised to meet up when they had both made it home, when they could.

'Stanley was called up into the navy after his year as a merchant sailor, and spent some time protecting the ships he once served on. But he didn't make it through to peacetime.

'When the war was over, I couldn't stay in Southampton. The parks he played in, the ocean liners we took passengers to see, our mooring for the Stanley B, it all reminded me of him, and the fathomless gulf his loss had left behind.

'The book he had made for me, it saved me. It let me feel close to him, that we were together still. So as soon as it was safe to do so, I set off on Stanley's journey, jotting down the dates in Stanley's table at the back, and I wrote to him in the notes. Told him about all the places. I tried to take a picture of all the little sketches he had done.

'I turned up at the address in the matchbook unannounced. I met Martha, and we had this photograph taken of us in front of Whitby Abbey. She had kept her word. She had waited for him. And when the news of his death reached her, it had hurt her deeply, despite only being with him for the odd few days when he was on shore leave. She had kept all his letters. Always would, she had said. More than two years on after his passing and she had still not started courting. I told her she must. He wouldn't want her to live a life on pause. She was a lovely girl,' she said, and took up the photograph of them both, tucking it back into the Whitby entry in the notebook.

'I got all the way up to Arbroath on the Angus coast that first year, before the weather started to turn. The Stanley B can take on swell, but she was never designed for storms out at open sea. Better safe than sorry, I moored up in the little harbour there and waited out the October storms and winter squalls.

'A short way from the harbour, barely a few feet from the ocean, was Gayfield Park, home of Arbroath FC. As luck would have it, they were looking for someone to help out the groundsman. They were sceptical at first that I could do the job, being a woman, so I said I would work for free for two weeks on the proviso that I would get the job if they were satisfied.

'They would make me roll the pitch with the heavy roller every day, help fix the stands in bitter, howling winds that came in off the North Sea and cut you in two. They had me fork mounds of cut grass onto a scrap of land beyond the far goal,' she smiled 'I proved my worth. Got the job, and spent the winter watching the Red Lichties battle the conditions and the opposition. It was fresh to say the least.'

I had watched the ball being buffeted on the wind up at Gayfield Park in my Cowdenbeath days. I had even seen our keeper take a goal kick, only for it to stall on the wind, be turned about, and drift out behind the goal for a corner. It was a bitter cold up there unlike anything else I had ever experienced.

'At least,' she said 'I could warm myself here in the cabin. She was built well. The heat from the stove kept her toasty even on the coldest of days.

'And then, when the seas calmed, I carried on. Up to Wick and its castle built by Norse Kings. Round the Orkney's, Shetland, the Outer Hebrides, where I saw a football match on one of the most beautiful pitches I have ever seen, away up in Eriskay. It looked out on a bluff, the wild sea, rubbled stone shepherd huts. I sat and watched as the visiting team from Barra arrived by trawler, climbed up the cliffs from the beach. There were more sheep and horses watching than people. It was wonderful.

'I carried on down to Mull, Skye, and Fort William where I climbed up to the top of Ben Nevis for him, tasted whisky in Oban, and everything else he had planned in his book. Until I reached Whitehaven, and by chance met Charlie. And the rest you know.

'The plan was always to finish Stanley's trip. I never meant for the Stanley B to sit here for so long. But one thing leads to another. My job, the gardens, Charlie, there was always a reason to put it off until next summer, the summer after that.

'It was always in my mind. Stanley, our boat, they were always in my mind. But then, when Charlie started getting sick, all my energies went into him, and then the years after his passing were overwhelming. Trying to keep everything up together. Trying to keep what had been built from falling away again.

'And here we are. And she is in a bit of a sorry state. I keep the cabin up together as best I can. Where I sit and think. Of Stanley.

'But maybe you, having discovered her, is fate? Maybe it is time?

'Maybe you can help me free her from the rest of this undergrowth, now that it has been started, and we can see what sort of condition she is really in. Maybe we can still save her from ruin. Though I wonder if the days of finishing Stanley's trip might be behind me now, I feel in worse condition than the Stanley B here.'

I shook my head, told her that I didnae believe there was anything she couldnae do, if she wanted to do it, and she smiled.

'Well, you wait till you turn seventy, with an aching back and limbs. Then you come see me, eh?'

She sat back and took a sip of whisky, looked about the cabin.

'Whether I can or not, it would just be something to get her up together again. At the very least, I owe her, I owe Stanley that.'

I told her that I would start first thing, that it shouldnae take more than a day or two to free her.

She nodded, looked about her.

'Thank you Gordie,' she said.

We sat for a time, Maisie rooting through the box, looking at pictures, leafing through a bundle of Stanley's letters bound together by a frayed piece of ribbon, while I marvelled at Stanley's notebook, at the level of detail and content on each page, lingering over the last dot. The last port of call.

I looked across at her. Asked why the imagined trip ended on Netton. If they hadnae intended to return to Southampton.

Maisie shook her head.

'No, Stanley had imagined a new life for us on Netton, taking tourists on sightseeing trips around the island. In the middle of the Blitz, with the bombs falling all around, flattening vast swathes of Southampton, many thought the city was finished, could never recover, be rebuilt. It seemed entirely plausible right there in the moment. It was terrible, terrible. Whole streets gone. Entire communities lost or bombed out.

'It felt like we were just waiting for our turn, for fate to deal us with a direct hit.

'We had only ever been on one holiday, Stanley and me. We just couldn't afford any more. We took the train, then the ferry across to Netton for four days and took a room on Westlyn Esplanade. We went on a bus excursion down to Freshwater on the southern tip of the island and had fish and chips on the seafront, walked all the way up to the lighthouse on Saint Catherine's Point. Stanley adored it there. He said that Freshwater, the bay, was the most magical place he had ever seen and would often talk about it in the months and years after. The pretty little cottages, the fishing boats in the harbour. The vast sea cliffs, the lighthouse on top among a sea of tall grasses that spread across the bluff.

'Whether he still thought it was the most magical place after he had been to New York, Havana and the like I don't know. I do know that he often wrote home while out at sea about our trip, about our new life on Netton. Those plans didn't seem to change after meeting Martha. She was simply absorbed into the dream, into his grand plan.

'He always meant for it to be the last stop. And a quiet, happy life for us. He thought that Southampton was forever lost. To be honest, I did to,' she trailed away, the memories of earth shattering, deafening bombing raids making her wince.

After a moment she snapped back, took a sip of whisky, looked about her.

'She has lived a life, this little boat,' she edged out from behind the table and stood up.

'Let's see if we can't let her live a little more.

'But right now, it is getting late. Until tomorrow then.'

She snuffed out the paraffin lantern, and by torchlight we shuffled out and away.

The work grew harder the closer I edged to the stern of the Stanley B. Stubborn root bowls clawed deep down into the soil as I tried to dig them out, branches and limbs getting thicker from years of being left to their own devices.

Finally, I dug out the Propeller from a nest of ivy and gorse. A run of iron railings at the rear of the deck had been prised out of position by a young Sycamore tree growing up between them. A slow, torturous pressure warping them until they buckled, came loose, rusted down to a dull, brittle red.

Beneath the railings, the faded outline of the words 'Stanley B, Southampton' revealed themselves with every handful of ivy torn away. The ivy's sticky talons that had fixed themselves to the stern had preserved the paint beneath; thin slivers of black among the worn lettering hinted at how striking it had once looked.

It was exhausting work, and after a couple of hours I would down tools, take the lawnmower to the paths for a bit of respite, before returning and cutting up what had been cleared. Wheelbarrows of logs were stacked up by the cottage in the woodshed to dry out, while the rest of the foliage was heaped up and burnt over a glass of whisky, the flames' shadow dancing across the Stanley B, making it seem as if it was pitching and tossing on the ocean once more as darkness fell.

With the work finally complete, and the Stanley B free at last from the tangle of scrub, Maisie slowly wandered around the boat, her hands exploring any damaged section of hull. A run of rusted gashes on the starboard side, just below the wheelhouse looked terminal. Time, water damage, heat and cold had prised them open and weakened the steel, turning it paper thin in places. A cursory sweep of a hand would see flakes tumbling to the ground.

'It's not as bad as it seems,' she said when she saw the look on my face 'She is still sound, by and large. We can fix this. She was worse when Stanley discovered her all those years ago. We fixed her up then. We can do it again I am sure,' and with that, armed with a sheet of scrawled notes, Maisie disappeared off into the cottage and got to work on the telephone.

A week or two later and a truck backed up to the cottage and dropped off welding tools, metal sheets, iron poles, wooden beams, boxes of fixtures, bolts, nails, all sorts.

'All right then,' she said as the truck pulled away 'Time to go to work.'

She was a force of nature. Whilst keeping an eye on the glasshouse and any visitors that needed tea and cake, she set about rubbing down any failing part of the hull, stripping the rust back, before treating it with a solution she mixed herself from differing canisters of chemicals. She showed me how to do it, and while she worked on the outside, I would climb down a hatch in the wheelhouse floor into a small hold and the engine room, and work on the hull from there.

That done, she had us both donned in protective gear, thick gloves and visors, and began welding patches over every hole. I would hold the new sheet of steel in place, and she would lean in, weld it to the hull, expertly angling the flame to direct the sparks away from us, just as I had seen in the shipyards whilst a rivet catcher.

Once in place I would step back, and she would go over it again, binding patch to hull so well it became hard to see the join.

The gear dwarfed her, appeared much too heavy for her slight frame. But she worked in it, hour after hour, skilfully binding the hull back together. Manipulating herself into the tiniest, most awkward of spots in the engine room to make the Stanley B water-tight and structurally sound.

'It's like riding a bike,' she said when I asked her how she had learned to weld like that, 'I picked it up when we first bought her. She was in a bad way, and we had no money to pay anyone to fix her. So, I learned how to do it myself.

'I got some looks in the boatyard while I worked, mind – a young single mother was bad enough to some back in the thirties, but a young woman doing mans' work like welding!' she smiled. 'I heard what they said. The only problem was, for them at least, I didn't care one jot what they thought. If you spend your time worrying about what other people think of you, you will end up doing nothing that you ever wanted to.

'I dare say that we have had the odd visitor wondering at this frail old woman lugging all this gear, whether she should be welding big sheets of steel. Let them wonder. It doesn't matter. Not one bit.'

Thirteen

As the weather improved and warmed, tourists began to come back to the Lake District. From the odd soul in winter, the gardens began to receive a steady trickle of visitors. First to see the vast blanket of bluebells in early spring that spread out beneath the trees. The Rhododendron blooms in May. The field of poppies that lulled beneath sunny June days. The maze of Fennel. The sea of vibrant Dahlias.

The gardens grew, and demanded more and more of my time, while tea and cake in the glasshouse prevented Maisie from donning her welding gear. Making the Stanley B water-tight became a slow, drawn out affair.

A snatched hour here and there, and welding by torchlight after dinner became commonplace – the spray of sparks creating a spectacular display in the darkness. A brief pause for a wee dram of whisky, locating the next spot to be worked on, then Maisie would drop her visor in front of her face, nod at me to get in position, and off we would go again.

It took months, but finally Maisie was satisfied that the job was done. Neat patches of welding littered the length of the boat and made the Stanley B whole again.

The fixes in the hold, the engine room, were as neat as those that could be seen on the outer hull – fixes that had had us blinking up into the daylight as we clambered back out onto the deck after an hour or two of work.

She stood quietly for a moment when it was all done, hand pressed against the bow on the trickiest piece that needed fixing. She nodded at the Stanley B.

'That's that,' she said, took a step back. Now then. Onto the next job.'

The warped wooden decking on the bow came out easily, and it was used as a template to cut the fresh replacement timbers that had come from a great oak in the gardens that had fallen during winter storms. A timber yard in Windermere had cut it into lengths, expertly preserving its beautiful grain.

A slow, steady carving away of the wood with a plane and chisel finally produced the curvature needed for the bow, hours of sanding making them smooth, sleek, just right, while wood stain on the finished timbers brought out the whorls and rings created over centuries of growth in the gardens.

It seemed right, Maisie had said, that a little piece of the gardens that had housed her for so long should go into her reconstruction.

'She will always have a piece of this place with her. I like the idea of that. That seems right somehow.'

The timber yard had come out to the gardens and spoken with Maisie, checked over the fixtures and housings that had once held the wheelhouse roof in place, measured up any pieces of the frame over the deck that needed replacing. And one day in early summer a truck arrived with more of that reclaimed oak tree. Carved and cut into lengths that slotted into the original steel fittings like an oversized jigsaw puzzle, mortise and tenon joints held the frame together, made snug with a few strikes of a mallet.

Across the top Maisie had ordered a heavy, waterproof canvas that we stretched as tight as it would go, nailing it into place. Flaps with mesh windows could be lowered and fixed to protect the deck and wheelhouse from the elements on bad days.

Once in place Maisie and I replaced any rotten deck boards with oak beams left over from the work on the bow. And while I treated the sturdy frames of the benches that lined the deck, she set about using her metalwork skills to bend and shape a new set of railings for the stern. Manipulating each length of iron into shape with flame, she welded them into place, soldering uprights to them in intervals to make the structure solid. Like they had always been there.

Every night, after a long day in the gardens, and an evening working on the Stanley B, Maisie would sit in the cabin and talk about the places she had stopped off at on her journey to Whitehaven over a glass of whisky. She would describe the enormous ocean liners docked at Southampton that she and Stanley had weaved between with a deck full of eager passengers on the Stanley B.

'All lit up at night, they looked like huge floating city skylines, like a run of grand skyscrapers from some faraway place, all the cabins and ballrooms illuminated. Lines of beautiful, coloured bulbs created a canopy above the decks, running on strings away up to the tops of the smoking funnels, they looked like firework displays frozen in time. Little shadowy specks flitting about the promenades, readying themselves for a journey of a lifetime. You couldn't help but gawp along with the sightseers at the illuminations, the vast hulls looming up over us, even though Stanley and I had seen it so many times before. It was always a breath-taking sight.

'When the great cargo ships piled high with tarpaulined crates would pull out to sea, Stanley would guess where they were going, and what those places might look like. He would imagine palm trees and ancient ruins. Strange ports and cities beyond. Camels, pyramids, mountains, remote islands.

'He always said that he would love to find out one day. Where they went. And he did,' she would pause for a moment. 'The places he saw.'

She would sometimes rummage in the ship's box, read a few lines from Stanley's letters home when he served in the merchant navy.

From Miami he described the sun as being so bright that it bleached everything white, apart from the ocean that was so blue and clear that you could see right to the bottom, see shoals of fish. Everyone was so beautiful, he said, suntanned and tall, toned to perfection, walking along the beaches like it was all so very effortless.

From Nova Scotia he described creeping into port through bays littered with icebergs the size of houses that clunked together like ice in a whisky tumbler. The terrifying, towering storms of the Grand Banks, south of Greenland, that could pitch up in an instant into a rogue wave far bigger than the monstrous seas already breaking across the bow with a force so great he was certain that the ship was going to go down. White water hitting the windows of the bridge. Wide eyes watching the great wave rolling away beneath lurching boards.

'He wasn't even twenty-one,' she would say. 'But what a life he lived. He was such a good boy. He would be so happy to see his boat coming back to life.'

By candlelight, and drowsy with sleep after a long day, I would write a few lines to Eilish in my cabin before bed, telling her about how the boat was coming along, and describing the piece of the garden I was working on. I would tell her about all the secret places, hidden pathways and clearings, the walkways in the trees. I had cleared and re-set, replanted frames of sweet peas that had been set out like another maze, complete with dead ends and a bench and a little pond at the centre that couldnae be seen until you were right upon it.

I would send them off on a Monday. And they would come back the next week. Until the late summer of that year.

One week there had been the familiar 'Return to sender' written across Eilish's address. Then came a few weeks where the letters didnae come back at all. Following that they came back with unfamiliar handwriting and 'Return to sender. Not known at this address.'

After a month or two of my letters coming back with this new note, a letter came from a Mrs Omand, explaining that she had recently moved in, and that she didnae know the whereabouts of the previous occupants, that no forwarding address had been left.

She said that she was sorry she couldnae help me further, and that she hoped I would find Eilish's whereabouts before too long.

And with that, Eilish was gone.

Lost to me.

I stopped writing the letters.

Fourteen

Summer flew by, working on the gardens and the Stanley B. By the time the weather turned, and the autumn storms came, all she was missing was a new coat of paint on the hull and an overhaul of the engine, the internal mechanics. All of which hadnae been tended to for close to three decades.

With the lashing rain and howling winds of November, I would take the bus on washed-out days where no work could be done in the gardens, and I would spend them in the library at Ambleside where they had located a manual for the kind of engine the Stanley B had.

I transcribed everything that seemed important, drawing and labelling all the different parts, where they went, and what they attached to into a notebook. Seeing things laid out in my own hand made it seem a little less daunting.

Engines, mechanics had never been my thing, and the names of each element were a new language to me. But drawing them out, jotting down their names helped a little, though I always felt a fraud when enquiring on parts for the boat, certain that I was pronouncing them wrong.

But slowly, I began to understand a little of how it worked. How one part connected with another, helped it do a certain thing. But the actual names of these engine components would always escape me, beyond my awkward initial enquiry.

My notes from the library would be propped up by torchlight in the engine room, where I would carefully take the engine apart that had remained lifeless when Maisie had tried to start it. Frozen solid.

I laid the parts out on the engine room floor like a puzzle, jotting down the names of those that had rusted away, perished, become stuck fast.

List secured, Maisie and I would take the train down to Barrow to scour scrapyards for replacements, quickly learning that new parts from the chandleries were much too expensive.

She thought that I couldnae see, but I could, the smirk on her face as I painfully tried to explain what we needed to the scrapper – the names sounding wrong, clunky, the second I called them out. He would smile, more to Maisie than me, lead us off to various sheds full of bits for cars, boats, lorries, tractors, you name it, and we would scrub about until the part had been found.

It was clear, right from the off, that Maisie knew that engine as well as she did the rest of the Stanley B. But for reasons unknown to me at the time, she stepped back, let me stumble my way through understanding how it worked at my own pace. Letting me learn from my mistakes, awkward conversations with patient scrappers.

Greasy box of parts secured, we would have dinner at our pub on Barrow Park, and if the floodlights were lit at Holker Street, she would ask the barman to stow our parts behind the bar, and we would take in a game.

I had always loved night games. They had always felt special, to watch, and to play in. My goal at Ibrox is elevated in my mind by the floodlights behind the Copland Road End, the dark skies beyond, the shadowy stands, the brilliant green of the pitch.

Crowds in the low thousands for a rain swept, cold, midweek Fourth Division fixture against the likes of Rochdale and Exeter felt charged in a way that some games on a drab Saturday afternoon could not. Beneath the lights, the magic of a night game possessed those present with an energy, with a hope, that little bit more pronounced for a team drifting dangerously down toward the foot of the league table.

Floodlights blotting out everything else, all the worries of the outside world lost in the darkness beyond, all that is left is the pitch, the stands, the game, us. All beneath those dazzling lights.

A little piece of grand theatre, inspiring those present to dare to dream.

It possessed Maisie too. She would become lost in the drama played out to a backdrop of gusting rain swirling about the lights. Storms off the Irish Sea sometimes dictating the trajectory of the ball just as much as the twenty-two out on the pitch.

She would watch and become lost. In the here and now. And elsewhere too. To games, days, people long gone.

They were the spectacles we hoped for, our night games. Goals, the ebb and flow on the pitch and across the terraces. Thrilling fingertip saves, shots rattling crossbars. Thundering tackles and raking passes. Shadows jinking and dancing across the camber of the pitch, mimicking the players' every move. Fog rolling in over the main stand from the sea, sweeping down, reducing the play to a ghostly apparition.

Ninety minutes of wilful distraction from a life beyond.

Whether a simple fact of a long day in the gardens, the engine room, Barrow's scrapyards, I always slept solidly after a night game at Holker Street. Being drawn into the action, willing the ball into the net, slumping at a missed opportunity, it always left me drained, struggling to keep my eyes open on the train ride home. Too tired to open up the canvas flaps and slide the box of parts inside, I would leave them by my cabin door, slip into bed without setting a fire to warm the place, the echoes of the crowd the last thing I heard before sleep overcame me.

On the days when wild rainstorms washed out any chance of visitors, or meaningful work in the gardens we would climb up underneath the canvas covering of the Stanley B and listen to the rain drumming on it, the baying of the trees overhead. We would treat the wooden decking, oil the wheel in the wheelhouse, the prop shaft joints, remove old parts, replace them with the second-hand pieces reclaimed at the scrapyards. We would look through the old photographs of the Stanley B from a life on Southampton Water, and I would watch Maisie lose herself rummaging through the box of bits on the cabin table, slipping away for a time into memory.

Beneath umbrellas we would inspect the hull, check for leaks in the welding. There were none. Maisie would run her hand across the metalwork patches, at the paintwork that we had sanded down that told the story of the Stanley B.

'You see that faint magnolia there, that was the factory colour Thorneycroft painted all their smaller builds in. It was treated and acted as a final seal to the hull. Whoever had commissioned for her to be built had the boatyard paint her in this red here,' she pointed to the bow, where a dull, faded red dominated.

'Whoever had her built never stepped foot on her. When she was launched for testing, she collided with the dock and ripped a hole in the bow here, ruined the cabin, flooded the engine. She was written off, scrapped. Which is where Stanley found her.

'We couldn't afford to paint her, as well as fix her. So, she stayed this colour, with a patchwork of fixes over it for a number of years. The sightseers didn't seem to care, and when we finally saved up enough, we painted her back to the Magnolia. Stanley chose it. He thought she looked really smart. And she did.

'It was painted this dark green colour here,' she said, pointing toward the stern, 'for a job. But it was done quickly and shoddily and faded just as quickly. We had planned to have her put back to Magnolia, but the war meant everything was put on hold. One thing led to another, and it was never done. So, she stayed like this. Time did the rest.'

On a trip to Barrow, a Chandlery managed to find a paint as close to Stanley's choice as could be, and with aching arms, we lugged four large cans from the bus stop down to the boat and stowed them away. And waited for spring.

The seasons in the Lake District were as predictable as they were beautiful. After the wind and rain of Autumn, temperatures plummeted, bringing with it snow that heaped in deep drifts, blanketing everything, damping down sound, the silence about the gardens making it seem as if the rest of the world had been lost somehow, or paused at least.

Windermere and Ambleside presented picture postcard wintry scenes of snow doused thatched roofs, cottages, narrow lanes lined with pretty shopfronts, and the glassy waters of the lake. All beneath the backdrop of great ridges and bluffs shrouded in cloud and deep snow.

Days were spent reading through my notes in the cabin on particularly troublesome parts of the Stanley B's engine that didnae seem to want to go back together.

Heavy flurries that dissolved the prayer flags and birch copse to faint outlines, and the heat from the wood burner had me lingering longer than was needed, putting off heading out into the bitter cold to clear snow from paths, the glasshouse, the Stanley B's canvas. Though, as soon as I was out in it, the cold seemed to fade away: so magical it felt to have such a beautiful scene all to myself. The gardens frozen, still, as if time itself had stopped.

Maisie and I would head into Ambleside and Windermere to do chores, take the train that inched along at a painfully slow pace down to Barrow to search for more parts. And on days where paths had been cleared and parts had been secured, long hours were spent in Maisie's kitchen, drinking coffee, and reading the sports pages of the papers sat around Maisie's table.

It was not the life either had envisioned, shorn of loved ones lost to us long before we were ready. But it was a life all the same. One of colour, of simple purpose, maintaining the gardens. Resurrecting Maisie's beloved boat.

Bed was met each night with weary eyes and aching limbs, and a sense of achievement, even if that achievement was simply keeping Five Acre Gardens in a kind of timeless stasis, as close a facsimile to Charlie's vision as was possible.

It was a life, forever framed by a withering sadness, anguish, and horror at losing Eilish. And Shannon. But it was also a life that had meaning, purpose, even if that purpose was trying to maintain someone else's dream.

When you had lost all of yours, it was the next best thing.

We were two plate spinners, trying to keep the hopes and dreams of others from falling. Their lives from turning to dust. But it was a life far better than the one I envisioned for myself when I stepped on to that train in Glasgow.

And it was a life of football at Christmas, where Boxing Day 1970 saw us up at Carlisle to see United take on Bolton. New Year's Day and we were down at Holker Street to see Barrow play Bournemouth. Roast dinners at our pub on Barrow Park. A couple of ales, the walk to the match where Maisie would twirl her scarf about her head with every goal. A pint and a dram to warm ourselves back up after a few hours on the bitter terraces, before making our way through the dark to the train station, the lights of Holker Street still burning up into the night – looking back, a halo rising up into the cloud-choked skies.

Among the long days of trying to realise Charlie and Stanley and Maisie's dreams, these new rituals, for a new life, began to exist alongside them.

It was an unlikely pairing, Maisie and me. But it worked. We managed somehow to sustain one another. We both knew to give each other the privacy, the solitude we craved.

But Maisie also had an unerring knack of appearing at my cabin door when the burdens of the past had grown too great for one day. And a glass of whisky, a bonfire at dusk, a conversation about anything, nothing, over a roaring flame helped, losing yourself for a time in the lick of the fire, watching embers drifting up into the sky, disappearing into the night.

Without consciously acknowledging it, we had both taken on each-others' past, and sought to nurture it, preserve it, like curators in a museum; celebrate what could be celebrated, nurse those parts that couldnae.

Snippets of happy times with Eilish. Wordless trips on glassy waters with Stanley.

And all because of an advert in a discarded paper on a train. A curious, overgrown path with a little faded sign that read 'Gardens.'

Fifteen

As the clouds of bluebells beneath the great oaks began to droop and die away for another year, the spring of 1971 began in a chaotic pattern of sunshine and showers.

Patches of warm sunlight, strong enough to make you shed your jumper, neighboured shaded spots, where bitter chills lingered.

Impatient to get started on the painting of the Stanley B, Maisie had dragged out an old marquee from a rarely visited shed, lugged it across the grass in front of the glasshouse much to the annoyance of the scattering, screeching peacocks.

Between us we managed to hoist it up over the bow, secured the guy ropes where we could, draping the rest of the marquee over the wheelhouse. And while the visitors to the glasshouse remained minimal, Maisie set to on a task she and Stanley had done some forty years earlier: painting and sealing the hull. It appeared a real meditative task to her, so I left her to it, watching as she slowly edged along.

When it rained, she would get visitors in the peacocks, who would settle under the frame of the marquee and watch her progress, shifting slightly, standing for a moment if she drew too close.

With every section completed, we would drag the frame further over the Stanley B, and Maisie, her onlookers, would shift along, settle back down.

When visitors began to arrive with more settled weather and the resumption of the ferries on the lake, Maisie found her time taken up once more with the baking of cakes, the heating of tea urns, and the welcoming of guests to the glasshouse. From then on, after dinner, I would often see the sweeping beam of torchlight spraying across the gardens in the darkness, the glow of paraffin lamps as they were lit beneath the marquee growing stronger, gently swinging on the breeze while Maisie painted for an hour or two.

Sometimes sleep would overwhelm me before I saw the lamps extinguished, the torch leading a path back to the cottage and bed.

The summer of 1971 was long and humid. Days were spent labouring in the gardens, my shirt sticking to me in the stifling, clawing heat. The air thick, still, limp. Not even the slightest of breezes to bring a little comfort.

I tended to the plants as best I could, watering them from the numerous butts dotted about the gardens. And when they ran dry, I would take my watering can down to the river at the bottom of the gardens and battle through the huge wilting gunnera dug in along the banks to fetch water. Much of the gunnera grew to well over six feet, huge prehistoric looking things with thick, leathery leaves large enough to sit beneath. And as the river level fell, and their roots no longer reached damp soil, they began to wither and fall in on themselves. The first casualty of the relentless sun.

The grass curled and yellowed and would crunch beneath your feet as you walked. Sunflower heads drooped. Large sprays of ornamental grasses rattled as you brushed past them. Humans, Peacocks, and plants were all relieved when the thunderstorms came.

With the air so thick and heavy, charged, when the cloud built up and the skies darkened to a dusk, the thunderstorms were immense. Brilliant lightning bolts sizzled and forked across the sky. Deafening thunderclaps made you jump, despite knowing they were coming. Torrential rains blurred the panes of the glasshouse, shadows lengthening about the pool as the storm outside closed in. The drumming rain making conversation impossible. Garden visitors, Maisie, me, when I had finally skittered inside, stood quietly beneath the storm, and looked on.

It was one evening during the heatwave that Maisie found me sat outside my cabin.

'Come,' she said. 'I think I've finished.'

In the long, light evenings of summer we didnae need torches to examine the Stanley B. Her new coat of paint lit up the marquee. Painstakingly neat black trim on the railings helped make the pristine hull shimmer, the varnished wooden frame of the wheelhouse and deck a rich, golden ochre.

It was hard to imagine that this was the same boat that had been cut out of the scrub some sixteen months earlier. Maisie nodded.

'I know,' she said 'it's amazing. Stanley would be so happy.'

We walked around her to take in all of Maisie's handiwork. The propeller had been coated and painted a dark green. The rudder fins that had been cut from the fallen oak had been sealed and varnished and hung suspended above the grassy floor as new.

On the stern she had repainted the boat's name, her home port, in the same colour as the trim. 'Stanley B, Southampton' stood out proudly against the sea of magnolia.

She looked such a handsome thing, and if you hadnae known her before, you would have assumed that she had only recently rolled down the slipway of the shipyard that built her, out onto the water for the very first time. Though any floating would have become aimless, with the Stanley B's engine deconstructed and scattered here and there.

At the height of summer, it had become almost unbearable to spend any time down in the engine room, the wooden decking absorbing the heat, leeching it below deck. Engine parts that needed cleaning or unfreezing from decades of inactivity were done from the porch of my cabin. Laid out on newspaper they waited patiently to be returned to their housing, as did the new fuel tank, oil lines, and a host of other bits that had perished below deck.

Transcribed notes were read, then re-read. Actions checked once, twice. The movements of the parts, how they were supposed to fit together were imagined on walks about the gardens, long hours sat up in the walkways among the Oak trees. And finally, as the heatwave succumbed and the temperature began to fall, those countless engine parts began to be fixed back into place.

One by one. Slowly. Mistakes being walked back until everything fitted together as it should. Pages in my notebook being ticked off. Until one day, in late October, there were no more parts left on the oily expanse of newspaper on my porch or lying on the engine room floor.

Checked over once, twice, with a final trip up to Ambleside Library to make sure that every step in the manual had been taken correctly, the final step involved a trip down to Barrow to pick up oil and fuel, decanting it carefully into the Stanley B, and waiting the couple of days suggested to let the oil make its way to every point where it was needed.

As we waited, I dug out a little trench beneath the propeller, just in case my naïve engineering worked, not wanting it to cut into the ground if the Stanley B sparked into life, and then, finally, with whisky glass in hand and in failing light, it was time.

Maisie took up a key from the box in the cabin, a crude metal fob attached made by Stanley Buchanan in a metal work lesson at school more than forty years earlier, 'STANLEY B' haphazardly inscribed in uneven typesetting.

She stepped up into the wheelhouse, sat down in the skipper's chair, placed the key in the ignition, looked across at me and smiled.

'Here goes nothing,' she said, and turned the key.

The engine spluttered, stopped, then roared into life with a great plume of smoke that had the peacocks scattering for cover in all directions across the grass, before the engine room calmed and idled into a smooth, steady rhythm. The floorboards beneath our feet reverberated, coffee in mugs on the cabin table below rippled. Every inch of the Stanley B, every board and fixing, the wheel and railings, the benches on deck, the cupboards in the cabin, all energised, re-animated by the rumble of the engine room. Blood coursing through her veins once more. The Stanley B come to life.

Maisie's eyes grew glassy as she looked at me.

'She sounds just like she used to,' she said quietly, memories of ocean liners lit up at night, a young Stanley jogging from bow to stern throwing lines, howling up into the sky as she was launched away from the boatyard, of evenings on the deck watching cargo ships pulling out to sea flooding her eyes with tears.

'I could listen to her all day,' she said, wiping at her eyes with the sleeve of her cardigan 'what a sound.'

After a few minutes, composure restored, she nodded toward the stern.

'Shall we see what else she can do?'

From a safe distance I watched as Maisie pushed forward the throttle, at the propeller as it began to spin, the prop shaft rumbling below deck. The look of astonishment on my face must have signalled to her that it was working, and she brought it back to idle.

Next, she slowly turned the wheel, first to port, then starboard, the port rudder swishing left and right while the starboard remained motionless.

After a few more minutes sitting, listening to the engine, she turned the key and the Stanley B shuddered to a halt, silence descending across the gardens once more.

'Just one dodgy rudder, after all these years. I can live with that,' she said and smiled. 'Thank you Gordie. Thank you so much, for bringing her back to life.'

I told her that it should be me thanking her, that it had been an absolute pleasure, and that I would take a look at the rudder in the morning. I was so pleased for her, I said. For her, and for the Stanley B.

She nodded. Wiped away a tear. Said goodnight, her fingers playing across the key fob and Stanley's uneven inscription. And with that she slipped away into the gardens, toward the cottage.

A trip to Barrow and a few hours scrabbling below decks had the rudder fixed, the final piece of the jigsaw in place.

With the work done, with the Stanley B up to scratch, there appeared a lightness about Maisie. A calm replaced the drive she possessed when the Stanley B lay in pieces.

And at the burning of the old, warped decking that couldnae be salvaged for some other purpose down by the river, she produced a letter to her son, dropped it gently into the flames. Something she hadnae done for quite some time.

She watched it ignite, flare, curl, its embers twirling up into the night sky on the thermals, disappearing into the darkness. A message up into the night.

Every night after dinner she would take long walks around the gardens, kicking through drifts of autumnal leaves beneath canopies of skeletal beeches and maple, always finishing at the glasshouse, the Stanley B. A hand on the hull, she would linger for a time, lost in thought, before heading home.

She had resisted my suggestions to float her on the river at the bottom of the gardens. It would have been wide enough for her, if I took some time to cut back parts of the riverbank that had grown too wild. That way she could take her out onto Lake Windermere itself if she wanted to.

'She is ready,' she would always say 'for the water. But I don't think I am. Let's leave her here, for the time being. For a little while longer.'

She would flick through Stanley's book in the cabin, read his entries on the places she had never reached. One of her next adventures would have been Anglesey and the vast cliffs of nesting puffins at the remote South Stack. He had drawn a narrow, wooden bridge suspended precariously over a sheer drop of churning seas and crushing rocks, spanning across to the small rocky islet that housed the South Stack Lighthouse. Being a location with a lighthouse, Stanley had added an asterisk at the top of the page for added importance.

'Can you imagine it?' she would say more to herself than me as she read Stanley's descriptions. She took the book with her to the glasshouse every day, sat with it, alone in a sea of mis-matched seats, tucking it away in her apron pocket when the odd visitor arrived.

As Christmas approached, trips into Ambleside were complimented with long walks up into the hills where she used to work – if the snows allowed. Paths that she had once tended lost among the clouds and freezing fog, littered with scree and wary sheep. She lingered on them. Stopping to take deep breaths of bracing air. To listen to the wind whipping at scarves and coat tails, looking out into sweeping valleys, mountain tops looming and fading among the mists.

Extra trips to Workington were planned, for no other reason than to catch the Workington Reds play Newport and Aldershot. The week or two before Christmas itself, and the busy football schedule it would bring, seemed equally elevated, far beyond the sum total of a couple of simple Fourth Division fixtures.

There was an excited bustle about the High Street adorned in lights strung across from one shop to the next. Carol-singers in front of a large, twinkling Christmas tree. The smell of mulled wine and roast chestnuts. And Maisie would have us linger for a time, sometimes from the window of a pub, before following the crowd away to Borough Park.

And, as always, Maisie allowed herself to get caught up among the cut and thrust of the game, channelling long lost Christmas fixtures away down at The Dell with Stanley.

And when Christmas came, roast dinners in Barrow Park, ding-dong matches on Holker Street against Bury, New Year's Day drinks outside Brunton Park in Carlisle preceded ninety minutes in the paddock, watching United play Orient beneath crystal clear, arctic blue skies.

Long, lazy afternoons in the kitchen reading the football results by the fire.

It was only after the fact that I saw what Maisie had been doing with those lingering walks in the gardens. Her quiet moments on the Stanley B, in the glasshouse. Walks up onto her old stomping grounds among the clouds. Extra trips to Ambleside, the football.

She had been saying goodbye.

Sixteen

It had been like any other morning. My walk across to the cottage for breakfast had been hurried by bitterly cold winds, and black storm clouds trailing ominous capes of rain behind them.

Stamping my boots off by the kitchen door, everything seemed so familiar, yet strangely askew.

The kitchen was as it always was, neat and ready to go.

But it was cold, lifeless. The fire unmade, the smell of coffee on the stove missing. As was Maisie.

I sat down at the table as I was always instructed to and waited.

After ten minutes I felt a knot begin to tighten in my stomach. Something definitely wasnae right.

The door from the kitchen into the rest of the cottage revealed a darkened hallway. To the right was a toilet that marked as far as I had ever been inside Maisie's home.

As generous and welcoming as she was, she also enjoyed her privacy. Her cottage, or the rest of it beyond the hallway, was her space.

Not wanting to head in any further, I called out her name, and listened to the hush. I called again, then, concern overriding the breaking of our unwritten rule, I stepped inside.

I finally found her, in a comfy looking sofa chair by a smouldering fire in the front room. A whisky glass had dropped from her hand into her lap, her head bent forward as if in a deep sleep. There was silence save for the slight, incessant ticking over of a little clock on the mantelpiece.

I righted the glass and held her hand that was cold to the touch – for how long I wasnae sure – watching her bowed forward, eyes closed. And when my knees began to ache from my prone position by her side, I clambered back to my feet, squeezed her hand one last time, then I called the police station in Windermere.

When they came, I was taken away, put up in a guesthouse for a few days, and told to wait. I didnae know it at the time, but that would be my last day in the gardens.

She was buried in a small churchyard near Troutbeck Bridge a week later. There were precious few people in attendance, and the hymns echoed about the church with a heightened sadness at an extraordinary life being laid to rest in such an underwhelming way. There was to be no wake, but I received a note at the guesthouse to meet with Maisie's solicitor in a small tearoom immediately after the service.

She sat with a briefcase laid across the seat next to her. Her smile was warm, and her condolences genuine. She ordered a large pot of tea for us both, flipped open the briefcase lid, and began.

Maisie had been ill for more than eighteen months. A condition of the brain, the name of which was too long and alien sounding for me to register. It could have taken her at any moment, the solicitor said. Just like that, she said. Like flicking a switch.

She hadnae told a soul. She had stepped out from the doctor's surgery in Ambleside, met me with her familiar smile and wave. The burden of what the doctor had said hidden, imperceptible. Whatever day the news came, I had no idea. There had been no hint. Either then, or any time after. The energy with which she set about fixing the Stanley B seemed no more than the typical, tireless fire that burnt within her.

Only now, after the fact, did it begin to feel like a personal race against her fate.

Maisie had no claim to the cottage, the gardens, the solicitor said. She had not wanted to inherit either. They were Charlie's, and his extended family's, and she made sure that Charlie left it to them, with the provision that Maisie could remain living there as long as she chose to.

The solicitor shook her head.

'She was a strong, independent woman, Ms Buchanan. She made it clear that she wanted no part of someone else's wealth. Even her beloved Charlie's. She would pay her own way. She always had, she had said, and she always would. She made that very clear.'

The solicitor apologised for me being sent away to a guesthouse so quickly. Upon Maisie's death, all and any employment on the estate instigated by her would be terminated with immediate effect. I would be allowed to return very soon to collect my things, she promised, and the room in the guesthouse had been paid up for another week. After that, she said, paused. She didnae need to say anything else.

'Which brings me to our last piece of business,' she said, and took out a thick envelope from her briefcase. She placed it on the table, slid it over to me. Registering the look of confusion on my face she nodded to me to take it.

'That is for you. Ms Buchanan didn't have much in the way of material possessions and assets. And what she did, she made provisions for in her will.

'She wanted that,' she said nodding down at the envelope 'to go to you.'

She closed the lid of her briefcase and snapped the clasps in place, then handed me her card.

'Everything you need is in there. But if you have any questions, please do contact me,' she smiled, stood up, shook my hand warmly.

'Take care Mr Macrae. Ms Buchanan spoke of you very warmly. I wish you all the best for the future.' She went to the counter, paid for the tea, nodded as she passed me, stepped out into the street, and was gone.

I sat there for a time, staring down at the envelope. I went to the counter to pay for another pot of tea, looking back at the table, its contents. When it arrived, I poured myself a cup, took a sip, then opened the envelope and pulled out a bundle of papers.

On top was a photograph of Maisie and me stood in front of the freshly painted Stanley B. She had asked a visitor to take it, though I had never seen it developed until that moment.

Looking at it, her smile in the photograph made me smile, my hand shaking as I took a sip of tea. It reminded me of the picture she had shown me, of her and Stanley, stood in a similar position on a dock after they had finished restoring her down in Southampton all those years ago.

On the back, in that familiar, flourishing handwriting: 'Maisie, Gordie, the Stanley B, August 1971.'

Underneath the photograph was Stanley's notebook. Beneath that a picture postcard of a Lighthouse sat on top of some steep cliffs. 'Saint Catherine's Lighthouse, Freshwater Bay, Isle of Netton,' was printed along the bottom of the card.

Where there was the space for a quick note to a friend or relative on the back, Maisie had written:

> 'Take good care of her.
> Finish the trip.
> Live a life that will make Eilish proud.
> Maisie.'

In one of the envelopes that Maisie used to put the windmill money in and give to me on a Monday bus ride into Ambleside, was the haphazardly inscribed key fob, the key to the Stanley B, and £500 rolled tightly together and fastened with an elastic band.

There was a document transferring ownership of the Stanley B from Maisie Buchanan to Gordie Macrae. Another detailed payment for the Stanley B to be moved by crane onto a lowbed and transported to a berth in Devonshire Dock in Barrow. Another showed that the Stanley B would be moved in a week's time, and that the berth had been secured for six months. There was also a receipt for a full tank of fuel, to be administered when the Stanley B had reached dockside.

I sat back, looked down at it all. I had been saved, by Maisie, for a second time.

It felt strange, going back to the gardens. They looked the same. But felt so different.

I walked the paths one last time, wandering from one spot to the other, secret gardens to hidden pathways. I clambered up through the walkways in the trees, wove through the birch copse, the oak woods where shoots had already begun to come up and would become that vast seas of bluebells before too long.

The peacocks sat quietly on the grass outside the glasshouse. Subdued, as if they knew something terrible had happened, they didnae even shift as I walked past them, they just looked on as I opened the glasshouse door, stiff in its frame, and stepped inside and sat down at a table to take it in one last time.

Mist drifted across the water. Snagged on lily pads. Silence. The cherub still undecided about taking the plunge.

It had always been such a tranquil, comforting place, the world outside and its worries on pause. Seasons came and went, snow flurries and thunderstorms. Drumming rain and baying winds. The damp earthy smell of moss and creeper keeping the worst of the summer sun out. It had been our little sanctuary, and I knew, along with everything else, that I would miss the glasshouse terribly. It was one of a kind, timeless, and its stillness would stay with me long after I had been made to leave it behind.

I found myself looking away to the kitchen, the door to the back room, half expecting Maisie to materialise with a slice of cake and a tea in hand, like she had done that very first day. A mournful cry of a solitary peacock outside, sounding forlornly up into the sky reminded me that she would not.

The solicitor had said the family were going to turn the cottage, the grounds into a high-end country hotel. Charlie's gardens would be manicured. Reigned in and pacified. The glasshouse pulled down to make way for a spa.

I took photographs of my favourite spots with a Polaroid camera bought in Windermere. I took shots of the glasshouse, labyrinthine pathways, all sorts. Though the pictures never seemed to do any of it justice. Just a pale facsimile. But it was better than nothing. And I had my memories.

I sat quietly in my cabin one last time. Took down my tattered prayer flags from the birch copse, folded them up neatly, fastened them with a band.

I collected Eilish's snow globe, that newspaper advert for the Lake District, all brittle and weather damaged, Charlie and Maisie's old pamphlet – 'The Gardens of Five Acre Cottage.'

I collected a few peacock feathers from the lawn, my envelope of Cowdenbeath memories and the only picture I had of Eilish. I took it all to the Stanley B. For the box.

Lighting the paraffin lamp in the cabin, it materialised out of the gloom. Sat on top was a penknife, already opened.

I smiled. Sat down. Took it up. I looked at Maisie's initials, Stanley's, others of unknown origin dotted across the box lid. I found a spot I was happy with, and carefully carved 'GM' into the stained wood, before stowing everything away inside.

I took one last look behind me, taking it all in one final time, before wandering down the path – down the way I had come three years earlier.

And with that the cottage, the gardens, the glasshouse, were gone.

My final week in the guesthouse was spent chasing ghosts. Bus trips up to Ambleside, boat rides out to the cove by Five Acre Cottage, sipping pints of ale, watching workmen taking down the little sign, blocking up the path to the gardens. Walks up to Troutbeck Bridge, to share a whisky with Maisie.

When the time came, I packed my things, left the guesthouse and Windermere behind, and took the train down to Barrow to find the Stanley B.

She looked so familiar, yet so strange out of her woodland scene, moored up at Devonshire Dock. A light scuff mark on her paintwork the only casualty of her journey down, she bobbed gently on the swell as boats came and went about her. Unrolling the canvas flap, I stepped into the wheelhouse, closed it behind me, and went down into the cabin, as the owner of the Stanley B.

With the last of the winter storms still playing themselves out on the Irish Sea, the sea state was still much too rough for the Stanley B. Days were spent huddled in the quilt Maisie had made me that first Christmas, watching the world go by out on the deck, checking charts and maps.

I got used to handling the Stanley B by untying her, pulling her out from the dockside, then slowly bringing her back in. I learned when to jump across to tie her back up, how to throttle out and away from the dock smoothly. I got the feel of the rudders, the wheel by taking trips out into the sheltered waters of Piel Channel, protected from the elements by Walney Island. I took her down as far as Piel Island, just shy of open water, circled round past Piel Castle and back.

Edging past larger shipping I imagined the Stanley B down on Southampton Water, and Maisie's stories of her and Stanley taking sightseers out to see the vast ocean liners moored along the docks. I felt a shiver every time we passed the great hull of a cargo ship, looming above me and the Stanley B like a great cresting wave frozen in steel. Heaven only knows how it must have felt among those transatlantic ocean giants.

On match days, I would head to Barrow Park for something to eat and a pint, before making my way to Holker Street to watch the football. I would stand where Maisie and I always did and look on as Barrow slumped down into the bottom four of the Fourth Division, where they would fail to be re-elected back into the Football League come the end of the season.

A cruel blow to the town, and a final marker that my life, as I had known it with Maisie in the Lake District, had come to an end.

And with those last days of spring behind us, and the mooring at Devonshire Dock coming to an end, it was time to fulfil a promise.

We edged slowly, the Stanley B and I, down past the mud flats of Morecambe, the illuminations of Blackpool, the sand bars of Rhyl, signing off in Stanley's notebook with every destination reached.

I moored for a few days on the Menai Straits at Bangor, took a train into Snowdonia, and explored the picturesque towns and villages of Llanberis, Beddgelert, and Betws-y-Coed that wound around gargling rivers, steep rocky bluffs, and thick pine forests. Little cobbled alleyways lined with tea rooms and bookshops, sharp, fresh mountain air that compelled you to breathe in deeply.

Stanley had had Maisie and him down to walk up to the summit of Mount Snowdon, but with my bad knee I took the little mountain train up and sat above the clouds. Crystal clear lakes below shimmered, rippled on the bitingly fresh breeze.

A spot of rough weather kept me in Holyhead for a few days. More than enough time to head out to South Stack and a spot of puffin watching; although nesting season had passed, and the cliffs were lacking any birds, so it was not quite what Stanley envisaged. The hair-raising bridge across to the South Stack Lighthouse was thrill enough, watching great breakers crashing on the rocks below.

The summer was spent sailing between picturesque coves and fishing villages, bays lined with sand beaches and small towns, finally mooring up for the autumn and winter after a scary journey between the mainland and Ramsey Island off the Pembrokeshire coast of Wales.

Rising seas that made the Stanley B pitch and lurch violently had me seek out a mooring on a small, sheltered estuary at the little village of Solva, and a part-time job washing dishes at the Bishops, an old, low-beamed pub in the nearby town of St. David's.

My time was filled up with long walks along coastal paths that snaked across the tops of vast cliff faces between Solva and St. David's, and sitting next to the stove in the cabin, reading Stanley's notebook and future stopping points.

Saturdays were spent watching the Solva football team playing on an exposed pitch high up on a bluff above the village. A rope barrier hitched around rusting poles hemmed the players in, keeping them from the precarious cliff edge a short distance beyond the far corner flag. Over the course of the winter a few footballs were not so lucky, tumbling down into the rocks and white water below. Some, remarkably, were retrieved.

The currents, in their own time, brought them up into the estuary, where they gently bobbed up on the tides to the slipway by the post office. 'Solva FC' had been inked across their panels, and whenever a ball materialised, it would be dropped off at the post office where the team's manager worked and would be put back into circulation the following Saturday.

As the winter storms raged, and the seas kicked up white horses and swell that would boom against the rocks at the mouth of Solva estuary, the anniversary of Maisie's passing was met with a large glass of whisky in a booth by the fire at The Bishops, and a silent toast into the flames that carried it away up the chimney and out into the night sky. And with a fair wind, I hoped, up to Five Acre Cottage, up to Troutbeck Bridge.

As the seas began to calm once more in the late spring of 1973, we left Solva and eventually the beautiful Welsh coast behind. We sailed across the exposed Bristol Channel where, for the first time on our trip, land receded to a vague haze and for an hour or so, it was just me, the Stanley B, and the lulling ocean.

As the rugged and beautiful coastline of Devon and Cornwall came into view, we skirted treacherous cliffs and picturesque fishing villages, down past the stunning Tintagel, Perranporth, St Ives and on to Land's End.

From there we ticked off the last few stops in Stanley's notebook, spending time at Porthgwarra to see the Minack Theatre – an open-air amphitheatre cut out of the cliffs. The bay, the shimmering sea beyond the stage as impressive as anything performed on it.

The penultimate page of Stanley's book had us stop just along from Penzance at Marazion, where I walked the causeway at low tide across to Saint Michael's Mount – a small steep sided island covered in trees with a great labyrinthine castle perched on top.

As the tide came back in, I rolled up my trousers and waded back to shore, and headed on toward Mullion, Lizard and Coverack, then out, into the open sea, toward the last page of Stanley's book, and the Isle of Netton.

I rounded the island past Westlyn, crossing the ferry route; the esplanade, the large, whitewashed houses along the seafront brilliant in the sunshine, mooring round on Shanklin Point as the sun began to set.

After an hour or so's sailing the following morning, Saint Catherine's Lighthouse grew out of the haze on the cliffs. Rounding the steep bluff on which the lighthouse sat, Freshwater Bay slowly came into view, and the sleepy little fishing village of Freshwater.

A huddle of fishing boats finished offloading their catch on the seafront. Crates of fish sat dockside between heaps of net and lobster pots, and as I drew close, a few calls to fishermen mending nets and hosing down decks pointed me in the direction of the harbour master, working to bring ashore the catch of a fishing boat further along the seafront.

He nodded when I asked if there were any spots to moor up, pointing to the mouth of the River Ebb that bisected the run of weather-beaten cottages dockside. He told me to pick any that I liked along the river. There were plenty to choose from, he said.

I pulled up in front of the last cottage along the towpath, though, in truth, it was nothing more than an old, disused shell of a building. It looked like neither it, nor the mooring had been used for some time. I cut the engine and tied up.

I took up Stanley's book, the Polaroid camera that I had bought in Barrow. I wanted to keep adding a picture of every sketch he had drawn down in the bomb shelters of Southampton, just as Maisie had done.

The Polaroid was more expensive than a normal camera, but I loved the sound it made, the shape of the pictures. I loved watching the image slowly materialise before me. And so long as I kept stocked up on cartridges, I could add to his book right there and then, on the spot that he had dreamt of visiting.

Or for this final entry, revisiting.

Walking back up the river, through the pretty, homely village of narrow alleys and tightly knit cottages, past upturned rowing boats and heaps of old lobster pots leaning to here and there, along the seafront and its line of old fishing boats, and up on to the grassy bluffs above, I could understand why Stanley had loved it so.

There was a calm, a timelessness, a peace about this little place a way off the beaten track.

Sheltered in the lee of the bay, it felt safe, welcoming, somewhere you would want to bring your mum to escape the horrors of the Blitz, the hardships of life.

Up toward Saint Catherine's Point, if you lie down in just the right spot, you could shelter from the buffeting winds, completely hidden among the swaying grasses.

The little patch of sunlight above, warm and soothing, the world hushed, muffled, the swell breaking against the rocks below, muted, the cries of seagulls faint, distant, as they coasted on the currents above, drifting beneath scuds of wispy cloud.

I took a picture of the lighthouse from a little way down the bluff, with the sun behind it, so as when it developed it was captured in silhouette, against a brilliant blue, rising up out of a sea of swaying grasses.

I fastened it with a paperclip to the page in Stanley's book, filled out the time and date in the last column, then wrote in the notes:

'To Stanley, to Maisie. We did it. From Gordie Macrae'

I closed the book, held it in my hands, sat at the foot of the lighthouse, for how long I wasnae sure. And as I walked back down, with my mission complete, I began to wonder what came next.

My life had reduced down to the smallest of pinpricks – the gardens, the Stanley B, the odd game of football, my wee cabin. Life had become so focused on fulfilling Maisie, Charlie, and Stanley's dreams, by boat, garden, and adventure, that I hadnae thought much on what came next.

On what happened once Stanley's notebook had been completed.

And as I walked back down, stowed Stanley's book in his box on the cabin table, I had no idea.

All I knew was that Freshwater seemed as good a place as any to linger for a spell, while I worked it out.

The shadows had grown long across the towpath when they appeared, two young couples looking tired and red faced after a long day walking the coastal paths.

Beyond the Stanley B, and the last tumble-down cottage, the towpath dissolved into a tangle of impassable bramble and scrub.

One of the young girls slumped down onto an old bench by the Stanley B's bowline.

'Oh dear,' she exclaimed, and wiped her brow.

I finished my toast to Maisie, Stanley and the end of their adventure, placed my whisky glass on the wheelhouse seat, and stepped down onto the towpath and asked if everything was all right.

They had missed the last bus back to their campsite, she had said, over at Colbridge on the far side of Blackwater Lake, pointing at the vast stretch of water opening out beyond the Stanley B.

It was a good five-mile walk round, she had said, and they were already beat from a long day on the cliffs.

'What to do?' she said with a shrug at her companions.

I scratched my head, told them that I could take them, or as far as I could, on the Stanley B. I didnae know the lake, I told her, but if I could borrow the map that she had been holding, then we would see what we could do.

She waved her hand, thanked me, but they couldnae ask me to do that, she had said.

I told her that it would be nae bother. That I had no other plans for the evening.

She looked at the others.

'Well, if you are sure, that would be amazing. Thank you.'

The girl handed over her map of Netton and pointed out Blackwater Lake, that it would be a straight trip across to the landing post at the camp site.

She said that they would pay me.

I said they didnae need to and beckoned them aboard, sprung the lines, and headed out onto the lake.

The girl found an old oil can on the deck that had been cleaned out and kept, just in case. She tied a piece of string to it, and hung it on a nail in the wheelhouse, dropped some coins into it, and motioned for the others to do the same.

'Our bus fare,' she said, then shut me down as I protested.

'You saved us from a horrible evening. So here is your fare. And a little extra, to have a beer on us.'

It was a pleasant trip, the rich, refreshing smell of pine drifted out onto the water from the thickset forests along the shoreline.

Lanterns twinkled among the trees, swaying gently outside beautiful log cabins that nestled in the woods. A pontoon to each stretching out over the water.

The Stanley B glided across the water, cutting through the glassy surface with ease, her wake fanning out behind her, reaching the shore long after we had passed. It was a far cry from the chop she had been used to all the way down from Barrow. And with it, her engine purred. The Stanley B liked Blackwater Lake.

At the pontoon at Colbridge they thanked me as they stepped across, the girl stopping, turning. She asked what I was doing tomorrow. I said nothing. She said that the four of them, and another group were heading over to Canford Cliffs on another walking party. They were going to take the bus, but it was so much nicer going by boat. Would I consider picking them up in the morning, taking them back in the evening. She would get everyone to pay, to make it worth my while.

I shrugged my shoulders, nodded.

In the morning there were twelve of them, who all dropped their coins in the tin on the way there, and again in the evening on the way back, some of whom asked if I would take them down to Freshwater the next day. Which I did. And then another group the day after that.

I didnae know it, but the girl from that first trip had told people at the campsite how nice it had been to travel around the island by boat.

Word spread. And with every pre-arranged pick up, there would be a few more people at the pontoon, hoping on the off chance to be taken across to Woodford, to Durnford Downs, wherever, for the day. All dropping their coins into the tin can as they boarded.

And with that, and purely by accident, the Stanley B and me fell into a kind of vocation on Blackwater Lake.

In no time, summer days became filled with ferrying people, and then things across the lake. To here, there, anywhere they wanted to go.

The Freshwater harbour master heard about our service and asked if I would take the days catch from his boat up to Westlyn every morning, drop it off at the various fish restaurants along the esplanade that bought from him.

In return he offered me the last cottage on the towpath, rent free, so long as

I fixed her back up to scratch. It would save him two jobs, he had said. And if I planned to stay on, he said, the cottage would keep me warm in winter. It had thick walls, and a big fire, he said. Cosy on a foul winter's night.

I agreed.

It wasnae quite the sightseeing trips that Stanley had envisaged, but it was close enough to the dream he had harboured for him and his mum, the Stanley B.

It was honest work. It was enjoyable work, seeing people get a kick out of being on deck.

Sailing across the deep parts of the lake, looking out at the dense woods, the little communities huddled along the shoreline, it was a beautiful place in which to earn a kind of living. It was a beautiful place to be.

And after the long journey down, and with nowhere else to go, without knowing what it was I was looking for, Blackwater Lake soon felt like it was it.

Just the spot for me, for the Stanley B.

So, we stayed.

I got into a routine on the lake, ferrying people, fish, motor parts, whatever, from here to there. And in between I fixed up the cottage, sat in the cabin of the Stanley B, looked through the box, at photographs of the gardens that would certainly have been levelled. At the glasshouse no doubt torn down to make way for that spa. At Eilish's snow globe. The photograph of Maisie and me. Everything.

Some evenings I would sit in the pub on Freshwater seafront with an ale and a glass of whisky for Maisie, and watch the sky drain of colour – in the winter white-crested waves colliding on a boiling sea beyond the headland. The sweep of light from Saint Catherine's Lighthouse illuminating bleak storm cloud, the twinkling lights of the fishing fleet bravely facing down the bitter swells.

On occasion I would even get the odd day's work on one of the boats, if someone had gone down sick. The extra money helped.

Arriving back on shore at dawn, hauling the crates for Westlyn straight onto the Stanley B, I would start on the day's jobs without any sleep, and with just a large flask of coffee to keep me going.

During the quieter months of the football season, if there was no work to be done, I would head up to Shooter's Meadow to watch Freshwater's team play in the Island League.

Sometimes I would take the team on the Stanley B to away games around the island. To Woodford, Canford and Westlyn.

It was enjoyable exploring the football grounds on Netton, some with much loved, weathered old stands, preserved year on year by a band of eager volunteers. Some with just a little clubhouse, a roped off pitch. And when the weather was bad, I would wrap up in Maisie's Barrow scarf and get lost in the ebb and flow at these precious little grounds. Just like we used to at Holker Street, Borough Park, Brunton Park.

I would look out at the scene, and beyond sometimes. Losing myself, and I would see Maisie among the crowd, glassy eyed, looking out herself on matches long gone, her boy.

I would see Eilish, up in the stand, waving down at the pitch. At me.

Memories. So far away. So close. In the same moment.

Young Stanley had been right. Freshwater would have been the perfect place for Maisie and him. And thanks to his notebook, to the Stanley B, to a kindly soul at the end of a little path between the trees, it had become the perfect place for me.

I settled into my new life working on the lake, tending to the Stanley B, the cottage. Taking my time during the off-season when there were precious few tourists to ferry about.

Making the few deliveries and pick-ups, that I did have, last. Sitting over a pot of tea in the café by the bridge. Wandering up to the lighthouse to watch the breakers far below.

I settled into my new life, and worked, and waited.

Waited for the day that a young boy would find his way onto the bench by our mooring. Would smile and wave as we pulled alongside, scrabble for the bow line as I threw it to him.

I worked. And waited. For young Tom Maskell. And another chance at redemption.

The Lives of Maisie Buchanan

Seventeen

I was fourteen when the Great War broke out, and on my seventeenth birthday I volunteered to help convalescing soldiers in a military hospital at Brockenhurst, deep in the New Forest.

All I had ever known before then was school and long summer holidays spent cycling out to Lyndhurst, Ashurst Bridge and Burley. Lying in the sun, walking deep into the woods, picking wildflowers, watching grazing donkeys, ponies, and cows. Taking the train from Brockenhurst back into town if ever I felt too tired to ride.

It had always seemed a beautiful little village, where the animals would often be found wandering the high street, taking a drink in the ford at the far end, oblivious to the comings and goings around them. But from 1917, the horrors I saw at the hospital would always scar my memory of the place.

My job was to cook, then feed those that weren't able feed themselves: wards of men lost in thousand-yard stares, waking comas. Unresponsive, forever staring out into some middle-distance no one else could see. Limbs limp; they did at least chew when I presented them with a forkful of food.

Other unfortunates elsewhere in the hospital were very much caught up in the here and now, howling with pain from beneath swathes of bandages, feeling for limbs that had been lost in some unspeakable scene across the sea. Clawing clumsily at mustard gas burns with blinded eyes, voice boxes reduced to a gravely rattle.

Trying to feed them, overwhelmed as they were with unthinkable pain, was traumatic at the best of times.

Some days the suffering of those poor men became too much, and I would have to take myself away for a few moments, so as they didn't see me cry.

Those days among a sea of writhing, convulsing agony, I yearned for the mundane, and posts tending to wards of broken arms and legs.

And when I was posted to cook at the nearby training camp, feeding those new recruits who had arrived malnourished, it was a relief of sorts. Though I couldn't help but look out at my table of expectant faces as I handed out dinner, knowing that as soon as I had fed them up enough, they would be heading out to the front line and their fate.

If they had only seen what I had seen in the hospital, I wonder if they would have been so eager for their extra rations.

I wondered if I would ever see those faces again, a few months down the line, among the rows of incomplete men across the way. If I did, I knew that they would be considered one of the lucky ones, returning at least with their lives, no matter the state of their bodies and minds.

Walking the wards, watching men relive the horrors they had seen; flinching at long silenced mortar attacks, muffling their ears with their hands at ground-dissolving bomb blasts, curling up into a ball in their beds, pleading for it to stop – it was overwhelming.

It seemed that the war would never end. The horror would never stop. We all yearned for some relief. For some hope.

He was a Lieutenant tasked with overseeing the running of the training camp for new recruits. He was always kind. Would always stop to ask after me. See if there was anything I needed.

His name was John Bunbury, he was twenty-six, and had served on the front line in the Royal Artillery, where he had taken a bullet to the hip and been sent back.

In a world of such cruelty and pain, he was the antidote I had been dreaming of, and we started courting a few months before the end of the war, when I was not quite nineteen.

After Armistice he was transferred to the hospital but would often have to travel to other posts along the south coast for a few weeks at a time, helping the running of other hospitals.

I stayed on, to be with him. He said that we would marry once the hospitals had been successfully run down and the patients discharged. No more than a year or two, he had said.

I fell pregnant just before Christmas in 1922. I couldn't wait to tell him in person, as he was away on assignment elsewhere, so I wrote to him with the news.

He would often not respond. Lost in the job at hand he would always say.

But after a week or so without any news I wrote again. Then telephoned the hospital, who told me that there was, and had never been a Lieutenant John Bunbury stationed with them.

I called all the hospitals that he said he oversaw. None had ever heard of him.

Weeks turned to months.

The war office had just the one record for a Lieutenant John Bunbury, twenty-six, of the Royal Artillery. He had accepted a posting out to India. Not long after my letter to him with our news.

A long post that had seen him take his wife, his two young children with him.

I was confused, numbed, and it took a little time to realise that I had been played for a fool. That he wasn't coming back to me. That I had been a simple, naive little folly away from home.

I had been waiting on him, all that time, to come back and create the perfect life for me. Instead, he had scurried away to India. With his family. It had all been a lie. He had had his fun, and then I had been abandoned, discarded like spent fish and chip papers.

It was the first, and last time in my life that I would rely on a man for anything.

I hid the bump for as long as I could, but when it became obvious the hospital sent me away. So too did my parents, horrified as they were by my 'condition.' I had brought shame to the family, though my only crime, as far as I could see, had been to fall in love with a man who said he loved me.

The last time I ever saw my mum and dad was through tear-stained eyes, watching them stand stony-faced on the doorstep of our home, as they sent me, suitcase in hand out to meet my fate.

They never knew, but my Aunt took me in, less than two miles away. And when young Stanley was born, Aunt Harriet helped me until I could just about help myself.

She had lived alone before Stanley and I and had made her money through stocks and shares on the exchange in London.

She was a fiercely independent woman who had been at the coalface of the Women's Suffrage movement. And though she had been granted the right to vote in 1918 due to her business acumen, her university degree, and being the owner of her own home, she didn't until 1928 when all women were given the right.

In me she didn't see a young girl who had brought shame, but a young, innocent child who had fallen foul of what could be a cruel and unforgiving world. She offered us her home for as long as we both needed, but I was conscious of Stanley's cries interfering with her work, her telephone calls to the exchange.

So, I tallied up all the money to my name, it was not much, and I took a room in a house down on the docks in the Chapel district of Southampton when Stanley was eighteen months old.

It was one of the poorest parts of the town and had suffered greatly with the sinking of the Titanic in 1912, as many of the ship's workers came from there. So many homes were shorn of their breadwinner, falling into destitution. Then the Great War claimed so many more.

And those streets that had survived the slum clearances, huddled together on the banks of the River Itchen and made ends meet.

It may have been poor, and a little rough around the edges, but it was full of more good people than bad, who looked out for one another. Who helped a young woman with a young child, and no more than a month's rent in her purse find work as a cleaner in some of the big houses in town.

I worked six mornings a week, carrying Stanley in a sling on my back as I went. He would sleep, or watch proceedings over my shoulder as I cleaned, never making a peep.

It paid for the rent, for the clothes on Stanley's back, for fresh apples and carrots to make him strong. And where it didn't stretch, I would miss a meal or two, making up for it on a Sunday when we would meet Aunt Harriet in Palmerston Park. I would eat as many sandwiches as she had packed in her picnic basket while she played with Stanley, wandering around all the flower beds in bloom.

When he turned three, Stanley stayed with a neighbour called Alice four afternoons a week while I worked in a small bookshop in South Western House.

It was a grand old building made up of high-end apartments, ornate tea rooms, plush offices, and a hotel that serviced passengers waiting to board the grand ocean liners of the day that moored in the vast deep-water docks across the way.

A train station just for the docks nestled at the foot of South Western House, beneath a vast canopy of iron and glass. The bookshop looked out onto the station, and the owner and I would pause as grand steam engines painted a racing green, a piercing blue, or a vibrant red would pull in with a shrill whistle. Great plumes of smoke billowing up into the rafters and in through the bookshop door. Ladies and gentlemen dressed in their finest stepping down from the carriages behind, weaving between porters lugging trolleys stacked high with rich wooden travel chests and cases.

Once Stanley started attending school, he would meet me at the bookshop after classes, wait patiently for me on a stool in the storeroom, where the owner would always have a comic or the like for him to read.

Mr Waters was an elderly man with a kind face, who would always tread carefully about his aisles of books, and talk in hushed, reverential tones, respectful of the insight and knowledge they contained, the great characters and their adventures crammed into his floor-to-ceiling bookcases.

After work, if it was a nice evening, Stanley and I would walk into the docks and climb up onto a wall, watch the shipping as it came and went. We would imagine where it might be going, and who was on board. What adventures they would have when they got there. The things they would see. He always adored it and would fidget with excitement as he imagined grand tales at sea, faraway lands.

He loved the boats. Far more than the trains that would rumble beneath his feet as he watched them pull into the station. It was always the boats. And with the extra money from the bookshop, I would take him across on the Hythe Ferry to the other side of Southampton Water, watching him slack-jawed as the little ferry charted its path between the huge, overwhelming hulls of the great cargo ships and liners moored dockside.

We would take the little pier train down into Hythe and eat a bun on the seafront, before heading back across the water, watching stevedores in rows of grand cranes loading crates onto those grand ships, unloading others onto towering stacks on the dock. He could have done the journey over and over, away and back, watching everything, if we had the money to spare.

I didn't know what I wanted my life to be. I never had a big plan like some do.

When the Great War came, I felt compelled to enlist in the hospitals, doing something to help.

And when Stanley came along, all I wanted was to make him happy, to bring him up to be everything that his father wasn't. To be a good lad, respectful of others, to be caring and kind.

Fate had found me to be a single mother, living in a single room in Chapel – and there were many derogatory labels that society tarnished me with because of it.

But with Aunt Harriet's help, and the friendship of those in the cramped terraced streets of Chapel, I came to learn that none of it mattered. If Stanley was happy, if I was happy, then everything else could go fish.

I enjoyed my work at the bookshop. I had time for my own thoughts whilst cleaning. And, sat on the docks with Stanley, we imagined the future, and what we would do with it. No matter how unconventional, or unbecoming in some peoples' eyes. Our dreams were our own.

It was Stanley who said it, who planted the seed one day as we sat watching the ships in the dock a little before his seventh birthday.

'Imagine if we had a boat,' he had said and paused, letting the idea sink in.

'It needn't be a large one, just something small. We could start our own ferry service. Take people to see the great ships.

'The Hythe Ferry always goes straight past. What if we took people out, went about them all slowly so as they could get a proper look at them. People would pay for that, don't you think?

'We would take a fare to pay our way, and we would learn all about the engine, about everything, so as we didn't have to rely on anyone else for anything. It would just be us. Our boat. The water.'

It was a great idea I told him, though I kept quiet about how expensive boats were.

And no matter how impossible a dream it felt, sat there on that wall watching the ships coming and going as the dusk fell about us, I wasn't about to limit him in his.

On the walk home we worked out how many pennies we might be able to save every week towards our boat. And every Friday, after all the bills had been paid, and groceries bought, if there were a few pennies left I would hand them over to Stanley.

He had an old wooden box that one of our neighbours had given him, where he would put any treasures that he had found on Weston Shore. Small fragments of rope from broken bow lines of the great ships he revered so. Gnarled and sun-bleached driftwood, pieces of glass, smooth and rounded from countless years being dragged up and back on the tides.

He had etched his initials in the top and kept it on his bedside table, and I would often watch him fall asleep at night while looking at it. Daydreams turning to the real thing, and adventures out to sea on his boat, following cargo ships away to who knew where.

He would carefully place the pennies inside, count them every week. And as the total grew, he would keep me apprised of the total.

'We're getting closer, Mum,' he would always say and smile. I would smile back, so proud of his passion, but heartbroken too. That one day, maybe, with such frugal savings, I would have to watch him see his dream fail.

When he wasn't dreaming about the sea, or our boat, he was dreaming about football. Our neighbours, Alice and Arthur, who took him in on a Saturday while I worked at the bookshop, would take him along to see the Thorneycroft works' team play in the Hampshire League.

Arthur worked in the Thorneycroft shipyard that built many of the great ships that plied up and down Southampton Water, and had once played for Thorneycroft's reserves in the Southampton League. He would always play down his endeavours on the pitch and would make Stanley chuckle by saying that he had been very accomplished at being a very poor player.

The Thorneycroft ground was a basic affair. Rope barriers lined the pitch. But it captivated him completely. He would crawl between the legs of the shipyard workers who often stood two or three-deep on all four sides behind the rope, following Alice and Arthur's kids, Callum and Nell, to the front, were they would sit cross-legged on the touchline and follow the play.

As I turned the corner into our street after my shift at the bookshop, Stanley would be out playing football with the other children. Letting Callum's little sister Nell, who could have been no more than five back then, and who followed Stanley and Callum around like their little shadow and adored them both, tackle him and take the ball for a moment, racing off until one of the lads poached it from her.

Racing around wildly, Stanley pretended to be the Thorneycroft winger Cyril Smith, who had become Stanley's footballing hero with his thundering runs and dribbles down the touchline, that were so close to Stanley that he could feel the rush of air as Cyril roared past just a pace the other side of the white line.

He had jet black hair that he slicked back, and his feints and jinks along the touchline tormenting defenders would prise strands loose, falling across his forehead until there was a pause in play, where Cyril would quickly sweep them back into place with his hand.

He was feared in Hampshire League circles as being one of the very best, and Stanley became transfixed by his pin-point crosses into the box, the trickery in his boots sending defenders the wrong way. His speed down the wing with the ball seemingly stuck to his boot.

He was a humble hero, Cyril Smith, who worked alongside Arthur in the great hangars at the top of Thorneycroft's steep slipways, fitting piping in the bowels of vast ships while the decks above them were being built. Fountains of sparks illuminating their gloomy position way down in the hull.

They worked at it five days a week, plus a half day Saturdays, before Cyril would make a dash for it to get to the game on time.

He was a quiet, but friendly man, who would always stop to chat, and watch the children playing football in the streets about Chapel, no matter how long his shift had been. And every season, in the week leading up to the big match, the children would follow him home, talking excitedly to him about Saturday. Asking what it was like to be a part of it. Cyril, an understated, benign pied piper of footballing dreams, would trail a chattering, animated crowd of boys and girls through Chapel to his door. They would slowly disperse after he had smiled, waved to them, and politely closed his front door.

It was the blue riband event on the streets of Chapel – Thorneycroft's Hampshire League game at The Dell, home of Second Division Southampton FC – and a fixture against Southampton Reserves.

For many on the breadline, it was a rare opportunity to visit the town's cathedral of football, that could sometimes be heard down in Chapel on match days, with a fair wind behind it. The guttural roar of 20,000 souls all at once, rising and falling at opportunities created, and then wasted. The clamour at the ball hitting the net.

It was a working-class game, with working-class admission. But even so, for some, there wasn't enough left for the turnstiles come Saturday. But there would always be enough when Thorneycroft got to play there.

I would wave to Stanley, to Alice and Arthur, Callum and Nell, from the door of the bookshop as they all proudly trudged up into town for the game. I would make sure that Stanley had enough to get in, for a programme, and a toffee apple from the stalls outside. And I would wait for him to excitedly rush into the shop at full time, bombard me with scattergun sentences, condensing ninety minutes of play into a few breathless lines. Of descriptions of main stands as huge as ocean liners. Of steep sweeps of terracing. Of Cyril Smith jinking down the wing beneath the shadow of vast banks of seats.

'One day mum,' he would say 'I'm going to play there. I'm going to play for Thorneycroft, just like Cyril Smith.'

And it was that dream of his that helped set us on our way to fulfilling another.

During the school holidays Stanley would spend some of his days with me, helping me to clean houses in the morning, stack books in the afternoon, reading The Boys' Football Favourite paper in the storeroom. Mr Waters would always be sure to leave that week's paper out for him, and he would devour it, over and over again, reading about the big teams of England and Scotland.

Other days he would spend with Alice and her kids. Arthur had bought them a brand-new leather football, and they would walk along the Itchen, take the floating bridge across to the shipyard, and play football on the works pitch across from the main entrance. They would go until the shift whistle sounded, and the workers poured out of the Thorneycroft gates, where they would meet Arthur and head for home.

It was after a day spent out with Alice and Arthur's kids that he came home breathless, animated, unable to get out his words. He grabbed my hand, started to cry.

'You have to come mum. You have to see.'

Stanley, Callum and Nell would take a rough path across some scrubland, once they had left the floating bridge, up and round the back of the shipyard where an enclosure housed all the scrap that was set to be sent to the scrappers yard.

It was a seldom used short cut round to the football field, and they would take it and play chase among the undergrowth as they went, sometimes scrabbling through the brush to peer through the railings of the yard, see what was going on.

It was a balmy July evening that time he came to find me, all breathless and teary, and he walked me without a word, hand in hand, down to the floating bridge and across. Up over their shortcut, to the railings.

'There,' he said, pointing away to a heap of large, six-foot tall empty spools that once held cabling. Metal offcuts, wooden pallets, rusting barrels, buckled steel panels and iron girders.

'There,' he said, 'can you see?'

Slowly, among it all, she began to materialise. The bow of a boat, a porthole, a stern, the rest obscured by all the scrap piled up against and over her.

'It's perfect,' he said 'that's the one mum. That's our boat.'

Stanley had to stop off at Alice and Arthur's on the way home, to ask Arthur if he knew anything about the boat. He didn't, he said, but he would ask at work the following day.

She had been a private commission, Arthur said over a cup of tea the next evening, a 40-foot leisure cruiser. They would do them from time to time.

Though with this one there had been an accident. When they sent her down the slipway to be tested, she had been steered into a heavy wooden groyne, cutting a great gash along her port side. She took on water that flooded and seized the engine and was not considered financially viable to be repaired, according to the underwriters. If she had been in deeper water, they would have scuttled her and sent her to the bottom, Arthur explained. But she hadn't been. So, she had been winched out and dumped. And she had been sitting there for a year or so, waiting to be sent off to the scrappers.

Him and Cyril had taken a look at her on their lunch break, Arthur said. Other than the gash, which looked worse than it was and could be welded, and the engine, that would need to be stripped and rebuilt, she was sound enough. A lot of the fittings had been cannibalised for other projects. But other than that, he shrugged, there was a boat under all that scrap.

'Do you know how much she would cost Mr Parsons?' Stanley asked. He shook his head. He would ask.

In 1931 £70 was a small fortune. A years' wage for the apprentice shipbuilders of Thorneycroft. More than nine months for skilled workers such as Arthur and Cyril.

Stanley brought the box to the table in our room, and we counted out our savings, Stanley looking on as piles of pennies began to rise up about us.

In three years of saving, we had managed to squirrel away just shy of nine pounds.

'Have we got enough mum?' he asked, looking up at me expectantly.

Not quite, I told him, but that it was a good start. We must keep going, I said, and then we would see. I didn't have the heart to be honest with him.

On afternoons that I wasn't working at the bookshop I would sit at our table, leant over an old ledger that Mr Waters had thrown out. The pages in the last third were unused, and on them I wrote out various financial permutations.

If we took ten passengers at a time out to see the liners, all paying five pence, did that twice a day, seven days a week while the weather was fine. If we took people out day-tripping to Cowes, to Ryde in between, and charged a Shilling a person. If we did it all, taking out the bare minimum for food and rent, it would take us a little under five years to pay back a loan of £70.

Satisfied with my numbers, and the hardships we would need to face to make it work, I wrote the sums out neatly, and carefully tore them out of the ledger.

And in the hour between my cleaning job finishing, and my shift at the bookshop beginning, I arranged appointments at every bank on the High Street.

Stony faced old men in starched shirts and suits listened to my proposal, glanced down at the sums put before them. But they seemed more concerned by my address on the letter of application, my position in society as a single mother, and my vocation as a domestic maid and shelf-stacker.

It was clear they had made their minds up the minute I stepped through the door, regardless of my sound arithmetic, though I continued with my speech, my business plan, right to the very last word, every time.

As I was ushered out onto the street after each appointment, the sound of heavy wooden doors closing behind me, and my eyes would begin to well.

Men of privilege were writing me, writing my son off, because of our 'situation.'

A situation created by the actions of another man of privilege.

A situation that left me proud of the boy that Stanley had become, our lives the richer for the friends I had made in Chapel.

Far richer than these stuffed shirts could ever know.

But sadly, it was these stuffed shirts who controlled the banks, and therefore our ambition, with their pre-prescribed notions of what 'people like us' should be. Should do.

Though I despised it, it was how the world worked. Never mind about all those left behind.

Solid ideas, invention, were not enough for people like me.

I would be sure to mask my anger, my despair when Stanley arrived at the bookshop after school. And we would continue to drop our pennies in the box every week, Stanley looking at me expectantly, me shaking my head. Not yet, I would say, and he would nod. And continue to dream.

I hadn't planned to show any of it to Aunt Harriet. She had already been so generous and kind to us that the thought of bringing Stanley's plan to her never crossed my mind. She had done more than enough for us already.

The papers had fallen out of my bag while we were in the park one Sunday, sat on a bench watching Stanley dribble his football between the flower beds.

'What's this,' she said, picking them up, scanning the title 'a loan proposal?'

It was nothing, I told her.

'It doesn't look like nothing Maisie,' she said 'Please, tell me everything.'

So, I did. How we sat in the docks watching the ships, and Stanley's dream for us. How he came across this £70 boat that was set for the scrappers yard, and my fruitless weeks in the banks on the High Street.

I rattled off the numbers that I had memorised by heart. All the trips, the fares, our five-year plan, how it seemed so cruel now, to have let him dream.

That one day he would have to realise that maybe big dreams weren't for the likes of him.

He was still too young for that, I said. So, I was doing what I could.

Aunt Harriet scanned each line, each figure as I talked, nodded, then looked up at Stanley. She called out, waved him over, and when he came dribbling back to us, she sat him down between us on the bench.

'Stanley,' she said 'tell me about this boat of yours.'

It did not take long for him to persuade Aunt Harriet to take the floating bridge with us, to see it for herself. Though I protested as Stanley led her through the scrub of the short cut in her Sunday best. The sound of fine fabrics grazing against clawing thorns made me beg them to come back.

'Don't be silly, Maisie, this is fun. We are on an adventure, to hell with the dress. Come on now, keep up!'

By the time I had reached them, Stanley was busy pointing out the boat to Aunt Harriet, having helped her clamber through to the shipyard's railings. He explained where the gash in the hull was, how Arthur said it could be repaired, and he should know as he worked on the ships.

He pointed to the portholes and said how Arthur and the footballer Cyril Smith had said there was a fine cabin behind them. That the engine could be rebuilt, and second-hand parts could be found in the yards up and down the Itchen. That they said she was sound and could be a fine boat. It would just take a little time and hard work.

She looked down at him as he peered through the railings of the yard, before following his gaze, placing a hand on his shoulder.

'Well,' she said to Stanley 'what a day young man. My first trip across the floating bridge, and I haven't explored among the brambles since I was a little girl. You have made me into quite the explorer. Though I think it must be time for tea and a slice of cake. What say you, Master Buchanan?'

He smiled, took her hand, and led her away.

A few days later, while ensconced in unpacking a delivery of new books at the bookshop, the doorbell chimed, and I turned to find Aunt Harriet stood before me. She smiled, hugged me as we always did, then she stepped back.

'Right then, down to business,' she said, handing me back the papers I had dropped at the park 'I have had a good examination of this, and I accept your proposal.'

I looked at her blankly. Not entirely sure what was happening.

She took out an envelope from her bag and handed it to me.

'Our agreement, written up by my solicitor,' she said 'and your £70 for the boat. Though I reserve the right, as your Aunt, to waive any interest on this loan.'

I stood blinking, unable to quite absorb what she was saying.

'You have asked nothing of me Maisie. When you very well could have. You have stood up on your own two feet, and you have brought up a lovely little boy along the way. You have worked every hour you can. You have sacrificed more than any young girl should ever need to. And I am so very proud of you. And this,' she said, nodding at my handwritten pages 'is a solid bet. So, I would like to be your investor.

'I would have been happy just to give you the money Maisie, but I know you like to pay your own way,' she said 'So, here we are.'

'With the right address, the right name, any bank should have taken you on. That they didn't is wrong and says more about their failings as human beings than anything else. So, I have righted that wrong. I am a businesswoman too. It is my prerogative.'

She smiled, nodded at Mr Waters when he came out from the storeroom.

'You are busy I can see. And I shouldn't take up any more of your time. We shall talk on Sunday,' she shook my hand, kissed me on the cheek.

'Until then,' and she turned, stepped back out onto the platform, wandered away as the shrill whistle of the train in the station sounded. Carriages shuddered. The rhythmic chugging of the engines sending great clouds of smoke up into the rafters as it slowly pulled out and away, smothering the platform, Aunt Harriet.

That evening I slipped the money into Stanley's box while he was out playing in the street, and after dinner I asked him to bring it to the table, to see how we were getting on with our savings. As always, he sat expectantly in his chair, watching me folding out our notes, piling up the coins, laying it all out across the table. He leant in as I totalled it up, wrote the figure down on a slip of paper, slid it across the table to him.

He read it, then again, his eyes widening as he absorbed the grand total of £80, 12 shillings and 6 pence.

'Have we done it? Have we really done it, Mum?' he said, leaping up to hug me when I said that we had.

We were going to buy his boat.

After my cleaning duties the following morning I walked to the Thorneycroft gates, asked to speak to the manager, and was ushered between a labyrinth of workshops, boat houses, and grand construction hangars to his office. I waited for a time until he could be found, then sat in a large leather chair across from him as he settled in behind his desk.

I slid the £70 across to him, that it was for the boat in the scrap heap, then offered another £2 for the hire of some welding gear to make her watertight. If he could see to her remaining in the yard while the work was carried out, I would be grateful, I told him.

He looked at me for a time, the envelope of money, and raised his eyebrows, leaning back in his chair. Then after what felt like an age, he nodded.

He said that she would be cleared of debris, and I could have my welding gear, a spot in the yard for two months, not a day longer. If she wasn't seaworthy by then, he said, and shrugged. Leaving our fate to hang in the air.

We shook hands on the promise that she would be ready for us on Saturday, and when the day came, Stanley and I, Alice, Callum and Nell arrived at the gates, and were shown how we were to access the yard.

The security guard left us standing in silence, as we took in our first look of her free from scrap, Stanley squeezing my hand tightly. She was beautiful, sleek, even in her damaged and incomplete state. The sweep of the hull made you want to touch it with your hand. Neat lines of rivets beneath your fingertips. The rich red gloss still fresh enough to give off that new paint smell.

She was due to have had an iron frame erected over the wheelhouse and deck, and a canvas cover to protect both from the elements. But with the accident the plan was scrapped, leaving just the fixtures. Though Arthur was adamant that a simple wooden frame could be made, at a fraction of the cost, that would do just as good a job.

While the children clambered up onto the deck, down into the cabin below the wheelhouse, Alice and I inspected the jagged gash in the port side, smiled as Arthur approached to arrange a first lesson in welding for the following morning. He had stowed some scraps for practising, and some that would cover the damage to the hull on the bow.

And on his only day off of the week, he went back to work and spent hours showing me how to create neat welds, binding one piece of steel to another, using the heat of the torch to dissolve one into the other. So as, when done well, you could barely see the join.

He showed Stanley how to stand, how to safely hold the steel in position while the welding took place. He did it all selflessly, patiently, despite the ribbing he got from work colleagues who thought the shipyard was no place for a woman.

Thankfully for us, he didn't agree, because it had to be Stanley and me that made her right again.

It had been just me and him, after all, for so long. And it was his dream. He found her. It had to be us who made it real. Confounding expectations. Proving to him that anyone could do anything, so long as they had the heart to see it through.

It wasn't easy. We heard the comments as we worked every hour we could. Cat calls and wolf whistles, coarse abuse and innuendo from the windows of workshops.

We said nothing, drowned it out with the roar of the welding torch, concentrating on the task.

We both collapsed into our beds every night, exhausted. The hours of toil on top of cleaning, schoolwork, and shifts at the bookshop made every muscle ache.

Soldiering on through rainstorms, missed meals, cold winds that set Stanley's teeth chattering, we must have looked a sight to any passers-by.

While it was far from a professional finish, the patches were strong and neat. The product of a good teacher, the willpower of a young boy in holding them in place with buckling arms, and the soothing effect of seeing the joins dissolving away. We had no money to paint them the same colour as the rest of the hull, but Stanley liked their patchwork pattern along the waterline, so we left them be.

Instead, we spent our money in the scrappers' yards along the Itchen on second-hand rudder fins, a reconditioned propeller, and coils of old mooring rope so as she could be steered and fastened in the water, even without a functioning motor.

And when the day came for her to be sent down the slipway into the water, as she was towed around to a mooring by Chapel, Stanley stood on the bow and waved and howled at all the windows in the workshops, at the shadowy faces framed within. Silenced.

We had done it, with two weeks to spare.

On Saturday mornings while I got ready for my shift at the bookshop, Arthur and Stanley would walk the scrapyards, coming up with parts for the engine – Stanley carefully counting out the money from our dwindling savings from his pocket.

Sunday mornings they would disappear down into the engine room for hours, fixing their new parts in place, writing a list of new targets for their next expedition while I tended to matters in the cabin or on deck. Fixing benches, cupboards, varnishing the wooden decking.

Of everything about our boat, it was the engine that was the most alien to me. I had never seen one up close. Had no idea how it worked, let alone how to strip it down and build back up. Stanley, on the other hand, had a natural aptitude for learning what went where, and what it did when in place.

He absorbed everything Arthur showed him like a sponge and would sit with me down in the engine room and go through each and every piece, explaining what it did, why it did it, and what would happen if it didn't. And between us, we took on Arthur's knowledge from a lifetime of toil in the Thorneycroft hangars, until we knew the boat, every cog and piston, as well as we could.

It was on a Sunday morning of polishing and fixing that Alice presented me with a set of cushions for the benches out on deck, made from felt pad off cuts from a local factory, and covered with a pair of old flowery curtains that had been thrown out at one of the houses she cleaned.

'Well, you'll want your customers to be comfortable on your trips, won't you,' she said as we slipped them on. They were perfect, and I told her so. She shrugged.

'It's just my little bit to help out. It is such a wonderful thing, all this. And the children love it so. They are always down here looking at it. They love seeing it come to life, piece by piece. A little bit of magic. Right here in Chapel.'

It took more than a year for her to come together. For the engine to be rebuilt, buying parts as and when we had saved enough for each one. For a wooden frame to be constructed out of the cheapest timber at the timber yard. Stanley and I were so careful as we marked out and cut the wood to size, carved out joints so as they fitted together, knowing that any error would take a month's worth of saved pennies to replace.

With the very last of the money from Stanley's box, we bought a selection of old, fraying, and faded grey canvas sails. And with Alice's tuition we set about measuring up and cutting to size the material, sewing it together on her little manual sewing machine, until a patchwork canopy for the wooden frame appeared. It stretched snugly over it, with flaps that could roll down in bad weather to protect the deck. And with that, she was done.

One fine afternoon while Stanley was at school, I bought a can of paint and, dangling over the stern on a swing made of a plank of wood suspended from two lengths of old rope, I carefully painted the boats name:

> 'Stanley B
> Southampton'

When he came home from school, I showed him, handed him the official papers that the Stanley B, home port of Southampton, was a licensed passenger ferry permitted to carry 15 persons.

It was his dream. He had found her, I explained. It seemed only right that she should be named after the boy who had saved her – Master Stanley Buchanan.

He beamed. Hugged me, and that evening we sat and ate fish and chips on the deck, before sleeping in the cabin. He put the papers in his box, stowed it behind the table in the cabin. And there it stayed.

We had to save for another month or so to afford a full tank of fuel. But on the few cans that we had bought to check that the engine ran, and everything worked, I practised manoeuvres on my afternoons off, along the Itchen.

I learnt how to edge her to dock, how to swing her out again. And by the time we had a full tank on board, I felt confident enough in both me and her.

On her proper maiden voyage, on the evening of the July 15, 1932, we invited Alice, Arthur and the kids, Aunt Harriet, and Mr Waters from the bookshop to join us.

Aunt Harriet brought a bottle of champagne, and she and Stanley smashed it against the bow for good luck before we set off out into Southampton water.

It felt both a dream – Stanley's vision come to life – but also a great vindication of hard work, perseverance, and belief.

It was a fairy tale, but one born out of minute detail and intricate planning, bruised hands and countless hours of back-breaking endeavour, tending to every inch, every fixture and moving part of Stanley's boat. It was a dream, but a dream founded in a stubborn, oily, wearying reality. And it felt all the better for it.

As dusk fell, we glided out into the still waters of the deep channel, past moored cargo ships being loaded and unloaded. Great crates of fruit and sugar from the Caribbean, containers holding motor cars from Europe, and all manner of other produce spinning gently as cranes laboured to bring them to shore. Stevedores gesturing up into the darkness, directing crane operators high up in their cabins, lost among the night sky as they stacked each ship's cargo dockside.

In the deep-water docks, the grand old ocean liners Mauretania and Olympic towered above the Stanley B.

We idled and drifted beneath their vast bulk, a tiny speck among great walls of steel. Ribbons of twinkling lights from the tops of their chimneys cascaded down to the bow and stern and shimmered on the water. Rows of cabins, all lit up, the odd silhouette of a soul taking the air. Too excited to settle, the prospect of a grand trans-Atlantic voyage and the Americas beyond, the odd one waved back to Stanley who sat cross legged up on the bow with Callum and Nell.

Beyond, the lights of Southampton rose up and away from the dock. Great warehouses, lines of grand townhouses, church spires and slanted rooftops all created a haphazard skyline that dissolved away in the darkness as we turned down Southampton Water, watching the thick canopy of trees on the western shore.

Down to Fawley Creek, Calshot Castle, we idled at the breakwater of the Solent and looked across to the lights of Cowes on the Isle of Wight, a cargo ship threading its way out into open water and to who knew where.

It took just the one trip for everyone to get Stanley's vision, and once we had a timetable printed up, Aunt Harriet handed them around her friends and colleagues.

Mr Waters displayed a poster in the bookshop window, and a pile of timetables by the register. Alice and Stanley took them to every point where passengers disembarked from ocean liners. To every bus and railway station, tearoom, chip shop and newsagent.

It worked right away. Every trip had at least half a dozen eager passengers waiting for us at the pontoon at Town Quay, next to the Isle of Wight ferry. More for the evening trips. Seven days a week.

Alice would accompany me on the morning trip, taking the money and throwing the lines while Stanley was at school, and he would take over for the afternoons and evenings.

And as business picked up, I taught Alice how to handle her, and she and Stanley would take her out while I was working at the bookshop.

We were able to increase our repayments to Aunt Harriet, as well as pay Alice, Stanley, and me a wage. And when business tailed off during the winter, we still had the shifts at the bookshop to keep us going.

We had become the masters of our own fate. We had believed in our dream. Ignored all those who thought it unbecoming of an unwed mother and a fatherless child to be welding, fixing engines, skippering boats.

It was a healthy living. No fortunes were made. But we never went hungry again. We never had to scratch about for rent. And Stanley and I moved into a little house of our own, a few doors down from our little room.

We had enough for fuel, for any repairs, and to pay Aunt Harriet back ahead of time. We had enough to buy Stanley his first pair of football boots. We had enough to pay Alice a wage that helped them take Callum and Nell on their first ever holiday and a week in Weymouth.

Callum started to work on the Stanley B on Saturdays and Sundays, earning his own money for the first time. And with that experience he went on to work in the merchant navy when he came of age, as did Stanley.

We lived a life in the fresh, briny air of Southampton water, beneath the shadows of the great ships of the Atlantic and beyond. We lived a life of squalls and rainbows, coasting gulls, shimmering breakwaters, waving to the skippers of the Hythe and Isle of Wight ferries. Stevedores on a break sat dockside, lost in their thoughts, legs dangling over the side, cigarette smoke trailing up into the sky. Deer on the western shore, watching us suspiciously before dissolving into the thickset trees.

Summer nights on the bow, looking up at the stars. Winter days in the cabin, keeping warm by the stove.

And all the while, as we took people out to see the sights, we would imagine where all the great ships were bound for, and what they would see when they got there, just like we did when Stanley was a little boy, sat on our wall in the docks.

We lived a life that was all our own. All because of one little boy's vision, among the brambles, pressed up against the railings at Thorneycroft.

And so it went, for seven years, until September 1939.

When war came nothing changed immediately. But it would. And our idyllic lives would be over.

Eighteen

When Stanley turned twelve in 1935, he had been going with Arthur to watch Thorneycroft play in the Hampshire League for close to five years. Five years of Cyril Smith tearing down the wings. Five years of walking up to The Dell to see them play Southampton reserves. Five years of looking up in awe at the grandstands and steep terraces. Of promising to play there one day, just like Cyril.

The summer of 1935 saw Stanley add football training with Thorneycroft juniors to his busy diary of shifts on the Stanley B, and playing football with his friends in the streets and parks.

After every session, he would polish the boots we'd bought him, leaving them as new by the front door, ready for the next time. He adored it, and took to it just as he had working on the Stanley B.

He absorbed tactics and training methods like he did the fixtures and pistons of the engine he helped overhaul. He practised over and over with the dedication that had seen him devour all the nautical books in Mr Waters' bookshop.

On Sunday afternoon trips he would tell Aunt Harriet, who would always join us, all about training, about the latest match he had seen.

Trip done, we would sit over a coffee in the cabin and watch him hunched over a football paper, devouring every word. And when he was old enough, Stanley started playing for the Thorneycroft juniors on a Saturday morning, after which we would rush down to the Stanley B and cast off for the first trip of the day.

Stanley would often take the money still dressed in his Thorneycroft kit and with muddy knees, only changing down in the cabin once we were safely out and away.

He was a blur of enthusiasm and smiles, Arthur would always say, out on the pitch. He was not the most talented player, but he was the cleverest. He knew how to anticipate the opposition play, how to find the right pass at the right time, when to tackle and when to jockey an opponent. He made a solid centre back for the team, where he could see the whole game in front of him, setting up attacks by breaking down the opposition, neat passes finding the more talented players on the team.

He loved the game, and I would always be sure to have cover for him so as he could take in the Thorneycroft Hampshire League match in the afternoon, if they were playing at home.

I had never been exposed to football before. I had no idea about it, or what it meant. Why people became so obsessed with it. And I imagine I never would have, if it hadn't been for Stanley, and my first trip to the Dell the Christmas of 1935.

We had had a good year. We had introduced extra day trips over to Cowes and Ryde, which had gone down very well. It was a joy to see Stanley playing on the sandy beaches, among the breakers at Ryde while our guests went on a walking tour. We would sit on the seafront at Cowes and eat fish and chips while they went up to the stately Osbourne House, royal retreat of Queen Victoria.

Sometimes we would walk up to Westwood Park above the town so as Stanley could take a peek at the home of Cowes Sports football club, and its beautiful wooden stand painted blue and white.

He would always tell me, like he had never told me before, that Cyril Smith once told him that Westwood Park was the best ground he had ever played in, if you took The Dell out of the equation.

'It does look a fine place to play, doesn't it, mum?' he would always say. And I would always nod in agreement. It did have a spectacular view over the Solent, that shimmered on a sunny day like glass. Though I didn't think that was what Stanley was seeing, his eyes lingering on the stand, the plush grass, the barriers about it. Though I would finally see what he was seeing that Christmas, and a Boxing Day match at The Dell.

It was a surprise, a thank you to Alice and Arthur, to Stanley and Callum, for all their hard work on the Stanley B: tickets to the big game against West Ham.

We had already spent Christmas Day watching Thorneycroft play Totton, their Hampshire League rivals from across Southampton Water, the cold, sharp winter air eased by Arthur's hipflask of whisky.

The shipyard had arranged for vats of mulled wine for everyone, and at the final whistle both sets of players and supporters milled about them, toasting everyone's health – Stanley and the other children looking up starry-eyed at the men still in their kits, caked in mud. Men who had turned a sodden field into a captivating spectacle – though I didn't understand much of what had been going on.

But I felt the excitement, the expectation as the play swept up and down from one goal to the other. The blood and thunder, the rise and fall of the spectators three or four deep at the rope barrier, craning to get a better view between flat caps and head scarves. Mixed with the whisky and then mulled wine, it had been a heady experience and it had me looking forward to our walk up to The Dell the following day.

The roads became clogged with supporters the closer we got, funnelling into the narrow, terraced streets surrounding The Dell. The sounds of a brass band parading up and down the pitch drifted out over the stands and onto Milton Road. The chatter of hundreds of different conversations milling about outside, the rich smell of tobacco, rattles firing off scattergun salvos in the hands of children, the clatter of the turnstiles, the thunder of boots on wooden stairs up into the bowels of the stands and seats by the half-way line. The pitch a brilliant green, the vivid strips of red and white and claret and blue as the teams ran out drawing the eye in.

The roar of the crowd at a goal, as the play surged forward and back; it was as thrilling as it was overwhelming to someone who had never been exposed to it before. And it didn't seem to matter that Southampton had been beaten by four goals to two. The occasion, of football on Boxing Day, seemed more important than the outcome. The act of coming together at such a time more sacred than any two points for the league table. Memories of the moment, not the game lingering on.

And at the final whistle, as dusk gathered, snow began to tumble from the heavy skies, The Dell fading from view as the flurry grew heavier, while the crowds dissolved away into the streets about it, Stanley pointing at names in his programme who had enthralled. Their endeavour mimicked in a kickabout with Callum and Nell in the street as soon as we got home. Their figures drifting and fading in the tumbling snow, the dark. Excitable shouts and calls muffled as Alice, Arthur and I huddled in their doorway, and toasted their health. The end of a lovely Boxing Day.

It had been more than enough of an experience to make it an annual event, inviting Mr Waters and Aunt Harriet along as well – the friends of the Stanley B taking the best seats in the house every Boxing Day fixture. Coming together to relax, celebrate achievements and friendships, and enjoy each-other's company.

Though we would go more often than that, Stanley and I, in the years that followed.

In the cold winter months, the Stanley B would run a reduced service. And even then, there would be occasions where there were no passengers waiting for us at the pontoon on Town Quay.

The bitter winds off the Solent, relentless slanting rain dappling the water, drumming on the canopy above the deck and falling like sheets into the dock dissuading all but the hardiest of sightseers.

If that happened on a Saturday, and Thorneycroft were playing away, we would tie her back up at her berth on the Chapel dock and head up to The Dell, rounding up Callum and Nell on the way.

We would stand on the Milton Road terrace, Callum, Nell and Stanley elbowing their way to the front, stationing themselves behind the goal, while I would stand toward the back, where I could watch the animation of the crowd, and keep an eye on the children as well as the play.

I saw the looks, but I didn't care. It was not the norm for single women to stand among the hurly burly of the terraces, and people would look across at me with confusion, suspicion.

But I liked the terraces. I liked the bustle. I liked seeing the action in the goalmouth up close.

And after an unwed mother, a welder, a grease-stained tender to an engine room, a skipper of a boat, what did it matter if terrace dweller was added to my list of unbecoming behaviour for a woman.

With every look I would smile and think of all the things Stanley and I wouldn't have done if we had succumbed to what was seen as 'proper' behaviour for people like us.

At every Southampton goal Stanley would push his way through the crowd back up to me, and wide-eyed he would hug me, before proclaiming 'what a goal,' even if it had been a scuffed shot.

Then he would bundle his way back down to the front.

It would be the same ritual if we were up at Thorneycroft, wriggling between legs to give me a hug before making his way back to the rope barrier in anticipation of the next goal.

No matter if he was at The Dell, or at the park next to the shipyard, he would talk of Cyril Smith and his fellow Hampshire League players with the same reverence he bestowed on Sillet, Hill, Briggs, and Osman of that Division Two Southampton team. Excitedly recounting their exploits to me with equal passion.

To him it was the endeavour, not the setting, that made the man. Anyone that could make the game sing became a hero of his, no matter where they did it. Autographs captured were treasured, no matter whether they belonged to International players, or Shipwrights.

For me it was the electricity of the atmosphere, the charged emotion of caring so much that you would howl up into the skies at a missed shot. It was thousands becoming one swaying mass, all willing their team on – anguish, frustration, joy all writ large across this sea of faces.

It was the almost telepathic connection between players, who found each other with the ball somehow on just a fraction of a glance. How attack became desperate defence in a heartbeat.

It was an intoxicating drama. A drama that Stanley wanted to be a part of, and he would daydream on our way home, that it would be him one day out on that pitch.

Though neither of us could have predicted how it would eventually come about.

In the lead up to the 1938/39 season Stanley was elevated into the Thorneycroft 'A' team, who played in the Southampton Junior leagues against men, even though he had just turned fifteen.

Being the Thorneycroft third eleven, they rarely got the chance to play on the main works ground that had captivated Stanley from such a young age. Instead, they played out on the practice pitch in the park in Woolston, overlooking Southampton Water.

With the firsts and reserves alternating playing at home every week, precious few spectators made it down to see the thirds, with most preferring the senior football on offer over a junior division four match. But I would always go when the work allowed, and anyone else alongside me on the touchline would think that it was the most important game in the country, given the concentration and work rate of their little centre back, a young Stanley Buchanan.

Despite their lowly status, Stanley took great pride in joining the ranks of Saturday afternoon football, where the biggest teams in the land would kick off at the same time as Stanley's team.

Arsenal's, Newcastle's, Manchester United's results displayed on a Saturday night in the local sports paper, the Football Echo, along with Stanley's team, though the Thorneycroft thirds would be right down among the small print.

He had become a part of the grand ritual. From the baying crowds of The Dell to the packed touchlines watching Cyril Smith, his little muddy, out of the way pitch down by the water was a part of this grand spectacle – the pride he felt, the result of his match in the sports paper proved it.

He adored getting back to the Thorneycroft clubhouse after a match, mingling with the firsts and reserves as a player of the Thorneycroft club, rather than a starry-eyed tyke from the touchline.

Men with pints would ask after the score of his game, how he got on, buy him a cola that he drank at the end of the bar, watching it all wide-eyed.

He would stop off at a Newsagents on his way home to pick up the Football Echo, and pore over it after tea, tracing his finger along the other results from the Southampton Junior Division Four. He would then flick to the pages of tables and see how they had affected the standings.

Thorneycroft 'A' were nothing more than a lower mid-table side, made up of eager youngsters and ageing players not yet ready to hang up their boots. But they were players, all the same, in this glorious spectacle that captivated the nation every Saturday afternoon.

And whenever Stanley's game got a brief write-up in the paper, he would read the line or so of text out to me with a big grin, before heading out to the Stanley B to cut and paste the results, tables, and occasional report into a little notebook stashed in his box.

He had neatly written 'Thorneycroft 'A' – season 1938/39 – Southampton Junior Division Four' on the cover and would write the date of each match above each collection of glued cuttings.

And while every other copy of the Echo would become wrappers for fish and chips, or liners for kitchen bins – the results and standings of lowly junior leagues forever lost to time – Stanley would collect these games played, cherish every moment and memory, and often flick through his little book during an absent moment out on Southampton Water. Proud at the part he had played for Thorneycroft, on a muddy little pitch down by the water.

He started the 39/40 season with the thirds, buying a new little notebook to capture the campaign, though it only lasted three matches before it ground to a halt with the outbreak of the war.

When football restarted a month or so later, life looked very different.

Men were called up to fight in vast numbers, decimating the footballing landscape. The junior leagues were scrapped, though the Hampshire and Southampton Senior Leagues carried on, to keep a semblance of normality, and bring a welcome distraction from the looming dread building with every report from mainland Europe.

At only sixteen, Stanley was too young to be conscripted, but he was trusted and respected enough to step up into the reserve team for a few months, until it was disbanded, while he helped me on the Stanley B carry out her last few months as a sightseeing vessel.

As the war effort intensified, there weren't enough men free from long shifts building warships to run a second team, and when it was mothballed

Stanley was thrust into the last remaining pool of players sustaining a side in the Hampshire War League.

He would play as often as he was needed, as often as he could, when we weren't too busy with our own personal war effort.

The Stanley B had gone from ferrying people on sightseeing trips to being conscripted into ferrying parts to and from the Thorneycroft shipyard, that had turned all its efforts to producing war ships for the Atlantic fleet and beyond.

As well as daily trips to the slipways and docks of Thorneycroft, we were charged with carrying propeller and engine parts further up the river to the secretive Supermarine factory building Spitfires that would patrol the skies, chase down ever-growing, strafing sorties from the Luftwaffe.

We were a small cog, helping to keep the wheels of industry turning, that built the warships and fighter planes that would try and protect us.

It was proud work, tiring work, that never stopped. So, neither did we.

But every game Stanley did manage to play, in between long shifts on the water, would be chronicled in his little book.

Newspaper cuttings of Hampshire League matches bordered worrying articles from the front line.

We were taking heavy losses and were losing ground. Countries were being lost, and notices of repatriation ships taking Americans back home and out of harm's way began to appear. Leaving behind what looked like a country soon to meet a similar fate.

But even among the creeping dread of a nation watching the merciless Nazi machine roll ever closer, Stanley needed to record each game played. A simple act of normality from a world that was quickly falling away beneath him. A stubbornness, that life wouldn't be so easily rubbed out and lost.

On Saturdays we go to the football, and then afterwards, we read about it in the paper, and no war will stop us.

So, Stanley played, collected the peppy match reports lined with adverts for coming attractions at the cinema, theatre productions, church sales, and pasted them in his book. An open act of stubbornness. Keeping life going. A little document of defiance.

'One day these might come to mean something,' he would always say. 'How we never gave up on all those things that matter to us.'

Every fixture, every page in his books became a celebration of sorts.

Every game played was a distraction for Stanley, as well as those watching. It enabled him to be that little boy for a short time, a boy full of dreams, a ninety-minute respite before reality came clawing back.

A reality that saw the last Thorneycroft team fold in January 1940, finally unable to spare eleven men every Saturday, who were desperately needed in the workshops and on the scaffolds round the clock.

Stanley missed it terribly and would look at the surviving results in the paper on a Saturday night with a quiet longing. Missing the escape that it brought, the sense of the everyday, and a time before conflict.

Thankfully, the war would not take football from him for too long. And when it returned to his life, it helped him fulfil another of his grand dreams.

In order to keep the Stanley B fulfilling the demand for parts along the Itchen, we took shifts to keep her running long into the night.

Stanley learned to skipper her, and he would take young Callum out into the docks until the early hours, when Alice and I would take over.

With the blackout in effect to prevent targets from bombing raids, he had to run with no lights. Weaving across the docks carefully, dropping off nuts and bolts, landing gear and nose cones, windows for cockpits that would face down the Luftwaffe over the Sussex coast and the white cliffs of Dover. All manner of fixtures and fittings for the ships that would careen down Thorneycroft's slipways and out into the bloody cauldron of the Atlantic.

It was on one of his late night runs that fate had him bump into his hero, Cyril Smith, while offloading a consignment of parts. Though nearer forty than thirty, Cyril was still a fearsome player, even if his runs down the wing had slowed a little over time.

He had always taken an interest in Stanley and his boat. He used to pop over to see us from time to time while we worked on the welding all those years ago. He would bring tea and squash, and stop for a while to chat, Stanley always star-struck into silence at a local footballing legend taking an interest in us.

He had been the first player to congratulate Stanley on his debut game for the third team, seeking him out in the clubhouse afterwards. He had encouraged Stanley during training sessions, as he was bumped and jostled off the ball by seasoned Hampshire League players almost twice his age.

And like many of the skilled workers in the shipyard, he was spared the frontline to help manufacture the vast war machine that was needed.

He had also been given special dispensation to turn out for Southampton on a Saturday in the hastily arranged War League, playing against the grand old names of professional football.

With fuel rationed, and unnecessary travel prohibited, Cyril's experience stretched no further than Cardiff City to the west, Brighton and Hove Albion to the east, and Watford to the north – endeavouring to fill the gap left by the many professional footballers sent off to war.

With the smattering of professionals left behind, and promising young talent not yet of conscription age, respected amateurs such as Cyril stepped up to provide some semblance of normality on a Saturday afternoon with War League South derbies against local rivals Portsmouth and Bournemouth.

After the war, their endeavours would be forgotten, not considered worthy enough to be included in the histories of clubs up and down the country. The supposed drop in playing standards, and the competitions haphazard nature made results and appearances unworthy of recording by many historians.

But for those people like Stanley and me, who took so much pleasure from an afternoon at The Dell, and who took great comfort from losing themselves in a simple game of football – even when the horrors from across the Channel drew closer – players such as Cyril and the teams they populated were a godsend. They helped us spectators breathe beneath the suffocating fear of what might be to come. Enjoying the familiar, comforting surroundings of a terrace, a grandstand, programme in hand.

They were cherished by us just as the pre-war favourites of Osman, Bates, and Briggs were. Their play and endeavour as welcome, as captivating. Carrying on bravely beneath air raids and the threat of falling bombs.

And for that, for playing on during such a dire time, in the face of invasion, and the loss of everything we knew, those wartime teams and players deserved better. So much better.

Cyril had heard that Stanley had played a few games for the cobbled together and now mothballed Thorneycroft Hampshire League team, and when their paths crossed, he asked Stanley if he still had his boots.

A few days later a letter came on headed Southampton Football Club paper, the club badge embossed in the top corner, requesting Stanley come to training on Wednesday evening by recommendation of 'Mr. C Smith.'

Alice and Callum covered for us, and I went with Stanley up to The Dell and we rang the bell, then waited patiently at the players' entrance, Stanley with his letter in his hand.

We were ushered in; Stanley directed away to the changing rooms, while I was shown through to the benches on the lower tier of the West Stand and was fetched a cup of tea by the doorman. And for a time, I was the only soul sat about that beautiful old ground; the stands and terraces, still, save for a couple of starlings flitting from seat back to seat back.

Sitting there, I couldn't help but remember those afternoons spent with Stanley across the way on the terraces. Afternoons from a simpler, safer time, where missed shots and bad refereeing decisions were all we had to worry about. Faces raised to the skies in anguish watching nothing but scudding cloud, rather than the sea of barrage balloons drifting on their tethers as Stanley and the Southampton team ran out onto the pitch.

He stood for a moment, dwarfed by the over-size kit hastily arranged for him, looking up at the stands towering over the pitch, before getting into line to start some drills.

He had a grin from ear to ear as he began, looking across to me and waving every now and then. He had done it: he was out on that Dell pitch, training with the Saints, and with Cyril Smith no less.

All the troubles and issues in getting games on. In cobbling a competitive squad together. In crawling slowly home from away matches beneath a blackout and air raid sirens. I got why they went to all that effort while I watched Stanley.

For the shortest while, transfixed as he smiled and dribbled and passed and tackled, the war faded away. And all there was left was a simple practice match, lurching from goal to goal. Shouts and cheers echoing about the rafters, the heavy thud of ball on boot, the satisfying ripple as a ball hit the net. And a young boy's dream coming true.

It was no more than a distraction. But it was very welcome and lasted all the way home as Stanley explained what the dressing rooms were like, the corridors beneath the stand, how he had been tasked with marking Ted Bates – one of the few professionals left in the side – who had played at some of the finest stadiums in the land in a Saints shirt before the outbreak of war.

It hadn't mattered that there wasn't a crowd there to see him out on the pitch, he said, just as long as I had been there to see it, that would do him.

But there was a crowd there, albeit a small one, the next time he stepped out at The Dell.

The letter came a few weeks later, on a Thursday, informing him that he had been selected for the reserve team that Saturday, and to report to The Dell at twelve noon.

I saw him off, then walked up a little before kick-off, passing through the turnstiles and taking my spot on the Milton Road terrace.

With the paper shortage the programme was a simple sheet of paper folded in half. The cover blue for some reason, even though Saints played in red and white, with an advert for a factory on the cover.

Beneath it was printed the date — April 17,1940 — and Southampton's Hampshire League opponents: Air Service Training Hamble.

And there he was inside — No. 5, Buchanan, in the team line-ups.

There were no more than a hundred people milling about the terrace, the same again sat up in the stand, all of whom gave a smattering of applause as he ran out in that oversized Southampton kit. Sleeves turned up to his elbows, folds of material stuffed into his shorts.

Despite standing wide-eyed before kick-off at the scene, he buckled down to the task at hand on the referee's whistle, and more than held his own.

His younger self stood down behind the goal would have been impressed, and as proud as his mother, who quietly wiped away the odd tear at Stanley realising another of his dreams. Even though the world about him was falling apart.

They won five — two, and neither of the goals against were down to Stanley. The match went by in a flash. And it seemed that no sooner had he trotted out, he was smiling and waving to me, and heading back in at the final whistle.

We celebrated with fish and chips on the walk home, before he jumped straight on the Stanley B and set off out into the darkness and another night's work with Callum.

And in the morning, as we sat and had a cup of tea before I took over, he smiled as he found my programme from the game tucked inside his notebook; carefully folding it to fit snugly alongside the match report from the paper. A report that had him down as a Southampton FC player.

It hadn't been for Thorneycroft in the end, his Dell debut. It had been bigger than even he had ever dreamed. He had played for Southampton.

And as if he didn't quite believe it, I often caught him staring down into his notebook in the cabin. Gently folding out the programme, tracing his finger across his name, the club badge, before carefully packing it all away again in his box.

He would play for Southampton again in their patchwork wartime sides, after receiving another letter requesting Stanley attend pre-season training in June. But not before the horrors of the war became all too real to us both.

The news had been bad. Day after day. Articles in the paper detailed enemy forces sweeping through Holland, Belgium and France, pushing back the British army and its allies until they were cornered in Dunkirk, with the sea at their backs and elite Panzer divisions bearing down on them.

The Luftwaffe bombed them mercilessly, while the last of the French Army tried to delay their seemingly inevitable obliteration at the siege of Lille. Forty Thousand men putting their lives on the line to save so many more.

The battered allied forces fought desperately in the Battle of Dunkirk to delay their fate, while we waited anxiously for news on the other side of the Channel. Waited for the fall of Dunkirk, and a Nazi tide to swiftly break on our shores.

When it came, the request for help, we jumped at the chance to try and do something, anything, though we didn't know what help we could offer.

An officer appeared dockside one day and requested ours and the Stanley B's help. If we were not prepared to travel with her, she would be requisitioned by the British Army for a mission he couldn't talk about. If we could travel with her, his majesty's government would be very grateful. They needed every able body they could find.

We dropped everything, packed some things, and taking the paperwork given to us by the officer, Stanley, myself, Alice and young Callum set off for Ramsgate on the Kent coast, not knowing what we were doing, or why.

When we arrived a number of soldiers hastily painted what could be seen of the Stanley B's hull in a grey green camouflage while we were told what to do — be ready to sail across the Channel. We could be off at any time. To try and save the army trapped in Dunkirk.

We waited and waited, long day after long day, then finally came the signal, and, under the cover of darkness, we took the Stanley B out among a flotilla of pleasure cruisers, fishing boats, paddle steamer ferries, fireboats, and yachts. Out into the English Channel. Out until land slipped from view, until it was just us, the grey sea stretching for miles around us.

At first it looked like a terrible thunderstorm up ahead. Great bruised clouds sparking with bursts of light, deep booms exploding and rumbling, crackling with a charged energy that rippled out toward us.

We stood silently in the wheelhouse as we drew closer, watching as our thunderstorm morphed slowly into an ungodly sight. What looked like thunderclaps slowly morphed into shell bursts, accompanied by great billowing plumes of smoke and fire. Bricks and mortar, sand dunes collapsing, then being hurled into the air as bombs gouged great smoking holes where houses, churches, life had once been.

The rumble of ordnance, their shock waves skittling over tiny dots along the shoreline, scattering for cover on a long, exposed, sandy beach. The Allied forces falling, one by one.

Overhead came tigerish Spitfires, hunting down the strafing sorties of the Luftwaffe, chasing them away from the beaches, dumping some into the sea in fiery tailspins. Giving a little respite, but not much, to those pinned down along the seafront.

How many of those Spitfire parts had been ferried across Southampton Water by our little boat to the Supermarine factory we didn't know, but as they soared above, Stanley and Callum shouted and waved, cheered for all their worth as they did their work, proud in having played just the smallest part in getting them airborne.

As we drew closer, we passed through a line of great navy vessels that could no longer reach the stranded soldiers. The piers and pontoons that had been streaming soldiers onto them long since bombed out, they idled helplessly, unable to reach the shallower waters without running aground. The barrage of fire from the frontline rattled the boards of the Stanley B as we slipped between the navy ships and in toward the shore, Callum and Stanley readying the rope netting to starboard as they had been shown in Ramsgate, while Alice and I brought the Stanley B as close to the beach as we could. They would then drop the netting into the water and help soldiers wading out to us up and onto the deck.

As soon as we were full, they would draw up the netting, point to the next little boat coming in behind us to the soldiers left in the water, and we would take our load out to the support ships, where they would climb up even greater swathes of netting and disappear from sight.

The beach, the waters shook with every bomb that fell, rattling your teeth, making your legs go weak for a second. Great showers of debris spewing up into the sky from somewhere in the warren of streets beyond the seafront.

Lined with restaurants and cafes, large paned shopfronts, Dunkirk looked like it had once been an idyllic place. It reminded me of Westlyn Esplanade, on the Isle of Netton, and mine and Stanley's only little holiday back when he was five. Lazy days lying on the sand, looking in at the pretty shops, walks out onto the piers and the penny arcades.

I went back, to Dunkirk, many years later, on holiday with Charlie.

We walked the seafront, sat outside cafes drinking small cups of strong coffee, lingered outside patisseries looking at colourful rows of macaroons and tarts. Young couples walking the esplanade, children playing at the shoreline, cigarette smoke, the rich smell of fresh baguettes from the bakery.

I never told him that I had been there before, and the circumstances in which I was.

I never told him how that little boat behind his glasshouse had been one of the little ships of Dunkirk.

I just wandered the quiet streets, the old shopfronts looking out to sea, that had somehow survived that onslaught of May and June 1940.

Because right there and then, as we helped to rescue what was left of the British Army from its breakers, it felt like days of coffee and cigarettes, reading the paper outside quaint cafes had been lost forever.

It seemed like we were watching the last days of Dunkirk, that it could never survive, that it would soon be wiped from the face of the earth as we ferried soldiers back and forth from shore to ship, Callum and Stanley dragging up soldiers, helping them shake off their waterlogged gear so as they could climb up. Helping to lift stretchers aboard, sometimes carrying mortally wounded men that their friends had been unprepared to leave behind, and had struggled through the breakers with, trying to get them home.

Alice would tend to those on the stretchers the best she could, holding their hands, cleaning their faces, whispering to them on their short trip out to the fleet, watching as they were lifted up and away.

Stanley and Callum would stand quietly, catching their breath, looking out at the sea of wide-eyed, haggard faces sprawled across the deck. All silent, save for the odd sob, unable to suppress the horrors they had seen and experienced.

We carried on, day and night, to and fro, dropping to the deck whenever a bomb landed close-by. The shockwave knocking you off your feet, the swell rocking the boat violently as we struggled to clamber back up.

It was worse at night. Claustrophobic. The burning fires rose up above the buildings of the seafront and choked the sky, the clouds closed down upon us. It was hard to gauge how far away the falling bombs were, and the soldiers wading out to meet us. All of a sudden there would be a cluster of pale, scared faces in the dark, arms above their heads on my bow. I would reverse the engines, back the Stanley B around so as they could climb aboard.

As the night wore on, we started to pick up soldiers fresh from the front line.

The positions at the edge of town were falling.

They would not last much longer.

They were coming, they said.

Dawn brought with it dread. The enemy had broken through. Dunkirk had fallen.

The order was given to sail for home, and the navy vessels began to turn out to sea. We were about to follow suit when Stanley shouted out, pointed away to our port side.

'There Mum, can you see?' he said.

I couldn't. I could only see smoke and rubble, breakers shifting the lifeless bodies of the fallen at the shoreline. He pointed again, and a small cluster of waving arms appeared for the briefest of seconds above the swell. Heads just about above the water.

I looked at the fleet turning away, then at Stanley, and throttled the Stanley B's engine toward the shore one last time.

Stanley's waving arms turned out to be eleven soldiers from the decimated Belgian army, who had barely the strength to climb aboard. Grabbing desperately at Stanley and Callum's hands, they were, one by one, hoisted onto the deck.

Whether they were the last evacuees from Dunkirk, we would never know. As we pulled out into deep water, we couldn't see any other boats behind us. Which, of course, didn't mean that they weren't there, somewhere among the chaos. But what I can say is that the Stanley B was one of the last to leave. And trailed behind the fleet for a good while until we caught up.

Our Belgian passengers looked back with horror as mainland Europe, their homeland began to slip away. Lost to German occupation.

Their friends and families' fates unknown.

Over the thrumming engines I could hear them sobbing, looking up to the skies at the Spitfires shepherding the fleet home.

They could only speak Flemish and looked blankly at Alice and Stanley when they asked if they were all right, if they were injured.

Alice cooked them up some soup and handed it out with chunks of bread that they ate like they hadn't seen food for days.

She gave them the last of our biscuits, tins of fruit, whatever we had. Then we stood and watched them, as they sat and watched us back, sometimes looking out into the wake of the Stanley B, the grey morning.

Stanley brought out his box from the cabin and showed them the lid, the carved initials. He pointed at his, then said 'SB – Stanley Buchanan.' He showed them mine, Alice's, Callum's, pointed at us in turn, said our names. Then he held out a little pocketknife, mimed carving into the wood, and handed the box around to all eleven soldiers, who etched their initials, said their names one by one.

I don't think any of us caught much, their accent being so alien, so strong, but there was an Albert, a Franck, a Hercule.

Stanley stood up and mimed playing football, scoring a goal.

'Football?' he said and held his thumb up, then down. They all held their thumbs up.

'Good, good,' he said and smiled. 'My team – Southampton. You?' pointing at Franck.

'Anderlecht,' he said to a couple of weak cheers from the others, who held their thumbs up in support. Someone else booed to muted laughter.

'Liege,' the dissenter said 'Standard Liege.' Another couple of thumbs up. Another couple of boos, some more chuckles.

Hercule, sat in the stern, held his hand up.

'Charleroi,' he said proudly, to a barrage of abuse and thumbs down, hands waving him away.

'No good, no good,' one of them said and held their nose, to which Hercule shrugged his shoulders.

'Charleroi,' he said again, tapping his chest 'Charleroi.'

Everyone laughed, a few closest to him playfully elbowed him in his ribs before the boat settled down quietly once more, the momentary respite from their situation faded away to distant stares out to sea, pondering if they would ever see their teams play again.

If they would ever see home again.

In the twilight before dawn, heads began to bow, the odd soul unable to keep their eyes open any longer, falling asleep sitting up.

And beneath leaden skies we edged toward home.

They disembarked at Ramsgate, following the lines of bedraggled soldiers from the other boats off into town, slipping away from view, nodding at us earnestly as they climbed up onto the dock.

They walked away to their fate. A fate that we would never know. Though I know that all four of us aboard the Stanley B never forgot them, or the scores of other faces that scrambled up her sides to safety.

All four of us pausing over their initials on Stanley's box from time to time in the months and years that followed, wondering about them.

We didn't sail for home right away. We couldn't. None of us had slept a wink for nearly three days. And the minute the harbour emptied of soldiers, and our task was over, the reality of what we had seen hit us all. I remember being unable to stop shaking, and when the tears came, they wouldn't stop.

We would all take ourselves off for a private moment, though none could smother the sounds of their sobbing completely. You would hear it coming up from the cabin, the engine room, dockside. Fuelled by images of the dying, deafening bomb strikes, scattered bodies. The war made real by scenes that could now never be unseen.

Stanley unfastened the net that had helped so many up, neatly folded it into an old hessian sack, and stowed it on a shelf in the engine room. After what it had seen, what it had helped achieve, it deserved to be looked after, kept safe, Stanley said. And there it stayed. For all time.

We never spoke of Dunkirk to others when we got home. When we pulled up at Chapel dock, we went right back to work ferrying parts to Thorneycroft and Supermarine as if nothing had happened.

Though out on the water we would talk about it, wonder on those who had graced our deck, where they might be. We talked out our nightmares, and the scars that had been left behind, the four of us. All changed from the experience, though none regretting it for a single second. Just that it had to happen at all.

Nineteen

As summer of 1940 wore on, the bombs started to fall on Southampton. It would be known as the Blitz in history books.

The air raid sirens would sound, and the cities' population would scrabble for cover in the shelters that had been built, or failing that, the nearest cellar or basement – people hurriedly ushering complete strangers into their homes, and down steep, dark steps beneath the stairs.

And there we would wait, listening to the sirens winding down as their operators fled for cover themselves. Silence. Then the deep, terrible drone of the bombers would grow louder and louder, even over the anti-aircraft guns dug in beneath great walls of sandbags as they opened up on them.

Southampton shook as the bombs fell. Any close by came with a dread whistle as they fell.

If you lost the whistle, you knew it was right on top of you, the shelters rocking violently as it hit. Pieces of masonry hurtling like shrapnel, a shower of dust and disintegrated concrete choking all inside, forcing us out onto the streets and a world transformed.

Neighbours' houses, corner shops, the local church, gone. A smoking tangle of wood and brick beneath a hellish night sky of flame and exploding gun fire, briefly illuminating the dread silhouette of droning bombers above.

If we were out on the Stanley B when the sirens came, then there wasn't enough time to dock and find shelter. We would throttle her out and as far away from the dockside as we could. As far away from the shipyard, the Supermarine factory as we could get. As far out into the deep-water channel as possible before dropping anchor and hunkering down in the cabin.

The shockwaves rattled the rivets in her hull, and the swell from the odd off-target bomb hitting the water made her lurch violently, as if on a confused sea.

My stomach would sink when Stanley and Callum were caught out among it all on their night shifts, when the sirens came. Stranded, with just the flimsy decking on the Stanley B to protect them, which was no protection at all if a bomb came too close, Alice, Arthur and I would rush to the dockside at the all-clear, and wait, and pray. And somehow, remarkably, the Stanley B would always bring them home, materialising out of the smoke and ruin drifting across the water.

Stanley would flinch with every bomb, wide-eyed. And despite his heroics at Dunkirk, despite long nights riding out the raids on the exposed Stanley B, he was still only sixteen, soon to be seventeen. He was a young boy. He was scared out of his mind.

He tried to block it out with another of his little notebooks, and a few colouring pencils. He would lean in over it down in the shelters and write and draw, sometimes showing it to the smaller children to help them take their minds off everything too.

It was his trip, around Britain, that we would take when all this horror was done with. Every page a new destination, a new drawing of some landmark, a few remembered sentences about it from a travel book he had read in the storeroom of Mr Water's bookshop.

Raid after raid he would add to it, flinching with every bomb strike, he would wipe away the dust from the ceiling and carry on, smiling weakly at me. He would show me the little maps he had sketched out, the illustrations.

He had drawn the last page first, our final destination, sketching out Freshwater Bay, Saint Catherine's Lighthouse, on the Isle of Netton.

We had only been there for a few hours, back when he was little. We had taken a bus from outside our little holiday let in one of the big townhouses on the esplanade down to the southernmost point of Netton, walked up the bluff to the lighthouse. The keeper had seen Stanley looking up at it in awe and invited us in. He had taken us up past his quarters, all the way to the top to see the beacon, the vast ocean of white-crested waves beyond.

We had laid in the long grasses and listened to the faint sounds of breakers on the rocks below the bluff, watching gulls coasting across crystal blue skies. We had sat and watched the fishermen bring in their catch on the seafront. Ate fish and chips. Wandered through the pretty, narrow, higgledy-piggledy streets of Freshwater with their old fishermen's cottages. We had walked along the river to the banks of Blackwater Lake, and the deep fresh pine forests that whispered on the breeze as we drew near.

It was the most beautiful place he had ever seen, Stanley had said. And it would be the final stop on our adventure.

'We could live there, in one of those old cottages. We could make a living taking people on sightseeing trips,' he had said. 'The cliffs are full of nesting birds. Some rare. They have even been known to have puffins. And people have seen seals, basking sharks, and other things. It would be perfect mum, wouldn't it?'

Beneath the roar of the Blitz, it *was* perfect.

With mainland Europe having fallen, and our enemy massing at the French coast. Beneath the firestorm from above, and repatriation ships taking Americans back home across the Atlantic, seemingly resigned to the fact that Britain would be lost at any moment, it was dreams like Stanley's that kept people going.

There was a stubbornness that, even in such dark hours, we would not fall. Hopes, ambitions, futures would not be lost.

After every raid, people would re-emerge and adapt. Would keep at the task at hand. Keep turning up for shifts at the factories, bakeries, hospitals and shops. The Stanley B would carry on ferrying parts. Daily life would continue as best as it could, even in such a precarious situation.

There would be adverts in the local paper for the cinema, displaying the latest releases. During the summer there would be reports of cricket matches played to a conclusion, despite 'interruptions' more sinister than any inclement weather.

No matter their severity, the air raids, 'interruptions' would be the language used by the staff writers at The Echo to describe them, choosing to focus on the life in between. There was plenty of room elsewhere in the paper for grim statistics and the reality of our situation.

This defiance in the face of such a bleak outlook permeated out beyond the pages of the paper, and into the war-torn streets.

Life, normal life, would carry on. And Stanley would play his part.

When the letter from Southampton Football Club came, asking him to report for pre-season training ahead of the 1940/41 season, Stanley found the time, and the energy to answer the call.

The Dell, and the matches played there had been such a source of relief the season before. A ninety-minute respite from the troubles beyond the perimeter walls, where among the simple, honest endeavour of a football match, life could be put on hold.

Stanley had been solid enough on his debut to be considered a worthy replacement for any of Southampton's Hampshire League team, should any of the regulars be unable to play.

And he turned up for training every Tuesday and Thursday evening and gave his all, even if his name didn't appear on the team sheets for the following Saturday's fixtures.

He saw it as an honour, taking part in training. And the novelty of playing out on The Dell turf always sent him bouncing down to the dock for his shift on the Stanley B, stowing his boots away in the cabin with a broad grin, waving as he and Callum pulled out and away into Southampton Water.

But his day finally came a month after his seventeenth birthday, and a reserve team start against RAF Southampton at The Dell.

Though it was like no other game he, or anyone else on the team had ever played in before.

For football to resume beneath the Blitz, concessions had been made. The Football League had been reduced to regional divisions to avoid any unnecessarily long journeys. Fuel was severely rationed, and travelling any distance was dangerous, let alone cross-country trips to play football.

Any match that started, but couldn't be finished due to an air raid, would stand as the final result, no matter how little of the game had been played.

Teams would attempt to complete as many of their fixtures as they could beneath the onslaught, and the league table would reflect the vast discrepancies in matches played by using goals for and against, rather than points amassed to create some semblance of a fair set of standings.

By Christmas of 1940, some teams had lagged a good ten games behind others. Victims of the raids, and players being deployed elsewhere.

It was chaotic, but better than nothing, and both player and supporter alike adapted to keep their beautiful game going. In some instances, for just a few minutes play.

The rules were that players and supporters should take shelter beneath the stands at the first sounding of the air raid sirens. Where there had once been adverts for beer and motor cars in the match programme, stark instructions on where to take shelter in the event of a raid replaced them.

But there were so many false alarms, wailing sirens that came to nothing disrupting the play that some supporters took to standing at the tops of the Milton Road terrace, so they could see the city skyline beyond.

They would wave and yell 'play on' if there was no sight nor sound of a bombing raid to keep the game going beneath the sirens, changing their cries to 'take cover' with the first sight of the anti-aircraft guns over Portsmouth down the coast lighting up. Great balls of black smoke ballooning as their shells exploded and bruised the sky.

Players would join supporters who had streamed down off the terracing and onto the pitch, scattering and running for cover beneath the West Stand, where they would huddle together, listening to the sickening drone of the waves of bombers above, the shuddering boom of ordnance hitting some part of the city, rattling the girders and stairwells, chattering the seat backs in the stand above.

Then, after the all-clear had sounded, those with the stomach for it took up their spots on the terrace once more and watched the returning players attempt to reach full time.

And if the all-clear never came, and the sirens kept sounding, the guns continuing to fire up into sea of barrage balloons above as darkness fell, the game would be called off by the referee. And we would wait by the turnstiles for the right moment, and then, in dribs and drabs, we would take our chances, and try to get home, players still in their kits and boots.

Stanley's first match of the season, on the 21st of September, fell foul of everything.

Kick off was delayed by an hour due to the sirens. The first half halted after twenty minutes as the supporters on the Milton Road end skittered down the terracing toward the West Stand.

We stood, Stanley and I, and listened to the bombs fall, Stanley smiling weakly up at me in his oversize kit, in a faltering attempt at reassurance. The rest of the team milling about, lost in thought, hunkered down in huddles with a few supporters, flinching with every detonation.

They managed half an hour at the restart until the sirens came again, and as dusk began to fall the decision was made to blow the final whistle with the RAF leading three one.

It affected me profoundly, that match, or the parts of it that happened. The bravery of the few hundred spectators, the players and officials, in doing what they could to keep that Saturday afternoon ritual alive, in the face of everything. It was deeply moving.

Looking back, it was inspirational. A two-fingered salute to the skies.

The report in the paper the following Monday concentrated only on the action, mentioning only a delayed kick off and shortened halves. Exalting pin-point crosses and powerful headers, last-gasp tackles and wicked shots. It was cut out and added to Stanley's books, the programme tucked safely inside. The symbolic meaning of it far more profound than the simple Hampshire League defeat that it covered.

The following week he played in a two all draw at Winchester City that lasted the distance, before coming home from training the following Thursday in a daze.

'The first team are short of defenders for Saturday mum. They've called me up, for the football league.'

It may not count in the 'official' record of the football club, Stanley's first team appearance; his war-time effort being seen as sub-standard to that which went before and came after it.

But in what it stood for, stood up against, in what it did to keep the city together, those players during the Blitz deserve that recognition. Never has a braver man pulled on the red and white of the Saints. Not before, or since.

And in the opposition that Stanley faced that early October afternoon, precious few would dare call them substandard.

In a quirk of fate, the war had transformed Aldershot from a perennial lower league minnow to that of the star attraction. Many of the country's great players passed through the town and its army training bases, and some of them would guest for Aldershot on a Saturday.

As young Stanley lined up in a defence supporting pre-war regular Ted Bates and his hero Cyril Smith, a bumper crowd of a couple of thousand had turned out to see the man he would be marking, the great Tommy Lawton of Everton and England, ably supported by other senior pre-war professionals in Hagan of Sheffield United, Crooks of Blackburn Rovers, and Swift of Manchester City.

He gave Stanley the run around with his sublime skill, the man who had scored the winning goal for England against Scotland the year before in front of one hundred and forty-nine thousand at Hampden Park, and had won the First Division title with Everton before the war. But Stanley stuck to his task ably and helped keep Lawton's and Aldershot's goal tally down to three.

Having to concentrate so hard on Lawton, let him forget about all the people watching, and the grand stage he was on.

He was even able to celebrate a Cyril Smith goal up the other end, shaking his hero's hand warmly as they trotted back to the centre circle.

I waited for him at the players' entrance after the game, and he excitedly showed me his programme that he had got signed by Lawton, Crooks, Hagan, and Swift, as well as his very own Cyril Smith. It was hard to see which caused him the greatest pleasure: the England international, or the Thorneycroft winger and shipbuilder he had grown up idolising.

To him, they were both great players, just on different stages. They could both make magic things happen with a ball. It was just that one did it at Wembley in front of one hundred thousand, while the other performed wonders on a muddy park in Woolston.

The newspaper report on the following Monday extolled the virtues of Aldershot's top-flight quartet. Amidst columns of print that tried to juggle the war and normal life, with articles on the last of the repatriation ships fleeing for America, keep fit classes for women at Freemantle Parish Hall, Sherlock Homes starring Basil Rathbone playing at the Abbey Theatre, and a 'mystery fire in Berlin,' Stanley's first team debut was squashed. He was even mentioned as 'showing up well against Aldershot's stellar front line.'

It was, along with his autographed programme, safely stowed away in his notebooks.

After the war, I would keep an eye out in the papers for those names Stanley played against, as they resumed their first-class careers.

Walter Crooks of Blackburn Rovers would go on to manage the Dutch giants Ajax, twice. For his second spell he left lowly Accrington Stanley to do so, becoming the only Stanley manager to ever leave the rarefied air of Peel Park for Amsterdam.

It would be some time before I heard the name of Frank Swift again, Aldershot's goalkeeper borrowed from Manchester City. He had become a journalist for the News of the World after his playing career and perished along with much of the Manchester United team in the Munich air disaster in February of 1958. He had been sent out on assignment to cover United's European Cup match with Red Star Belgrade but would never see his article in print.

I remember sitting in the cabin of the Stanley B, behind the glasshouse at Five Acre Cottage after I heard the news, leafing through Stanley's books until I found his programme, looking down at Swift's autograph. I remember thinking, had one man not experienced enough already, to be made to suffer such an end?

The following Saturday after his Aldershot baptism of fire, Stanley was included in the first team eleven for an away fixture with Brighton and Hove Albion.

He set off in the early hours, walking up to The Dell and the team bus straight from a night of deliveries on Southampton Water.

After a three-hour bus trip, they managed barely fifty minutes in front of a crowd of no more than one hundred. The Goldstone Ground's sweeping terraces being far more exposed than The Dell, and with little shelter, an afternoon watching The Albion was fraught with danger during the Blitz.

In the little two penny programme that Stanley had neatly folded away in his trouser pocket, the air raid notice gave little comfort:

> *Patrons are informed that if an air raid warning is sounded during any match, the referee has been ordered by the Football Association to stop play immediately, and to recommence only after the raiders past has been sounded if light permits. The exit gates will be opened for those persons who wish to leave the ground, and those who remain are advised to spread out round the terraces. It must be understood that money cannot be returned once patrons have paid for admission.'*

They played in fits and starts beneath an afternoon of raids to an ever-dwindling number of scattering supporters, until the referee called a halt in the failing light with the game still goalless.

The team bus crawled home in the dark, unable to use its headlights due to the blackout, until close to midnight it came upon a Southampton skyline on fire, swathes of burning buildings, a battery of spotlights sweeping desperately back and forth across clouds stained orange and red from the destruction below.

Ribbons of tracer rounds flailed up into the sky from all across the city, desperately trying to find the bombers, whose great silhouettes occasionally materialized out of the plumes of smoke and cloud. Blinding flashes as bombs found their targets.

With it being too dangerous to drive any further, the team got out, said their goodbyes, and made their way home into the burning city any way they could.

Stanley, Cyril, and a few of the boys who lived by the docks made their way to the Itchen River where they found the floating bridge had been halted.

With no other way to get across they hunkered down by the waters' edge, and flinched as they watched the bombs fall, the city shaking, the sky roaring, the flames rising.

As soon as the floating bridge started up again at first light, the bombers slipping away with the dawn, Stanley and his exhausted team-mates slipped through the rubble and home.

'From outside, it looked like the town was finished mum,' he said over a cup of tea. 'It looked like it had all gone up in flames. That the sky itself was on fire,' he shook his head. 'I thought it was all finished.'

But it wasn't.

Beneath the onslaught, life carried on as best it could. Fires were put out. Damaged buildings were cleared, propped up, their inhabitants re-homed. Films kept rolling in cinemas, shops remained open, people kept attending dances at the Atlantic Club on Grosvenor Square. And Stanley kept turning out for Southampton.

He played in back-to-back Hampshire League fixtures against RAF Calshot in the weeks after the Brighton match. The away game was played on a field across from Calshot Castle that we used to see every day on our sightseeing trips before the war, down on the Calshot peninsula that jutted out into the Solent.

After the game they were shown around the hangar where the great Sutherland flying boats were stationed, before the pilots they had just played against were scrambled into the air, as air raid sirens across Southampton Water began to wail.

Not long after, Stanley and his team-mates stood helplessly and watched as a formation of bombers materialised out of the clouds, sweeping across the Solent and on toward Southampton.

Somewhere among it all, some of those players for RAF Calshot, in the thick of it, their planes diving and rising up into the clouds.

Whether they ever made it back safely to play another game, we would never know.

Stanley played one last Football League match in a depleted Southampton team in early November, going down four nil to Watford in a rare, uninterrupted ninety minutes of football.

It was a walloping, but the news report couldn't fault the inexperienced Saints' effort and application. It had been another fixture fulfilled. Another Saturday afternoon's entertainment for those in attendance. A little slice of life, preserved for another week. And, beneath the onslaught from the skies, that was far more important than any result.

And it was another week of young Stanley living one of his grand dreams.

It would turn out that Stanley's footballing fate would become entwined with that of The Dell's. His career ended as that grand old ground, that he held in such esteem, that had been the pinnacle of his footballing ambitions, finally succumbed to the Blitz.

After Stanley's match against Watford, the air raids had become longer in duration, and ever more sustained and devastating. Wave after wave rolled in relentlessly and lit up the sky with their deadly payload.

Many evenings we couldn't even put the Stanley B out to work, instead running for the shelters and spending long nights crammed in with similarly ashen faces; Stanley turning to his notebook and our trip around Britain's coast to try and keep the horror out.

Training at The Dell was abandoned and replaced with a letter on a Friday morning detailing where and when to report if you had been selected.

The 23rd of November saw him off with the reserves to play an away fixture against Air Service Training Hamble, getting home just in time to dive into the shelter before the worst of the night's raids.

The next two weeks would be known as 'Southampton's Blitz,' so badly hit was our poor town in an attempt to snuff out Spitfire and warship production.

On Saturday November 30 Stanley was selected to play in the Hampshire League side against Cunliffe-Owen.

The paper on the Friday ran a story on how the young Saints would be coming up against Southampton's pre-war goalkeeper, Sam Warhurst, who was turning out for his works' team.

Stanley was so excited.

He had stood behind Warhurst's goal on the Milton Road terrace so many times before the war. He had seen him acrobatically turn away vicious shots, dive bravely at centre forwards' boots to snuff out goalscoring opportunities, punch away dangerous corners to the roar of twenty thousand approving souls.

To be out on the same pitch as Warhurst was a thrill. An honour for young Stanley.

I took my spot on the Milton Road end, from where I had seen Stanley crane his neck to get a good view of the action as a young boy. Where he would kick every ball, chatter animatedly to Callum and his football chums, twirl their scarves above their heads with every Southampton goal. With every fingertip Warhurst save, Stanley would call out 'Great save, Sam,' and every time Warhurst acknowledged his praise with a wink or a wave, Stanley would work his way up to me to see if I had seen. His eyes wide with joy.

And then, there he was, out on the pitch with another of his heroes, the great Sam Warhurst, witnessed by 100 or so brave souls beneath a leaden November sky.

We didn't know it at the time, but it would be the last time I would see Stanley play a game of football. And it would be the last game played at this grand old ground for quite some time.

After an uneventful one all draw, darkness fell, and with it came the single most devastating night of bombing that Southampton ever saw.

We sat it out in our shelter in Chapel, listening to the ground shaking around us, the piercing whistle of falling bombs, the terrible, deafening explosions making our heads ring as if we had concussion. Until everything went black, a roar, and the shelter roof caved in.

We felt for one another, those around us, helped those we could, looked on at those we couldn't, before we scrambled up and out onto a burning street of splintered homes and warehouses.

We joined the line passing buckets of water from the dockside to the fires, in a desperate attempt to save some of the burning buildings. And as the bombing subsided with first light, the new day revealed a smoking ruin of a city, and a soundtrack of pealing bells of fire engines racing here and there, we made our way home. Or where home was.

It had taken a direct hit, our little house. One of four on the terrace that had been levelled as if they had never been there. No trace of it had been left behind, just a gaping crater of mud and brick. We had to count the house numbers to be sure, so surreal was the sight. But number nine had gone.

I felt Stanley's hand in mine, and we turned, and hurried for the dockside. Where, amongst the choking smoke and shattered hulls of cargo ships, the Stanley B materialised, untouched.

How our little boat had made it through Dunkirk, and then worked on beneath the Blitz unscathed, I will never know. But she did, and we sunk onto the benches in her cabin and slept, for how many hours I couldn't say, until Alice and Arthur found us.

It was not just our house that took a hit. A bomb had found the Milton Road goal at The Dell, creating a 16-foot crater where Stanley, Sam Warhurst had been defending only a few hours earlier.

Had it landed during the game they would have been lost immediately. So too all of us stood on the terraces behind, the shockwave killing us instantly.

The result wasn't even featured in the paper on Monday, just the terrible devastation that the city had suffered. Newspapers from London and beyond declared that Southampton had been destroyed, that it was finished, so thorough the flattening it received.

Poor Mr Waters and his bookshop perished that night. He hadn't wanted to leave it and was found a few days later.

Stanley was inconsolable at the funeral. He had been so kind to Stanley.

Stanley never knew it at the time, but Mr Waters knew that he had been reading lots of the books on the shelves, hiding them behind comics to make it seem like he wasn't. Mr Waters would smile, wink at me, wave me away whenever I apologised, saying 'it is not for me to stifle an enquiring mind. He looks after them like they are the Crown Jewels themselves. Let him read.'

He would always sit and listen to Stanley telling him all about the work we were doing on the Stanley B. About all the places he thought the ships in the docks were going, what they would see when they got there. He would always save any brochures for the great ocean liners left behind by customers for Stanley, and they would sit in the stockroom looking at the brightly coloured posters advertising grand adventures around the globe. They would read through all the itineraries together, detailing exotic places and wonders of the world.

He didn't need to be so kind. It was a place of work. He didn't need to be so generous as to let an employee's son hang around the place after school and during the holidays.

He was a kind man, who judged the measure of a person by their empathy and consideration for others, by their acts of humility and humanity, and he had been one of the first people Stanley asked to invite to the Stanley B's maiden voyage.

His loss hit Stanley hard.

A piece of a happy childhood lost forever.

The Dell had been crippled too, there would be no more football played on it. Though the Echo declared that the Saints would somehow carry on. The Football League team would play the remainder of their fixtures away from home, the Hampshire League team, sadly, was to be disbanded for the foreseeable future.

When he could, Stanley kept on attending training, which had been moved to the common, a large park in the centre of town; though he received no more letters through the post. With that direct hit, his Southampton career was over.

To some, three first team appearances and seven in the reserves may not amount to much, especially in the cobbled together wartime leagues.

But to Stanley, to me, to Cyril Smith, and all those other brave players and supporters during the Blitz, it was some career, as important as those that went before and came after, in keeping the beautiful game alive during such an ugly moment in time.

I have never stopped feeling so proud of him, for what he did. On the Stanley B, at Dunkirk, playing his football, in the merchant navy, on D-Day.

And it would be the merchant navy for him next.

We lived on the Stanley B that winter, keeping warm by the stove, that we used to heat up the cabin before the blackout meant we had to snuff it out. Sleeping on the benches beneath blankets, the first one woken by the cold at first light would relight it, the heat slowly thawing us out.

When the call for recruits came Stanley joined the merchant navy in February 1941 along with Callum. And when he left for his first posting, I took a room up by Saint Michael's Church in the French quarter of the city.

The streets about the church had been left unscathed, the medieval city walls and Tudor buildings surviving another moment in history. Grateful recipients of the Luftwaffe using the church spire as a way point to begin their turn toward their targets across Southampton.

It was a twenty-minute walk down to the dockside and the Stanley B, where

I would meet Alice and her youngest, Nell, who helped us keep our little war effort going.

Nell would leap from boat to dock to tie her up, and lug boxes all day long.

She was a tireless little thing who had spent her young life trying to keep up with Stanley and Callum, trailing after them to the park, pleading with them to join in their kick about until they relented. Running around with a big grin, lashing at the ball. The hem of her old play dress covered in mud. You would often hear Alice's cries of anguish up the street as Nell bounced in through the front door in such a state after a day of playing and scrubbing about with her elder brother and Stanley.

I hated being so far away from the Stanley B, living by the church, and would sometimes sleep on her if we had a late finish, or an early start. And whenever the air raid sirens sounded, I would sit in the local shelter nervously, feeling helpless being so far away. Though I knew she was being looked out for.

Alice would tell me how, as soon as the all-clear had sounded, Nell would run down to the dock to check on her. And was ready to run across town to fetch me if anything ever happened, which thankfully it never did.

She had been no more than five years old when Stanley discovered the Stanley B in the scrappers yard and had clambered over it that first day with her brother after we bought her.

She had seen it transform into our little boat and been on its maiden trip around the docks.

She loved coming with us on our sightseeing trips and would sit on my lap and steer when we were out in the deep channel.

She had seen dreams come true with our efforts on the Stanley B, And, just as Stanley had never given up on his, and had become a skipper on a boat, had played up at The Dell like he said he would, Nell saw that anything could happen with an open mind, and a stout heart.

As a young woman she started a school for destitute children, and taught them, among many things, their own self-worth. That great things could come from humble beginnings.

She taught them in the classroom, fed them in the kitchen, and kept them safe and warm in bright, neat dormitories. She formed a school football team, and they would play school teams from around the area and would win as many games as they lost.

She would fix them up with apprenticeships and jobs. Her door would always be open.

What she did helped so many, our little Nell of the Stanley B.

Working the boat helped Nell forget just how much she missed her big brother when he went to sea. They had been thick as thieves all their lives, and she would read out his letters home while we sailed between pick-ups and drop-offs.

Stanley and Callum had been assigned to different ships in the Atlantic fleet, carrying supplies back from the Americas.

It was dangerous work.

U-boats lurked beneath the waters and could bring devastation to the exposed merchant convoys. Tales of ships being picked off one by one, despite the navy escort doing its best to protect them were common.

Stanley's letters home wouldn't focus on the perils out at sea, he didn't want to worry me, or think about it himself, so he would write about the things he saw when they came into port, providing endings to all that wondering as a little boy, watching ships heading off out to who knew where.

He had bought a little camera and sent home photographs of the places they stopped, which would help him when he couldn't find the words.

In one letter he sent a photograph of the Manhattan skyline as they were coming into dock in New York. Bleak storm clouds had snagged about the vast looming skyscrapers, their lights from countless floors dissolving beneath a thick fog. It was a scene of towering shadows and dusky menace, a city bracing for a storm about to hit.

'We went to New York,' he wrote 'just look at the picture.'

The crew would make the most of every minute of shore leave that they were given, even if it was just for a few hours, celebrating their safe passage where others hadn't been so lucky.

New York was a regular stop-off, and all would hone their routine to make the most of every minute, visiting their favourite haunts with a military precision.

Stanley would send back pictures of Times Square, all lit up at night, with grand buildings lost behind walls of neon advertisements rising up into the dark. Streams of yellow cabs, trams and people blurred on the streets with the bustle of a city that never slept.

From the top of the Empire State building Stanley's pictures showed me Central Park, the five boroughs, the Statue of Liberty, far, far below.

He showed me the grand canopies along Broadway. Famous names up in lights above famous shows playing out in the plush theatres beyond ornate wooden doors. He showed me newsstands decked in *The New York Times*, *The Washington Post*, *The Boston Globe*, and all-night diners with figures hunched over cups of coffee and jukeboxes. He showed me the peculiar Flatiron building on 5th Avenue, the vaulted ceiling of Grand Central Station, steam rising from grates in the road.

But it was Ebbets Field in Brooklyn that Stanley was most animated about in his letters, and he came to love the most about New York, and it would be there that he often tried to reach, if the stars aligned.

It came from a tip from one of the stevedores loading up the ships one hot summer's day, when Stanley asked him where he would go to see the real New York.

'There's only one place,' he had said to Stanley, in a deep, gravelly New York drawl. 'If I didn't have to be here, I'd be over there, across the water, watching the Dodgers. *That* is New York, if you ask me. Here.'

He had handed Stanley a folded newspaper from his back pocket, turned over to the sports pages. He tapped the picture of four young men dressed in baseball uniforms, all with a bat slung over their shoulders, smiling at the camera.

Above it the headline 'Dodgers ready for the Reds.' Below the photograph a caption that read 'Dolph Camilli, Pete Reiser, Pee Wee Reese, and Dixie Walker are ready for Cincinnati Reds series, starting today at Ebbets Field.'

'Take it,' the Stevedore said. 'Take the Brooklyn ferry at the end of the next pier, then follow the crowd. You won't regret it.'

Stanley wrote home about Ebbets Field in the way he talked about The Dell.

He wrote of a grand façade. Of vaulted glass windows and rows of pillars. Of crowds milling about outside with an expectancy that was electric.

He wrote of sitting in the cheap seats, called the bleachers – baseball's version of the terraces – shaded from the heat of the day by the grandstands above, looking out on centre field.

Hot dogs and sodas. Organ music ditties while the next batter took to the plate. The sweet crack of ball on bat, accompanied by the roar of the crowd. Children stood at the front of the bleachers, straining to catch foul balls and home runs as they sailed into the stands. A sea of worn catchers' mitts flailing above their heads. One lucky glove plucking a bright, white baseball from the skies that was stared at with an awe and incredulity. A little piece of the Dodgers, all for them.

He wrote of three old-timers sat together, studiously noting each pitch, and its fortunes, on a scorecard. Sipping at a beer with their shirts opened to try and catch a little of the wilting breeze.

Cigarette smoke, expectant faces, hope tumbling down the steep rake of the grandstands and into the cheap seats.

It was intoxicating, he wrote, though he didn't entirely understand what was going on out at left field, or third base, or anywhere out on the lush green baseball diamond.

But he recognised the awe and joy on the jostling kids' faces about him as one of their heroes thundered past on the way out to second base, hurling their mitts in the air at a home run sailing up and out of Ebbets Field and into the lots beyond. The ripple of applause at a wicked pitch making a Cincinnati Red swing at fresh air, miss, the thud of the ball in the catcher's mitt, the umpire yelling 'strike,' to add insult to the batter's misery.

The stevedore had been right, Stanley wrote home, cutting out and tucking that picture of the four Dodgers inside.

This was Brooklyn, New York, America. More so than the bright lights of Broadway. This is where the people were. People like you and me, he said.

And though he had never been there before, and was so far away from home, it felt familiar.

It was a comfort, he wrote, and he could see himself in the kids down at the front and imagine me looking on from the rows behind.

The passion, the reverence, the feeling that you were where you belonged, it made him feel closer to home, to me, to our life before the war.

It was a surrogate for the roped off Thorneycroft pitch, The Dell, and all the joys that they had brought, and he would go to Ebbets Field whenever he could.

Over the course of 1941 and 1942 he managed another six visits to see the Dodgers. And whenever he went, he would send home his ticket stub and a thin programme full of impenetrable batting and fielding statistics, league standings, small player profile pictures and line-ups, fixture lists and past results. Inside he slipped photographs he had taken: the Ebbets Field sign all lit up at night looking out on Sullivan Place.

Grinning kids in the bleachers, holding up their gloves and captured bounty for the camera. Rows of shadowy faces looking out intently at the play. A snatched picture of those three open-shirted old timers hunched over their scorecards, beer in hand. The grand columns flanking the main entrance. The field of play, a blurred runner making for second base.

He would attach a little note to the front of it all – 'For my box,' he would write, and I would duly place them inside for him, for when he came home.

He also sent home three baseball caps for me, Alice, and Nell, with the note 'For the fearless crew of the Stanley B!' They were cream in colour, with a dark navy blue bill, above which had been embroidered a large black 'B' for the Brooklyn Dodgers.

Nell adored them and insisted that we wear them whenever we were working. We sent him a photograph of the three of us sporting them, stood in front of the Stanley B, and he kept the picture in his wallet. He said we all looked so handsome and found great pleasure in learning that, whenever anyone asked Nell about them, she would proclaim that they had come all the way from New York, from the home of the famous Brooklyn Dodgers, and had been sent by a very good friend of hers who was away at sea.

And away at sea he was, for months at a time. His letters would detail trips across the treacherous Grand Banks of the North Atlantic, where the giant, unpredictable swells protected them from the U Boats. Though with forty, fifty-foot breakers rising out of the darkness and crashing over the bow, and steep, terrifying troughs in between, he sometimes wondered what was more deadly.

He would write of weaving between carving icebergs on the frigid seas of Nova Scotia, the land lost beneath huge snow drifts in winter.

He sent pictures home of grand art deco buildings on the streets of Miami, and vast brilliant white beaches, boulevards lined with palm trees and beautiful, tanned, young people.

Snatched moments of other worlds in between long hours loading motor parts and tyres from New York, huge bags of wheat, maize and flour from Halifax, Nova Scotia, crates of dried fish, oranges and beet vegetables from Florida, sugarcane and coffee from Havana, Cuba, where he would meet his Martha from Whitby.

She had been working for the British Embassy, helping to secure stocks to boost the war effort and the ration books of everyone back home. Along with sugarcane and coffee, she had been tasked with helping with the import of rubber, for the countless parts and machines being rolled off production lines up and down the country.

They had met by chance one evening at the famous Copacabana Club and hit it off right away, Stanley said. After that, he would spend every free hour he had taking long walks with her along the Malecon, watching the shipping coming and going as the Caribbean lapped against the sea wall that seemed to stretch on and away forever.

They would sit in the parks at dusk, beneath sweet-scented Magnolia trees, watching old timers playing chess through a haze of cigar smoke, mosquitos and rum.

They walked the narrow streets of the old town, listening to the intoxicating sounds of salsa, rumba, and cha-cha-cha drifting from open windows. Young couples in doorways slow dancing, heads resting on each-other's shoulders.

She was funny and kind, he said, and so very beautiful. She had given him her address back home, on the lip of a match book, and they were to meet up when the war was over. They were in love, he said. They would wait for one another.

He wrote and asked what I thought of inviting Martha to join us on our trip around Britain on the Stanley B. To become a part of our new life on Netton, in Freshwater. I told him that he must. That I was so happy for him. That I couldn't wait to meet her. That I would keep that matchbook safe for him, in his box, when he sent it home.

When I finally met her, she was everything Stanley had said she was. A beautiful girl with a warm smile and an infectious laugh. A strong, brave, intelligent woman who had indeed fallen in love with young Stanley.

When she spoke of him the tears flowed freely, and she showed me some photographs he had taken. One was of her leaning in, watching a chess match intently, her face partially obscured by a plume of smoke. It was his favourite, she had said. I could see why. Her face a vision, lit up with a blissful joy for life. That sparkle in her eyes dimmed a little when I met her, a victim of the ravages of war.

She would never forget him, she said. You could tell that she wouldn't.

Every four or five months, Stanley would get an extended shore leave, a week or two, and would appear out of the blue at the dockside. Wearing a huge grin, he would leap aboard before Nell had her tied up securely, and he would hug us all as if his and our lives depended on it.

He would help us with our work and tell tall tales of life out at sea to Nell, who would wait on his every word, spellbound. Tales of giant rogue waves blocking out the sky, of icebergs looming out of the darkness, of warship escorts launching torpedoes at an unseen enemy, Stanley watching them zoom under the hull of his ship and away until the sea began to writhe and boil. Great cheers going up across the convoy if debris began to surface, or a mass scattering for cover if the klaxons sounded at the sight of incoming fire silently streaking just beneath the water.

He would want to know everything that had been happening and would nod as we told him of repairs that we had made to the Stanley B, of neighbours that had been lost on the front line, and at home. He would love to catch up on the football news, and if there was a game on, we would head over to the patched-up Dell to see Cyril play.

He would always take the time to visit Mr Water's grave and spend an afternoon with Aunt Harriet.

He would lose himself in his box in the cabin, looking at Martha's matchbook, his Dodgers programmes and photographs, his notebooks of a football career that seemed a world away, and his trip around Britain that he hoped was not too far off.

He would sit and trace his finger across the initials carved into the box lid and wonder about what had become of our eleven Belgian soldiers from Dunkirk.

He would sit with Alice and Arthur and listen to how Callum was doing on supply runs down to North Africa, where he would write home of being able at night to see the battle on the front line lighting up the sky a hellish orange.

Their leave never seemed to coincide, Stanley and Callum, and these two good friends would be destined to never see each other again. Whenever they were home, they would write notes to one another, and leave them on the cabin table. Snippets of their lives at sea, well wishes and messages of good luck, memories of their night shifts beneath the Blitz out on the Stanley B, and playing together in the streets of Chapel.

Stanley was home when the terrible news came. That Callum had been lost at sea in March of 1943. His entire convoy sunk off the coast of Portugal. There had been no survivors, no time to send out a mayday. Seven merchant navy vessels, and two navy protectors, more than fifteen-hundred men.

Alice, Arthur, and Nell were inconsolable. As were Stanley and me.

But we had no time to mourn. The bombs kept falling. The war raged. We had no choice but to carry on. Though our work would be carried out in silence, red, tear-stained eyes, blank faces looking out into the wake left behind by the Stanley B. Lost in our own, terrible thoughts.

When the call came, he didn't blink. Stanley enlisted with the Royal Navy in the June of 1943, two months before his twentieth birthday. He told Alice and Arthur that the first shot fired would be for Callum, and every shot after that would be for them.

Because of his experience on the Stanley B, he was assigned to skipper one of the landing craft used to get soldiers from one ship to the other, or onto dry land. When not tasked with those jobs, he was a support gunner out on deck, and would ferry shells to the anti-aircraft guns during battles. He would duck and weave between swivelling mounts as they chased their prey across the skies.

He would write home and wonder how many parts he saw in action had once been ferried by our very own Stanley B, before becoming a piece of these great warships.

He wrote of bombers and fighters smoking with a direct hit, falling away into a spiralling nose-dive, and exploding into the sea.

He wrote of the deafening sound of the cannons as they opened-up. You weren't able hear yourself think, you just did what you had been trained to do, everything else around you blurred and distant. And he would lug his cases of shells, the battle around him fogged beneath a barrage of noise.

Twenty

No one knows that they are going to be a part of history. It just happens. To a special few. From time to time. We knew that something was happening. Something big.

In May of 1944 American and Canadian troops started flooding into Southampton, filling Southampton Common with tents, latrines and mess halls. So many that not all could be accommodated, and some were bivouacked along Western Esplanade, by the old walls, blocking the road completely.

Hunched up with nowhere to go, these GI's of Western Esplanade sang songs and heated coffee on little gas stoves outside their tents.

The letter box up on Bugle Street became clogged with letters home to family and sweethearts. So much so that it had to be emptied twice a day. And on an old brick wall that lined the road, and gave them shelter, names and dates, regiments and hometowns were carved with penknives to pass the time.

There was a W Wright, born 14/03/09, and a Lawrence Mathis born 23/11, but no year given. Alice wondered if he had signed up before his eighteenth birthday, giving a false birth date. It happened quite a lot: young lads wanting to get a piece of the action before their time. And now here he was, all the way over in Britain, still not wanting to give the game away, in case some officer noticed and sent him home.

There was a T/S Robert M. I never learnt what the T/S meant, but it was important enough to Robert M to take the time to carve.

HL Eatherington came from Zion, Illinois. We looked it up: it was a small town of fifteen-thousand souls north of Chicago, up on Lake Michigan, close to the Wisconsin state line.

About him the names of Joe Hammond, Dave Pa, James Henley, Bill Urban, WM Mellor, and the initials NH were carved. Maybe they were from the same company, huddled up together against that wall, carving out their names side by side, like they would be in battle.

We would never know.

When they finally marched away into the docks and the waiting ships, they took their futures with them. Their stories on Normandy beaches, among the towns of St. Lô and Caen, the Battle of the Bulge and beyond, lost to us.

All that was left were their names and nicknames on an old brick wall that would, in time, become a shrine to the bravery of those young men who were unaware of what they were about to do. Their fates, and the fate of my Stanley unknowingly intertwined.

He came home for a few days in May, his ship moored in Gosport where he had been running exercises with the landing craft. Something was happening, he said, though he was not sure what. But the amassing of troops suggested to him and his shipmates that a grand assault was in the offing.

He would come with us on the Stanley B, and silently watch as more ships came into port. More troops thronging the dockside, and all the way up to the Common at the north end of town, its sea of tents bursting out into the surrounding streets.

When he felt mine or Nell's gaze on him, he would snap out of his reverie and smile at us, pull Nell's cap over her eyes playfully and slip down into the cabin with a chuckle.

And that is how we spent our last days together, on his beloved Stanley B, out in the docks. Just like he had always imagined.

Days of tall tales from out at sea, evenings sat in the cabin looking over his box of memories and plans, cups of coffee up on the bow, looking out at the lights of the docks, large ships silhouetted against the night sky. He would flick through his notebook and tell me about a place that we would be visiting on our trip around the coast, or the types of nesting birds we would see on the cliffs of Netton. And when it was time for him to leave, he did so like he always did, planting a large kiss on my forehead and refusing to say goodbye.

'There's no need,' he would always say 'because it is just a "see you later".' And with that, with his kit bag slung over his shoulder, he waved, slipped away from Chapel dock between the streets and warehouses. And was gone.

The 6th of June 1944 came and went like any other wartime day. We were busy transporting parts across to the shipyards and factories, long into the evening, Alice, Nell, and I. The long days of high summer pushing dusk further and further back.

We heard no radio broadcast, saw no papers.

For us it was the rhythmic chug of the Stanley B's engine, and crate upon crate of parts and fittings, before falling into bed exhausted.

It wasn't until the following day that we learnt of the D-Day landings at Normandy, and a massive assault on Nazi occupied Europe. Arthur brought us the paper before he headed off to Thorneycroft, and we finally learned where all those soldiers, where Stanley had been destined.

I always thought that I would know, somehow, that my instincts would tell me if some harm had come to Stanley. The bond between mother and child so strong that I would feel something.

But I didn't.

I worked through the day Stanley died as if it was any other day.

Completely unaware.

Focused only on throttling back the engines at the right moment, easing the Stanley B dockside slowly and gently to let Nell jump across safely and tie her up.

I went to bed. Slept soundly. Drank my coffee in the morning. Donned my Brooklyn Dodgers cap, waited for Nell, then set off on another day on Southampton Water.

It was Alice's day off, and both Nell and I looked on surprised as we saw her, and Arthur, stood on the Thorneycroft pontoon as we came alongside. I remember we waved.

I didn't register why Arthur should be holding Alice up, who was doubled over, both of their faces stained with tears.

Alice couldn't speak. Neither could Arthur, who simply took the unopened telegram Alice had been holding, that had arrived for me, and passed it over. They had received one before, for Callum. And they knew what it meant.

I read the words, then my mind seemed to fog, and I remember little else.

From what I have been told, I fell backwards, Nell grabbing me, and we both toppled to the floor with me in Nell's arms. She wouldn't let go of me and helped carry me back aboard the Stanley B while sombre shipyard workers looked on, taking off their caps and holding them to their chests.

It had been the 8th of June, and Stanley had been dead for two days, falling during the terrible battle of Sword Beach, in the first wave of landings.

It would take another week to learn how Stanley had died.

He had been skippering one of the landing craft taking soldiers to the beach. The currents had been stronger than expected, and had pushed the craft further to the east, leaving them exposed to the bombardment from the beachhead.

To protect the forty men on his lander, he swung the craft to port as it beached, so as they weren't directly in the line of fire; the starboard wall of the lander giving them a few extra metres of protection from the hail of bullets. By doing so, he had left his position up at the wheel exposed, and he had taken a bullet before he could pull back out to sea. He died instantly. Two months shy of his twenty-first birthday.

In the weeks and months after, I found myself down at that brick wall on Western Esplanade quite a lot, letting my fingers brush across the roughly carved names.

I would imagine that it was HL Eatherington of Zion, Illinois, the possibly underage Lawrence Mathis, born 23/11, Bull Urban, Dave Pa, and T/S Robert M who had been on Stanley's landing craft. That had benefited from Stanley's selflessness, and had somehow taken that extra shelter to get them safely up the beach.

That Joe Hammond and James Henley, NH had, thanks to a young man whose name they would never know, survived where so many others didn't.

It was unlikely, to say the least. But someone had benefited from Stanley's actions, even if it had been for just a few extra steps. Why not let it be them, who I could visit, make real?

I spent the first few weeks after Stanley's passing with Aunt Harriet, who had been broken by the news. She had always been captivated by his effervescent spirit and had loved him like he was her own.

We managed between us to keep each other fed and consoled, taking it in turns to discover the other crumpled in a flood of tears in the small hours of the morning; grief inducing a cruel insomnia, where the days seemed to drag by with a terrible slowness.

We would take a trip across to the military cemetery where he was buried after the war, standing quietly among a sea of identical headstones that seemed to stretch forever, in all directions.

It was a comfort of sorts, to place my hand on the neatly manicured grass beneath his headstone, to see his name etched into the granite. To know that he was there, safe from harm.

But it didn't make me feel closer to him. It was a strange field in a strange land, that neither Stanley nor I had ever been to before. He was here, but he wasn't here.

To me, Stanley was back home, on the Stanley B. In every board, every moving part, sat behind the wheel in the wheelhouse, on the benches down in the cabin, by the bow line. That is where he was in my minds' eye. Where I felt him in my heart.

On his beloved boat, Stanley could never leave us.

And because of that, I would never leave it.

I would make the trip back to his headstone many years later, with Charlie. But I would take time every day to sit in the cabin on the Stanley B in its new position behind the glasshouse at Five Acre Cottage.

I would leaf through his box of bits and feel myself transported back in time. The tactile, rough pages of his notebooks. His handwritten notes and pasted newspaper clippings, those Southampton programmes sporting his name. Sights and sounds, smells would materialise, people and places, Stanley himself. So vividly, for a second, that it felt real. That then was with me in the present. Or I was back in the past. Clear as day. For a moment. It was the only memorial I needed.

It was a precious place, and down in that cabin beneath the clawing forest, I would talk to my Stanley. And he would reply in kind, from his box, drawing memories out. Of Netton, Christmas matches at Thorneycroft, Mr Waters' bookshop, watching the boats from our wall in the docks.

From that box of memories, he would talk, and I would listen.

After a few weeks with Aunt Harriet, I stayed in Alice and Arthur's spare room, and saw out the war on Southampton Water. On the Stanley B with Nell.

When VE Day came our celebrations were muted – happy that the war was over, but mindful of the terrible price we had all paid for our freedom.

Aunt Harriet came down, and we sat in Alice and Arthur's front room, and with Nell we toasted Callum and Stanley with an expensive bottle of whisky. Harriet took a couple of drams, and we walked to the Stanley B, and she and Nell poured them out on the bow. One each for the boys.

With peacetime I spent a while fixing up the Stanley B. She had taken some damage under the relentless workload placed on her, and the engine needed an overhaul. Thanks to Stanley's patient teachings, and a little help from Arthur, I replaced all the worn parts, and then bolstered the hull in dry dock until she was right as rain. And waited for the summer of 1946.

I knew that I couldn't stay in Southampton. Around every corner was a memory, some good, some bad. And often it was the good ones that hurt so much. Echoes of the boys playing football out in the streets, marching off to the floating bridge with young Nell trailing behind them. Stanley and Mr Waters in the back room of the bookshop at South Western House, leaning into some book or other as thick as thieves.

Stanley had not wanted to stay, even before he had met Martha.

The Blitz had affected him profoundly. It left him always on edge, as if he could never truly relax, flinching at any out of the ordinary noise. He could never unsee the terrible devastation on building and human alike that had lain strewn amongst the rubble.

I would spend long hours leafing through his notebook, reading through all the stops he had planned for us around Britain, and his dream of a new life in Freshwater at the end. And he would talk about it in his letters home while in the merchant navy, and then the navy.

Stanley never saw limitation in anything. He dreamed, then he made dreams come true. In his twenty short years he did more than many could only hope to achieve in a lifetime.

He dreamed of us owning a boat, then he found the Stanley B. He learnt everything there was to know about her and helped make her real.

He dreamt of playing football for Thorneycroft and playing at The Dell. He did both.

He dreamt of places beyond the docks, where great ships sailed, then he visited them in the merchant navy.

And then he dreamt of our trip, exploring castles and coves. Abbeys, grand feats of engineering and ancient sites. Of taking sightseers to see the puffins, Saint Catherine's Lighthouse. He dreamt of a small cottage, and long walks up on the bluffs, away on Netton.

It was to be a grand life.

I felt I owed it to him. To at least set off, to work through his notebook. To undertake the one dream of his that he hadn't been able to fulfil. I would set off, and then see what happened.

So, I readied the Stanley B, and waited for summer.

I told no one of my plan, until it was time. And when I told Alice and Nell that I meant not to come back after it was done, we hugged one another and cried dockside when they came to see me off.

The Stanley B had been such a big part of Nell's childhood, and her brother's, that she placed her hand against the hull, rubbed it gently, like she was saying goodbye to a beloved pet.

She would miss me, The Stanley B, she said.

And I would miss them.

We had seen so much together from the wheelhouse. We had lived through the best and worst of times on deck. We had become independent businesswomen, with a stern bristling with sightseers.

We had rescued lives from the beaches of Dunkirk and kept our war effort moving ferrying parts to the factories on Southampton Water.

We had seen first Callum, then Stanley fade from view, and dealt with the grief together, on the Stanley B.

It was hard, pulling away from Chapel docks that final time, leaving behind such good people. I waved back at them until the docks and distance swallowed them up. Then I turned, and looked forward, and didn't look back again. Out past Fawley Creek and Calshot Castle and into the Solent. Past Cowes harbour where we had sat and ate fish and chips. Past Ryde where Stanley had played in the breakers. On toward Stanley's first stop in his little notebook.

Past Dover we took a detour on a calm, limp summer's day in July, leaving the coastline of Britain behind to jog across the Channel, to Sword Beach, or Luc-Sur-Mer, Normandy, as it was known in peacetime.

We idled, for how long I don't know, looking out at a beautiful stretch of golden sand, the scars of D-Day healed by sweeping tides. We pointed toward the shore, nodding gently on the rolling swell toward where Stanley fell. Where HL Eatherington of Zion, Illinois and the men on that Southampton wall met their fate.

Then I turned the Stanley B about with a tearstained face, and we set off back the way we came, and on to the next stop on Stanley's adventure.

I meant not to go back. To Southampton. But I did twice. I would write postcards to Aunt Harriet, to Alice, Arthur, and Nell when I could on my trip. And after I had met Charlie, and moved to Five Acre Cottage, we would write to one another quite regularly.

In 1953 I received notice that Aunt Harriet had passed away and took the train down for her funeral.

The place had changed so much in the seven years since I had left.

The streets of Chapel that had survived the Blitz had been levelled in the final tranche of slum clearances implemented after the war.

Where Stanley, Callum, and Nell had played, where people had lived and died, warehouses, chandleries, and aggregate plants now stood. Streets and street names had simply disappeared, and Alice and Arthur had moved across the water to Weston, to a neat little house with a back garden of fruit trees and rolling lawn.

I stayed with them overnight and would do so again in 1960 when news came of Arthur's sudden passing.

He was six months shy of retirement when he had a heart attack at work, down in the bowels of a ship he was working on. He died as he had lived and worked, next to his friend Cyril Smith, who held his hand in the dark as they waited for help.

Cyril remembered me at the funeral, and talked warmly of young Stanley, and their short time as team-mates at Southampton.

I told him that Stanley would be made up to know that his hero remembered him.

That I would have to listen to Stanley for hours on a Saturday evening over a fish and chip supper, as he talked me through the trickery Cyril had performed on the wings for Thorneycroft that afternoon.

I told him that he had given Stanley the courage to put on that famous Southampton shirt, and step out during the Blitz, to keep football going in the face of everything.

He had smiled, blushed, embarrassed that someone still remembered his humble career, and said that he always tried his best.

A few months after the funeral, I invited Alice and Nell up to Five Acre Cottage, and we went for long walks around Windermere, up into the hills and mountains where I worked, across the great lakes on the ferries. We would have tea and cakes in the hotel at the end of the narrow, winding path from Five Acre gardens, looking out on the still waters of Lake Windermere. The odd sailing boat drifting past.

We would spend long evenings sat up on the Stanley B behind the glasshouse, beneath the grand canopy of trees. We would talk about memories on board, of Stanley and Callum. We would pore through Stanley's box of things, at the initials carved on the lid. We would reminisce on anything and everything.

They had both said how good it had been to see the Stanley B, that she was still here, after all these years. Nell even took out a small parcel from her bag one evening, and carefully unwrapped it to reveal her old Brooklyn Dodgers cap gifted to her by Stanley.

'I could never throw it out,' she had said, and put in on again for old times' sake, which made us all laugh.

'It should go in the box,' she had said 'don't you think? It should be with everything else,' and she gently, carefully placed it inside.

The Stanley B is a testament to what can be achieved, if you just give someone that tiniest of chance, open the door a jar to let a little light through.

Stanley Buchanan had been forsaken by his father, by his grandparents, from before he had even been born. His standing, his worth determined before his very first breath. But if they only knew what he went on to do, I wonder what they would think.

He was a boy who saw the good in life. Who didn't see a rainy day, but the perfect conditions for sliding tackles at the park.

He didn't see a small one room flat in Chapel, but a home right on the docks, where we could sit and look at all the boats, and dream.

He didn't see scrap when he discovered what would become the Stanley B, he saw those dreams coming true. He saw afternoons down by the water playing for Thorneycroft A in front of the odd passer-by as *the* match of the day. And turning out for Southampton at The Dell in front of a few hundred souls during the Blitz was as dizzying and magical as those Christmas matches, crammed together in a sea of thousands.

And just that one chance, that one loan from Aunt Harriet to buy the Stanley B, and look what he achieved.

He helped build our little boat back up from scratch; a boat that then helped two families make a living. Made skippers of those who could never have dreamed of such a position.

His boat helped rescue countless soldiers at Dunkirk and saved the lives of those eleven Belgians left behind in the surf. His boat helped build Spitfires and warships and kept his spirits up down in the shelters as the bombs fell.

His experience on the Stanley B helped him join the merchant navy, and travel to far flung places full of skyscrapers and bleachers, palm trees, sweethearts and icebergs.

It enabled him to become that hero at Sword Beach, forsaking himself for the benefit of others.

That one break, that one opportunity, and look at what he managed. All in 20 short years.

And as I dutifully sailed from spot to spot in his notebook, I steeled myself to make good that one final dream of his.

Though I never thought that it wouldn't be me to finish what he had imagined.

He would have liked Gordie, I am sure. They would have been good friends in another life. He would have gravitated toward this lost soul as it washed up at the glasshouse. He would have given him a break, that sliver of light. He would have seen the good, even when Gordie couldn't.

He would have given him the shears and the trowel, the hoe and rake.

He would have done it, and so that is what I did.

There had never been any grand design. Any plan to nudge Gordie in the direction of the Stanley B. It was purely fate that had him discover her.

I had always intended to finish what had been started myself. But time was not on my side.

Putting things off for another season, not wanting to let the gardens fail and wither caught up with me.

And then along came Gordie.

Nothing is truly yours forever. You have to give everything up eventually. But you don't have to let it crumble away to dust. You can try, at least, to find some way to breathe more life into an idea, a hope.

And that is what I did.

I will never know if Gordie took my gift of the Stanley B. If he ever rounded that headland to see Saint Catherine's Lighthouse. If he ever finished Stanley's trip.

I can only hope and lean on my intuition – that tells me that Gordie is a good person, with a good heart.

That his time among the gardens of Five Acre Cottage, the glasshouse, the terraces of Holker Street and those long Sundays in my kitchen were as genuine as they felt.

And that he cherished them as much as I did.

That all his selfless work on the Stanley B, helping me get her right as rain was born out of a simple joy at seeing another human soul come to life, blossom with every engine part fixed, and hull breach made sound.

I can only hope that he took the Stanley B, and lived the life he deserves.

That somewhere out there is our little boat, finding smooth sailing on calm waters.

The ghosts of all those whose initials are etched into Stanley's box, who lived and loved her, finding a fair wind and a warm sun, up on the bow.

That somewhere out there, tucked away in the cabin, there is still Stanley's box of memories, and that Gordie is adding to it.

All you can do is open the door a sliver. Let a little light through.

But I have faith. I believe.

A young boy called Stanley taught me that.

The Left Back

Twenty-One

After my day with Gordie, I spent the rest of my time on the Island drifting from one spot to the other, gathering my thoughts and further material for my article.

I walked up onto Freshwater Bay and wandered around the base of the lighthouse, looking down at the breakwater below, and the village huddled in the lee of the bluff.

I sat in the sun on the seafront watching fishing boats bob. A brazen cat would come right up to me on my bench, look at me with a disdain that suggested that I was in its spot, circle about for a few moments, then curl up in a lesser spot nearby, one eye monitoring my position.

I wandered about Shooter's Meadow, sitting in the old stand, drinking coffee in the little café that used to be Freshwater FC's clubhouse.

It was quiet enough for me to weave between the seats, taking in all the pictures on the walls – a century of footballing history played out across team photos, action shots, celebrations of trophies lifted where caravans and motorhomes now stood.

Faces ghosted across faded black and white images, sepia tinged with old age, slowly materialising into colour in the early '70's. A few faces re-appearing across the walls, young men in team line-ups ageing into track-suited trainers, managers, bucket men standing at the end of the line. Then again into elderly gents in suits: fixture secretaries, groundsmen, chairmen. A lifetime of faithful, willing obscure footballing servitude jumping from one frame to another.

I lingered at the washed-out picture of the 1984 Freshwater Gold Cup Final team, with a very young Tom Maskell beaming back at me, his secrets as safe now as they were before I began in on his story.

I rode my bike around Blackwater Lake, all the way to Woodford, away on Shanklin Point, to find the home of Woodford FC, where Tom Maskell played his first senior game.

It was not easy to find. The little wooden sign pointing the way down a narrow, overgrown track had long been obscured by bramble.

And as everyone on the island who needed to know where this obscure little outpost of island football was already knew its location by heart, no one bothered to rescue the faded sign with the club's name on it.

At the end of the stony track that popped and cracked beneath the bicycle's tyres, a small clubhouse appeared. Large windowpanes covered with an iron trellis to protect them from wayward balls looked out on a pitch littered with seas of daisies. Nets in each goal had been hoisted up and tied to the crossbar, keeping them safe, ready for another season of Island League football.

Thickset trees surrounded the pitch. Low lying branches brushed across the corrugated roof of a stretch of covered standing on the far side like a dull, tuneless xylophone. Birds hidden among the woods accompanying with staccato song.

What a place to play your football, and a perfect venue to start a football career.

From the tables outside the café on Woodford dock I saw Gordie and the Stanley B gliding across Blackwater Lake, then, again, the following day on my way up to Westlyn, where I had arranged to meet Rory Hamilton – one time player, trainer, kit man, tea hut attendant, committee man, and gate man for Westlyn Town FC.

Now ninety-six years old, Rory is simply a supporter these days, who can be found, come rain or shine, up in the stands for every home game. But back in the day, he had been the man who arranged with Gordie the away travel for the club's Island League side. He had also saved Gordie a programme from any match that young Tom Maskell played in.

Rory would take a daily constitutional up to Seaview Park, walk slowly round the pitch barrier a couple of times before a quiet moment in his spot in the stands.

He remembered Tom well. He had promised Gordie to keep an eye out for him on away trips to the mainland and would always be sure to sit close to him on the ferry, and on the team bus the other side. He would engage in aimless conversation with him, cracking jokes, talking about the opposition, anything.

Being so young, and quiet, Tom didn't sit at the back of the bus playing cards for money like most of the players did. He would be up the front where the old timers from the supporter's club sat, and he would often while away the long trips by looking out the window at the world passing by.

'We've had a few players move on up into the football league from Westlyn,' Rory had said 'Mainly with the local teams, and rarely for a sustained period. They would try, do their best, and within a season or two, find themselves back in the Western League, either with Torquay or Exeter Reserves, or back with us. And there is no shame in that. That is a decent career that many could only dream of.

'I thought that if that was to be young Maskell's lot, then it wouldn't be talent that would hold him back. He had that in spades.

'But sometimes, players just don't take to leaving the island. It is a different pace of life to the mainland. I have seen so many players preferring to play out their days in the Island League, or with us here at Seaview park, be slightly bigger fish in a smaller pond, rather than be unhappy, a little rudderless, lost, at a higher level. And that is perfectly fine. Contentedness comes in many guises. And Tom seemed so happy here, with Gordie,' he trailed away.

'The simple answer is, I don't know what happened to young Tom. I don't know where he is, or why he didn't continue in the Football League; though I have often wondered, over the years.

'Wherever he is, whatever he is doing, if he is half as happy as he was out on Blackwater Lake, on that boat. If he is half as happy as when he was turning out for Freshwater, for us, then that would be some life indeed.

'I just wish we knew, one way or the other, for Gordie's sake, if no one else.

'Just to know that he was all right. That really would be something.'

After Rory I met with Westlyn Police, then the Netton Gazette. Neither had anything to add that hadn't been gleaned from talking to those who knew Tom. Nothing to help with the mystery of his disappearance, or where he might be.

And as I sat on the pontoon in front of my cabin, waiting for Gordie to pick me up, take me across to Colbridge and the ferry home. As I sat in the faint light of early dawn, watching the mist drift across the expanse of black waters before me, creeping out from the shadows among the thickset trees on the far shore, I hoped that Gordie was right.

That Tom would come back to him one day, would be found sitting patiently on Gordie's old bench. That, unable to choose between a life on Blackwater Lake and his dream of professional football, he found a third way. And that one day he will come back to tell Gordie all about it.

If I were able to write the ending to this story, then that would be it. I would write it gladly.

As we neared the pontoons of Colbridge, Gordie throttled back the engines and I stepped across to tie her up. Still no expert, but there is hope yet, Gordie had said with a wry smile.

We shook hands and I promised that I would be in touch, and just before I set off for the ferry I stopped, pulled out a paper from my bag, handed it across to Gordie.

'What's this?' he said.

It was the team sheet, from Tom's reserve team debut, I told him, complete with his very first autograph as a professional footballer.

'It should be in his box, with all his other things,' I said. 'It should stay on the boat, don't you think?'

He smiled, nodded.

'He would like that, very much. Thank you,' he said, looking down at it in his hands, then waved as I turned away.

'Safe journey,' he said, and with that Gordie, the Stanley B quickly slipped away behind all the caravans and tents pitched dockside. The sounds of her engine throttling out from the pontoon in the still of early morning, gradually fading away to nothing as it slipped back out onto Blackwater Lake.

The feature came out ten days later, in the weekend sports magazine. It looked really smart and was adorned with those few images of Maskell that existed, and a couple of shots I had taken of Shooter's Meadow and Seaview Park.

The stills team even managed to track down that photograph of Gordie Macrae scoring for Cowdenbeath at Ibrox, all those years ago, and it sat next to a picture I had taken of him standing on the towpath in Freshwater, in front of his boat.

I sent him a couple of copies of the magazine, as I had promised. One for Gordie, and one for young Tom and his box of memories.

And that, after everything, was that.

The story of Tom and Gordie sat among a sea of other articles, other weekend supplements, and slipped into piles of recycling up and down the country on the Monday morning.

And while I received a few messages, from Town supporters and complete neutrals expressing how much they had enjoyed the article, it shed no new light on what became of Tom Maskell. Nothing to follow up on. And with that the story was filed in the archives along with the rest.

Though I hope that it isn't the end of the story, even if I never get to hear it.

Like Rory Hamilton, I hope that one day Gordie and Tom will meet again, set off once more across their Blackwater Lake. Just like old times.

That is the ending that Gordie, young Tom Maskell deserve.

I'm just sorry that it wasn't me who could give it to them.

Not yet at least.

The Rangers Reject

Twenty-Two

When the article came out it caused quite a stir across Netton. Our little island isnae the sort of place people write about.

The Gazette picked up on it, and did an article on there being an article, and over the following weeks I bumped into a few old players and supporters who wanted to stop and chat about it. About old times. About young Tom.

They arranged a get together up at Shooter's Meadow and we sat and drank and talked about games gone by. Funny stories about some of the characters we had seen playing for Freshwater, or one of the other island teams.

Those who had memories of Tom talked fondly of him. Of crunching tackles far greater than his frail frame should have been able to produce, of darting runs down the wing and wicked crosses into the box.

Robbie Pardoe, the centre forward for Westlyn Town during Tom's one season there talked about it being the best season of his career.

'I never scored as many goals in a season again, after Tom moved on. I knew I just had to get in the box and Tom would whip the ball across, and I would just stand there and nod them in. He made me look very good. Which was a problem the following year when he wasn't there. Because I looked God-awful again.'

The Gazette came down and took a photo of all of us as we hung Tom's article above his picture on the old clubhouse wall.

Westlyn Town had paid for it to be framed, and it looked so smart in a wooden frame made from driftwood found along Shanklin Point. Tom would have loved that, I told them.

The evening went on with a bottle of whisky, people milling about the pictures on the wall, chatting in groups at memories they evoked. All united in the warmth they felt for Shooter's Meadow, for Freshwater FC, chuckling at recollections of a young Tom Maskell drowning in a Freshwater kit, while others seemed ready to burst out of their top.

Anecdotes of away trips on the Stanley B, trying to dodge Tom collecting fares.

'Though no matter how hard you tried, he would somehow appear at your side, rattling that damn can.'

Memories of the crate of beer that would be waiting on the boat for the team, no matter the score, helping to pass the time on the trip home.

Stories of trying to carry a live lobster home after a man of the match display. Horrendous pre-season sprints up to Saint Catherine's Lighthouse, heaving into the long grass with the jeering of your team-mates ringing in your ears. The fear of a sliding tackle away at Canford Cliffs where, on a wet day, you could slide right under the pitch-side railing, and much too close to the cliff edge for comfort.

At some point someone said how sad it was to see Shooter's Meadow the way it was, with the little wooden stand beginning to rot away. That before too long, it would be lost forever.

I told them how much Tom loved that stand and would sit in it and replay the Freshwater match from the previous Saturday when he was a very young lad, running through the moves and goals, some of which were created and finished by people gathered together here.

They were Tom's heroes, I told them, that they had inspired him to be the player that he was.

After a moment of quiet contemplation at learning that they had been someone's hero, a voice piped up.

'Then we should do something about it. We should preserve that old stand. For posterity. And if not in the name of Tom, then for our own vanity. We are heroes, after all!'

And that is what they did. A small working group begged and borrowed materials, man hours and expertise, and over the course of the summer replaced rotten boards and rafters, panels and pillars, finally giving the stand a new coat of red Freshwater FC paint.

In late August, on the weekend that the Island Football League started back up for another season, a group of us gathered at Shooter's Meadow to celebrate what had been achieved. We toasted the revamped stand that was playing host to the last of the holidaying children from the campsite, sitting quietly as a movie played out on the screen before them.

It looked good as new. Tom would be made up, I told them. It was a fitting tribute, to him, and the club. And maybe, one day, he might be able to thank them in person.

With that, we retired up to the café, and Sandy poured us all a dram, and we sat quietly looking out at the pitch, the failing light, listening to the faint soundtrack of the kids' movie. The beam from Saint Catherine's Lighthouse sweeping out across Freshwater, across the bay.

It was a month or so later, after a long day of taking fish up to the restaurants and fishmongers on Westlyn Esplanade. Of picking up boxes of car parts from the ferry and taking them down to the garage in Freshwater. Helping to remove a couple of old wardrobes from one of the cabins on Blackwater Lake, resting them on my trolley and haphazardly wheeling them down onto the pontoon and toward their next stop at a charity shop in Woodford. Before taking an elderly couple across to Canford Cliffs for a spot of hill walking.

It was a long day, and my back ached in my chair in the wheelhouse as I steered toward home, the sky an array of fiery reds, oranges and pinks as the sun set behind the shadowy rise of Durnford Downs. There was a chill coming off the water that hinted at Autumn and had me yearning for another warm sweater from old Andy Widdett and his sheep, while the Stanley B cut through the layer of fog that had crept out from the forests; thick enough to hide the chop on the bow, our wake fanning out from the stern.

As I drew closer to home, my heart sank a little as a figure sat on my bench on the towpath materialised out of the fog.

A job is a job, I had thought, though my bad leg was aching from the day's exertion, and I was due up at Shooter's Meadow for one last dram with Sandy, before she shut the café down for the winter now the camping season had come to an end.

As I came to, I throttled back and edged up to the towpath, stepped across with a wince to tie the boat up, then nodded at the figure on the bench.

'Good evening,' I said 'Do you need taking somewhere?'

She was a pretty woman, slight, middle-aged. Her hair was tied back in a ponytail and had a streak of grey running through it from her right temple. She stood up and pulled her cardigan about her, then she stepped toward me.

'Are you Mr Macrae?' she said in a quiet, faltering voice.

I nodded.

'Gordie Macrae?'

I nodded again.

'From Govan? Who used to work in the shipyards? Who played for Cowdenbeath?' I told her that that was me, and she pulled out a copy of the magazine from her bag, opened it at the article, at the picture of me and my goal at Ibrox.

'An old work mate of yours, from the shipyard told me about this. I met him completely by accident, out of the blue.'

I nodded, and we stood silently for a few moments before she spoke again.

'You see,' she said, pausing. 'Well, I was at that match, when you scored against Rangers. Though I dinae really remember anything about it. I was too young.

'And I was too young to know that you wrote to me every week, sent me birthday and Christmas presents every year. I never knew.

'And until this,' she said, holding up the article 'I didnae even know if you were alive.'

She wiped away a tear that had begun to roll down her cheek.

'What you did, for this Tom Maskell. It was a wonderful thing,' then she paused.

'My name is Eilish,' she said.

'Hello Dad.'

The Girl in the Stand

Twenty-Three

It is fitting that one of my first memories is of watching the stars in the night sky, seeing as I have spent the rest of my life listening to them.

I couldnae have been more than three.

I remember a dark, narrow stairwell that felt ominous enough to have me reaching for my dad's hand, holding it tightly.

I remember a heavy door that opened up onto the roof of our block of flats, revealing a vast sea of stars above. Or, at least, those that could be seen through the light pollution.

My dad knew nothing of the constellations, but I remember as clear as anything him pointing out Cassiopeia, with its distinctive 'W' shape. Though he called it a sideways 'E.'

'E for Eilish,' he would say 'The stars are talking to you.' He could have no idea that they would, for more than thirty years.

We would sit on clear nights and track 'E for Eilish' on its path above us. Sometimes low in the sky, obscured by other buildings, we would catch partial glimpses. But in the most part, it stayed high enough to see. And in the summer months it sat right on top of us, so as you could lay on the floor and watch it without your neck aching.

To me back then it was just a pretty pattern in the darkness. Now it is one of many examples of the awe and majesty of the universe that I have had the pleasure to explore. My 'E' littered with astronomical wonders: Schedar, an orange giant star two-hundred and twenty-eight light years away. Gamma Cassiopeiae, a blue star more than six hundred and ten light years distant. Binary stars more than sixty-five million years old, rare yellow hypergiants, and star clusters ten thousand light years from Earth.

When I was old enough to write, I would drive my teachers to distraction by writing my E's as I saw my 'E for Eilish' in the sky – with a slanted top line followed by a zig zag to complete it. No matter how they tried to school me, I remained stubborn in how I wrote it, etching what looked like an ancient rune.

A subliminal symbol of those happy, simple nights spent with dad up on the roof, all that was left of him after mum and I left.

I write my E's like it to this day, as natural a rhythm as breathing.

Despite not knowing dad beyond my fourth birthday, those moments in time watching the stars are not the only memories that I have of him.

And despite being told how scared I was of him, when he went into himself, I have no memories of that at all. And you would think that I would. But I havenae.

All the snapshots of life back then – little bursts of moments, places and sounds, whirring like an 8mm projector in my subconscious, are benign and soothing, worthy of losing yourself in for a moment.

I remember the Saturday ritual, of going to see him play football. Though I have no memories of games and the like, I remember the excitement of getting the train. The heavy clunk as doors slammed shut, the worn carpet-like fabric on the seats smelling of tobacco, feeling rough, grainy to the touch, that would tickle your face if you laid your head down to sleep on the seat next to you.

I remember the walk down Cowdenbeath high street, following the stream of people to the football ground.

I remember the stand from a certain angle, pillars and beams frozen in my mind's eye like a Polaroid picture.

I remember yelling and cheering, though I don't know why.

I remember waving down at the pitch when instructed to by mum, though I couldnae see dad among all the other players. I remember Mum had a big warm coat with a black and white pattern that I would snuggle into.

I knew that it was a big deal, Dad being out there, though again, I didnae know why.

I remember corridors and changing rooms that smelt of liniment and cheap aftershave, wet mud caked around studs on football boots that cracked and clattered on the hard floors.

I remember Dad meeting us at the door, behind which the clamour of team-mates laughing and shouting. I remember falling asleep on him on the train journey home, the rise and fall of his breathing, the familiar smell and rough weave of his jumper as soothing as the clack of the train rattling along the tracks.

I have been told that I was in the stand when he scored against Rangers at Ibrox, in front of more than forty thousand people, though I have no recollection of it, being a little too young.

I don't remember it, or anything else to do with him.

Just pointing at the stars, waving to him unseen, way down on the Central Park pitch, train rides home.

And that was that. Nothing more.

I waited every birthday, every Christmas after we left, for some message, a card, anything. But nothing came. Or rather, nothing was ever given to me. He was seemingly lost to me, and I, lost to him. Though I hoped that he might think about me, wonder after me, just as I thought and wondered after him.

He was never spoken about. Erased from the face of the Earth. For the rest of my life. Or so I thought.

Despite my errant inscribing of the letter E, I loved reading and writing. I devoured books from the library. Mystery novels, ghost stories, books on mythical sea beasts from the deeps were my favourites, and they would send a tingle down my spine as I pictured the spooky scenes within, otherworldly adventures. Peering into the unknown, often with bedsheets pulled right up over my nose for protection, it had me captivated. What was out there among the fog? The stars? Beneath the waves? What was that lurking deep in the woods? I came alive as I explored those questions through the pages of books borrowed from the library.

I was fascinated by The Abominable Snowman, UFO's, deep sea creatures and the Loch Ness Monster, that would sometimes crop up in my grandparent's newspaper with a grainy picture and a claimed sighting.

For a young girl from Glasgow, it was effectively a few hours up the road, and had my full attention.

I would ask my Grandfather and his old work cronies when they came round for a few tins if they had ever seen it. Most would just scoff. A hard life working the Govan shipyards stripping them of any romantic notions of mythical beasts. Though one did humour me enough to bring round a couple of books he had found at a jumble sale: *The Mystery of the Loch Ness Monster*, and *The Story of the Loch Ness Monster*. Both pulpy paperbacks designed to reel in tourists and excitable children alike, full of photographs and drawings, anecdotes of sightings of something lurking out in the deep waters.

I kept them beneath my pillow and would flick through them before bed. And I would wonder, imagine, ponder all that we didnae know, and the places where all that we didnae know might be lingering, just out of sight, somewhere among the shadows.

I loved stories. And the places they took me. *The Kraken Wakes* by John Wyndham, *Journey to the Centre of the Earth* by Jules Verne – they were two of my favourites, and I would visit them regularly. Captivated by spine-tingling adventures, the unknown, looming just round the corner.

English was by far my best subject at school. That and history and religious studies, where both were another source of stories and tales from far flung lands.

Maths and science, much to my frustration, remained unfathomable, no matter how hard I tried. It seemed that 'practical' endeavours could never settle and bed in in my mind.

So, when I was offered a scholarship to go to University to read English Literature I jumped at the chance and spent every hour of every day in its beautiful-vaulted library reading tales from Homer, Sophocles, Coleridge and Virgil. Dante's Inferno, Dr Faustus. The heart-breaking lyricism of John Berryman, George Eliot and Virginia Woolf.

Though it was the stunningly hypnotic Sylvia Plath, and her breath-taking poetry that spoke to me the loudest. Emotions and evocations blossoming out of the page with every word in vivid flash-bursts of imagery. The weight of bristling emotion, even if I couldnae quite fully comprehend the meaning, stopping me dead in my tracks. Transported for the briefest of moments into Plath's soul.

The line *"Her blacks crackle and drag"*, from her poem *"Edge"* – the last poem she ever wrote before her death – staying with me forever. An image of a woman in turmoil, vulnerable, lost. Powerful beyond words.

Powerful enough for me to write about her for my dissertation, visit her grave in a pretty little graveyard in the equally pretty and cobbled village of Heptonstall.

Perched high up a devilishly steep hill, looking down at Hebden Bridge and the Calder Valley below, it seemed a restful enough spot, overlooking the ruins of an old church destroyed by a gale in 1847, a little square, lined with weaver's cottages, hand looms resting beneath large windows to make the most of the natural light.

With its cobbled streets and quiet cottages, time seemed slowed in Heptonstall, and my few days there were spent drinking tea in the tea rooms, wandering the woodlands of Hardcastle Crags, complete with towering chimneys from long lost mills, and reading Plath's poetry in the window of Stag Cottage, the oldest house in the village that dated back to the 16th Century, and came available to rent with a dungeon that was once used as the local lock-up.

Every day I would find myself wandering back to her gravestone, littered with pens, pretty stones, and posies gifted her by fellow lovers of her poetry. Solitary figures standing for a time in their own thoughts, before weaving away, always looking back over their shoulders, one last time, before Sylvia slipped from view.

At university I was nothing special. A solid, honest, hardworking student who did her background reading and got her essays in on time. Who attended every lecture and seminar. Who absorbed as much as she could, and took advantage of the gift that was my scholarship. Though the social side of things were a struggle, always preferring the company of books to humans.

I would try. Turn up to parties and dances. Walk about and smile, to be seen. Have a drink in the corner, stand awkwardly for a time, then slip back out and away. It was fine. I liked it that way.

When my studies drew to a close, I didnae know what to do next. All I knew was that I loved the little town that engulfed the university. I loved the narrow streets lined with higgledy old cottages that had stood for centuries. I loved walking up to the old church that looked down over rooftops and smoking chimneys. I loved wandering along the riverbanks that lined the river Ouse that gurgled and eddied as it bisected the town in two. I loved being able to wander up little paths lined with hedgerows and finding myself in the countryside. Dappled thickets of trees. Vast fields of bright yellow rapeseed. I had loved my time there, and I didnae want to let it go. I wasnae ready.

I had paid my way, working evenings and weekends at the little market store near campus, stacking shelves and working the tills. But with the subsidised rent of student halls gone, I needed something else if I wanted to stay on for a little longer.

It was pure chance that I came across the notice pinned up on a board by one of the campus refectories.

It had got swamped by newer notices pinned across the top of it, and it would have remained lost to me if not for an idle moment over a pot of tea, with nothing better to do than flick through the tangle of papers.

It said rather vaguely "Research Assistant required. Telephone 273459".

Professor Bethany Standing's office was on the top floor of one of the oldest and most remote buildings on campus. The wooden steps bowed and creaked as you took them, making you hold on to the handrail, just in case, as you passed through five floors of shadowy, abandoned lecture rooms and offices.

It very much felt like professor Standing had been left behind, while the rest of the campus had grown and moved on into newer settings. Both her and her work marginalised, left to fend for itself beneath bowing roofs. Cold and the dampness in the walls only kept at bay by grand hearths dotted about her rooms on the top floor. Hearths that would become my first port of call every morning, for decades to come, carrying armfuls of firewood up those rickety stairs to keep Professor Standing's rooms warm and welcoming.

We would both take some time every week to wander the woods behind her building, gathering and chopping fallen limbs, stacking it in the lean to round the back of the building to dry out.

'For she who chops the wood, warms herself twice,' she would always say.

Bethany, or Beth as she preferred, was a thin, middle-aged woman who lived behind thick rimmed glasses, and beneath greying hair tied up in a knot, that always had a couple of pencils sticking through it for when she needed one quickly.

At our first meeting she looked me up and down. Smiled, and asked me about my interests. I told her of my studies.

'Any background in science?' None, I told her. She nodded. 'Probably just as well,' she said, 'as this job will ruin any standing you might have in that field. This job is not one for building a reputation,' she paused, shrugged. 'Well, at least, not a good one. Do you have any interest in astronomy? Space? The planets?'

I told her about nights on the rooftops looking up at the stars with my dad. About Cassiopeia, E for Eilish, and how I still write my letter E's in the shape of the constellation. I told her I loved old b-movies about UFO's and monsters. And looking up at a full moon.

I told her how I loved the unknown, mysteries. How I had once stood as a child on the shores of Loch Ness, for hours, trying to catch a glimpse of the monster.

And how that was it.

But I was a fast learner, and a hard worker, and I had become proficient at research during my years in the library.

She nodded, smiled.

'Well Miss Macrae, believe it or not, but staring into Loch Ness counts as some considerable experience for this job.

'And despite little to no knowledge of astronomy, and no background in science, the fact that you have been the only applicant for a post that has been advertised for more than a year holds you in particularly good stead. When would you like to start?'

The pay was terrible, but the job did come with a rent-free room with a private bathroom in the north eastern corner of Professor Standing's floor of the building.

We would be roommates of a kind, she told me, pointing to a door surrounded by heaving bookcases behind her desk. Her bedroom.

I moved in that weekend, ready for a Monday morning start, still not sure exactly what my new job actually entailed.

'There will be plenty of time for all that on Monday,' she had said, handing me a set of keys for all the doors from the ground floor up to my new room. 'Welcome.'

I sometimes wonder if my passion for the unknown, for mysteries stems from not knowing what became of dad. If thinking about UFO's and giant monsters of the deep were just a part of that conscious and subconscious yearning to know what became of the man who took me to see the stars, and was so comfortable to sleep on, where curled up on his lap on the train I never felt safer.

After all, conversations or questions about him were always shut down, the subject changed. The dad I remember receding into myth and legend, and the fog of old memories.

I wonder if one desire fuelled the other, and ultimately gave me the mindset to want to delve through all those papers on that noticeboard, right the way down, until I came across Professor Standing's old and yellowed notice.

It is possible. It makes sense. It feels right.

Either way. No matter how I got there, come Monday morning, I found myself sitting in a chair in Beth's office, waiting to learn just what it was I had signed myself up for.

When she appeared from her room, she made us both a mug of tea.

'Come,' she said, and beckoned for me to follow her down a creaking corridor to a door to what used to be an old lecture room.

Inside was a mess of tables stacked high with papers, books, and reams of printouts that had once chuntered through a row of three printers in the far corner. Taking up paper from a box behind them, the printers whirred and chattered noisily as they spat out new stacks onto the floor, folding back up on itself along the perforated line that joined the ream together.

Beth extended her hand out, an invitation to explore, and I wandered between the heaped tables, stacks of printer paper scored with row upon row of numbers – mostly ones and twos, the odd three and four. A set of unfathomable co-ordinates, the date and time stamped down the side of each page.

On the walls, charts of star constellations overlapped one another, pins placed on particular stars, some charts choked with pins so dense in parts that they obscured the contents beneath almost entirely.

All of it, the tables, charts and printers orbited two desks, placed back-to-back in the middle of the room. Old monitors, speakers, machines with flashing lights, keyboards and headphones filled up nearly every inch; monitors raining the same pattern of numbers as the printouts down its screens in a stiff, juddering, staccato fashion. On and on. Never stopping.

'Here,' she said, offering me a seat at the desk, handing me a set of headphones. 'Put these on.'

She took up a pair herself and held them up to one ear.

It was a hiss, almost like static on a television set, interrupted by pops and scratches, an intermittent crackling that set lines on a monitor on the desk spiking and dipping with every sound as it travelled across the screen from left to right. A soon as they reached the right-hand side they reappeared again on the left and started their journey across the monitor again, over and over; a mountain range spiking with a burst of activity, before subsiding to a near flat line across the bottom of the screen when just static.

I looked up at professor Standing and she nodded.

'That,' she said 'is the sound of space. All the energies swirling about the heavens, captured by receivers far, far away, and transmitted here for us to observe.

Radiation, gases, gravitational pulls, atmospheres and collisions in deep space. Supernova, dying stars exploding, matter reforming, building new stars. The chaos of the universe ripping itself apart, rebuilding itself, living and dying, light years away, all in your headphones.

'I like to think that if chaos is good enough for the universe, then it is good enough for my filing system, no?' she said and smiled, looking about the clutter.

'Come,' she said, pointing at my headphones 'take those off and I will explain. Follow me.'

I had wondered where the door next to my bedroom led but hadnae felt comfortable enough to explore that first weekend, not wanting to do anything to offend Professor Standing.

It led to the roof and a small, sturdy looking box of a machine with a dish attached to the top.

'This,' she said 'is a poor example of what we do, but it is all we have. So, we treat it with all the love and respect it is due. It is called a portable spectrum analyser and,' she said, pointing up 'it listens to the stars.'

'It is old, and outdated, and has come all the way from Ohio State University in America. It was gifted to me by some professors who felt sorry for my lack of equipment.

'Give it to me, or let it perish away in some lock-up. That was the option. They thought it almost an insult, offering it to me, it is so outdated and weak by comparison to what is used now. But to me, it is so precious. A direct line to space. Right here. That we can use whenever we like.

'The dishes they use now, they are thousands of times stronger than our little dish. They can scour the skies faster, and with better clarity. But even then, they are only able to listen to the tiniest fraction of space. And our dish, it can only listen to the tiniest fraction of what the newer dishes can,' she shrugged.

'No problem I say. It is listening. And that is all that really matters. To me, at least.'

She nodded at the dish on top.

'I calibrated it over the weekend, just for you. What you were hearing in the headphones, that was Cassiopeia, or "E for Eilish" as I now know it to be called. Sounds that have travelled hundreds of light years to reach us, and will continue on past us, for eternity.

'It is something, is it not, to comprehend. One light year spans five point eight trillion miles. How far they have travelled, those sounds. Having been made centuries ago, they finally reach us, then carry on, and away.

'They are fascinating, wondrous things. But they are not why we listen.

'We are looking for patterns among the chaos of space. Patterns created, sent out by deliberate, intelligent design, just like the patterns the radio transmissions we emit here on earth make, travelling ever out into the darkness.

'Miss Macrae, with our little dish here, we are searching for intelligent life among the stars. We are looking for messages from extra-terrestrial beings. We are waiting to see something appear among those printouts, spike across our monitors, ring out in our headphones. A repeating, manufactured pattern among the chaos. A pattern that would signify the most profound discovery in the history of mankind. Evidence that we are not alone in the universe.'

She paused, smiled. Clearly amused by the look on my face, my slack jaw.

'Well,' she said 'I suppose if you are going to run for the hills, now would be the time to do it. I wouldn't blame you. I'd say you've done pretty well to make it this far without bolting down the stairs.

'So, what say you, Miss Macrae? Do you want to stay, peer through the looking glass?'

After a moment, I found myself nodding.

'Good,' Professor Standing said. 'Let's get to it. But first, a cup of tea and a bite to eat, and some rudimentary theories I think.'

We took a table in the corner of the windowless refectory beneath the library, and while we ate iced buns and drank tea, she took a napkin and began to draw.

'This equation is the cornerstone of everything that we do. By a great man called Frank Drake. I actually attended the lecture he gave at Green Bank Observatory in West Virginia, way back in 1961, when he announced his equation to the world. The handout from that lecture, I had him sign it. It is framed and behind my desk,' she pointed vaguely behind her in the direction of our building.

'The equation is to determine the number of civilisations in our galaxy with which communication might be possible. That is shown by the letter N,' she drew a large N on the paper, followed by an equals sign.

'So, the equation goes like this. We need to determine the average rate of star formation in our galaxy. 'And from those stars, how many of them have planets.

'And from those planets, how many can potentially support life.

'And from the fraction of planets that could support life, how many actually develop life.

'And from those planets, how many develop intelligent life.

'And from those civilisations, how many develop technologies that release detectable signs of their existence.

'And finally, the length of time for which civilisations release detectable signals into space, or in other words, do they destroy themselves in a nuclear arms race and disappear into the ether before anyone can detect them.'

She sat back and looked at the equation, each symbol a factor in Drake's hypothesis:

$$N = R* \cdot fp \cdot ne \cdot fl \cdot fi \cdot fc \cdot L$$

She slid the napkin across to me, where I had been feverishly jotting down her every word in my notebook, and I leant in over the line of letters and symbols, their meaning I would come to learn by heart, complete with all its possible permutations.

'So,' I said, after a while spent peering at that line of letters 'How many might there be, that could be sending out signals for us to try to hear?'

She shrugged.

'No one knows. For sure. Because anyone trying to answer the equation is doing so using educated guesses at best. People disagree. They love to disagree. But Drake and his colleagues believed that one star would be formed every year, during the life of a galaxy. And of those stars, between a fifth to a half would have planets. And from those planets, one to five would be orbiting at a distance from the star conducive to creating life. And they believed that if a planet could create life, it would do so, and that it would develop into intelligent life. After all, we only know of one planet that has ticked all the above boxes – Earth – and it has developed in this way, so we must assume that the pattern could be repeated. That life in the Universe will have a habit of persevering.

'And of all those intelligent civilisations, 10% – 20% would be able and trying to communicate out into space. And those civilisations would last between one thousand and one hundred million years.

'And if all the above comes to pass, then Drake and his colleagues believed that, based on his equation, there could be between one thousand and one hundred million planets with civilisations in the Milky Way. Which seems quite a lot no?

'But consider, the Milky Way is roughly two hundred thousand lights years in diameter, with between one hundred and four hundred billion stars, with at least that many planets out there somewhere. And the Milky Way is but one of millions of galaxies out there. Even with the biggest dishes and receivers, it is like looking for a needle in a haystack.

'But what a needle eh? And what a fascinating haystack to be looking in.

'It will take a lot of luck, pure chance, and so much perseverance. But to finally answer the question: "is anyone else out there in the universe," that would be worth all the years of listening in on static, no?'

It would, I said, and we sat quietly for a time before heading back. The napkin with the equation, Professor Standing's sweeping inscriptions, seemed too important, too profound for the bin, so I snatched it up and stuffed it into my pocket.

I would go on to get it framed, just like Professor Standing had done with her notes from Frank Drake himself, and it hung above my bed for so many years that it left a dark patch on the wallpaper when it finally came down, the pattern all around it faded through time and countless afternoons of sunlight pouring in across it.

But in the weeks after my induction in that poky little refectory, the napkin would stay in my pocket, and became a point of reference whenever the sea of data and algorithms became too indecipherable. When the probabilities and distances we were working in became too overwhelming.

Along with my scribbled notes, it was a layman's pick-me-up, that helped me to understand that what I had got myself into was fascinating, vital work. The basic premise as exciting as any mystery from my childhood books, even if the minutiae of the science behind what we were doing often passed me by.

To her credit, Beth eased me in gently to life 'among the lunatic fringe,' a title that had been given to her life's work by a group of academics she once overheard at some long-forgotten function.

To start off with, my days would be spent ensuring there was enough firewood stacked next to every fireplace, and a steady stream of tea for us both.

I would regularly check the printers and swap out any reams of paper that were getting low. It would be my last port of call every evening, so as the radio signals that Beth tracked from dishes in distant lands could be recorded through the night. Appearing as yet another stack of paper on the laboratory floor the following morning.

I learned to swap out old printer cartridges, hooking up the spare printer first, so as there would always be three machines on the go – translating and regurgitating cosmic noise being received at three separate locations around the world.

And, as I replaced the printer cartridge, serviced the machine as best I could, as I stacked and labelled the printouts by date, the location of the receiver, and celestial point of origin, I began to make some sense of the chaotic towers of papers that loomed over Professor Standing – who would sit almost motionless, for hours on end, at the bank of monitors in the middle of the room. Headphones on, she would listen to the noise of deep space with her head cocked to one side, as if trying to listen out for something just out of reach.

I started by stacking the reams of paper alphabetically, arranging them by constellation first, then star cluster second. Then I backdated them all the way to the 1960s and Beth's earliest work, creating piles of readouts in rows across the tables around us that could be located and retrieved more easily through my basic filing system.

After weeks of sorting, labelling, and moving, Beth appeared at my shoulder with a mug of tea, nodded at the stacks and explained that they had no pertinent scientific value, having recorded no abnormal signals among their countless pages.

'Most observatories and listening posts just bin them. But I never could. They are records of distant stars, nebula, the firmament in all its glory. They are precious. To me at least. You have mapped the stars Eilish. Our own paper tower night sky that we can walk through. It is beautiful, or I think it is. Thank you,' she said, and she gave me a warm hug.

Among my daily chores, Beth would stop me and get me to take up the spare set of headphones for an hour or two, where she would help me to interpret the buzzes and whirs, pops and crackles, explaining what each one was, until I started to be able to tell the difference between solar flares, radiation, the gravitational sweep of planets, moons, and great asteroids.

'It's important to know what it is we aren't looking for, so as you can focus on what we are' she said.

'This is all the beautiful chaos of the universe. What we are looking for is pattern where there should be none. A repetitive signal, a prolonged burst, intelligent design of some kind. Anything out of the ordinary – if you can call the music of the universe ordinary.'

Long afternoons listening with Beth, learning to understand the sounds of deep space, would often be accompanied by anecdotes and stories that began to form a rough history of this rogue science, and her part in it.

Tales of trips to the Arecibo observatory in Puerto Rico and violent tropical storms the like of which she had never seen before. Deafening thunder, blinding rain and lightning bursts. The birds in the trees and crickets in the scrub, their chirps and squawks that were constant background noise normally, growing hushed, then silent as the storm rolled in off the sea.

She told of the vast one-thousand-foot dish that spanned a valley covered in and surrounded by lush, dense rain forest. The heat that would beat down onto it, drenching you in seconds, standing in awe at the edge of this monstrous miracle of engineering as it searched deep space.

She spent a couple of semesters at Frank Drake's Green Bank observatory in West Virginia not long after he published his equation, assisting some of the earliest attempts at listening to deep space, and worked on Project Cyclops in 1971, set up by NASA's Search for Extraterrestrial Intelligence, or SETI Institute.

She then spent a full year at 'The Big Ear' at Ohio State University, a dish that would go on to record the 'WOW' signal on August 15th, 1977.

'I missed it by a year,' she said over dinner in our little kitchen one evening, shaking her head.

'The guy who took over from me, Jerry Ehman, he found it, among all the chatter.

'The only signal we have ever received to date that hasn't been disproved or explained away. No one knows what, or who, made it.

'It has become the most studied and critiqued signal from space. And after all that, we only know for sure what didn't make it.

'When he found it, Jerry circled the signal on his printout and wrote "WOW" alongside it. So, it became the "WOW" signal.

'It lasted seventy-two seconds, and it came from the constellation Sagittarius. The closest star to the signal's origin is called Tau Sagittari.

'Seventy-two seconds and then it stopped. And hasn't been detected since. Unique. Baffling. The best evidence of an alien transmission from space. Wow,' she said and shook her head.

She rolled up the sleeve of her shirt and laid her arm on the table palm up. Running down her forearm was a column of tattooed numbers and letters:

6
E
Q
U
J
5

'That is what the signal read. Among a sea of one's and two's, and the usual thing we see on the printouts.

'I'm afraid I got rather carried away and had this tattoo of it done. And I find that I can often lose myself, looking down at it, wondering, at what it might possibly mean. Where it came from, and who or what might have sent it.'

After The Big Ear she had visited the Allen Telescope Array near San Francisco and worked at Jodrell Bank in Cheshire before settling at the university.

'You know it used to be called the Jodrell Bank Experimental Station. How glorious does that sound? Back when people weren't scared to push the envelope and dream big.'

Her three printers, her bank of monitors, were wired into the dishes of Arecibo, Green Bank and the Lovell telescope at Jodrell Bank. The grants she received for the data analysis she did for those stations barely kept her operation in business. It was the funding she received from private philanthropists that kept the university compliant, leaving her alone to do what she did.

Her fundraising gatherings were legendary. The talk of the university.

She would invite interested parties and ply them with wine. She would set up telescopes on the roof of our building and have them directed at points of interest, such as Sagittarius, from where the 'WOW' signal emanated. At Proxima Centauri, a mere 4.2 light years away, that many in the field believed was a strong candidate for discovering another moment worthy of exclamation.

She would then take them down to the monitors and let them listen in to what they had just been observing, waxing lyrical about the pops and crackles, explaining that they were spectacular nebulae, the gravitational pull of Saturn and Venus, stars exploding, comets trailing into deep space, and that, one day, among it all, they would discover something else coming through. A pattern among the chaos.

'To have facilitated that, to have funded that discovery, the most profound discovery in the history of mankind, well that would be quite something, no?' would be her line to finally hook them in. And more often than not, after an evening of drinking and peering into telescopes, monitors, chuntering printers, the cheque books would come out, and Beth would have the funding to keep the university quiet for another year or two.

It was astonishing to watch, especially considering how socially awkward she was in every other facet of her life. Where simple interactions at the refectory, at the supermarket where we went to stock up on a Friday afternoon were littered with stunted, faltering interactions over where the washing powder was located.

It would not be uncommon for Beth to open her purse upside down at the tills, watching in horror as coins spilled out across the stone floor. The jangling clatter exacerbating her torment.

But put her in her own environment, and she could put together a spellbinding lecture to donors right off the top of her head. And she would do, sometimes at the base of the towering dish at Jodrell Bank, where she would bring her funders once a year, to properly hook them in with some serious hardware and a tour of the facility.

She could beguile anyone. Inspire even the biggest cynic to dream, focusing in on the one doubting Thomas in the group, she would explain to them all, but make it seem as if she were talking only to them, the sincerity, belief, and sheer focus in her eyes becoming almost spellbinding.

She would lean in and talk of 'The Great Silence,' or the Fermi Paradox – that if the Drake equation was correct, and there must be abundant intelligent life in the universe, then why haven't we found it?

She would then answer her own question by talking about the vastness of space, the accepted notion that intelligent civilisations would probably exist for only six and a half thousand years or so before either destroying itself or succumbing to disease. That the window of opportunity to broadcast and be heard, in celestial terms, was but a fraction of a second.

Look the other way, and they would be gone, trailing ever on into the infinity of space.

Then she would counter herself with the belief that habitable planets could certainly sustain at least four rounds of intelligent civilisations coming and going. Evolving and crashing among the vastness of space. That if life occurred, and it does, we are the proof of that, then it wouldnae occur just the once. It would persevere. Begin again.

That the Fermi Paradox was simply a waiting game, that contact would happen, but only if we kept looking and listening. That their donations would do just that, she would say.

'You never know, it might even be my voice that we detect. I might be the first sign of extra-terrestrial life!'

She would smile at their confusion, before going on to explain that her voice, reading "*At the Bay*" by Katherine Mansfield, her favourite short story, was a part of the Arecibo Message that had been beamed into space in 1974.

'It was sent to the M13 Globular Cluster in the constellation Hercules, some twenty-five thousand light years from earth. The cluster contains hundreds of thousands of stars, and therefore possibly hundreds of thousands of planets.

'The accepted belief is, that if anyone hears our signal, their first attempt at contact might very well be to send our own message back to us. It could be my voice that they send!

'And, if you follow me, I have a real treat for you. We are going to observe M13 through one of the world's most powerful telescopes. And who knows, maybe as we stare out, something could be looking back at us.'

A few times every year Beth would make trips out to Arecibo or Green Bank, to meet and work with Professor Drake and others in the field.

While she was gone, she would task me with monitoring the signals, studying the printouts for tattooable anomalies.

'You know what you are looking for,' she would say 'Keep listening. Keep watching. Make history,' and with a hug and a smile, she would be gone. For weeks at a time.

Knowing that she trusted me with her work, that she had faith in me, had faith in the way I had devoted so much time to learn everything she had taught me, it meant so much. And I pored over the printouts from the night before, meticulously, the sounds of the here and now bristling in my headphones.

If the weather was fine, I would wrap up warm, take a mug of tea up onto the roof and spend an hour or two plugged in to our little portable receiver, listening in on Cassiopeia while I leant back in a deck chair and watched 'E for Eilish' in the night sky above.

I would think of dad, of those snippets of happy memory, and I would wonder if, somewhere, he was looking up at it too.

Our lives, Beth's and mine, were those of hermits. We never had visitors, save for the delivery man who dropped off boxes of printer paper every other week. Though he didnae have to, he helped lug the boxes up to the top floor, where Beth would eye him suspiciously as he helped stack them next to the printers.

Save for our socially awkward trip to the supermarket, and the odd tea and bun at the refectory, our lives could have played out solely on the top floor of our rickety, old building. If I let it.

Beth had never talked of days off, time off, when I took the position. The thought had never entered her head, her vocation having long since become all-consuming.

But whenever I asked for a few days away to visit home, or an afternoon or evening off, she never said no.

'Of course, you must take some time. Absolutely Eilish. I insist. As long as you like.'

She would not even argue when I suggested she came out with me. For a few hours. For a change of scene.

She was always so focused on her work that the notion of doing something else never came naturally to her. But when she did come out with me, she did it with a wide-eyed enthusiasm, and an open-minded wonder that must have been forged by a life's work constantly being dismissed as a waste of time and pointless. How could she then not appreciate these things, if it meant something to someone else, if it nourished them the way her work did her?

I took her to the little picture house in town to watch *ET: The Extra-Terrestrial*, and she sat absorbed by the story, not once picking apart the science of the movie. She cried at the end when ET went home and came willingly on our next trip to see a re-run of *Star Wars*, where life in a galaxy far, far away had her on the edge of her seat.

She came with me too to watch the odd game of football down at the town's modest non-league club, who despite their lowly position and only being part-time, were a decent little team, who could really play.

Sitting all wrapped up in their humble, creaking wooden grandstand on cold midweek evenings, she enjoyed the ritual of a tea and chocolate bar at half time. She often commented on the floodlights, how stunning they looked in the night sky. She loved the halo they created above us, blocking out the rest of the world, elevating the endeavour out on the pitch.

She knew nothing of the rules, though that didnae seem to matter. She saw the poetry in sleek passing moves and applauded every goal, no matter which team scored, which sometimes drew daggered glances from the few regulars sat about us if it happened to be the visiting team. She would carry on regardless, oblivious to her faux pas, lost in the moment.

For someone so cerebral, so scientific, she seemed to enjoy crunching tackles the most, gasping as players crashed together.

'Gosh!' she would exclaim, grabbing my arm, before applauding again. And as we walked away at the end of the game, she would often look back at the floodlights burning up into the night.

'Well, that was certainly something,' she would say and smile.

Sometimes I would find her up on the roof of our building afterwards, looking across the trees and rooftops, back at the halo of light.

'All these years I've wondered what that was,' she would say, shaking her head, before turning back to her telescopes.

'Here,' she would say 'I have something for you,' stepping away from the sight so as I could peer up into the stars. Nebulae, stars, planets in tantalising detail came into focus. The cosmos slowly revealing itself to me. A picture to accompany the sounds.

Twenty-Four

My first trip to see the football at university wasnae planned. It just seemed to happen. The ground was situated on the edge of campus nearest the town. It was a short walk from the halls of residence, across a bridge that spanned a slow-moving river, a tributary to the River Ouse, thick with a dense reed bed that undulated and flowed in front of the canteen and post room, and on toward a small block of lecture rooms.

The bridge was the unofficial end of campus. Beyond it a park with large willow trees lining the river finally gave way to the old town, with its centuries-old rows of cottages and town houses hugging narrow lanes — a warren of twisting alleyways that led up to the church on the hill overlooking the town.

On the far side of the park, a row of tall, old, thickset fir trees accompanied the path. Beyond them stood the football ground.

I had thrown myself into my studies, forgoing most of the social side of things for a few extra hours with my books. I knew the librarians by their first names but struggled to remember those of people on my floor in halls.

As a result, I had precious few people I could call a friend, meaning walking into the campus bar or canteen usually resulted in a few minutes of awkwardly sitting over a drink or meal on my own, before finishing up and heading out for a quiet walk through the park.

It was one such Saturday afternoon that I heard the familiar sounds of a football match warming up. A crackly tannoy system distorting a popular song, trainers barking orders at the players, the thud of football boots connecting with footballs, the clack of a turnstile hidden in a cut in the trees.

Those bursts of memory, those Polaroid pictures and 8mm snippets of my childhood — afternoons away at Cowdenbeath — melted into the present, so familiar those sounds were to me, so primal they had been in another life, fusing together with the here and now. And without knowing what I was doing, I found myself drawn toward those snapshots of another life, joining the small queue, paying my money, and slipping inside.

For the socially awkward, a football ground is heaven. Where you can be a part of something just by being in attendance. Where witty banter is purely optional, and can be circumvented with a smile, a shrug of the shoulders, a raised eyebrow at a withering critique of a player's performance.

And in non-league grounds, where attendances often peak well below two hundred, just paying your money, taking the time to frequent such a small-time institution more than once gains you a tacit acceptance, an allegiance with everyone else inside.

Smiles and nods with the programme seller, the old-timer in the tea hut, the gate man, build up, week on week. Waves goodbye at the final whistle, until next time – wordless friendships, definitely feeling more profound than simple acquaintances, helped fill a void, kept loneliness at bay, and helped me to settle into university life. They became precious to me, these nods and smiles, friendly waves and snippets of conversation, as Ford Park became a regular haunt.

The old man in the programme hut, his quiet little assistant no more than twelve years old, who would peer over the counter at me from behind thick-rimmed glasses, a beanie hat pulled down as far as it would go, loved that Cowdenbeath were the team I mentioned when asked who I supported. Brothers and sisters in the small-time.

I would buy a programme, hand over the change to the boy, stand and chat about this and that, sometimes sharing my chocolate bar with the little assistant. A minute or two, no more, every week. Waves and smiles, nods about the place. It made you feel like you belonged, that you were valued, wanted. Such small gestures that meant so much.

It was one of the things Beth found most captivating in joining me at a match, watching her quiet little assistant sharing greetings and the odd quip with so many of those in attendance.

To me it felt homely. It felt comforting. Being the girl in the stand once more.

The old wooden steps leading up to rows of rickety seats felt familiar, as did the smell of tobacco drifting from old-timers who leant in to watch the action.

Hunched forward as if in prayer to some footballing God, who rarely answered them, they would burst into animation with the odd miss or refereeing decision, before settling down once more, their grumbles joining together like Buddhist monks in incantation.

Apart from their accents, the rest would seamlessly blend in with my memories of watching Dad away in Cowdenbeath. Happy memories that, along with our star gazing, never seemed to dull, despite the bitterness and hurt I had felt at his absence.

It was a terrible paradox: my comfort in those memories I had of him sitting alongside the anger at being abandoned, the hurt at not being worth staying around for.

Back then all I knew was that he was gone. That he had had an episode as Mum called it. And was gone.

As a little girl I would wait every birthday, every Christmas, hoping for a card, anything.

And his silence stung. No matter what else appeared beneath the Christmas tree, it was what wasnae there that I remember. It just didnae chime with the memories I had of him, his abandoning me, and it made the pain all the more acute. An open wound that could never truly heal.

I don't blame Mum, in doing what she did. She didnae know of depression, no one did. All she knew was the man she loved retreating into an impenetrable shell. Locked in, with no means of communication. It must have been scary. I am sure it looked it, menacing even, with a proper diagnosis. And she had a little girl to protect.

Though there was, in truth, nothing to protect me from. Dad was just lost, benign in his thick fog of illness.

My memories of him carried the truth. He loved me, and Mum, very much. He just couldnae reach us. And we him.

I don't blame Mum for taking us away to live with Nan and Grandad. It was an awful decision to have to make, and she did it with the best intentions. But not passing on his letters, his birthday cards and Christmas presents, that was a mistake.

Only learning some forty years after the fact that he had written to me every week up until we moved away, it was a hammer blow. All that pointless anger and bitterness expended.

All that animosity clashing with my 'E for Eilish,' my Central Park memories – it had been exhausting, confusing, upsetting.

She had never opened them. Had just returned them to sender, never mentioning them to anyone. Possibly too afraid to see if Dad had spiralled even further, to let that back into our lives.

She had done it to protect us, she said.

It didnae feel that it had.

But again, I have to put myself in her position – a frightened young woman with no idea what had happened to her husband who had grown dark and distant. Anguished.

She had been genuinely scared of him.

It wasnae her husband any more. And she didnae know what to do.

In situations like those, what does the right answer look like?

She did her best. He did his best. There was no malice, or ill intent. Just fear. And in the middle was me.

It was overwhelming: fifty years after it had been posted, to finally receive the Christmas present Dad had sent me that first year that we had been apart.

He had taken out this old box of bits, rummaged through it, and pulled out a worn paper bag with a Lake District address of a gift shop printed on it. In time it would be replaced in the box by Beth's Drake equation napkin and a few sheets of printout from deep space, my initials joining the others on the lid. The remaining contents of the box collapsing down into the gap the bag, my overdue Christmas present had left behind. Memories settling back down in the darkness.

It was a snow globe, containing a miniature glasshouse with a pool, tiny peacocks stationed outside. When I shook it, the two of us watched the flurry swirl and settle, and he told me how it snowed so heavily there, at Five Acre Cottage, that those whiteouts looked just as beautiful, as dizzyingly intense as my little snow globe.

He told me that he had worked in the gardens where the glasshouse stood for a good few years, and when it snowed, he said he would look up at the flakes tumbling against the glasshouse panes and wonder if I were looking up too. If I could see what he was seeing. A moment together.

He told me that he had written his letters to me in a little cabin on the far side of the gardens, and that a very wise lady had shown him how to get his letters to me when they had been returned. That he would drop them into a fire and wish the embers would find me, to pass on his love.

While I had my 'E for Eilish,' my afternoons at the football with my little university town team, Dad had been looking up at the falling snow all the while and had been thinking of me.

I canae tell you how wonderful it felt to learn that. That my stubbornness in preserving my little Polaroid pictures of Dad were well-founded. That I had been right to hold on to them so tightly.

Those happy memories of Central Park, busy corridors beneath the main stand, train rides home tucked into the rough weave of Dad's jumper.

That idle moments looking up at the falling snow from the stand at Ford Park had been laced with a greater meaning, though unknown to me at the time.

And that was why it hurt so much, when my little adopted football team folded in 1996.

It felt like a bereavement of sorts, losing those afternoons among subliminal memories of Dad, and my new-found nodding, waving friends dotted about that pretty little ground.

There had been some dispute over the land the club sat on. There had also been some mismanagement of funds that saw this little team with barely two hundred supporters facing a bill no one could afford to pay. Property developers saw an opportunity to build expensive student halls, and among this maelstrom of legal writs, our little club folded.

That our little community of kindred spirits had been made homeless was one thing – I would sometimes see the old man from the programme hut sat in the window of a tearoom on the High Street. From the window of the university canteen, I would sometimes see his little bespectacled assistant walking alone through the park, kicking through piles of leaves on his way home from school, peering across at the dormant turnstile, redundant floodlights peeking above the trees.

Every now and then I would see one of the regulars from the stand in town, and we would smile weakly at one another, wave. But in the most part, my little band of familiar faces, who had come together to keep each other company on a Saturday afternoon, they were lost to me. They were lost to one another. Many I simply never saw again.

That was bad enough, though it was losing that connection to my memories of Dad, of Central Park and those Cowdenbeath matches that hurt the most.

Afternoons letting memories rattle about the sparse terracing of my little non-league team had become a comfort greater than even I had understood. Those childhood snapshots mingling with the present had brought me a peace. Had helped me feel whole. Feeling a connection to a life I had never wanted to give up on, had never wanted to end, playing itself out like some ethereal wisp, a dream, faint apparitions of then drifting across the here and now. Pencil thin outlines of Central Park, and games long gone, ebbing about the dimensions of Ford Park.

For a time, being neither here nor there. Dad somewhere out on the pitch among the scramble of bodies, supporters applauding a goal, the ghosts of Central Park rattling about my off-campus haven.

But with boarded-up turnstiles, snatched glances through fences at an overgrown pitch, and a decaying main stand that would last three more winters before a wild storm scalped it – the roof caving in the seating below, my memories had no home.

Walking past that tumble-down relic that would stand for five years before developers finally got their way: it hurt.

What had once been so important to those who frequented it, for many different reasons, being left to fall into ruin was very sad to see. And though it felt good to walk past it, to feel some kind of connection, it felt worse to see what had become of it, what had once been such a nourishing, homely place fallen into such terrible disrepair.

I felt sorry for it, for my smiling, waving friends, and for me. I missed my memories. I missed my little club, and the kindly characters within.

At least I still had my stars.

Professor Standing and I would listen in on them. Day after day. Collecting their sounds in reams of printer paper. Listening out for that one rogue signal that could change everything.

Days, weeks, months, years passed plugged into our headphones – every morning charged with the thought that maybe today would be the day. Breakfast hurriedly eaten, we would lean in over our printouts looking for an anomaly as wow-inducing as the one that adorned Beth's arm, switching to the headphones once they had been scanned and catalogued, archived.

Though as the years passed, our system of tabletop filing of constellations and clusters became too precarious; towers of paper grew up around us and looked set to topple and bury our little operation in an avalanche of galactic chatter.

I cleared out the adjacent rooms to our base of operations and began the process of transferring Beth's lifetime of listening into them. Every morning transferring the latest piles to the corresponding star system dotted about the rooms.

Days in the lab, evenings up on the roof looking through Beth's telescopes, interspersed with the odd trip to the cinema – time passed without us really acknowledging the day to day, so lost in the celestial were we. Birthdays were forgotten, seasons came and went among our all-encompassing blips and fizzes, our distant points in the night sky, our stacks of papers. It was just me and her, and our work. Year after year.

And among it all, Beth became more than just my boss. She became such a good friend to me.

She had a wicked sense of humour, and a dry wit that could have me bent-double with laughter. We truly enjoyed each other's company. Conversation came easily, as did protracted silences in front of the fire, or up on the roof looking at stars. We were both comfortable enough with one another that we could respect each other's desire for quiet.

We would wander down the hill into town to the supermarket, the pictures, or a football match chatting and laughing. It was a happy life, spent in the company of a warm, compassionate, fiercely intelligent, and driven woman.

The purpose and meaning I found in our work fulfilled me in so many ways.

Long days and nights listening in to the great unknown, in the company of such a vivacious spirit as Beth, it was everything to me. It made me so happy.

And after our first few years together, I became sad at the prospect of leaving Beth alone over Christmas. She would wave me off back up to Glasgow, then see out the holiday in complete isolation.

Before long I made the decision to stay with her. The thought of her sitting all alone next to the Christmas tree that she would carefully decorate with baubles, tinsel and lights in the lab becoming too problematic for me.

From then on, we would open little presents to one another that we would place beneath her tree, before making Christmas lunch together and sitting in the kitchen with paper hats from our crackers at a jaunty angle, drinking a bottle of red wine as the light drained from the sky. And then we would link arms and go for a walk through the woods behind our building, ignoring the cold if it had snowed, pausing to take in the pretty scene of the laden trees, the building drifts, a brilliant white illuminating the dusk, the shadowy recesses of the forest undimmed with an eerie, spectral glow.

It was one such Christmas that little Rosie came into our lives.

Beth had been away an awful lot that year. Long trips out to Arecibo and Green Bank meant that I was left to carry on the work alone, sometimes for months at a time. They were a part of the research grants that kept us going, and Beth loved them; the chance to share findings with the brightest in the field, to work with ground-breaking new equipment, to peer deep into the cosmos with state-of-the-art telescopes. It was pure heaven for her.

But she would always feel bad that the funding couldnae extend to a second plane ticket for me.

'You deserve it,' she would always say 'given all your hard work. I wish I could afford to bring you along out of my own pocket. But,' she would shrug. The knowledge that she barely had two coins to rub together writ large across her darned cardigans and patched trousers that she would keep viable for years after they should have been put out for rags.

In fact, the meagre wage she paid me made me the senior financial partner of the operation. And every Christmas I would spend some of that money on a new pair of trousers, or one of the simple blouses she liked to wear underneath her cardigan, a pair of khaki shorts for the heat of Puerto Rico, wrapping them up and placing them under her tree.

Rosie came along a few days before Christmas, with news of a four-month trip away in the New Year.

'I thought you could do with some company while I'm gone,' she said, ushering me through to her office. 'Lord knows I appreciate how lonely it can sometimes get up here. So, let me introduce you to little Rosie.' She nodded into the corner, and a carry case.

I crept toward it, knelt down to peer inside, and found two large eyes peering back out at me, hunkered away in one corner. A thin, timid little tabby cat cowering in the shadows.

'She had been abandoned, the poor thing. One of the maintenance team found her in the garden of one of the student houses, bless her. They didn't know what to do, so they brought her back to their shed by the post room. I was picking up my post, and as soon as I saw her, as soon as I heard what happened, I offered to take her. For you.

'I took her to the vet. She is fine. A little malnourished. A little skittish. But nothing a little bit of love and attention won't fix. She is two years old or thereabouts the vet said. He gave me a big bag of bits. Food, litter and the like that had been donated to them. He said she just needs someone to love her. I thought maybe you could keep each other company?'

Resettled in a quiet corner of my room, she didnae come out of her carry case for two days, creeping out to the open door to have her breakfast and dinner when she had the room to herself. Empty bowls proof she had ventured that far.

But slowly, steadily, Rosie the little tabby cat, revealed herself. First by sitting in the doorway to my bedroom, looking down the corridor at the line of doors, wondering at the whirring of the printers. She would turn tail if either Beth or I came out into the hallway, slipping back into the safety of her case.

Then she started to get a little braver at breakfast and dinner time and would wait for me outside her little shelter – a frail half-meow and a flick of the tail, her saucer eyes looking up at me as I prepared her bowl.

Finally, after a few more days, I woke in the middle of the night to find her curled up in a ball against my legs, fast asleep. The following morning there were purrs as she climbed onto my chest for a cuddle, burrowing under my chin while she allowed me to rub her tummy.

From then on little Rosie grew in confidence, and began to explore the rooms on our floor, following me from one to the other. Scampering to keep up, she would jog along, then sit behind my legs and look out at the new landscape, watching Beth at the monitors, or a newly lit fire spitting and popping.

It didnae take long for her to pad down the stairs after me every morning, where she would climb the log pile and chew at the long grass as I gathered up wood for the fires, and when they were lit, she would stretch out in front of one and bask for hours on end.

In her more playful moments, I would be disturbed from my studying of printouts by a little face peering round the door frame. With her ears flattening, and a wiggle of her bum, she would skitter across the wooden floor and pounce on the trail of paper at my feet, kicking it with her back paws and batting at it as I let it gather on top of her. Then there would be an explosion of paper, and she would race away, skidding around the door and down the corridor, before her little face reappeared in the doorway once more.

I would hear Beth giggling every now and then, followed by the rolling of a ping pong ball down the corridor. The thundering of little paws after it, a blur of fur and claws before the moment of capture. If Beth was busy, or absent, I would often hear the ball set in motion down the hall by a paw, followed shortly after by a racing Rosie hunting it down.

At Christmas, Beth and I would hear the jangling of baubles, the rustle of tinsel, the chinking together of tree lights, before an ungodly scramble of cat up trunk, quickly followed by a crashing cacophony. We would wander into Beth's office to find her Christmas tree at sixes and sevens, baubles scattered across the room. Rosie sitting all innocent and angelic, looking up at us with those big eyes that seemed to say 'Oh my, what has happened here? I am sure I don't know.' We would laugh and pretend scold her, fix the tree back up, Rosie unable to stop herself from launching at an errant strand of tinsel.

Most days she would curl up on my lap as I sat at the monitors and half-heartedly batted at the lead from my headphones, before comfort consumed her and she settled down with a stretch and a sigh. And when she got too warm, she would make a nest for herself among the strewn papers across my workstation and keep me company from there as I listened in on the stars.

She loved heading up and out onto the roof with me, and it would become an evening ritual, where she would chase moths and gnats in the summer months, bat at snowflakes in the winter, and sit in the doorway when it was raining, sniffing the moisture on the air. I would sit on the step below with a cup of tea, and we would watch the rain drumming on the roof for an hour or so before Rosie decided that there would be no outdoor play for her and padded back down the stairs.

In the summer, when my room could get stiflingly hot, Rosie would struggle. In the night she would gently paw at my face and cry until I woke up, and we would head up onto the roof to cool down a little. She would pace in front of the door while I got my dressing gown on, and then scamper up the stairs and wait for me to open the little roof door.

I would settle in a deckchair and watch her as she rolled around on the cool floor and purred. After a while I would listen in to our little portable receiver, and often fall asleep to the faint hiss of deep space. A stiff neck or leg would finally wake me in the half-light before dawn, Rosie curled up on my lap. The world at an absolute dead calm. I would gently pick her up and rest her over my shoulder to a sleepy grumble of a protest, and head back to bed for a few hours.

She couldnae meow properly. Instead, she would 'hee,' and we would chat to one another all day, her heeing down the corridor towards me after a long nap, I would tell her what I had been up to while she had been sleeping.

It would make Beth laugh. She said we were like Huckleberry Finn and Tom Sawyer, thick as thieves, off on some little adventure together as we went about our business.

She would shake her head and proclaim that she had created a crazy cat lady as an assistant.

She was right.

Our secluded life at the top of our rickety old building had made me proficient in the language of space radiation, quasar chatter, and the ebb and flow of vast gravitational forces. It had also made me an expert on Rosie's hees': when she was hungry, playful, hot, wanting a cuddle, or just some company. There was a certain kind of hee that came with a swish of her tail and would be accompanied with a scratching at the leg of my chair. Knowing the drill, I would stand up and she would scamper down the corridor and sit nose pressed against the door to the roof. It was play time.

Her nuances were as complicated as space, and with the code cracked, we had a wonderful friendship.

She had been a Godsend, arriving not long after my little football team had folded. And along with Beth, our work, she had become everything.

We would both skulk around the edges of Beth's fundraising gatherings. Me topping up glasses and passing round nibbles, Rosie sitting in the doorway of our bedroom, glaring at excitable potential donors, standing her ground as they headed up and out onto the roof for some stargazing.

And when they were all gone, she would sniff around every room, making sure that none had been left behind.

It was, to my mind, the perfect life.

I had stumbled across a fascinating field of work that fuelled my love for the unknown. I had met an inspirational woman in Beth, who had forged a path in a male dominated world that few women had been able to take before her, but many more would in her wake. And I had Rosie. As best a friend as anyone ever had.

The seasons would come and go. Autumns of clearing leaves from our little receiver, with a little helper skittering about my feet. Christmases where we would share our Turkey three ways with an impatient Rosie pacing in front of the oven. Long summer months where Beth would invariably be out in the field, Rosie and I would pad about the place, past wafting windows and rippling stacks of papers – growing tubs of cat grass on the roof that Rosie would devour whilst purring ferociously.

She would climb the woodpile and bat at bees as I chopped wood in spring, and scrabble about the undergrowth as I collected berries from the bramble that grew up against the side of the building.

If the door to our top floor had been left ajar, she would sneak down to explore the empty floors below us, ignoring my frantic calls when I couldnae find her.

As I came down to search for her, she would scamper up the stairs with a flag-pole tail, heeing loudly, telling me all about her adventures. She would purr on my lap as I brushed all the cobweb from her back and whiskers before a well-deserved snack for being so brave.

It was a life. It was our life. And I was happy. Batting away the scepticism from home, from other departments on campus, that we were wasting our careers listening out for something that wasnae there.

We had our Drake equation. And we knew the odds.

And we also knew that if you didnae listen, then you would never hear. The most significant event sailing past our little planet and on into eternity. Opportunity, understanding, lost forever.

Listening to, observing the stars that Beth would bring into focus for me with her telescopes – it was a privilege.

Believing in something, the ramifications of which were so profound, it made every day exciting.

Laced with anticipation, our office was the vastness of space and time.

And the astonishing spectacle that began to reveal itself with the Hubble telescope, and a series of vivid images of deep space, added colour to the objects we had been listening to in our little corner of campus. Majestic nebulae, swirling galaxies, and exploding stars all brought into stunning focus.

We studied, logged, and listened, waiting patiently for our own WOW moment.

Though for Beth, that WOW moment would never come.

It had been just another semester out at Arecibo. Nothing out of the ordinary. Or as ordinary as a life spent listening out for alien life could be.

She left as she always did, early in the morning. Opening a tin of tuna as a special treat for Rosie, she sat and chatted to her over a cup of tea, like she always did the day she left.

She told her to look after me in her absence while Rosie wolfed down the fish, and with that, Professor Bethany Standing was gone.

She would write every week, detailing the work they were doing, the sights they had seen in the observatory. She would send back photographs of her and colleagues stood next to the vast Arecibo receiver stretching across that vast, spectacular rain forest valley.

She would write of life among the humidity. Of breath-taking thunderstorms pounding on the roof of her little hut. Brilliant prongs of lightning illuminating black, tumbling storm cloud. How the birds and the monkeys in the trees would grow hushed as the storm began to claw its way across the island. The air growing thick as shadow began to stretch out from the dense forest.

She wrote of sitting in the doorway of her hut, shrinking beneath the violence of the storm, yet unable to take her eyes off it, being so beautiful, and utterly terrifying at the same time.

She would always write a line to Rosie before signing off, commenting on the size of the moths outside her hut, that they were perfect for chasing, and how she missed her.

Those few short pages, read out to Rosie over a mug of tea, filled the lab, our rooms, with Beth for a short while. The words, as if she had read them out herself, charging the atmosphere with her infectious passion and drive. And for the shortest of moments, she wasnae on the far side of the Earth any more.

It would be the highlight of our week, my walk down onto campus, past where my beloved football ground used to stand, across the park and over the bridge to the post room and canteen, to pick up the post from Beth.

I would try on Thursday, and if it hadnae arrived, I would head back on Friday, where it would invariably be waiting for me. Sometimes a letter, sometimes a small parcel with a t-shirt with the Arecibo Observatory logo, or NASA's, or SETI's.

She knew I loved them, and I would wear them with pride. So, Beth would continue to post them home.

'They just hand them out,' she would write 'for free. You can just take as many as you like!' We would both live in them until the logos faded away in the wash, then Beth would bring new ones back. And so, it would go on.

The week everything changed, I wandered down to the post room on Thursday, then again on Friday, but didnae think too much of it when there was nothing for Rosie and me on either day. It sometimes happened. I would try again on Monday.

It was only when I received a telephone call from the Dean's office on Saturday morning that I knew something was off. They wanted to see me. Right away.

We never got calls from the University.

I don't remember much. I remember deep leather armchairs that you sank into and an old looking portrait of a jowly man with thick grey chops dressed in his University robes above the fireplace.

The Observatory had called. Beth and a few others had been on a flight across to Miami to get supplies. One of those small single prop island hoppers. A storm had come in suddenly. One of Beth's great thunderstorms.

The plane had gone missing.

On Tuesday.

There was no wreckage. No mayday. One minute it had been there on the radar. The next it was not.

They had been searching for four days. With not even a speck of a sign. They had followed the currents from the plane's last known co-ordinates right out into the Gulf Stream. The plane, its pilot and passengers, Beth, had seemingly vanished off the face of the earth.

The Observatory informed the University that the search had been scaled right back. The chances of survival out at sea for so long being slim. That Beth and her colleagues were slipping into the realm of the missing, presumed dead, out at sea.

It made the newspapers — four scientists hunting for extra-terrestrial life gone missing in the Bermuda Triangle — it was a reporter's dream. The lack of any wreckage only fuelled the mystery and elongated the news cycle for days.

Papers included maps with other prominent missing ships and planes from the Bermuda Triangle, tales of vanishing vessels and squadrons of fighter planes. Theories of otherworldly dimensions, abductions, phenomena that could take a huge tanker without so much as a snippet of a distress call.

Planes vanishing into cloud, never coming out again.

Ships slipping from the face of the Earth by some unknown force.

Such speculation neither helped nor hindered.

I kept going to the post room. Day after day. Expecting what I am not quite sure. Something. Anything.

That she had disappeared, had not been found, helped in some way. They could have been forced to land on some tiny, uncharted, uninhabited island. They could still be out there, Beth and her colleagues, waiting for some remote ship to spot them.

It made grieving hard. Impossible. No one knew that she was definitely gone. They just knew that she wasnae where she was supposed to be.

Some days I would sit with Rosie and cry, the emptiness of our floor without Beth almost suffocating. Others I would scour the library for books on the Bermuda Triangle, and theories on what becomes of the missing. I remembered reading about this mysterious place in my books as a girl, and as I reacquainted myself with its mysteries, the irony was not lost on me.

That a woman who dedicated her life to exploring the skies for alien intelligence found herself mixed up in notions of portals and time slips to other dimensions, folds in space and wormholes to distant galaxies, it seemed fitting. Worthy of Beth's extraordinary life on Earth, these theories of how she may have left it.

And though it was a little comfort, something to cling to, that maybe, if some of the more outlandish theories on the Bermuda Triangle could be true, Beth may have found the answers to her life's questions, it didnae make her absence here on Earth hurt any less.

It all came down to faith. And some days I had enough to muster a little hope, that even though she might be lost to us, she might not be lost completely. Just enough faith to stop the otherwise overwhelming dread and sorrow consume me entirely. My own little Drake equation of probability, that somehow, somewhere, her story is carrying on.

And with no definitive proof either way, my equation held enough water to sustain me, to shine the faintest of lights through my darkest thoughts.

Some would call it denial, a prescribed stage of dealing with loss. Beth would have called it 'exploratory thinking,' looking beyond the accepted, where great scientific discoveries have been made throughout the ages.

Whatever it was, I didnae know what else to do but sit tight and wait. Carry on with our work, whilst caught in a terrible emotional limbo.

We sat and listened, Rosie and I, to the skies. We studied the printouts, and the sounds of deep space. And waited. For a sign. For something. Anything. I don't know.

We waited for weeks, months, collecting up reports, filing them away. Then slowly, one by one, the monitors grew silent.

The printers stopped.

The signals and data from Arecibo, Green Bank, the Allen Array ceased.

Without Beth, the grants had been cancelled. Our work was over. We had been shut down.

What had once been a dizzying place of chuntering printers, monitors displaying radio waves rippling from left to right, the hiss and chatter of deep space filling the room, now stood still. The silence more deafening than the never-ending whirring of machinery that used to lull me to sleep every night. Banks of screens flatlining from left to right. Over and over in the stifling vacuum.

Rosie felt it too, padding from room to room looking for the sights and sounds that had become so familiar to her, pawing open the door to Beth's office, looking forlornly for her old pal, before quietly carrying on her search in another room.

I didnae know what to do, so I did the only thing that felt natural, that I thought Beth would have approved of – I went up onto the roof and carried on listening through our little portable receiver. Rosie at my side.

Though that didnae last long.

As soon as the grants had been confirmed as cancelled, the letter came. A notice of eviction. Without the protection of Beth's reputation and the money it attracted, the university had no need for a rudderless department of left-field experimental science.

I had a week, then I had to be gone.

I had become institutionalised to our remote life out on the fringes. It was the only thing I knew. It made me happy. It inspired me every day: our search. It was a warm, nourishing place where I truly felt safe. Truly felt home.

The company I kept. The work we were doing. It could have sustained me for all time.

Instead, I was tasked with deconstructing it, abandoning it to its fate. Turning off monitors and printers, speakers and screens. Breaking down all that Beth had built up; it was heart breaking to have to do. It felt cruel: someone so invested in it being made to pull it to pieces.

I had so little time; there was no way of preserving the stacks of printouts. A life's work carried mournfully down the stairs and placed in rows of waiting skips. Monitors were broken down and stacked in one corner, other equipment in another, Beth's books and personal effects boxed up and left in a third.

I packed a small bag with clothes, my favourite t-shirts from Beth's trips, the picture frame of her Drake equation napkin. I tore the last few pages from the printouts, including the one that ended abruptly, the shower of numbers across the page stopping suddenly. I folded them up and stuffed them in my pocket. A memento from decades of her searching the skies.

I carefully packed up Beth's little receiver into its carry case on the roof, and somehow managed to get it down the stairs without causing myself some serious injury.

Then Rosie and I wandered around our floor one last time, looking in on rooms that we feared we would never see again. Staring at them one last time, trying to absorb as much to memory as possible.

It was so familiar, and yet so alien shorn of Beth, all the equipment, her reams of celestial chatter, of the comfort of knowing that it was ours. Our home.

Without her, the sounds of our industry filling the air, it had become a dream already, even though we were still standing in it.

I wrote my mother's address and telephone number on a piece of paper and put it on Beth's bare desk, just in case. Still hanging on to the notion that she might re-emerge from her vanishing and reclaim it all, bring me back to our little corner of paradise.

And with that, I enticed Rosie into her carry case with a few treats and tried to console those big saucer eyes peering out at me that we would be all right. We would find somewhere new, I told her. We would carry on with our work. We would set our little receiver up toward the M13 cluster and listen out for Beth's voice coming back to us, reading out her favourite short story.

I didnae know where, I didnae know how. But we would keep searching. For Beth. For us.

The walk down to the train station was painful. Rosie's little mournful 'hees' breaking my heart, while bags and carry cases knocked against leg and rib. With not much money in my pocket, staying on, finding a new place, and some kind of employment wasn't a viable option. Walking about the town, the campus, chasing ghosts – watching Ford Park fall into further disrepair, looking up at Beth's building all dark and boarded up, the woodpile empty – I think it may have caused more hurt than comfort. Like forever picking at an open wound.

And I knew that it would always be there, that pretty little town, its leafy university campus. That I could visit, for old times' sake, anytime I liked. Like one of those comets we used to track, gravity clawing it back from deep space and decades lost on a long, distant orbit. It would always find its way back. Back home. And so would I, when the bittersweet pull of nostalgia became too much. It would all be there for me, waiting.

I sat on the platform with little Rosie's case on my lap and looked in at her cowering at all the strange noises. I fed her treats and cooed and chatted to her to try and console her. Though the breaking of my voice with emotion did little to reassure either Rosie or me. And when the train to Glasgow arrived, I lugged everything on board, and we settled down in a window seat, and watched as our little university town faded away with the station master's whistle and a shunt of the engine.

I opened a little tin of food for her, opened the door to her carry case and popped it inside, stroking her gently as she ate. When she was done, she hunched up next to my arm, rested her chin on my wrist, and settled down as best she could.

By the time we arrived at Argyle Street station I had no stomach for the buses, so joined the queue at the taxi rank. When it was our turn, an elderly man got out from behind the wheel and helped with getting the receiver in the boot.

I slumped in the back seat and stared in at Rosie, paying no mind to the outside world as the taxi began to thread its way across the city.

After a while the driver spoke up.

'Excuse me Miss, but I have to ask. Your name isnae Eilish by any chance?'

I nodded.

'Eilish Macrae?'

I nodded again.

'Daughter of Gordie Macrae?'

I nodded a third time.

He slapped the steering wheel, which made both me and Rosie jump a bit, though his broad smile in the rear-view mirror at least soothed me a little.

'I knew it,' he said 'I never forget a face. Though it took me a little while to put a name to you. It's been forty years or more I dare say.' He stared back at me through his little sliver of mirror.

'But I never forget a face.

'I used to live a wee way from your grandparents on Oban Street. I used to take them to the bingo every Thursday. Up at the Apollo.

'I'm pretty sure I took you and your mum along with them as well for a time. And before I became a cabbie I worked with your dad at the shipyard. We went to see the Rangers up at Ibrox together a few times. Before he was signed up by Cowdenbeath.'

He shook his head.

'We lost touch after that. When he had his troubles. A very sad affair all round, no?

'My God. How strange is this. First that article appearing, Gordie resurfacing. Now you. After all these years'

He must have seen the confusion on my face.

'Have you nae seen it? The article?'

I shook my head.

'Oh my,' he said 'I have it here somewhere. I couldnae throw it out. It's not everyday someone you know appears in the papers.'

He looked back at me.

'But you should have it. If you'd like it. It is your dad after all. Let me fetch it.'

He dropped me off at a café. Rummaged around his glove box, pulled out a magazine supplement and handed it to me.

'Here you go love. Are you sure you dinae want me to wait for you? Take you the rest of the way?'

I shook my head, thanked him profusely when he refused payment.

'No, no, no. This one is on me. You take care of yourself Eilish. It's been so nice to see you,' he nodded at the magazine 'All the best, eh.'

I took a seat beneath a neon sign in the corner and ordered a pot of tea and a tuna salad, scooping some of the tuna off onto my saucer and popping it in for Rosie.

Then I took a deep breath, opened the magazine to the contents page, and found the article – *The Left Back Who Never Was.*' I began reading, pausing at an old black and white photograph of dad scoring at Ibrox. A picture inset of him in a Cowdenbeath team photograph.

An old man, smiling weakly in front of a boat.

Dad.

I phoned Mum from a payphone by the toilets. She had seen it when it came out a month or so earlier, she said.

She had not known what to do.

She had wanted to tell me, but not on the phone. That hadnae seemed right, she said. It had all been so overwhelming. So much to consider. She burst into tears.

She told me that he had written to me every week, when I was a little girl.

Had sent birthday cards and Christmas presents, which had only stopped when we moved with Nan and Grandad to Fisher Street, and he no longer knew where I was.

She had sent them all back. She had been so scared. She thought she had been protecting me. Doing the right thing.

But reading the article, maybe she had been wrong. All these years.

That all that love he had invested in that young lad – it should have been mine.

'I thought I was doing right by you Eilish. That is all I have ever wanted to do. I thought I was protecting you. Protecting us. But now, I just don't know any more. I'm sorry love. I truly am. I truly am.

'He came through the other side. He found himself again. He helped that little boy. Maybe if I had just waited by him that little bit longer, it would have all been yours.'

I told her that life is easy in hindsight. That she had only ever done what she felt was best for me. That she had been a great Mum in very tough circumstances.

There was no right. No wrong. Just best intentions. She had lost everything too, I told her.

I told her that I loved her very much. And that I would see her soon.

I waited outside the café for my taxi, sitting on the receiver, hugging Rosie's carry case to my chest. Among the light pollution, Cassiopeia was just about visible, shimmering in the night sky.

E for Eilish.

And when the taxi arrived, the driver helped me with all my stuff, before looking back at me from his seat.

'Where to Miss?' he said.

'Argyle Street Station please.'

The light was beginning to fail by the time I found the little towpath by the bridge. Keep going until I couldnae go any further the barmaid from the pub had said. There is a little bench, with a bell. Wait there and he will be along soon enough.

The path was uneven and littered with the odd stone that seemed to find the wheels of the receiver's travel case with annoying regularity, making it lurch from side to side, taking me along with it.

At the end of a run of small fishermen's cottages the towpath dissolved into undergrowth, and I found the bench, the bell. I rested the receiver, my bag, alongside it, before setting down Rosie's carry case on a patch of grass and opening the door.

At first a tentative snout sniffed the grass, then she looked up at me.

'Go on,' I said softly. 'You are fine. Stretch your legs. Just keep away from the water.'

With a little hee she trotted out and took in her surroundings. Eating a little grass before weaving between the legs of the bench, padding toward the brush at the end of the path.

'Not too far mind,' I said. She looked back at me and hee'd, before slipping into the shadow.

It was a beautiful spot, looking out at a lake surrounded by dense forest. Thick fog crept out from the trees and drifted across the still water, and as dusk grew deeper, the sweep of the lighthouse became more prominent from way up on the bluffs behind us.

It was so peaceful. The evening still, save for the odd rustle of an exploring cat.

The fresh pine smell of the forest carried with the fog and felt so rich and pure when taken in deep breaths. Wisps of mist snaking across the towpath.

Though deep breaths didnae do much to calm my nerves, my hands shaking in my lap as I waited patiently.

Until, finally, the faint sound of an engine began to grow.

First the glimmer of port and starboard lights began to pierce the fog. Then, slowly, a hull began to materialise out of the gloom.

I scrabbled behind me for my bag and stood up, feeling for the magazine inside.

I watched as the boat grew more distinct out of the fog and dusk.

I took a deep breath.

And watched.

And waited.